THE
SUNKEN FOREST

Where the Forest Came out of the Earth

A Novel by
R. Barber Anderson

Pangolin Books ♦ *Charlottesville, Virginia* ♦ *2018*

THE SUNKEN FOREST

Where the Forest Came out of the Earth

For information write:
Pangolin Books
PO Box 2257
Charlottesville, Virginia 22902

Or call: 434-996-2457

Email: bob.littlerhinostudio@gmail.com

If you are unable to order this book from your local bookstore,
or have difficulty ordering from Amazon.com,
you may order directly from the publisher.
Quantity discounts for organizations are available.
Call: 434-996-2457

Library of Congress Catalog Card Number:
ISBN 978-0-9715941-5-9

Cover design by Rick Bickhart
Staunton, Virginia

Cover art: photograph by Manuel Sanchez

First Edition
Printed in 2019
in the Czech Republic

THE SUNKEN FOREST

Where the Forest Came out of the Earth

For
Jacob and Elias Anderson

1 – PRELUDE

A Gaboon viper lay loosely coiled on the forest floor. Virtually invisible to the untrained eye, the broken up colors and shapes of the snake's body had become completely lost within its setting of rotting leaf litter, vines, and squirming roots; a cubist composition, evolved over millions of years; one of Nature's true masterpieces in camouflage.

This specimen was large, perhaps five feet in length with a weight of almost forty pounds, at least fifteen of which were the result of the large rodent it had consumed in the early hours of the night. Its pupils were tightly contracted indicating that it was asleep, and the loose coil in its posture was allowing it to digest the unfortunate creature gradually working its way down its digestive tract.

Suddenly its pupils dilated to full size. The viper's body had sensed a subtle vibration through the ground; a warning that an intruder might be approaching. It remained motionless, but its eyes rotated toward the source of the signal. Seconds passed, and then an almost inaudible hint of movement followed as a dark indistinct shape emerged from out of the dimness. As the intruder neared, its form broke apart, revealing itself as two separate entities; two humans.

One was taller than the other, and each carried a short spear. The tall one, much older than his companion, wore a simple pull-down cap with rolled-up brim made from the skin of a golden cat, and he carried across his shoulder, a long wood shaft. They were pygmies, a grandfather and his grandson, and as they approached the snake it became evident that their course was in direct line with the position of the reposing serpent.

1

As they drew to within one or two more strides of stepping on the viper, the elder pygmy casually dipped his spear in the direction of the snake, and then changed his course just enough to avoid disturbing the watching serpent. The younger pygmy's eyes shifted toward the snake as they silently glided by, regained their original direction, and then gradually faded into the maze of trees and vines. The viper's pupils retracted, and it returned to its former state of sleep and digestion.

When members of the pygmy tribes travel through the rainforest, they are most likely going from one known location to another on a specific mission, or they are hunting, searching for honey, mushrooms, ground nuts, or edible roots. When hunting and gathering, they usually work in groups, or, if alone, they are connected to a family unit that is never far away. They also tend to follow existing game trails formed by animals or their own people.

On this day, however, these two pygmies did not appear to be following any established trail. They were also alone. There was no hunting or gathering group nearby, but the older pygmy led on with the certainty that he knew exactly where he was going; as if some internal mechanism were guiding him; some connection that was an essential part of his whole, that bound him to the all that was his world—the sounds, the smells, the very energy that emanated from the animate and the inanimate.

The forest was very old here. The trees were large with trunks that reached upward like sentient giants, uninterrupted in a cycle initiated in the earliest beginnings of time. The continuous canopy of interlacing foliage above resulted in a perpetual gloom that dominated this realm, obscuring the fact that the ground level was surprisingly open and relatively easy to walk through. Yet, with little sunlight to provide a source of direction, navigation through such a world was a complex enterprise.

Through this primeval world the old man led on, not driven so much as drawn—drawn to some destination that was essential to him and to his grandson. And as they progressed, the grandson, like his grandfather had in the past, created his own internal map of where he was going and where he had been. Each ran his eyes back and forth, scanning everything that lay in their direction of travel as well as outward, to each side, down to the ground, and up into the midstory above. They stooped to pass under a descending vine, stepped or hopped over roots and fallen branches, then altered their direction to circumvent the larger tree buttresses, many of which far surpassed the older man's height. They were in tune with every sound and every smell that sifted through the air.

The day was half over when the pygmies arrived at the edge of an escarpment, where the ground dropped off abruptly. Looking downward, their gaze followed the descending flow of the forest floor to where it quickly evaporated into a dark entanglement of massive trees. Trees whose trunks appeared to reach down, extending their lengths deep into a bottomless confusion below while their crowns remained level with the forest that grew above.

The younger pygmy stood close to the old man, whose hand rested on his shoulder, and the two stared in silent contemplation. The older pygmy breathed deeply, then leaned his spear against a tree and grasped the wooden shaft with both hands. It was a primitive forest trumpet with an open chamber, split into two branching stumps that projected out from one end like small antler stubs. He lifted it to his mouth and began to sing into the open end. His voice became amplified through the instrument as it flowed outward and filled the forest. The sound grew deeper—the long melodic timbre unbroken until the old man paused to refill his lungs. He began again, and this time his grandson joined in. Now, as the old man's song returned, it was deeper than before, originating in his chest and projecting out as a deep bass. In contrast, his grandson's voice came from his head—the sound much higher—the voice of a boy. And, it came out as a yodel, rolling smoothly at first, then breaking into a fluttering of atonal sounds. He began to add occasional whistles and clucking embellishments, as the two wove their voices into a cyclical roller coaster of polyphonic complexity—a sound, not so much human, but something almost mythical and otherworldly. It played on and on, circled back to the original unbroken harmonious movement, then returned to the yodeling, and finally to a stuttering mix of clucking, clicking, and shouting. They were singing to the forest and as their song slowed, the breaks between sounds became longer and the intensity began to soften, settling finally to mere whispers and then, together—they stopped. Total stillness hung in the air. Seconds, which seemed like hours, passed, and then a single beetle clicked, a bird began to sing, soon joined by others, then a chattering of monkeys and the distant trumpet of an elephant, as the forest sang back. And deep within the darkness below, the eyes of some creature stared out— bright gold lanterns against the blackness. They disappeared for an instant, then reappeared.

Far above a gust of wind rushed through the upper branches, spreading them apart and opening, for a brief moment, a doorway to the sky. And as the branches parted, a single shaft of sunlight slipped down through the canopy and sent a dancing shimmer across the chests of both man and boy. The two looked up, and as they did, a spec of light appeared. Followed by a thin, continuous cloud, it travelled in a perfectly straight line as it sliced across the sun, then disappeared behind the foliage. A sudden gasp escaped the old man's lips. He and the boy stared at each other—the boy's eyes questioning. The old man returned his gaze to the sky, but the branches had once again closed. The two stepped back from the edge where the ground dropped away and the boy looked at the old man who reached out and hugged him gently. The boy asked what it was that they had seen in the sky and the man replied using a word from the language of the tall Bantu people because certain words did not exist in their own.

"*Bobé*," he said. "Evil," he repeated. The boy saw a fear in the old man's eyes such as he had never seen before.

2 – THE BODY

The morning when Kutka Volkov's frozen body was discovered and dragged up into the tiny vestibule of the old Orthodox Church, the temperature was minus-eighteen degrees and a foot of new-fallen snow was on the ground with more still coming down.

All thirty-four residents of the village were there, for in the middle of winter in a remote mountain village like Dersu, Sunday morning church was the major, and, for some, the only event of the week. Seven of the community elders were squeezed into the vestibule, talking in muted tones around the body, as children of various ages squeezed into the doorway, straining their necks to get a glimpse. Everyone else stood back in the nave gathered around Anna Samardziza, the old spinster who made her living gathering ginseng, and the one who had discovered the body earlier that morning. Anna, her eyes wide, was speaking nervously and shaking, unable to shed the cold. She had never before been the center of attention of so many people.

The priest, Batushka Petrov, was standing alone on the front porch, flapping his gloved hands against his sides in a losing battle to beat off the brutal chill while each gust of wind blew through him as if he were naked. He was anxiously looking up the road when an old KAMAZ dump truck belched and grumbled its way into view. Three people were huddled together in the cab as the truck ground to a halt directly in front of him. The driver, a robust, gray-bearded man dressed in army surplus fatigues with a light-brown fur Ushanka hat, flaps pulled down tight over his ears, climbed out.

Petrov greeted him by name, "Boris, has the local Militsiya got you working as a chauffeur now?"

"Zolnerowich's fancy government-issue pickup wouldn't start this morning, and I must have been the only one stupid enough to get out of bed when he called around for help," Boris responded. "Besides, Chachy is almost extended family you know. How could I not come?"

By then, Junior Sergeant Pavel Zolnerowich, the district police constable, and Chachy Volkov, Kutka's wife and now widow, had come around from the other side of the truck. All three of them scurried up the steps to the priest who took Chachy's gloved hands between his. Her eyes were red and filled with apprehension and fear. The priest took her in his arms and held her close, then with one arm still around her shoulder, looked at the other two and said, "Come on! Let's get inside."

The elders gathered around the body moved back into the nave as Betushka Petrov and the newcomers entered. Chachy immediately dropped to her knees and cried out, "Kutka!" as she leaned over to embrace his head, only to bolt back suddenly as if she had been given an electrical shock. Her eyes opened wide, and her chin retracted back into her rigid neck, the veins and tendons tightening. The expression on her face went from fear and destitution to horror and confusion. Kutka was frozen solid; his body solid as stone. His bodily fluids had all become ice and had swelled both inward and outward, causing a grotesque bloating with the skin beginning to crack in places. Ice had glazed up over his face giving the impression that all of his features had been partially erased, and his eyes were wide open, bulging out of their sockets, the pupils and irises almost nonexistent as if all color had leaked out. His thin mustache had become a pair of icicles sprouting outward above his mouth, which was wide open as though fast-frozen just as he had gasped desperately for his last breath of air.

Chachy's hands trembled. She flung them upward and violently grabbed at her own face while a sickening, choking sound rose up from her damaged soul, attempting to force its way out. Boris, who was closest to her, immediately stooped down beside her, pulled her

6

hands back from her head, then wrapped his arms around her and gently drew her to his chest.

By now a stillness had fallen across the people of Dersu. Everyone stood motionless in the nave, staring toward the vestibule, hardly breathing, trapped in a mass hypnotic trance. Beyond the door Chachy, now completely limp, began to sob as Boris rocked her gently back and forth and all succumbed to the enveloping winter silence, broken only by a cold gust of wind that pushed against the building around them. A branch broke in the forest nearby, roof battens rattled over head while the muffled cry of human despair drifted like a fog into the nave, filling the air and rising into the onion-shaped dome above. The silence of death lingered interminably until finally one of the younger children began to cry—and then another joined in, followed by several of the older women who started into their slow moaning dirge of shared grief.

Pavel Zolnerowich cleared his throat, coughed into his hand, still gloved, and asked, "Who found him?"

"Anna Samardziza," someone replied.

He looked around until he locked eyes with Anna, then nodded to her, stepped through the nave door and asked, "Where did you find him, Anna?"

Slightly over six feet, the junior sergeant towered over Anna Samardziza by at least a foot, and, even though she had known him since he was a child, his overwhelming physique when combined with the aura of authority implied by his dark blue-black policeman's overcoat, black boots, belt, and pistol only added a sense of intimidation to her emotional state. Her eyes flitted back and forth, and she was unable to maintain eye contact with him as she attempted to speak.

"I—I saw the s-smoke," she stuttered in reply.

"Smoke?" he asked.

"Ye-yes. C-coming from the place where he stays—sometimes— sometimes Kutka stays there. If … if he's been hunting."

"Ah, you mean the abandoned farmhouse going up the old logging trail," affirmed Pavel.

7

"Batushka g-got three of the others to help, and they d-dragged him b-back here," continued Anna.

"Will you come and show me exactly where you found him?" asked Pavel.

"Y-yes, yes, of course," she said as she pulled a heavy wool scarf from her pocket and wrapped it around her head.

As he gently placed his hand on Anna's shoulder, Pavel turned to the priest and said, "Batushka, you know, none of these people will be going home soon. Maybe you could get some of them to join in—cook up something warm for everyone. We won't be long."

"Yes. Good idea," the priest responded, and as Anna and her police escort stepped around the frozen cadaver and exited the building, Petrov's voice could be heard asking for volunteers, followed by a sudden surge in excitement that helped drown out the droning of the mourners. As Pavel was about to shut the door, a thought crossed his mind. He leaned back into the building and addressing the entire group said, "Let's keep the door between the nave and the vestibule closed. We don't want Kutka thawing out yet. You'll never be able to dig a grave with the ground frozen like this."

The snow continued to deepen as the old woman and the policeman began to walk. "Tell me, Anna," the sergeant asked, "What caused you to go up to the old cabin? You said you saw smoke?"

"Yes," she replied, "I saw the smoke so I knew Kutka was probably there. I was on my way to church, and since he is usually alone when he stays there, I thought to invite him to come along." The effort it took Anna to trudge through the cold and the deepening snow allowed her to forget her apprehension, and she had stopped stuttering. Holding tight to Pavel's arm she looked up and without his noticing gave him a little smile.

It took only ten minutes to get to the log cabin, and although the smoke was no longer rising from the metal stovepipe projecting above the roof, the odor of smoke still hung in the air. The new snow had already covered most of the tracks made when the body had been dragged up to the church, but Anna seemed pretty certain of where she had found Kutka.

"He was here in this ditch," she said. "I tapped on the door first, and when he didn't answer, I opened the door and looked in. He wasn't there, and I thought maybe he had gone into the trees to relieve himself, so I just closed the door and was about to go back when I saw him. All covered in snow. At first I thought it was a pile of branches or something in the ditch, but it didn't seem right. I was scared but told myself he had just passed out from drinking or something. I went to shake him but could tell right away that he was completely frozen. He must have been lying there most of the night—oh, God!"

Pavel pulled her closer, his own subtle gesture of comfort, then said, "Let's take a look inside." They entered through the cabin's only door and quickly shut it behind them. The stove still radiated some heat, but it was well below freezing in the dark, dingy cabin and almost impossible to see anything. One window was covered in old newspapers, and the other had a makeshift burlap curtain nailed to the frame above. Pavel pulled down the curtain to reveal the minimal setting of the cabin's interior. What furniture there was consisted of an old straw-filled mattress lying on the floor in one corner, two wooden chairs, a short bench, and a table. Kutka's hunting rifle was leaning against the wall next to the door, along with his old Soviet army backpack, and the partially skinned carcass of a deer was laid out on the table, a large blood-smeared knife next to it, and a folded-over wad of money. He opened the wad and saw that it consisted of American dollars. Kutka's job was unique in that he was paid in American dollars directly by the international conservation organization that funded his work. Pavel thought to himself, *Kutka made more money in one month than I make in four.*

And then there were two empty vodka bottles, one standing upright on the bench and the other on its side on the floor below. Pavel picked up the bottle from the floor, looked at it and shook his head, rolling his lips inward ever so slightly.

"OK, Anna," he sighed. Let's get back to the church. I'm going to have to get Boris to drive me back and then I'll need to make a report." Just before opening the door, he picked up Kutka's backpack. It was heavy, and using both hands, he emptied it onto the floor where out fell a couple extra pairs of socks, two cans of sprats, a clip of cartridges for his rifle, and the radio tracker and monitor he used for tracking tagged wildlife. He then replaced everything and slipped the money in as well, muttering to himself, "I need to give this to Chachy. She's going to need it now."

As the two of them began their walk back to the church, Pavel Zolnerowich thought to himself, *fucking vodka*. He knew what he was going to write in his report. He would say that Kutka Volkov, former member—no, former, *decorated* member of the Primorsky elite anti-poaching ranger brigade, had died as the result of an accident. He had tripped and fallen into a ditch that was concealed in snow and hit his head on the frozen ground that caused him to lose consciousness, eventually leading to his death from exposure. He just wouldn't mention the possible role of the vodka. Too damn many Russians seemed to die every year from excessive drinking, and Kutka Volkov had been one of the good ones.

Had Pavel Zolnerowich been more experienced as an investigator, he might have noticed a set of unusual tracks that led away from the cabin and up into the forest. They were almost hidden by the snow now, but still discernable. They were the tracks of a snowmobile, a piece of equipment that no one in Dersu or the surrounding district had ever owned.

3 – THE BLIND

Twenty-four hours earlier, Kutka Volkov had been perched alongside another man in a most unusual metallic cupola-like structure extending from the top of a very large, tracked military amphibious personnel carrier. It had been painted white, much of the armor had been removed, and where small gun ports, vision blocks, and optical devices once pierced its armored skin, there were now several thin, horizontal windows. The original truncated cone turret had been replaced by a hexagonal structure that resembled a large crow's nest. The bottom half was constructed from solid metal panels with steel pipes rising from each corner of the hexagon, supporting a wide, flat roof and leaving the upper half wide open on all sides. Both men were bundled in Russian military parkas with fur-lined Ushanka hats and heavy gloves. Kutka, who was descended from the original indigenous people of the region, the Udege, wore a traditional tunic, just visible under his parka. His black hair, sliced with occasional streaks of gray, was tied up in braids to each side, and he had a long, thin face, accentuated by a pair of large, protruding ears and a forehead that slanted back sharply, revealing deep brown, almost black eyes. His companion was well over six feet in height. The light reflecting from the snow gave his pale grey-blue eyes an eerie appearance, as if they had no irises. Kutka's parka and hat were both camouflage army surplus while the other man's were modern winter white with white sable fur linings; he was a man of means.

The companion rested his elbows on a wooden armrest that capped the top of the crow's nest's enclosure as he looked at something with a pair of binoculars.

11

"Ah, yes—I see it now. That big pine tree," he said. "Those are definitely scratches. Man, you got eyes like a hawk. I don't know how you could have seen that."

"You just need to spend more time in the woods. When you've spent your life in these mountains, you get to where you see all the little details."

The head of a third man popped up from an open hatchway in the cupola floor. He lifted a glass filled with a clear liquid and said, "Oleg, tiens—voila, pour toi," he spoke in French. "Keep you warm up here," he added, now in English."

Olegushka Levkov, the man with Kutka, bent down, took the glass, gulped its contents in one quick shot, handed the glass back without a word, then continued to scan the area around the tree through his binoculars. Glancing back at the man in the hatch, he said, "Martel, tell Viper to get on the tracker. Looks like we might be getting close."

"You see tracks?" asked Martel.

"Fresh scratch marks on a tree over there. Get Viper on the tracker."

Without a word, Martel's head dropped back through the hatch and into the vehicle's dimly lit interior where two more people, a man and a woman, sat on wooden fold-up benches. The woman had just finished pouring French Napoleon brandy into some vodka glasses and pushed one across the table to her companion. The man who was seated further back into an unlit corner of the cabin with his upper torso completely concealed in the darkness, reached out, grasped one of the glasses, then lifted it back into the shadows. The sound of his swallow could be heard, followed by a heavy sigh of satisfaction, then his hand reappeared, plopping the empty glass down on the table.

The woman emptied a jar of caviar onto a plate, then reached up and offered a glass to Martel as he stepped off the ladder. As Martel took the glass, he motioned toward the front of the vehicle with it and said, "Viper, Oleg thinks we're close and wants you to turn on the tracker."

"Huh—OK," grunted Viper. He quickly reached out, tapped his empty glass, and the woman refilled it. He gulped it down, leaned

12

forward, and looked up toward Martel. As his head rotated into the light, part of it appeared to glow, like an eclipsed moon moving back into the sun's exposure. His scalp was clean shaven, and the left half of his head was entirely coated in a confusion of reptilian patterned tattooing, the split running vertically from the top of his spine, up and across his cranium, then down between the eyes and along the length of his nose, at which point it was swallowed up by hair. His baldness was counter-balanced by a thick black beard that hung down to his chest. The division across his head rendered an imbalance to his eyes, which emitted a deep sense of meanness.

Viper hesitated, took another drink, swallowed it, then shifted up to the driver's seat, switched on a radio-like device and began rotating one of the knobs, making adjustments as a pulsing light appeared on the face of the monitor.

"Here, Martel, take some," said the woman holding the plate.

"I can't eat that shit now. I do not have an appetite with that fucking stench in here."

"The question is, does the stench come from pig shit, or is it Martel?" asked the woman with a smirk on her face.

"Watch your mouth, *salope*, or you'll end up with your face getting rubbed in that pig shit," responded Martel as he pointed to something toward the back of the vehicle. Viper chuckled, and the woman lifted her glass as if toasting him.

They were all speaking in English, but each had an accent, and each accent was different. Martel was French, but Viper was obviously Russian, and the woman was American. She also spoke some Russian, which she did with Viper, making occasional short comments, peppered with sarcasm that had the tendency to alienate Martel, who did not speak Russian. The conversation would switch languages in mid-sentence, going from English to Russian to French, occasionally resulting in some confusion, and with the drinking, voices grew loud, and Martel had a tendency toward paranoia.

"Keep the noise down, you idiots!" came Oleg's voice from above. "Viper, are you looking at the tracker?"

"I am, boss." Viper answered as he continued to manipulate the device in front of him. Then, raising his hand, he said in a loud whisper, "Hey! Everyone quiet!" Then a little louder, "Boss, we're almost on top of him. Shit!"

Martel and the woman set their glasses down and turned to look out the windows as Oleg jumped down into the compartment from above. Moving toward Viper he said, "Let me see that thing." He nudged Viper aside as he looked at the screen, "Oh yes! OK, everyone, this is it! He's really close—really close!" Then looking back up into the cupola he called out, in Russian, "Kutka, down here!"

Kutka quickly descended into the compartment as Oleg turned to the Frenchman, "You and Aziza get the door. Viper, you and Kutka go ahead and move our friend out there. Hurry up everyone! I'll give you two a hand with the crate."

The three quickly put on their coats, hats, and gloves, and then Martel flipped the latch on the large sidewall door while the woman, Aziza, assisted by grabbing the handle on the lower panel. Together they pushed it open, the top half gliding upwards and the bottom, with its non-slip foot treads, dropped out and down to form a sloped walkway. As the outside light illuminated the darkened area toward the back of the vehicle's compartment, a deep grunting sound followed by a series of ear-wrenching squeals erupted from a large wooden crate. Oleg, Viper, and Kutka pushed and pulled the crate to the opening where the other two, now outside, helped to slide it down the lower door panel onto the snow-covered ground. By this time, the squealing had gotten much louder, and the crate was shaking back and forth. Kutka jumped out onto the ground, flipped a wire that had been securing one end of the crate, dropped open the end panel, reached inside, and with his right hand wrapped around a rope, pulled a squealing pig out into the snow.

Viper followed the cage out onto the ground as Kutka looked at him, then back over his shoulder, motioning with his head up toward the clearing that went off the upper side of the logging trail, and said, "We need to get him to the sapling out in the middle there." One small isolated ash tree sat eighty to a hundred feet away in the middle of a long, narrow clearing. Kutka pulled the pig by the rope and Viper pushed from behind.

While they were struggling with the pig, Martel and Aziza had disappeared back inside the vehicle, returning almost immediately, each holding an AK-47, aimed toward the two sides of the clearing. By this time, Oleg was back up in his cupola with a lever-action Browning BLR pointed toward the far end of the clearing, over the heads of the two men and the squealing pig.

The pig seemed to understand that it was about to become part of something very unpleasant, and it resisted, pulling back as hard as it could on the rope as its squealing intensified. The two men were strong, and within five minutes they had the animal securely tied to the base of the sapling. They immediately turned and ran quickly back to the personnel carrier, Viper slipping in the snow at one point and almost falling on his face. As he regained his balance and continued on he could be heard laughing to himself—like an adolescent delinquent who had just pulled-off a mindless prank.

Once everyone was back inside the vehicle and the door shut, a complete silence fell over the clearing and the forest around. The pig had stopped its wailing and now was trying to burrow into the snow. Kutka and Martel joined Levkov in the cupola while Aziza quietly positioned herself below at one of the windows that faced out toward the clearing and the foredoomed pig. Viper was back on the radio tracker. "He's moving," Viper whispered. "When we went out the monitor showed that he was about five hundred yards to the far-right side of the clearing somewhere. Now he's moved in really close. Can you guys see anything?"

Kutka set his gun aside, took up the binoculars, and scanned the dense snow- covered brush on the right side of the clearing. "I see him," he said. "He's low to the ground—crawling on his belly; looking straight at the pig now; slowing down. Get ready, he's going to go any second."

"I don't see him yet," said Oleg, "but I'm positioned to get a shot off to the right side, assuming he keeps coming that way. This gun holds three shots, so no one else shoots unless I mess up and don't get him right away. Kutka, stay on the binoculars and keep talking to me. Martel, just be ready." He glanced quickly at Martel, realizing that he'd been speaking in Russian. He repeated himself in French.

"Stopped moving," said Kutka. "He knows we're here or at least knows something is over here. He's very still. Just moved his head toward us—now back to the pig. Get ready! He just drooped his head and tightened up. He's gonna spring!"

Without a sound, the blurred form of a large Amur tiger shot across the clearing as if it had been launched from a powerful catapult. If Oleg had blinked his eyes at that instant he never would have seen the huge cat until it was on top of the pig. He fired his rifle once, and an explosion of snow kicked up on the far side of the clearing, the shot was behind the cat. He cocked and fired again. The tiger had half the pig's head and neck in its mouth by then and suddenly flinched, jerking its head upward and arching its back as the second bullet tore off a piece of its spine. It dropped the pig and tried to turn back toward the cover of the forest, but the pain in its back caused it to arch upward again as its body went into a spastic gyration, then finally, Oleg got off his final shot which knocked the cat over onto its side where it remained still.

"*Merde*!" exclaimed Martel. "I can't believe how fast that fucker was moving, man! Can you imagine—if you were standing down there and he was coming at you? I would have shit in my pants before I could pull the trigger. Oh, *mon Dieu*!" He was shaking but he howled with laughter.

The side of the personnel carrier opened, and everyone filed out and started walking, with caution, toward the two dead animals. Kutka led the way with his AK-47 held ready, aimed at the motionless tiger. The others held back several feet while he prodded the cat with the end of his gun. He then leaned his rifle against the huge body of the cat, grabbed it by its two ears and lifted the head up. "There's your trophy, Oleg. This is a big one; could be over seven hundred pounds."

"Nice shot," said Martel.

"Nice three shots," added Kutka. "Good follow-up shots, Oleg. You tracked him, and you stayed with him."

As everyone now looked at Oleg, he straightened into a commanding posture and said, "OK, everyone, let's get this cleaned up and get out of here."

◆　◆

It was dark, Viper had just shut off the engine, and the personnel carrier now sat at the intersection of two old logging trails. The hatch to the canopy was shut tight to the falling snow, and everyone was gathered around the portable table between the two benches. Oleg had just counted out a pile of money—euros—and handed it over to Kutka. "Here you go my friend. Not bad for five days of your time, huh? You gonna retire now?"

"Either that or he's gonna get himself a shitload of vodka and disappear 'til spring comes around," said Aziza with a chuckle.

"What you people need to do is take your trophy and disappear now," responded Kutka. "You know if anyone ever got wind of this and connected me to it, they'd cut my manhood off before they sent me to Siberia for the rest of my life. Even Putin is now in on this conservation kick. Last summer they had a phony photo set-up of him supposedly releasing an injured tiger back into the forest."

"You're gonna be all right, Kutka, and you know that," answered Viper, who was seated next to, but slightly behind him. Viper stared intensely at the Russian, his right eye twitching slightly while he plucked hairs out of his nostril, an unpleasant habit he fell into when he assumed no one was watching.

"I'll be straight with you people. I need the money. This is not what I want to see happen to these animals. I've spent twenty years chasing poachers and trying to protect them. Not just the tigers, but the leopards, the boars, the wolves. They won't take this lightly if anyone ever finds out."

"Kutka, Viper's going to take you home on the snowmobile while we get over to Vadenka." Oleg laughed to himself and added, "Yeah,

17

we're supposed to be assessing what's left of our timber subsidiary over there. Viper, you can catch up with us by morning."

"I don't want to go to my place now," said Kutka. "You can drop me off at the old hunting cabin I use just outside of Dersu. It's closer anyway."

"OK then, Dersu it is. Martel, you help Kutka get the snowmobile out while I look at the map with Viper. I want to make sure he knows where he's going when he gets to Vadenka."

As they opened the side door up, Oleg handed a knapsack to Viper. "The radio tracker's in here along with a couple bottles of vodka. Maybe you can celebrate a bit with him when you get him to his cabin. He's a potential loose end that I don't think we want to be worrying about."

With a subtle hint of a smile on his face, Viper took the knapsack, stepped out of the personnel carrier, and joined Kutka who was now waiting next to the snowmobile.

Five hours later, Viper was straddling Kutka Volkov's motionless body, both of his hands firmly grasping the back of Kutka's head, pushing it down into the snowy bank of the ditch that ran along the old logging trail just across from the cabin at the far end of the village of Dersu. Dersu, one of the most remote villages to be found along the western slope of the Sikhote-Alin mountain range, almost dead in the center of Primorsky Krai, and a few miles south of the newly formed 72,000-hectare Sredneussuriisky Wildlife Refuge, one of the last protective holdouts for the highly endangered Amur tiger, still known by some as the Siberian tiger.

4 – THE TRACKER

"Home Base, this is Peregrine 3, do you read me? Home Base— come-in, Peregrine." The short-wave radio on the table next to the young woman with short-cropped chestnut hair had suddenly jumped to life. The woman coughed, spilling a mouthful of coffee down the front of her sweatshirt. She quickly placed the cup on the table, grabbed the microphone next to the radio and flipped the switch on.

"Peregrine 3, this is base and I read you, but lots of static. Is that you, Tim? Over."

"Yeah, Abby, it's me. We had a little bad luck here—had to go back to Advanced Base Camp. Problem with one of the clients."

"Oh shit. That's not what I want to be hearing. We were expecting you guys to be summiting in a few hours. What kinda problem?" she responded.

"Client Koufax got AMS and it came on fast. Before we realized what was happening he started flipping out—ended up with what might be a busted ankle. Almost killed himself and could have taken some of us with him.

"Nooo," she muttered to herself, "Acute mountain sickness. Could turn to cerebral edema, and we'd have a dead body on our hands." "Not good, Tim," she responded. "Hold-on—let me get Billy." She turned in her seat toward an open doorway and shouted out, "Billy, get your ass in here, quick. Tim's on the horn, and they got a problem!"

Through the doorway came a creaking sound followed by a heavy thump on the old spruce flooring, quick shuffling feet, an animal-like moan, and then the burly head of a large black-bearded man, eyes blinking as he tried to adjust to the light. "What's going on?"

"He says they were about to summit when the guy from Chicago got AMS. He must have started to hallucinate or something. Sounds like maybe a broken ankle too. They needed to evacuate him right away and got him back to Advanced Base Camp, which is where they are now."

"Let me talk to him," said Billy, taking the microphone as Abby slid out of the chair. "Tim, Billy here. How is the guy now?"

"We pushed some pills into him soon as we saw what was happening. We're at the ranger's tent, and the medic's checking out his foot now. It's swelled pretty bad, but the AMS may still be a problem. He hasn't responded the way he should to the pills. Medic here seems a bit concerned—wants to get him down to a lower elevation as soon as possible. Everyone else is in great shape, though."

"What are your conditions up there?"

"It was nineteen below at High Camp but a little warmer here. Wind's a bit breezy now—twenty, maybe twenty-five miles per hour. Sky's crystal-clear—not a cloud. It's beautiful man. Rest of the team's really pressuring us to get back up there, and it don't get no better than this."

"All right." Billy looked at the clock on the wall. It was exactly three minutes after six. "Make sure the rangers can evacuate Koufax, then get the clients back up to Advance Camp. Go for the summit again tomorrow."

"Not that easy, Billy. Rangers' helicopter's out of action and they can't get another one for at least forty-eight hours. I was thinking about sending de Rycken down the mountain with Koufax. What do you think?"

"Tim, see if a couple of the rangers can help get him past Windy Corner. Even with the sled you'll need someone to rope the thing down there. If you can get someone to help with that, then go ahead and get the expedition back on track. Meanwhile we'll have a team start up from Base Camp to intercept de Rycken at one of the low camps. That'll be a long-ass haul, but that's the best we can do. Least the weather's not gone haywire. OK?"

"All right, Billy, we can do that. Got it."

"I know I can count on you two. Tell Zee to check in with me as soon as they're down. Thanks Tim—and have a great summit."

"OK. We'll check in again as soon as we hit the top, assuming I can get through. Over and out."

"Shit, Billy," said Abby. "Koufax is big. He must be forty or fifty pounds heavier than Zee. You think Zee can get him down alone? Could be over eight thousand feet of descent before they run into the guys from base."

"Should be a piece of cake for my little Zee," said Billy, as he turned, walked out of the room and pulled out his cell phone.

♦ ♦

Carver Hayden was already awake at ten minutes after six when his phone started playing the opening notes to Beethoven's Fifth Symphony. "What now?" he grumbled as he put his glasses on, found the phone and picked it up. "Carver here," he said as he started to pour his first cup of coffee.

"Carver, it's Billy," came a voice on the phone.

"Billy, what the hell, man. This is Sunday morning, dude. The sun's hardly up. What's up?"

"You're asking me? What are you doing up so early?"

"Can't sleep. This Africa thing's really tearing me up. I'll be honest with you, Billy. I'm scared. They got me booked on a flight to D.C. tomorrow, then the Congo the day after, and I don't have my shit together."

"Timing is tight, but maybe I can help. Carver, the tracker I told you about is suddenly going to be available. You said this was a super urgent situation for your people. So, as it happens, Zee de Rycken's pulling some sick dude off Denali as we speak, and they should be arriving on the glacier sometime tonight. How'd you like to go up and introduce yourself in person when they arrive?"

"You can get me to Denali base camp by tonight?" Carver asked.

21

"If you can get to the hangar in Bellingham by ten, we got an air taxi making a run up there this morning and I can get you on. You up for it?"

"Billy, this is great. I need to check in with the office so they know what we're up to, then I'll be in my car and on my way. Will you be there—or, who do I ask for when I get there?"

"No, I'm not going. Just ask for Mark when you get there. He's new, but a super good pilot. I'll let him know you're gonna be there."

"Thank you, Billy. This is really important! Later, dude."

◆ ◆

It was 9:45 a.m. when Carver Hayden drove up to the security gate at the Bellingham International Airport. There had been almost no one on the road, and he was able to drive from the north suburbs of Seattle up to the airport in Whatcom County in less time than it would have taken to drive south and wait for a flight out of SEATAC. A guard pointed him toward a private hangar area, and within minutes he found himself standing in front of the Peregrine Expeditions hangar. A small turbo prop was sitting just in front of the hangar, and two men were in the process of loading it up with large waterproof cargo bags.

"One of you guys named Mark?" asked Carver as he approached.

"That's me," said the nearest man. "You must be Carver." They shook hands and Mark guided Carver into the plane. "I thought I was gonna be alone today so it was good to hear from Billy that you'd be coming. It's not that long a trip, but always nice to have someone to talk to."

Ten minutes later the plane was airborne, and within another fifteen they were settled into their cruising altitude. "What kind of plane is this?" asked Carver.

"Otter," answered Mark. "Biggest plane that can land at Denali Base and the only one with enough range to make it up there from Bellingham. Most people have to fly into Talkeetna from Anchorage or Seattle, then switch to a Beaver for the final leg. Hiring me and getting this Otter was a big jump for these guys. Billy's hoping to double the number of expeditions by next year. This is becoming a really competitive business and this plane is just one more way to give us an edge on some of the other outfits.

"So Billy says you're going up and then coming right back, maybe in the company of one of our guides?"

"That's right," answered Carver. As odd as it may sound, I'm going up to offer a job to one of your guides. Problem is, I need him now and he doesn't even know I'm coming. You know Zee de Rycken?"

"This is my first season with the company so I don't really know everyone yet. I haven't met Zee but definitely heard the name," answered Mark.

"How many guides you guys have on Denali now?"

"For Denali we've got three expedition teams, and each team's got two guides; I think one team has three. They each do two expeditions during the season. It's short you know—May through July. Before May it's too cold, then by July it gets too stormy. Small window, and each expedition can take up to thirty days. They're just now finishing their last trip for this season—which leads me to ask: what makes you think Zee will want to go running off on another trip? These guys usually need a good break right about now, not another expedition."

Carver didn't respond but just sat staring out the window, nervously gnawing at his upper lip.

They remained quiet for a while, Carver continuing to look down at the passing landscape, but not really seeing it. Mark broke the silence again, asking, "So what's so important that you got to come up here in person to hire a guide?"

"I work for a big international corporation and we had a really high-profile research team suddenly disappear on us. The guy leading the team is a close friend as well as a colleague, and I've been given the job of finding them. I need a very special kind of tracker to pull it off. Apparently their lives are in grave danger; in fact it's possible they might not even be alive now. Billy told me this de Rycken was the person I needed to pull the job off—said they knew each other in the army."

"Talking to the other people working for this outfit, I understand Billy's a real class act. The guy's smart, fit like a rock and really has a knack for choosing the right people. If Billy says the guy's your man, he probably knows what he's sayin'. How d'you know Billy?"

"We were roommates in college—played football together. I was more into academics—went on to grad school. Billy was a third-round pick in the NFL but had this strange need to go into the military. I think 9/11 had a really profound impact on him as a kid and he never got over it. He was in Special Forces. That's where he met de Rycken. Says de Rycken was the best tracker anyone had ever seen."

"So where you guys goin' then? I mean, where did this crew disappear?"

"Africa."

"Africa?" shouted Mark, "you're kidding. You come up to the top of the coldest place on earth to find someone to guide you into Africa? Kilimanjaro?"

"No, the Congo. Right in the middle of the damned Congo."

◆　◆

Their touchdown on the southeast fork of the Kahitna Glacier was a textbook landing. Carver helped Mark and Jacob, a coordinator at the base camp, unload the plane. The airport was unique. The runway was compacted snow and there were no permanent structures of any kind. There were two smaller planes sitting off to one side, and then several groups of tents set up in random clusters around the site. When they finished unloading, Mark flew off with the plane to get it refueled at a nearby landing strip and Jacob led Carver over to one of the tents where he picked up some binoculars and outfitted Carver with a parka and snow boots. From the tent, they walked out to the edge of a vast downward sloping area that was strewn with spines of granite, and there, Jacob began scanning the far side.

"They're coming from down there?" asked Carver.

"Yeah—Heartbreak Hill. Last leg of the journey after climbing all the way up and then back down Denali is uphill. It's a real ball-buster. Here," he said, as he passed the binoculars to Carver. "Keep looking. I'll go get a thermos of coffee ready. They should be showing up any time now and they'll be wiped out."

"See anything?" asked Jacob as he returned.

"Just white on white," answered Carver.

Jacob took the binoculars again and within seconds broke into a smile. "There they are—just popped up over that ridge. Looks like they got the client on the sled. De Rycken's coming up behind—must be wiped out by now. Here, take a look." He handed the binoculars to Carver and then helped get him oriented.

"Yeah, I think I see them. Yeah. There's one guy alone behind the others with the sled. Looks tired too—like he's walking in slow motion. Oops, they just disappeared—went into a dip or something."

"Zee's gonna be in bad shape when they get here. They've been moving for fifteen hours nonstop, descended twelve thousand feet in one day, at least four thousand pulling that guy. Let's go—more help the better. Here, you want to carry this?" he said to Carver as he handed him the thermos. "You are OK with a little hike, aren't you?"

Without waiting for an answer, Jacob took off and Carver followed as the two started down the long slope of Heartbreak Hill.

It was almost midnight when they finally ran into the two men towing the sled. After a quick greeting the rescuers continued their ascent with the sled and the injured man in tow; Jacob and Carver continued on. Within five minutes de Rycken, like a dark phantom backlit by the arctic midnight light, came into view, head down, and legs slowly dragging the cumbersome boots through the powdery snow.

Obviously exhausted, de Rycken seemed to have drifted into a semi-hypnotic state. As Jacob and Carver got closer they could hear the long, deep hissing of inhalations and exhalations, perfectly harmonized to the rhythm of the churning legs. De Rycken almost ran into them, but stopped short just in time and looked up as Jacob held out the now-open thermos and said, "Thought you could use some warm caffeine about now."

De Rycken ripped away goggles and helmet with one hand,

grabbed the thermos with the other and with head thrown back, began drinking, emitting short moaning sounds with each swallow of the warm liquid. Carver stood dead still and just stared. "What the... You're Zee? Zee de Rycken?"

"Zora's my name. Zora de Rycken. Who the hell are you?" she asked.

5 – THE MISSION

The distant glow of the midnight arctic sun crept southward across the landscape, barely keeping pace with the Otter and its six passengers. Mark finally broke the silence: "Look down there. We're just passing over Mt. St. Elias. You can see it rising up out of the ocean—eighteen thousand feet, straight up. Spectacular!"

Carver, the only passenger who had not fallen asleep, looked out the window. "Yeah, spectacular," he said with a sigh.

He watched the view for several minutes until some clouds got in the way, then settled back in his seat, took his glasses off, closed his eyes, and slowly massaged them with the thumb and forefinger of his left hand. He looked at his watch and mumbled to himself, "Twenty-two hours." He turned and glanced back at Koufax who was knocked-out from painkillers, and in the darkness of the plane's tail, the sprawled out forms of three returning climbers, lost in post-expeditionary slumber. He turned back and looked at Zora who sat in the seat across from his, slumped over, her head resting on the window. He had been looking at her constantly—ever since the Otter had finished its climb and leveled off. *I'm fucked,* he thought to himself. *She shot me down— like I was talking to a wall.* He closed his eyes once more, went through the routine of massaging his eyes again, and then turned his gaze back to the girl.

She had shed her heavy climbing wear as soon as they boarded the plane and now wore nothing but her thermal underwear—long johns with a buttoned-up long-sleeved top. He could see that she was fit; that didn't surprise him given her current job description. Her pitch-black hair was cropped short, *functional*, he thought, *not very fashionable, but not bad—maybe an army thing.* Her complexion seemed naturally dark. At first he thought it to be the result of high-altitude sun exposure, but then he caught a glimpse of her bare mid-section when she was pulling her sweater off. *Latina*, he thought. *Definitely Latina—with those big brown eyes—almost black. Name doesn't fit though—Billy mentioned she'd been married—husband killed in Iraq.*

"Little air turbulence coming up," said Mark, interrupting his train of thought.

Within seconds the plane shuddered as it slipped into a wall of dense clouds. "Thanks for the warning," said Carver.

"Shouldn't last long. Supposed to be pretty clear all the way down—not very typical for this coastline."

"Carver's your name?"

Carver's head snapped quickly back toward Zora. She was awake, sitting up straight, and looking at him. "Yes—Carver Hayden."

"You OK, Carver? You look—how should I say?—ill at ease?"

He looked at her, rubbed his hand back and forth across his mouth, then said, "I guess I'm a complete wreck about now. The man who's been my mentor and best friend these last couple of years is missing and might be dead—I have to find him, and I have no idea what the fuck I'm doing." He looked down and ran his hand through his hair, then looked back at her and continued. "He's in some remote jungle in the middle of the Congo. Billy said you were a guide—a tracker. He said you could help. I came all the way up here and you—you hardly give me the time of day then—you're out cold. I understand—it's just—"

"I guess I should apologize. I didn't mean to be so short. I'm just so god-damned tired."

"Of course," said Carver. "Just that after the build-up I got from Billy, I didn't expect you to just shut me out like that—and I am at the end of the road. I don't know where to turn."

Zora looked out the window for a minute, then at her watch. She turned back to Carver and said, "So Billy sent you, huh? We've got over an hour 'til we touch down. Why don't you fill-me in. I'll sleep later."

As Zora opened the coffee thermos and took a long swig, Carver began, "I work for Norton Timber International, or NTI, as you might know it from the initials on our building in Seattle. We're rated as one of the top five timber stocks by market cap. In the U.S., we manage 5.3 million acres of forestland and are licensed on another 12 million. We're actually owned by an Australian-based corporation which maintains holdings in all kinds of commodities, but they originally started in timber and still consider it as their primary interest."

"Sounds like you take great pride in being part of this company. Since we both know the bottom line for most corporations is profit, that would suggest you're not necessarily a tree-friendly individual— which leads me to ask how you and Billy ended up such good friends."

"Trees happen to be one of my passions in life, but we can talk about that and my relationship to Billy and to the company later. For now, let's focus on where we need to go and why."

"Fair enough. Go on."

"In addition to NTI, Norton also owns timber operations throughout South America, Asia, and Africa. One of those subsidiaries, CATI—Central African Timber International—is active in Cameroon, Gabon, the Central African Republic, the Democratic Republic of the Congo—commonly referred to as the DRC—and Congo. Now I understand from Billy that your African experience was in the DRC, which is politically the worst cesspool in Central Africa. Billy said that I should make it real clear to you that the DRC is *not* where we need to go. Our concern right now is the Republic of the Congo. I hope this will provide at least some relief to one of your concerns."

"To some degree."

"Five days ago, our top field scientist, along with one of our two in-country managers and a support group of half a dozen locals, just dropped-off the face of the earth while doing a highly crucial survey, somewhere in that region. The exact area where they disappeared is one of the least populated areas in the Congo basin and one of the least explored land areas in the world today. Now Billy swears to me that if I had to find a needle in a hay stake, and the hay stack was a jungle anywhere in the world—you would be the one person who could find it."

Zora looked at Carver with her bloodshot eyes for a minute, then let out a sigh and took another swig of coffee that leaked out and down one side of her chin. As she wiped her sleeve across her mouth, she continued. "If Billy hadn't sent you, I wouldn't listen to another word. Anyway, so what were your people doing in this remote area?"

"Our company uses satellite-aided technology to map areas that we have timber leases on as well as areas we are interested in for potential future leases. For quite some time, we've had really accurate documentation on literally every acre we have leased in North America and Asia. Now we also have pretty accurate maps of even the most remote areas in South America and Africa. We also have software that can tell us with a pretty high degree of accuracy, what tree species we are looking at in these areas. Recently, we have been able to obtain a whole new layer of info thanks to a system known as Lidar technology."

"Yeah, I've heard of it—light detection and ranging technology."

"Right. It directs pulses of light from a constant altitude of around two thousand feet toward the ground. Most of the light bounces off upper surface of the forest canopy, but several manage to penetrate to the ground. In both cases the light returns to the source where the difference then is measured. The information obtained allows the creation of topographic maps. My colleague, Russell Hoyt—the one who's gone missing—has managed to enhance this technology in a most interesting way. Basically, he developed a digital model that shows both the topography of the ground and—simultaneously—the topography of the canopy. His program then generates a mapping overlay that provides the heights of trees. He began using the program to analyze dense forested areas that would normally be difficult to access and in doing this, he has discovered an anomaly that, quite frankly, would appear to be impossible."

"And what would that be?"

"This area we're talking about in the north-west of Congo is filled with some kind of tree that looks like a form of Moabi—that's a highly valuable timber product from that area. But there is something remarkably unique about these trees—mainly, they're too tall—not just for the Moabi but for any species that could exist in this area—or anywhere in Africa."

"And how tall is that?" asked Zora.

"The data we've come up with is telling us that the trees in this part of the forest are possibly as tall as a redwood or a sequoia," said Carver.

"As Billy told you, I've spent a lot of time in jungles," said Zora. "Most of it's been in Costa Rica, but also, Columbia, Honduras and, as you know, the eastern Congo basin. I know trees can get big in the rain forests, but the tallest I've ever seen or heard of, would be around two hundred feet, less than that in the Congo, I would guess. From what I know, redwoods can get up to around three hundred feet. I don't see how something like that could have gone unnoticed in this day and age. What makes you think your information is reliable?"

"Hoyt was certain, but we just couldn't accept what we were seeing. We asked our field managers in the Congo to check on it for us and they told us, the area's extremely hard to get to and is completely unexplored. They didn't have the time or resources to access it. That's why Russell went over in person."

"And what kind of background did Russell have that led him to think he could go somewhere that his own field people couldn't get to?" asked Zora.

"He's got two degrees in forestry, and he did extensive field work in Thailand. He's also a great climber. He's fit—climbs trees, sort of like you climb mountains. He and I have the same basic credentials, both technically and physically. I climb also. I've done Baker and Rainier. I rock climb and also, I climb trees—that's why they want me to go find him, and to get the expedition back on track. And I know my trees," he added.

"I think I understand. If this forest really has trees that even come close to being as big as you say they are, the market value must be through the roof. So—it's about the money, again—more so than the lives of these people who've disappeared."

"I don't disagree with you on that at all. I know that the company is just licking their chops thinking about the potential value of a forest like this falling into their laps. For me personally though, it goes way beyond that. My colleague was—listen to me, I'm already talking like he's dead—*he is* a close friend. Like I said, he's my mentor. He got me this job—we hang out together. Billy knows him, too. He's family to me, so my personal interest in this expedition is to find Russell—that's what's driving my anxiety. That and the fact that the only rain forest I've ever been in, is on the Olympic Peninsula. I need your help."

Zora sighed then asked, "Did Billy tell you about our little adventure in the Congo."

"No details. But he told me the both of you were part of a hush-hush special-ops thing in the eastern end of the DRC, and it sounded like he shares your aversion toward that mission and that particular area. Where we need to go is at least a thousand miles away in the north of Congo—Brazzaville-Congo."

"OK," she said as she looked back out the window. Several minutes of silence passed, then she began to speak again, still staring out the window, "I swore on my mother's grave I'd never go back there." She shifted back toward Carver and went on, "I texted Billy before we took off. He said this was really critical—lives at stake. I owe him. He sort of saved my life, you know. And to be honest, I have heard him mention your name. I know you guys are close. I don't care about the money, and I know it's not the DRC." She leaned forward, her forehead touching the back of the pilot's seat and spoke into her lap, "The danger doesn't bother me—it's dealing with low-life human scum."

No one spoke for several minutes, then one of the passengers in the back erupted into a sudden snoring bout. Zora and Carver both looked toward the sound, then at each other. She raised her eyebrows, smiled, and then resumed where she'd left off. "Don't get me wrong, I can deal with the scum. I just don't want to be put in that position again."

"Don't worry," Carver replied, "this place is totally uninhabited—with the possible exception of a few pygmies."

They both remained silent for several minutes. Carver tilted his head back, ran his fingers through his hair and sighed nervously. Zora shifted her eyes back to him. She continued to look, blinking softly, immersed in thought. He shifted nervously as she closed her eyes and slowly shook her head back and forth. After what seemed to Carver like an eternity of silence, she opened her eyes again, blinked, cleared her throat, and looked back at Carver. "OK," she said, speaking in a soft tone, "So, if I were to agree to help you, how would you proceed?"

He hesitated briefly as if attempting to organize his thoughts then, began talking. "As soon as we get to Bellingham I can drive you to your place. You get your passport and anything else you think you might need that we can't pick up along the way. Then while I'm driving us back to Seattle, you make up a checklist of what you think we'll need and we'll text it to my office—include any shots you might have to update. Send them your size if you want boots, clothing, jungle-gear of any kind. I have my passport with me so we'll go straight to the airport where someone will meet us. They're already alerted to this, so we'll be given a bag or two to cover at least part of what you'll have on your list. The rest we'll pick up in D.C., including visas. A corporate jet will get us to D.C. From there we'll fly commercial, either through Geneva or Paris. We can be in Brazzaville within the next twenty-four hours. Our people there will be able to provide any weapons you think we'll need."

"Weapons?" asked Zora. "You said the area was unpopulated." She shrugged her shoulders and settled back into her seat.

They both fell into silence again. Zora closed her eyes while Carver continued looking at her. After several minutes had passed, Mark called out, "Look out the left side and up ahead of us a little.

Those lights are Vancouver. Everyone's startin' to get up—it's a new day. We should be down in less than thirty minutes."

Zora straightened herself, stretched her arms and yawned. She faced Carver again and said, "Billy saved me when he forced me to climb Baker with him. We both did mountain training together at Hood, but Baker was really my first high mountain. We stood at the summit and I found myself speechless. I felt like I could see forever. The air was so fresh and clean. I'd been in deep depression for over a year, and in that instant, it just evaporated. I was suddenly reconnected with the earth, and I knew I could go on living. It was an amazing high. But, you know what, Carver?"

"What?"

"Nothing makes me feel more alive than being in the forest— the rain forest. That's where I spent most of my childhood. That's where my mother's family came from. Probably where I belong." She leaned closer toward him and went on, "So, maybe—just maybe, your friend is still alive. You said it was five days ago that you got his last message—probably six days now. If that's the case..." She paused, still looking at him, then said, "I think we need to go find him."

34

6 – THE MUSEUM

Small particles of dust floating in the long strips of sunlight gave the air an ephemeral quality as each ray sliced downward into the obscured volume below. Two parallel rows of clerestory windows provided the only source of natural illumination in the space where the high contrast of light against dark made the unlit areas almost invisible to the naked eye. Where the sun fell across the upper walls, a confusion of faint cobweb-like cracks gave the plaster finish a texture suggestive of marble, and through the darkness the faint lines of the architecture suggested a modest-sized basilica where the window walls were supported from below by rows of round columns connected by arches. Through those columns and to each side flanking the central chamber, much darker spaces with lower ceilings lay tucked away. A number of varying-sized inanimate forms sat on the wider floor between the columns, and there appeared to be objects mounted on the outer walls beyond the columns.

Barely detectable, the sound of chattering magpies crept through the well-sealed clerestory windows, offering a subtle relief to the cold stillness of the space. And then that stillness was broken by a single mechanical click followed by a low, pneumatic hissing sound and a sudden shot of bright light flashed out from the center of one of the side walls and across the floor in the shape of an acute triangular wedge. A series of recessed light fixtures in the ceiling along that same side became instantly activated by an unseen motion detector and illumination began to fill the perimeter spaces in sequencing waves that fanned outward to each side from the central initiating point.

"Welcome to my little museum," Olegushka Levkov said as he, Martel, and Aziza entered the space. "Martel, of course, has been here many times, but today I want you both to see the latest addition to my collection—as you two were so instrumental in my efforts to obtain it. Come along, it's out here, the new focal point of my menagerie." He raised his left hand and with his thumb, tapped a remote device and the entire central gallery came to life. An assortment of concealed spotlights, carefully focused on their subjects, pulled each of the floor-mounted inanimate objects from out of the darkness and into full view.

"Holy shit!" Aziza's eyes widened as she broke into a smile, scanning her eyes back and forth across the chamber.

"I've been in here dozens of times, but I'm always—how do you say it—in awe?" said Martel.

"I bagged every single one of them myself," Oleg boasted, as the corners of his mouth turned upward into an adolescent grin of self-satisfaction. As they walked directly into the middle of the central chamber where a large grouping of tiger displays were clustered together, Oleg continued, "With the Siberian we nailed this past winter, I now have almost every species of big cat on the planet. All the tigers are in the center here. Look, that's the Sumatran I got two years ago. There's the South China—there's actually fewer of them than there are Amurs. My biggest regret is that I never got a Java tiger. They went extinct while I was still in my youth."

They stopped in front of the largest of the tigers. "Here he is. My pride and joy—750 pounds on the day I shot him. That's not too far off the all-time record. Now he's all mine, and he rules here—my king!"

As they paused in silence, Aziza reached up and gently stroked the fur between the cat's eyes, then ran her hand down to its nose. "It's been almost a year now," she said. "I'll always remember the way he just shot out from nowhere—like a fuckin' jack-in-the-box. We all knew he was there, and we all knew he was gonna pop out, but it still made you freakin' jump when it happened. I've seen a lot of shit in my life, but never anything like that—fuckin' jack-in-the-box."

"I couldn't believe how cool you stayed, man. Took all three shots

36

with the big gun and wham." Martel stood on the other side of the cat, both hands caressing as he leaned over to inspect it closer. "Who did the taxidermy for you? Same guy?"

"Ah, yes—the Italian—the little greaser from Milan. An absolute artist—does museum work—those dioramas you see in natural history displays. His cousin used to clean money for us—but, those days are behind us." He looked at Aziza and added, "Everything we do now is legitimate, as you know."

Again, the three stood in silence for a few minutes, looking at what had recently been the 480th remaining living member of its species. His fur was dense and full, and his coat gave off a light sheen, the result of the shampooing process the Italian "artist" used to finish off his work. Finally, Aziza spoke, "I think he might not be as good as you think he is, Oleg."

"What do you mean?"

"Looks like he spilled a drop of glue or something here—near this eye," she said, smiling. "Looks like a tear."

Oleg chuckled while Martel laughed loudly.

"Ah, but I told him to put it there, and it is a tear. After all, he was the king you know—until I got him. Now Olegushka Levkov is the king." He waved his arm around the room. "They should all be shedding tears—every time I enter this glorious chamber."

"Now you're taking me for a *yutzi*, hey, Oleg? I think your wop taxidermist fucked up. Don't you agree, Martel? Ha!" She laughed as she stepped away from the display and started toward another. "I see you got a white tiger over there."

"That was my first tiger," said Oleg as they shifted over to the next display. "He was one of the few legal kills I've made. An Indian gentleman I used to do business with had his own private reserve near Mysore. He bred white tigers. Kept some in cages and then released a certain number into the reserve. The population needed thinning at one point and he invited me and another former business colleague to spend a week helping out. I got this one along with a leopard, a couple buffalo, and a chital deer."

37

"Look at these," Martel called out from across the room. He had wandered into a grouping of lion displays. "I was with Oleg when he got these two." He was standing in front of a lion and lioness that had been set-up together as a pair on the same pedestal. "These two came from India too, but they sure as hell weren't legal. I remember paying off, I don't know how many—wardens, government functionaries, even a local farmer who acted as our guide."

"Lions in India?" asked Aziza.

"Gir lions," answered Oleg. "The Forest of Gir in the north west of India. It's the only population of lions left outside of Africa."

Like a tour guide, Oleg continued on, strolling through his menagerie of stuffed feline specimens, Martel and Aziza in tow. He pointed at one and then another, speaking in a clear tone of authority as they progressed. The perimeter walls were hung with trophy heads, all cats, but not the big cats—fish cats, margays, lynx, a serval, a golden cat, and, when any species occurred in more than one color, each of the variations was represented—the jaguarundi came in black, gray, and brown. The central gallery had all of the big cats, and they were all complete specimens. Each had been meticulously stuffed and mounted on simple rectangular pedestals and the displays were grouped according to species—lions, leopards, jaguars, tigers, and pumas. The jaguar and leopard were both represented by the black and the tawny-yellow variations. Stopping at each specimen, Oleg expounded on his hunting prowess, the rarity of each of his possessions and usually some brief anecdote associated with each conquest.

"And now I think it's time for a drink, wouldn't you say?" he asked, as they arrived back in front of the door.

"I'm ready," said Aziza. "We've already discussed the diamonds, the timber, the caviar—enough business—but you know I didn't schlep over here just to talk business. It's time to start thinking about my big hunt."

"Yes, yes," added Martel. "It is your turn, Aziza—and from what Viper has told me, this should be one that I will not want to miss."

Oleg popped open a small metal panel that was set into the deep recess of the door opening, then with his back turned to his two companions, he quickly punched a code into a key pad, and the door hissed its way open.

"Oleg, I hate to keep bringing this up but you need to have some kind of emergency back-up to access some of these rooms," said Martel. "What if something happened to you? You're the only one who can get in or out of the vault."

"You mean like sharing the code with you, Martel?" Oleg responded with a little laugh. "Maybe someday." Then looking at Aziza, he added, "Martel has access to the house and Viper's studios below. Now he wants the code to my museum—not so he can play with the cats, but because he suspects there might be something else hidden away in here."

As the door closed behind them, they started up a wide hallway toward a large, well-lit room and their chatter continued. A tall, well-endowed Eurasian woman, dressed only in a G-string and a pair of black leather spike heels, greeted them as they entered the room.

"Vanessa, has Viper come back yet?" asked Oleg.

"No, monsieur, I haven't seen him since early this morning."

"OK. Why don't you bring us a plate of olives and a chilled bottle of Grey Goose with glasses—a glass for Viper too. We'll be on the veranda."

"Of course, monsieur. Right away."

While Vanessa quickly exited, Oleg ushered his two guests across the expansive great room. The space was classic in its architecture; early twentieth-century classic revival, but with decoration and furnishings that were modern, including original paintings by Botero, Picasso, Francis Bacon, and a grouping of Robert Crumb cartoons. A larger-than-life, bright glossy red acrylic sculpture of a pit-bull terrier sat on the marble floor immediately in front of three sets of tall French doors that opened onto the veranda beyond.

Oleg opened the middle door and they were immediately hit with the scent of lavender, and a cacophony of birds backed up by the scratchy drone of cicadas. The stone veranda was flanked by plantings of flowering shrubs, a dense backdrop of bamboo on one side and a small orchard of plum and cherry trees on the other. The main thrust of the veranda was outward and away from the house where it terminated at an infinity pool with a spectacular drop onto a series of lower hills smothered in olive orchards, and even further, the northern outskirts of Nice and finally, the deep blueness of the Mediterranean.

"Make yourselves comfortable. Pull a couple more chairs over by the table there. I'm going to grab some cigars," said Oleg as he stepped back into the house.

Aziza chuckled and shook her head. "He's too much. You guys are too much."

"Too much what?" asked Martel as he settled into a chaise lounge.

"This life. His harem. His obsession. I love it all."

"What do you mean, *his* obsession? How about yours?"

"Mine? We all have them—Viper, me, Oleg. I don't know about you, Martel, but then, you and I have only known each other for a short time. Maybe you got some delicious little secret I haven't learned about yet." She looked at him and grinned. "Probably not as twisted as ours, huh? Ha!" she chuckled. "But then, that's why we get along so well, isn't it? I guess you're just obsessed with power and money. No—forget the money. Power—that's our common denominator. Oleg's thing, though—I don't know if it's the cats or the illegal hunting he gets off on most, although…"

"You're as obsessed with hunting as am I, aren't you my dear Aziza?" came Oleg's voice from behind them. Viper was at his side, hair wet, as though he had just come from a shower. "At least that's what Viper seems to think."

As the four of them pulled their chairs into a semi-circle, Oleg opened a box of Cuban cigars, passed it around, and they each took one. He then passed a cutter and as he held out a box of wooden matches, Vanessa stepped through the doors with a well-laden silver tray.

"Thank you, Vanessa. You can just leave that. Close the door when you go back inside and tell the others we don't want to be disturbed. Actually, if you see Isaac when he gets back, tell him he's got a little job to take care of in the studio."

"Wait," said Aziza. "Tell Isaac to wait. I want to take a look down there first." Winking at Viper, she added, "You know I've been looking forward to seeing some of your fine work."

Oleg looked at Vanessa and nodded to affirm his approval and as Vanessa started back inside, Oleg began to puff on his cigar, attempting to get it going. Settling back into his chair, he let out a long stream of smoke, cleared his throat, hocked something up and expectorated off to the side. He then leaned forward, resting his elbows on his knees and spoke, looking at Aziza. "This next hunt is supposed to be your hunt, Aziza, and that's what we need to talk about now. We know that you've been looking forward to maybe another hunt in Poland, but—I've had something come up—an opportunity ..."

"Hold on, asshole," Aziza interrupted, "you just had yours. Are you suggesting that...?"

"No, no, no—let me finish. I realize you've only been with us for a little over two years now, and we all have this unwritten agreement that we each get our turn—and this year it is your turn. This is special though. We have an opportunity that should impact both of us—and I know you're going to love it. We can both be going after our own prey at the same time, on the same trip. It's a place where none of us has ever been—a place where both of us also have legitimate business happening right now—and the prize for each of us is potentially more fantastic than anything we've ever even thought about."

"Where?" Aziza snapped back.

"The Congo," said Martel.

They all looked at Martel. Aziza then stared back at Oleg. "I thought you'd already bagged every cat species that exists in Africa."

"Except the albino lion that ended up dying of old age before you could get to it," added Martel with a sarcastic grin.

"That was Botswana," continued Oleg, leaning forward again and speaking in a lower tone, "We're going to the Congo. This is like the albino lion, but it's much better. It's a melanistic lion—a black lion—

41

and if we can get it, it will be the most spectacular prize in the history of big-game hunting."

"It most certainly will," said Martel, "considering that it would be impossible. Black lions don't exist. In fact, lions are only found in drier more open terrain—like savannahs—they don't even exist in rainforests, and the Congo is all swamp and rainforest as far as I know. Where are you getting this from, Oleg?"

"I first heard about this a few years ago, but I didn't give it much credence until I started getting similar stories from totally unrelated sources, including our own people down there with the timber company. One report came out of Brazzaville from someone who had been looking around for new potential timbering sites in the north of Congo, then another report came from bushmeat hunters who were supplying loggers in Cameroon. They had been across the border and had strayed into a remote area of Congo, but from the other direction. Each source pointed out the same general area on the map, but each source had been coming from completely opposite directions and neither one had any contact or knowledge of the other. Then, if you look at other odd reports, there is a pattern of them that goes way the-hell-back—usually from local natives who'd been warned by the pygmies. At first it was just assumed that the pygmies were trying to scare off local tribes people who have a reputation for exploiting the pygmies. With these new reports, I think it's time for us to go find out for ourselves if this cat really exists."

"That whole region where northern Congo, Gabon, Cameroon, and Central African Republic come together is an area of interest to our timber business now," said Martel, "It wouldn't be a bad idea to run down there and check up on the situation in any case."

"And that's about as wild a place as we'll find anywhere today," added Viper.

"And where it's wild, it's also open season to doing all kinds of interesting things," said Aziza. She sipped her vodka, then continued, "I think I know where you're going, Oleg—you got my imagination working now. You have a map we can look at?"

Oleg blew a line of smoke out toward the pool, then flicked what was left of his cigar off to one side and stood up. "I'll go dig up my maps. While I'm doing that, Viper, why don't you take everyone down to the studio? Apparently, you've been telling Aziza a lot about your recent video interests, so I'd say it's about time for her to get a firsthand look and—as I understand it, you actually have some recent work she can take a look at."

"I'll join you for that," Martel said, as he stood up and flipped his cigar off after Oleg's.

Oleg led the way back into the house and held the door for the others. As they entered he held his hand up to Martel and stopped him. "You're going to need to stay here when we take off on this next trip, Martel."

"What do you mean?"

"We could be gone for a lot longer than we were on any of our past trips. You're the only one who knows everything about what we do—how we function. You're the only one I can trust making decisions when I'm not around—I'll need you here." He patted Martel on the back and winked at him as he added, "I might even have to give you the code to the museum vault."

Martel nodded, "Understood. How long you think you'll be away?"

"No idea—could be a while. It's a complicated place down there, and we'll be looking for something that most people don't believe exists."

Martel quickly caught up with the others as Oleg disappeared into a wide hallway with a grand staircase beyond. Martel, Aziza, and Viper proceeded along the same corridor that Vanessa had taken into what appeared to be the service area of the villa.

Viper led the way, and as they started down a dark stairway, Aziza asked, "So Viper, my dear, what is this recent work Oleg just mentioned? Or maybe I should be asking, how old was she before you got a hold of her?"

7 – BRAZZAVILLE

The first Europeans to arrive in the Congo were the Portuguese. They came in a small sailing vessel called a caravel in the year 1482, and every other European man—only men came in those days—who came to the Congo in the next four hundred years came by boat. It may have been a very long trip for those who first arrived, but they at least had the advantage of being able to acclimate themselves gradually to the oppressively heavy, humid climate that relentlessly shrouds Central Africa. Arriving in Brazzaville in an air-conditioned Air France Airbus did not offer that advantage. As soon as the airplane's engines stopped, so did the air-conditioning system, and almost immediately the atmosphere within the passenger cabin became unbearably stale and warm, but even that sudden transition in air quality did not prepare Carver Hayden for what awaited him as he stepped out through the first-class door onto the stair platform beyond.

"Jesus," he muttered to himself. His glasses had fogged up so he removed them and held them in one hand with his briefcase as he gripped the handrail with the other and slowly descended the steep stairs to the tarmac below. He turned when he got to the bottom and looked back at Zora as she almost bumped into him. "Welcome to the Heart of Darkness. Is it always like this?"

"The Heart of Darkness is really much further upriver from here. In any case, this is my first time here. My previous trip to this part of the world was at least a thousand miles to the east and maybe a couple thousand feet higher in elevation." She gave him a slight smile and took his arm, guiding him away from the stairs. "Wait 'til we get in the jungle. It's at least ten degrees cooler when you get under the tree canopy—but in fact, the heat isn't really the problem. Even though we're almost on top of the equator, the temperature always stays between 70 and 85 degrees. It's the humidity—and it's here to stay so you might as well get used to it."

Following the line of passengers ahead of them they entered the terminal, a modest-sized, modern-looking structure consisting of a series of elongated tubes of glass, overlapped by sheets of steel, rolling down onto the tarmac like a wave on a beach. Although it was very early in the evening, there were no signs of a sunset. The sky was pitch-black in contrast to the well-lit airport building.

It took no more than twenty minutes for them to retrieve their luggage—two large duffel bags. They quickly passed through customs, each with one hand gripping the end of a duffel bag, slung over one shoulder and the other hand carrying a briefcase. They were greeted by a muscular man of medium height, dressed in rugged tropical attire of khaki cargo shorts and shirt, a battered, wide-brimmed safari hat, and sandals made from recycled tires. He had a broad face with what appeared to be initiation scars on his right cheek, and he held a handwritten sign with Carver's name on it, but he had obviously identified them as soon as they came through the doors.

"Mr. Hayden, I presume, and Miss de Rycken." He held out his hand, and they each shook it in turn. "My name is Prince Abiola—CATI."

"Prince, yes—thank you for meeting us. I'm Carver Hayden—just call me Carver and Miss de Rycken here is Zora."

"I detect a slight accent Prince," said Zora. "Nigeria?"

"Yes, but educated in the U.S. I did my undergrad work at Virginia then went on to Cornell where I studied forestry. The company recruited me there." He reached for Zora's duffel bag, which she relinquished to him with a smile. "How was your flight?"

"Long," answered Carver.

"I've probably done that flight a dozen times in the past few years—long is a good way to describe it," Prince said as he stepped ahead of them and pushed open a pair of glass doors. "This way—the car's right here."

A black luxury Citroën was parked, idling, directly in front of the terminal doors. A tall, bearded man with a New York Yankees baseball cap, short-sleeved white shirt, lightweight trekking trousers, and Nike basketball shoes was leaning against the car. He stood upright and started toward them as soon as they came through the doors.

"This is Lucas Dubois," said Prince as he handed him Zora's duffel bag. Lucas is my right-hand man here and due to the sensitivity of this mission, he will be our driver."

After quick introductions, Lucas placed the bags in the trunk then joined the others in the car. "La villa?" he asked as he put the car into gear.

"*Oui. On les laisse se reposer un peu. Ensuite, on pourrait aller au Croco,*" Prince responded. Then, turning to face Carver and Zora, he continued in English, "You speak French, Carver?"

"Not a word. I speak a little Spanish, but languages are not one of my talents. Zora, on the other hand, seems to be quite fluent in French—and, as I discovered coming through passport control, she apparently speaks some Lingala as well. I should have known," he continued, looking at Zora, "Billy told me one of your many talents was linguistics."

"Yes," she said. "It was my major in college."

"But Lingala?" asked Prince. "Nobody from Europe or the U.S. just learns Lingala, except maybe Peace Corps people. Where'd that come from?"

"I did a mission in the DRC two years ago when I was in the army. I was assigned to the operation as a translator."

"So the American army teaches Lingala?" asked Prince.

"You could say that," she replied. "At least they arrange for it to be taught—when they think they need it."

"They arrange for it?"

"They had two women come in and give me a lesson over several hours before we took off, then they gave me a set of discs to listen to on the flight over. It gave me a bit of a base to start from."

"There are so many dialects of Lingala. I still only speak it marginally—my native languages were English and Yoruba. I did a one-month intensive course in French before coming here and now, after three years in the country, I'm just getting to where I can communicate on a basic level in Lingala—but—that's with people who come from the Brazzaville region. You go up north, and it sounds like a different language—and you say they gave you a short lesson and then you listened to discs? And you went to the DRC—they must have a dozen different dialects over there, not to mention Swahili."

"That's why they sent two instructors for me—one spoke Lingala, the other, Swahili."

"So you speak Swahili too?"

"Not as well as Lingala."

"Where'd you go in the DRC?" asked Lucas, as he attempted to look at Zora in the rearview mirror.

"Way out in the middle of nowhere—not far from the borders with Uganda and Rwanda. We flew out from a military airfield north east of Kisangani on some old Blackhawks. By the time we'd landed, I'd had another two hours to talk with a couple of DRC soldiers who helped me hone in on the dialect. I was able to converse on a rudimentary level by the time I left. I was far from fluent."

Lucas had stopped the car at a stop sign and had been looking at Zora again through the rearview mirror as she spoke. His head jerked slightly as a car horn blasted at them from behind; he mumbled something under his breath, then took his foot off the brake and accelerated the car, cutting into moving traffic with a slight squeal of rubber. Once the car was moving smoothly again, he said to Zora in Lingala, "You might need to talk pygmy where we're going."

"Your Lingala seems pretty good," she said. "Your French tells me you might be Belgian—how long have you been here, Lucas?"

"You are good! Yes, I am from Belgium originally. I came here when I was twenty years old. My wife is Bantu. This has been my home for the past twenty-five years now, so I really don't think of myself as a Belge any more—*Merde! Putin!*" he shouted suddenly as another vehicle cut them off.

"Keep your eye on the driving, Lucas," said Prince as he looked at Carver. "These people are tired, and they're not used to the way we drive around here. See if you can get us to the compound alive."

"Ha!" Lucas chuckled. "Tell us who's had the most accidents in this town, my Prince."

♦ ♦

Thirty minutes later the car pulled up in front of a deco-style black steel security gate and stopped as a man stepped out from a small guard booth on the far side of the gate. He flashed a light on Lucas, then nodded his head, returned to his booth, and activated the gate. "This is the nerve center for all our operations in Central Africa," explained Prince. "We have guest quarters here for any of the big shots who come in—which includes you two, of course. There's a bar, a swimming pool, media room, full commercial kitchen, dining and entertaining facilities for up to fifty people. Considering where we are, it's pretty well got everything covered."

"With our schedule we probably won't get to see much of the swimming pool," said Carver.

The car crept slowly up a long narrow driveway, nicely lit by elegant colonial-style street lamps. It was dark and hard to see too far beyond the lamps, but the driveway appeared to be lined with tall palm trees and lush flowering gardens on both sides. Lucas stopped the car in front of the grand entrance to a two-story, stucco building with corrugated metal roof. It was very French colonial in style and well maintained. "There's always an attendant at the front desk—just like a first-class hotel," said Prince. "Security includes two full-time armed guards with a dog. We have a cook with one helper and when anyone stays over, the cook sleeps out back in case you need anything late at night. He'll be here tonight, even though we expect to be out of here early tomorrow. Come on, I'll give you a quick tour, then show you to your rooms. Lucas, please be so kind as to take their bags up to the first floor—everything here is based on the French system—what you call the first floor is the ground floor here, and our first floor would be your second floor." Then, calling after Lucas, "They'll be staying in Ayous and Sapele. All the rooms are named for trees—we are in the timber business, after all."

Prince ended the tour at a room with the sign, "Ayous" above the door. The door was open and both duffel bags had been left on the floor at the foot of a king-size bed. The room interiors, like the rest of the building were simple and contemporary in style, but with furnishings and decor that were purely Central African—hand-carved wooden chests, pottery, baskets, batiks, paintings and drawings on the walls, and tropical plants in every corner. The room had a high ceiling with a fan and a large window with a hand-carved wood grille insert that looked out into an atrium below. The sound of a bubbling fountain could be heard through the window, accompanied by the scent of blooming plants. "Smells like gardenia," noted Carver.

"OK—the other room is straight across the hall and keys to each room are on the bedside tables. Lucas will be going with us tomorrow. Since he lives a good two hours out of town, he'll be staying downstairs tonight. He'll meet you both downstairs in about forty-five minutes and will drive you to a restaurant where I'll be joining you for dinner and whatever final planning we might want to do."

"Perfect. Thank you, Prince," said Carver. "Thank you for picking us up and for everything. I do need to check on one thing though before you take off. When my predecessor, Russell Hoyt, came through here last month, he was supposed to have left something in a security safe. Can you show me where that is?"

"Of course, come. See you soon, Zora——at the restaurant."

"Yes, see you soon," she responded. "I'll put your stuff in the other room, then I'm going to jump in the shower. I'm taking the room that's next to the fountain and smells like gardenia. Oh—Carver. This security safe—anything I need to know about?"

8 – LE CROCO FOU

"This is Le Croco Fou—the hottest new place in town," said Prince, as he shook hands with a Bantu doorman sporting an open Hawaiian aloha shirt, exposing his rippling washboard abdomen, the butt of a revolver just peeking out on one side.

After a friendly exchange of words in French, the doorman turned to Zora and Carver with an enormous, gleaming white smile, and in a deep baritone voice, greeted them in English. "Welcome to The Crazy Crocodile." He stepped to one side and rolled his arm outward with a slight bow, ushering them in toward two concrete statues of crocodiles standing upright on their tales. "Americans are always most honored here as our guests," and looking directly at Zora, "especially such beautiful as you, my lady."

Zora returned his smile along with a friendly nod, and the three passed the crocodiles and entered through a pair of heroic wooden doors, hand-carved in what appeared to be a traditional motif of hunters with elongated heads, carrying old-fashioned blunderbusses and surrounded by a frieze of tropical plants, animals, and birds.

Inside, they were immediately greeted by an attractive young hostess—tall, traditional attire, large circular earrings in silver that shimmered in the light, elegant against her pitch-black skin. "Your usual table, Monsieur Abiola?" she asked.

"No, since it's not raining tonight, let us sit out on the patio," he responded. Then as they followed the hostess, he said to Zora and Carver, "This place is what they call a *nganda* restaurant. That means that it is both a bar and a restaurant. And this place, like most *ngandas*, offers a more gourmet style of food. You must see the view here from outside, and since it is not raining tonight, we should take advantage—it is also more private."

The patio, lit by torches, was surrounded on three sides by columns that opened into dining spaces on two sides and an extensive bar, and what looked like a dance floor with a low stage for musicians beyond on the third side. Part of the bar extended out into the patio under a thatched roof. Bougainvillea cascaded down from balconies above, and the patio itself was landscaped with an assortment of small palms, banana trees, and flowering shrubs. The fourth side of the patio was open to the river. The hostess led them in that direction.

"Do not put your hand in there," said Prince as they passed an elliptical, waist-high rock wall, well integrated into the patio's plantings. Zora looked in and noted that it contained a pond with lily pads and a dozen small crocodiles. "This is the owner's idea of maintaining a sustainable facility. He minimizes waste by throwing all the leftover fish and meat in here late at night after all the guests have gone home."

They stopped at a low stucco wall that defined the end of the patio and prevented inebriated customers from falling down the steep embankment that led to the river below. Despite the fact that it was almost ten at night, and the moon and stars were totally blocked by the consistently heavy cloud covering, the view was, in fact, dazzling in an eerie and mysterious way. The artificial light from Brazzaville bounced off the low cloud cover and then settled across the surface of the river where its reflection off the rippling water danced like a muted light show.

"Look at that," said Lukas. "Kinshasa is only about four miles straight across, but with the kind of visibility we have now you can't even see the lights. It's over four and a half times the size of Brazzaville—one of many reasons why the company located our offices here. It's a bloody mess over there. They have nine million people while we have less than two million. The place is crawling with beggars, prostitution is rampant; there's lots of money, but not

51

everyone benefits from it. Everyone, from the most powerful to simple traffic cops, is on the take. Everything's dirty and rundown, like their airport—it's a complete dump compared to ours. How'd you like the new airport, anyway?"

"Pretty impressive—not at all what I expected," answered Carver.

"Come on, let's sit down here. What do you drink? Zora?"

"Just soda water for me," she replied.

"No, no, I can't let you do that. They make fantastic drinks here."

"Mr. Prince is right; you must try one of our specialty cocktails," said the hostess, who was holding Zora's chair as she sat down.

"Sorry, boys," said Zora. "I've been climbing the highest mountain in North America for twenty-something days, then I think we've been flying for at least twenty-five hours over the past three days, and tomorrow we get dropped into the middle of nowhere. I want to eat and get a good night's rest."

"Hmm," snorted Carver.

"What are you trying to say, Carver?"

"I don't know. I mean, Billy—he always gave me the impression you Special Forces types could drink one night, fight the next morning, and never blink an eye."

"In case you haven't noticed, I'm not a type. You might as well get used to it, Carver. I've been told that I defy almost every stereotype out there. In spite of my military service, I grew-up in a pretty sheltered environment. I'm a bungling ignoramus when it comes to contemporary social mores. Alcohol has just never been part of my culture."

"OK," said Prince, "Bring the lady a soda water. I'll have the house margarita—how about you, Carver?"

"I'll take a Scotch. Whatever you've got—on the rocks."

"No, no, not whatever they've got," said Prince. "Carver, if you're a Scotch drinker, they can do better than that in here."

"Guess I'm not really a big scotch drinker," said Carver as he looked from the hostess back to Prince. "I like Scotch but am not what you would call a connoisseur."

"Bring the man a Cragganmore—twelve year, if you still have it," Prince said to the hostess. Then, placing a hand on Carver's arm, he said, "You're going to like this, Carver. This might be the only place outside some of the Embassies where you can find it."

The hostess started to turn when Zora reached out and touched her arm. "Wait," she said, "Maybe I will try a real drink. What do you recommend?"

"Our famous Croco-boom-boom—mango juice, a touch of orange, 151 rum—you like mango?"

"I'm half Costa Rican," answered Zora, "Of course I like mango. Give me a Croco-boom-boom." Then, nodding at Carver with a slight smile, "There—."

As the hostess left, Lucas joined them with a bottle of beer in one hand. With the other he handed Prince a large folded up map. "Here, you left this in the car."

"Ah yes, the map," said Prince as he unfolded it across the table. "Tomorrow we take the company plane up to this town near the Cameroon border—Ouésso—it's on the Sangha River. We keep a couple of helicopters there—it's central to a lot of logging on both sides of the border and also to areas we're surveying for future operations. We then take one of the copters down here to where we dropped off Hoyt and his team."

"How many were there in his so-called team?" asked Zora.

"Eight. We have two copters up there, a Sikorsky Superhawk and a Bell 430. Since the landing area we were trying to drop them into seemed pretty sketchy, we sent them out on the Bell. It only carries up to eight passengers, so that's how many we sent out."

"What kind of people were they—what kind of experience?"

"It was Hoyt, one of our field managers, and six other guys— all with good back-country experience—one of them spoke some Baka. He was supposed to put together some porters from the pygmy camp. They were dropped off in an open area about half a mile from a pygmy hunting camp we picked up from a satellite photo. Your guys in Seattle sent us the photo. I said it was sketchy because any open area you can find up there is usually a swamp at least half the year."

"I already asked Carver this," said Zora, "but I'll ask you too—this place seems too far away from any areas where they might have had refugees coming in from problem spots in DRC or Central African Republic—but how about poachers or bushmeat hunters?"

"Not so likely," said Lucas. "No roads, no rivers large enough to take anything bigger than a dug-out, and no place to land a helicopter—other than this little open patch we found. The poachers—they focus on elephant clearings along the larger rivers and the swamps around Likouala, here to the east."

"Elephant poaching is getting bad," added Prince. "They come in by helicopter from Cameroon and DRC—other side of the Ubangi. We did see elephants in the clearing so maybe we shouldn't rule them out."

"Elephant poaching's getting bad, you say? Don't you guys sort of promote it when you move in to log an area?" asked Zora.

"No, of course not," Carver quickly replied.

The three of them stared at her, then Prince continued. "We've got bands of guerilla fighters coming down from Central African Republic now too, but they're way up in the north along the border. All the trouble seems to stay up north. There's nothing in this place—it's empty—except for the pygmy camp. But still—poachers—guerilla fighters. These days we need to worry about all of them."

"And this village," continued Lucas, "it's about five days by dugout from the pygmy camp. It appears to have some permanent huts in it and the pilot said there were Bantus there as well as pygmies. The Bantus trade with the pygmies and this place is at least a week away from the next village downstream, so they probably do a little bushmeat trading with the pygmies, but that would be it."

"I know what you're asking," said Prince, "but I just don't see any threat that might be coming from human sources. The government lists this area as having a population density of one human per square mile or less. If we didn't see this village here, I would say the density would be closer to zero."

Their drinks arrived; they ordered appetizers and dinner, then looking at Prince, Zora continued the conversation. "Did the helicopter just drop them off or did it hang around a while?"

"They got dropped off, but the pilot was there long enough to know that they did hire a few pygmies to help carry gear. When the pilot went back a week later hoping to find them, he was told the pygmy porters had returned, but without the rest of the expedition. They claimed that they were forbidden to go beyond some point out there. Based on what the pilot was able to decipher from the pygmies, they had left Hoyt at approximately where they were when they sent out their last satellite radio communication. The pilot flew around the area of the last communication, went back to the clearing and waited five more days, then left and came back again five days later. That's when we got in touch with Seattle."

"So, according to my notes here," said Carver, "It's been twenty-nine days now since they got dropped off at the clearing and twenty-three days since we lost communications with them."

"Yeah," said Zora, "That's a little more than the seven days I have in my notes which are based on what you told me." She threw a hard look at Carver, who glanced back at her and shrugged.

Dinner arrived, everyone ordered another round of drinks, and the conversation shifted to the food, then to local social and political issues. Lucas ranted about how the Chinese had cut a deal with the government to build a new municipal building, but then brought all of their labor in from China. "Not a single job went to a local and now, all the Chinese laborers—they're still here. Somebody got paid off, but those who needed jobs got nothing, and now Congo is just another place that's soaking up China's over-population problem. Government flunkies!" he exclaimed.

"Of course the Chinese paid someone off," added Prince. "This is Africa after all—if you do business here you have to be sticking euros or dollars in someone's back pocket." He turned his head toward Carver, and their eyes connected for a brief instant.

As the plates were cleared, Prince ordered another round of

drinks, and Lucas, who had been eyeing a young woman at the bar, excused himself and went to get another beer. "Let's get back to the business at hand," said Prince as he pulled the map back out onto the table.

"Lucas and I will both be flying up to Ouésso with you tomorrow. After the drop area, I'll be going back to Ouésso. Lucas and a four-man military escort team will be continue on with you."

"Military escort?" asked Carver.

"Yes. Required for anyone going into the backcountry."

"Even if you don't expect guerillas or poachers?"

"Yes. It's dangerous out there," said Prince. "When you don't know anything about a place, you really have no idea what might be out there. Those guys just disappeared, and we don't know why. To me, that makes it more dangerous than if we knew there were poachers."

"Four of Brazzaville's finest," said Zora, "Just what we'll need. They'll end up slowing us down or getting in the way."

"Sorry but that's the law here. I had to get a permit to go up there, and you can't get the permit if you don't have a squad of soldiers lined up. And, on top of that, I wouldn't be able to sleep at night if I knew you two were wandering around up there all alone."

"You don't need to worry about us, Prince," said Zora, "Your job is to get us up there. Mine is to find these missing people. You'll just have to take my word—I know what I'm doing, and I've done it before—in worse circumstances. The escort can come along for the helicopter ride, but they're just going to be left behind once we hit the ground."

Prince looked at Carver and asked, "Who the hell is she supposed to be? I was told she was some kind of consultant." Then looking back at Zora, "When I say this place is dangerous, I mean it's dangerous—you don't know what you're talking about—you don't know what you're about to step into," then back at Carver, "Is she telling you what to do?! Neither one of you has a clue what this place is like!"

"Prince, she knows exactly what she's doing. That's why the company's paying her to find Hoyt. Christ! Her plan was to go alone.

I mean alone—without me. It wasn't easy to convince her that I had to go too. If something's happened to Hoyt, I still have to obtain the data he was sent to gather."

"Have you ever even been in a jungle before, Carver? Do you know what a green mamba is? Is she going to keep you from walking right into a cobra?"

"As long as he does what I tell him to do, he won't run into any mambas or cobras," said Zora. Then, glancing in the direction of the bar, she caught the waitress's attention and raised her empty glass. The waitress nodded and as she turned toward the bartender, Zora suddenly smiled, motioned with her head, and said "Look at Lucas over there, he seems to be quite the ladies' man. I thought he was married?"

"He is," said Prince, "Just can't resist the ladies."

They all looked toward the bar and as they did, Lucas acknowledged their sudden attention by lifting his beer to them. The woman immediately next to him waved, then Zora noticed a man behind them who appeared to be part of their group but was looking at himself in the mirror behind the bar. A little taller than Lucas, with light-blond hair, graying on the sides, he was wearing what looked like a white silk jacket over a black designer tee shirt and tan silk trousers. Lucas nudged him, and he looked toward them, nodded with a smile and lifted his drink.

"Always with that same woman these days," said Prince, "The one with the colorful head scarf and long gold earrings—she's a beauty. I don't know that guy—must be new in town. Judging from the way he's dressed—some executive hotshot." Then, turning back to Zora, "I don't mean to sound short-tempered about this, but you have to understand, this place where we plan on dropping you—other than this little village that hardly shows up on the satellite photos—you're a hundred miles in any direction from any known human habitation, and nobody we know of has ever been in this place—no hunters—no researchers—no soldiers—no one. These people have disappeared, and we don't know why. Why is it no one inhabits this entire area—a single pygmy hunting camp? We don't know what's up there, and this whole thing gives me the creeps."

"We're aware of all that…" and before Zora could continue, the waitress showed up with her drink.

"This has been sent to you mademoiselle, with the compliments of the gentleman at the bar—the one talking to Lucas and Monique."

With a light chuckle, Carver looked back toward the bar and said to Zora, "Well, well, now, Zora, you seem to have an admirer."

"And here he comes," added Prince, as the tall man, accompanied by Lucas and his two lady friends started walking toward them.

All three of them stood as the man approached. Zora leaned over to balance herself with one hand than held out the other, which he took as he made a slight bow. Before he could say anything, Zora introduced herself and her companions, "My name is Ssora—" Her words slurred some, and she hesitated briefly, then continued, "De Rycken. And these gentlemen are my colleagues—Carver Hayden and Prince Abiola."

"Delighted," the man said. "I hope you can excuse my intrusion, but I have been talking with Lucas, here and it appears that we all have some common interests. I understand that we all are involved in the international timber business." Then, looking directly at Zora and bending ever so slightly with a bow and smile, "And you, my dear, are without question, the most attractive young woman I have seen in a quite a long time. My name is Olegushka Levkov. Please call me Oleg."

9 – LOSS OF INNOCENCE

"Feeling any better?" asked Carver, as Zora sat down across from him. A table had been set for them on a long terrace that stretched across the back of the villa.

"Yes, I think so," she answered.

"I ordered tea and orange juice," he said. "I noticed you always took tea on the plane." He smiled at her and added, "I guess that's something we have in common."

"Thank you. Don't know if my stomach can take it, but I'll give it a try. Where are the others?"

"Lucas said Prince is going to be delayed a bit so he went off to talk to the pilot who's supposed to ferry us up north. Said we can order breakfast, but I told him we'd wait for them. Guess we can relax for a few minutes."

"Breakfast? I'll be happy if I can just drink the juice and tea." She let out a sigh, sat back in her chair, and looked at him. He returned her gaze and they sat staring at each other until the tea and juice arrived.

Zora took a sip of juice, swallowed it then finished the glass without stopping. "That was good," she gasped as she set the glass down. Once again she settled back into her chair and looked at Carver, but said nothing. She rubbed her eyes, rocked her head back and forth, then took a deep breath, cleared her throat.

"You're my client, Carver. Your company might be paying me, but as far as I'm concerned, I'm working for you, not the company. I hope you understood that when I agreed to do this."

"Of course," he said.

Zora went on. "Once we get into the bush, there might be times when your life will depend on me. You're my responsibility, and last night, I was not very responsible."

"Oh, come on. I was just as responsible for that as you. I saw you getting drunk and I did nothing to stop you."

"I don't lose control like that," she said, her eyes looking down at the table. "I'm not a drinker—I don't even like the taste of booze. I never should have started drinking in the first place—I didn't want to, but—I changed my mind and I don't even know why." She looked back up at Carver and continued, "I have only vague memories of what transgressed at the table last night. I barely remember that sleazy Russian showing up."

"You certainly didn't hesitate to speak your mind, that's for sure. And, I wouldn't worry about what you said. I think most of us were thinking some of the same things you were saying. That's not such a bad thing, you know."

"Carver, I've lived through some pretty harrowing experiences. I thrive in a jungle where most people can hardly survive. It's partially due to my awareness. I've always had a powerful sense of awareness, and that awareness requires a certain amount of control—control of my body, my senses, my thoughts—everything. I know there will always be people or things in the environment that are beyond my control, or anyone's. But still, I do seem to be able to manage situations and unknown places without too much effort. In spite of my lack of social experience, I manage to read people really well. Being aware is part of who I am, and I've always been able to depend on it. Last night I lost it all, and it's really freaking me out."

Carver reached across the table and put his hand on hers. "Zora," he said, "you didn't lose anything. Everyone has to take a break once in a while, and that's all you were doing. You were exhausted, wound up tight. If you don't stop and just let everything go sometimes, you'll just explode. You needed to completely stop, do nothing, and let the world go by. You're not a machine, after all—you're a human—like me. No, you're not like me. You're—I don't know what you are actually." He withdrew his hand, sat back and went on, "You're unique." He smiled, a sheepish smile. "I guess everyone says you're unique." He looked away and added, "I don't know what I'm saying," then looking back at her, "I like you, you know. I have total confidence in you."

"Thank you," she said. "I guess I like you too—a little bit. Just don't try to hold my hand again." She smiled and added, "—at least until this is all over."

They sat in silence again for several minutes as they each began to sip their tea, trying to avoid each other's eyes but stealing quick glances at one another. She emptied her cup, put it down, sighed then looked toward the far end of the terrace as if in anticipation of the others' arrival.

Finally Carver put his empty cup down and broke the silence, "I looked at my watch and did some quick calcs before I came down here. You realize it's only been forty hours since I introduced myself to you back there? The temperature is ninety degrees warmer, and we've gone halfway around the world since then, and, for most of that time, you've been the only human being I've had any contact with. And yet, I don't know anything about you except for what Billy told me. And, what he told me was so limited that I assumed you were a guy at first. Ha!" he chuckled.

"What do you want to know?"

"I'm your client. I should know something about my consultant, don't you think?—Just a little background. Are you Costa Rican or American? How did you end up in the army? You know, basic stuff, like that."

"Well, my family name is Dutch. I kept it when I got married—it's my father's name. Through him, I'm descended from the original Dutch settlers in New Amsterdam. The first de Rycken who came to America, came specifically to trade with the Indians. The fact that I'm approximately one-sixth Mayan Indian adds an ironic twist to the family history so I kind of like keeping the name. My father—he was a career army officer—West Point grad. So was my grandfather on his side. My mother—she was from Costa Rica. She was killed in a

61

car wreck when I was three. I was the only child, and it was pretty much assumed that I would follow along the family tradition, so I went to West Point as well." She paused as she looked into her empty cup, then looking up with a smile, added, "I did not have a typical American upbringing."

"That I could have guessed." Carver smiled and leaned forward. "Sorry. Go on."

She cleared her throat and continued. "When my mother died, her mother—my grandmother, stayed with my father and me for a year so I grew close to her. When my father was deployed to Iraq, I lived with my grandparents, and by the time he got back it was decided that I would continue to spend at least part of each year—whenever I wasn't in school—with my grandparents. My grandfather's the director of a national park in one of the most remote rain forests down there. So, you could say, I was brought up in the jungle.

"My friends consisted of a couple of rangers and an array of conservationists and researchers who came and went over the years. One of the rangers taught me how to use a knife, another showed me how to make a sawed-off shotgun, and track animals—and people. The researchers taught me everything you'd ever want to know about rainforest biology—trees, water, monkeys, snakes—you name it. In all that time I only had one friend my age—Manuel. He was one year younger than I so I sort of became the initiator of whatever we did."

"Initiator? I would say the difference in age had nothing to do with it. I'd wager to bet you were a super-alpha from birth—ha!" he chuckled, "Look at me. I'm ready to follow you into some kind of black hole in the middle of Africa, but ... keep going. Tell me more."

"Manuel and I followed the rangers once. We watched them chase some illegal gold miners. They never knew we were there. And one time, we tracked a female jaguar back to its lair—I must have been about twelve then.

"You referred to me as an alpha? I always considered myself a tomboy. From the beginning I excelled in anything athletic, but I was also a loner so I stayed away from team sports. I did tae kwon do, swimming, and gymnastics. By the time I went to West Point I was a third-degree black belt in tae kwon do." She looked Carver directly in the eye and added, "I can also climb trees."

She stopped talking briefly, looked down into her empty cup, then back up at Carver. "Is that enough? You just got at least half my life in only three minutes."

"What about what happened in the DRC with Billy?"

"That was the worse time of my life," she said, as her face grew stiff, "Maybe even worse than finding out Justin had been killed by a road-side in Iraq. I don't talk about that."

"What could be worse than losing your husband like that?"

She remained silent again, then looked at him and said, "Loss of innocence, Carver."

"What? Were you raped? No, sorry—you don't need to tell me. You've told me enough, and now I'm getting out of bounds."

"I had to kill a man, Carver."

"You shot someone?"

"Shot someone? No—I cut his throat with a knife."

10 – LEVIATHAN

"You look lost, Carver," said Zora. "Guess I told you more than you expected to hear." She picked up her empty orange juice glass and tapped it down hard on the table. "Could use some more of this." Then, focusing again on Carver, "It took my shrink a month to get that out of me. It only took you forty hours. Maybe you should consider changing professions."

"I'm sorry, Zora. I really didn't mean to push you."

"Oh, that's all right. Better to get some of these things out now, I guess. What about you, though?" She stretched her legs out, leaned back in her chair, and stared at him. "As my client, you owe me a little glimpse at your bio. How did a tree nerd get stuck in the body of a jock?"

Before he could respond, they were interrupted by the sound of footsteps entering the far end of the terrace. "Just in time," said Carver under his breath, as Prince and Lucas arrived, followed by the waiter.

After a quick greeting, the two sat down and everyone but Zora ordered breakfast; she asked for a refill on her juice. Prince opened a satchel he had been carrying, pulled out a laptop, plopped it down in the middle of the table, then addressing Zora, asked, "And, how are you feeling this morning?"

"Couldn't be better," she answered.

"Good," he said, now with a big smile on his face. "That Russian guy—he was really coming on to you like he was certain he'd be taking you home with him and the next thing—no way! Ha!" he let out a short laugh, then went on, "You were starting to feel those cocktails by that time, but you had this intimidating way of looking at him—he just seemed to shrink away—I don't know what the guy thought when you asked him if he'd just had his eyelids lifted. He was obviously not too happy." Looking at Carver, he added, "It was a relief for all of us when you suggested it was time to call it a night."

"The Russian was a sleaze," said Zora, "That much I do remember."

"Zora, I have to confess," said Prince. "For a while I was starting to get a bit concerned about the way you were handling him, but this morning after talking to Lucas, it turns out you were right on target."

"When I was over by the bar," Lucas started in, "He came on a little too friendly. It felt like he'd been waiting for me, and as it turned out, someone must have told him who we are. He pried me with all kinds of questions related to the business. Turns out he's one of our major competitors in the area—and a nasty one too—SBP."

"Société des Bois Précieux," added Carver.

"That's right," said Prince. "They're listed as a Cayman Islands company, but they're run out of Nice. And get this—our friend Oleg, is not just with SBP, he *is* SBP. He owns them plus dozens of other companies—timber, metals, banks, high tech, you name it. They're all owned under his holding company, APEKS. The guy's a billionaire several times over—one of those one-percenters you hear people whining about all the time back in the States."

"And they say," Lucas continued, "he originally got his start in human trafficking. That wouldn't surprise me, based on some of the tactics we've seen them use here. We pay people off—they make people disappear."

At that point, Carver interjected, "Did you say anything to him about where we're going?"

"I didn't trust the way he was meddling—didn't really tell him much, although I did mention that we were about to go into the jungle to look at potential concession sites, but I didn't say where, and he didn't ask. Didn't mention our missing expedition. We've all been told to keep that under a tight lid. In any case, once he spotted Zora he lost interest in the topic of timber. He just wanted to know who the attractive woman was at our table. He obviously thought of himself as a real ladies' man." Then, looking at Zora, he added, "He insisted that I introduce him to you. You know the rest."

The conversation reached a pause as the waiter showed up with their food. Zora gulped her juice down as quickly as she did the first glass, then she spoke as Prince and Lucas ate. "In any case, I do apologize for overdoing it last night. To be honest, I had no idea rum could do that to you. What was that stuff called?"

"151," answered Lucas. "Not the real thing though—151 is from Puerto Rico—what you had was our local version. It's 151 proof— you might as well have been drinking what you Americans call moonshine—and you knocked off enough for all of us." He gave Zora a slight grin.

"Anyway, I'm not concerned about the Russian—at least not right now," said Prince. "I do wonder what someone at his level is doing down here, though. We can speculate on that later. Between our uninvited guest and Zora's sudden lack of focus, we didn't really get far with our intended discussion last night. So—," He turned the computer on and pushed it toward the others. "Let's take a look at where we're going."

Everyone pulled their chairs closer together, leaned in toward the laptop, and watched as Prince began searching. "I downloaded the program Dr. Hoyt brought with him. Since you worked with him on the development of this," he looked at Carver and slid the laptop over to him. "Why don't you go over what you two found?"

Carver took over and began to manipulate the program. His fingers tapped away with the sound of Lukas slurping his coffee in the background. "Here we go," he said, as he pushed the laptop out where the others could see. "This is the general area we're talking about. If you look carefully you can see a few villages scattered about. They're small—no roads anywhere. Only access is by small boats."

"Pirogues," added Lucas. "You probably know them as dugouts. Everything out there's surrounded by water. The equator runs right by the spot where Hoyt got dropped off. The north has its rainy season

66

from July through December and the south from January through June. In other words, rainy season is all year."

"This maze of streams and rivers," said Zora, "It's worse than the eastern DRC. No wonder no one lives out here."

"Now, you can see the border with Gabon overlaps our area of interest," said Carver as he continued. "If you draw a circle that connects these three villages here, you've got maybe a 300-square mile circle of jungle that's got no roads, no villages, and no people. And this line here represents a national park—it projects into the area we're talking about."

"This park exists on paper only," said Prince, "As far as we know, no one's ever been into this part of it—except maybe some of those pygmies."

"Some National Geographic guy who walked through this part of Africa sixteen, seventeen years ago, might have come close," said Lucas.

"That guy walked something like two thousand miles," added Prince, "from just below Central African Republic, across northern Congo, then across Gabon. It took him over two years and according to him, a huge part of the area had no signs of prior human presence. Apparently, he came across animals that showed no fear of humans— as if they'd never seen them before. His trek came close to our area, but as far as we can tell, he didn't get down this far."

Carver shifted the laptop around to get better access to it, did a quick search for something, then rotated it back to the others. "Now look at this. I've turned on an overlay that shows contours. At this distance each contour represents a twenty-five-meter change in elevation. Now we zoom in a little and they go to five-meter intervals. Look here."

"That's almost a circle," said Lucas.

"Right, but you would think the center would be the high ground. It's not—it's the low ground."

"A volcanic crater?" asked Zora.

"It was. Millions of years ago," Carver continued. "When Hoyt first discovered this, he showed it to me, and the two of us spent days trying to understand what was going on. He referred to the formation as a caldera, which I guess it is. You can see where the circle breaks down some at this end. Being a depression, it was obviously a large lake at one time. This was where the lake had its main outlet that, over time, expanded until the entire depression was pretty well drained. It still has a lot of water—a lot of it is probably swamp, but here's the thing that really got us. Let me flip this thing on here."

Carver turned off the topographic layer, tapped away again and another overlay appeared. "This shows the elevations of the tops of trees." He hit another button. "And, this gives us the ground elevations. Now, as I initiate this function—the program calculates the tree heights. Look—these numbers we get are impossible." He looked at Zora and said, "This is what I was telling you. The trees in this area are almost as high as red woods—some could even be higher. In addition to this, our analysis of the photographic data tells us exactly what species each tree is. Again, more surprises—a lot of mahogany—in an area where we normally wouldn't expect to find it, but also, bigger than any mahogany anyone has ever heard of. Then we have several other species, like Okoume, which does get pretty big but never like this. Most of the taller ones though, are completely unknown.

"Up until now, anyone looking at this area on satellite photos would see that the tree canopy is relatively even across most of the area. The tops of the trees inside the caldera are level with those outside. There is a dip in the tree top level, but it's not abrupt the way the ground drops off, and it all just looks like the same jungle going on and on with only minor changes in topography. In fact, what we have here is a large depressed bowl that is filled up with jungle— jungle like no one has ever seen anywhere before."

Carver pushed the laptop back to Prince. "OK, show us where Hoyt dropped off the map."

"Hoyt found this open area here." Prince switched to a highly enhanced satellite photo and zoomed in. "This was the closest potential landing site for a helicopter any of us could find. It's open here, but it's wet—the area was most likely opened up by forest elephants. Open areas like this are known as bais. Now this smoke coming up from below, not quite a mile away, is a small pygmy hunting camp. Although most of the pygmies are moving into Bantu villages now, we still find some who are subsisting in the old hunting and gathering tradition. These are obviously still hunter-gatherers but, the interesting thing is, this group is way out from any of the major tribal areas, and they don't seem to have any association with any known tribes."

"They're hundreds of miles from any other group," added Lucas. "We have the Aka in the far North East, along the border with Central African Republic; the Baka, along the Cameroon border, and the Bakola, a small group, further south on the border with Gabon. This group is a complete anomaly. They don't seem to be part of any major tribe. The pilot said he thought they called themselves *bisi ndima*, which an anthropologist acquaintance told me, means, 'forest people.' We've been referring to them as Bakaya."

"Yes," continued Prince. "So, when they landed at the open area here, a small band of these Bakaya showed up, attracted by the sound of the helicopter. Lucas, since you and the pilot talked with them, why don't you continue?"

Prince slid the laptop to Lucas.

"I went out with the copter on its second attempt to find Hoyt, and was able to talk with one who spoke a little Lingala. We didn't get much from him, but the pilot was there when Hoyt's guy was negotiating with some of the pygmies to go along as guides and porters. When the expedition took off, several went along. The landing site's extremely wet so the pilot didn't want to stick around any longer than he had to. He stayed until the expedition started off and said they took a game trail that went in the general direction Hoyt wanted to take—it was about here." Lucas pointed to a spot on the screen. "They were able to contact us the first night, just after they'd set up camp, and they gave us their position." Lucas looked to Zora and added, "Prince sent you the coordinates for each of their encampments." He zoomed out a bit, scrolled to the left, zoomed back in and went on, "This was their first camp. Appears to be about three miles from the landing spot. Over the next five days we got regular reports. Then they just went dead and we never heard another word."

"I thought Hoyt had—what was it—six or seven men with him?" Zora asked. "I ask myself why they wanted porters, especially pygmies? They wouldn't have the same carrying capacity as one of your Bantus or the soldiers. I have to assume they wanted a local guide and the pygmies would be familiar with game trails in the area. Let's zoom back to the landing spot for a minute." Zora reached in front of Lucas to the laptop and asked, "May I?"

"Of course," he said as he pushed it over to her.

She zoomed in a little, then started scrolling along one side of the forest edge. "I see at least three separate game trails along this side." She zoomed in a little further, focusing on what appeared to be a subtle gap in the wall of foliage that lined the open area, then continued, "This larger one was probably made by forest elephants or buffalo," then she scrolled again, "this one was made by much smaller game, as you can see."

"I don't see anything that looks like a trail there," said Carver.

"Very slight opening in the lower brush here," she smiled at Carter and continued, "and the grass leading up to the opening from the clearing is worn down. That suggests recent use—animals or humans. This is probably where they started. It's in the general area you pointed out, Lucas, and is pretty well aligned with the direction of the hunting camp, which happens to be in the same direction as Hoyt's first camp. This is where we'll start."

She slid the laptop back toward Prince while the three men sat looking at her in silence. Finally Prince cleared his throat and said, "Like Lucas said, that's about where they entered the forest, according to the pilot."

Another short silence followed, then Zora asked Lucas, "You said six pygmies went with them? How many in the village, any idea?"

"Not sure but the pilot said they actually had what looked like a big

70

disagreement among themselves. They speak their own language and not many people understand it, but a couple of them could converse a little in Lingala, so Hoyt's people were able to communicate on a very crude level. Apparently some of them were afraid to go into the area Hoyt was interested in. They had some kind of belief. You have to understand that this area, in fact a lot of the Congo basin, has a history of superstition and myths—usually involving a monster of some sort."

"That's right," said Prince, "they've got one about a swamp monster that dates back to the late 1800's and covers a pretty wide area, from Lake Tele, east of our area, to the swamps on the other side of the Congo. It's usually referred to as *mokele-mbembe*. There've been multiple claims of sightings. They range from some British doctor to a group of pygmies back in 1960 who boasted that they'd killed and eaten one. It's Central Africa's Loch Ness Monster."

"This one's a little different, though," said Lucas, "They say this one's a big black thing that can take down a forest elephant. Most of these reports have come from the area north of our target—from poachers hunting for bush meat they sell to loggers up north. But every now and then you hear something that filters down from the Muambo or Bassa people. They live in remote villages further east and to the north. The ones from the north are the most interesting. They claim it's a large black lion."

"That's a new one," said Prince, "Ha!—a big black Leviathan that's sprouted legs and runs through the jungle, eating people. Think that's what the pygmies were worried about?

71

11 – AN EARLY-MORNING CRUISE

Two long trails of cigar smoke drifted off the stern of a large river cruiser floating quietly in the dark Congo night. Viper and Aziza each sat comfortably stretched out on folding deckchairs, Aziza with her eyes half closed and Viper, gently running his fingers through his beard while staring blankly into the emptiness beyond. The air was thick with humidity and the putrid stench of rotting vegetation. The only sound, a constant rhythmic squawking—like the nighttime rant of some large river bird. This was not the sound of a bird though, nor was it the sound of an ape or any other creature that inhabited the island nearby. It was coming from below the cruiser's deck and was the sound of human beings, copulating.

"They sound like a recording that keeps looping back on itself, over and over—what was that shit you put in their drinks? Viper asked.

"Like ecstasy, only better," Aziza answered, "This guy in Brooklyn—my pharmacist—he developed a special recipe, just for my use."

"My cigar's almost finished, and this is what I call a one-hour cigar. That means they've been going for at least an hour without any let up. Did you ever try this recipe yourself?"

"Yeah, but only occasionally, and under the right circumstances."

"I hope it doesn't take too long to wear off. I want him fully present when we finish him."

"It's about one a.m. now, and you'll need some daylight—he should be totally aware by then."

They sat in silence again for several more minutes. Finally Viper flicked his cigar butt into the river, then lit up another. "Want one?"

"No thanks. I'm going to get a little sleep. Wake me when they're finished."

Viper responded with an affirmative grunt, and Aziza rose, stepped back under the cruiser's canopy, and climbed into one of the four hammocks strung across the deck. "Roll down that mosquito net when you're through with the cigar—they're starting to get in here." Then looking toward the bow of the boat, she called out to a man wearing a black beret and military fatigues, leaning against the cabin, and staring up at the stars, "Denis, you might want to get a little sleep too."

"Thank you, Madame—I am fine," he answered.

Aziza fell asleep, but not for long. She was awakened by a sudden scream. The dull constant grunting of the copulates below deck had switched gears, the rhythm speeding up and the groans now laced with short shrieks coming from the female. Her partner now joined in with his own series of deeper, more guttural grunts, and both began to gain in frequency, building and getting louder until a frenzied peak was achieved. Aziza rolled out of her hammock, looked at Viper and said, "OK—time for act two."

♦ ♦

"*T'as pris ton pied, mon ami?*" Viper asked as he guided the shorter, heavier black man into one of the deck chairs.

"Speak in English, if you don't mind," requested Aziza as she appeared from below. "English or Russian—or Yiddish," she said with a short laugh.

"You are my friend for life!" the man said, looking at Viper. "That was crazy good, man—I mean really crazy fucking good! What did you just give her?" he asked Aziza.

"Something to help her sleep. She should be out 'til we drop her off in Ouésso later." She unfolded another chair and sat down so that she and Viper both faced the man. He turned around for a second as he heard Denis, the soldier, lighting a cigarette. Denis had positioned himself behind the man where he quietly leaned back against the cabin wall and folded his arms.

"Jean Paul," said Aziza, "Did I ever tell you how much I love the sound of your voice?"

Jean Paul looked up at Aziza and smiled like a Cheshire Cat with a wide gap between his front teeth.

"You have one of those deep baritone voices, and Viper says your French is without any accent. You must have studied in France. Where did you go, Jean Paul? The Sorbonne?"

"No, no, I went to L'école Superieure de Commerce—in Paris."

"Ah yes, that's right, you're a professional bureaucrat. But that voice, man. I can imagine you as a radio or TV announcer—even an opera singer."

"A famous TV host—yes!" added Viper. "Say something for us, Jean Paul, like a TV host would say it."

"What would you like me to say?" Jean Paul asked.

"Good evening ladies and gentlemen, tonight we are going to talk about—pussy!"

"Ah, ha ha!" Jean Paul laughed, then repeated. "Good evening ladies and gentlemen, tonight we are going to talk about pussy!" He laughed again and repeated, shouting, "PUSSY!"

"Jean Paul," said Viper, "I always wondered how come you got a name like Jean Paul and not some Bantu or Lingala name."

"My father's favorite movie star was Jean Paul Belmondo. So, he named me Jean Paul. He used to go to all the French movies that came to Brazzaville. One of my sisters was named Brigitte—after Bardot—one brother was Alain, after Alain Delon. That brother died of hepatitis when he was a kid. My youngest brother is named after Johnny Holiday."

Aziza cleared her throat, got up and stepped back into the cabin. She returned with a towel which she dropped into Jean Paul's lap. "We need to talk business, Jean Paul—and I don't want to look at that little pig's tail of a dick that's peeking out from under your fat belly."

Denis let out a light chuckle, causing Jean Paul to turn and look at him again—this time with an angry scowl on his face. He then looked down into his lap and stared quietly for a minute, his mind still dulled from the drugs.

His hosts watched in silence until he finally looked up—then Viper began. "Jean Paul, you are indeed quite a specimen—and you like pussy, don't you?"

A grin spread across Jean Paul's broad face. "Viper, *mon ami*—"

Viper cut him off. "We're through talking pussy for now my good friend. Aziza and I want to discuss the timbering concession permits you're supposed to be securing for SBP."

"Yes, yes, of course—"

Viper cut him off again. "We've given you five million euros—so far—and we understand you've already put in an order for a new Mercedes, and you're giving the old one to your oldest son. I like that, Jean Paul. You take care of your kids. That's good—that's very good."

Viper's eyes shifted to Aziza, then to Denis, then back again to Aziza. They stared at each other for an instant, then she looked at Jean Paul. "You know, of course, that you are not our only friend at the Department of the Interior. In fact, we have several friends—not only there, but in every important post in Brazzaville, including the army. Same in the DRC—we have lots of friends—all over Kinshasa—everywhere."

"And they've been telling us things about you, Jean Paul," added Viper.

"Things that don't make us so happy," continued Aziza.

"You…you can't listen to what others—"

Once again, Viper interrupted him. "Jean Paul," he paused for a second, then repeated, "Jean Paul—we understand that you sold our contract to the Germans—for seven million euros. Now when were you going to tell us about that, Jean Paul? When?"

Jean Paul's shoulders drooped, and his head appeared to sink into his body as he shrunk back into his chair. He looked up at Aziza, then back at Viper. He was sweating profusely now, and his eyes had gone from half closed to wide-open, pupils dilated. "You—you know you are my friend. I...I..."

"Yes," said Aziza, "we know you're our friend, Jean Paul."

"Th-there's a reason...I...I...you—you don't really want that concession," he blurted out, I have secret information..."

"Secret information?" asked Aziza, "How can you tell us secret information? We know everything; we own everyone. You understand? There are no secrets we don't know about."

"No, no—yes, I do. The Americans—it's about the Americans—it's about CATI."

"CATI's owned by an Australian. They're not American, Jean Paul. You don't know shit," said Aziza.

"I know, I know. But it's the Americans who run the company. I mean they got a local guy. He's a Belge, and some Nigerian guy. But it's Americans who run things—from Seattle—that's in the U.S.—an-and they found something. They're doing everything they can to keep it quiet."

"What did they find, Jean Paul?" asked Viper.

"Nobody really knows, but one of their people came from the U.S. over three weeks ago. No one talked about it. Then he went out into the interior. A whole group of them went—very secret. Then they disappeared—never came back. Now two more Americans are in Brazzaville getting ready to go find the first one. Nobody's talking, but my spy—my man who works for them—he told me."

"He told you someone went off into the jungle and disappeared? Fuck, you idiot! You're not telling me anything." Viper leaned forward, his face hovering over Jean Paul's, and laughed, spraying spittle across Jean Paul face.

"No—no, I know where they went. Up north, near the border with Gabon, below Cameroon. It's a big empty hole up there. The government hasn't given any concessions up there because it's too far away. No one wants to waste time going up there—just swamps and jungle. They even declared part of it a national park or something. It makes the UN people, the internationals—happy. Good PR that doesn't cost them anything."

Viper pulled back away from Jean Paul. "You not only look like a pig, but you stink like one too. He pulled his own shirt up, covered his face with it and began taking long drawn out breaths through the fabric. "Wipe yourself. There, take the towel Aziza gave you and wipe some of the stink off yourself."

Jean Paul looked into his lap and slowly lifted the towel, running it up and down his face, then across his chest, down his belly, and then back into his lap. "My spy said the guy who came from the U.S. was a bigshot tree expert. That tells me they've found something—some kind of timber source that would make it worth going all the way up into that jungle. The money you paid me we can use that to secure this area for you. The Americans—they do all the work and you—you get the concession. Big joke on the Americans—or the Australian! You see?"

"OK, Jean Paul," said Aziza, "this really does sound a little farfetched, but maybe there's something to it. We still don't like you taking this little action behind our backs—taking our money, then selling us out to the faggot Krauts." She leaned over sticking her face in front of his and added, "You realize I'm a Jew don't you, Jean Paul? That's a real slap in the face for you to fuck-me over for a Kraut. I hate Krauts, you know—and Arabs too."

"But Ziza, why do you get so upset? Viper told me you are his friend, but you don't even work for SBP."

"That's true, JP…you don't mind if I call you JP do you? Jean Paul is too long for me—its un-American, if you will. So—JP—I don't work for La Société des Bois Précieux." She paused, gave Viper a quick smirk, and went on. "I'm in the diamond business—but the fact is that Viper is my very close friend. You realize he is the closest thing I have to a brother?" She paused again. "Well, that makes it my business—so now I'm pissed." She emphasized the *s* sound in pissed, like a snake hissing, "And like I said, I hate—fucking—Krauts!" She was shouting now. "And I hate fucking Arabs. In fact, I hate anyone who gets in my way, and I hate anyone who tries to fuck over my friends." She looked at him in silence for a minute, then continued, "JP, Viper is right—you really stink. Why don't you jump in the river and wash off before we go on?" She backed away from him and looking from Denis to Viper, said, "Viper—Denis? Come on. Let's help JP into the water."

Jean Paul sunk back into his seat again, pushing the chair back with his feet. "No!" he screamed. A nearby animal echoed his scream, causing Viper to giggle. "No!" Jean Paul repeated, "Not in the river! I—I'm working for you … I …" He began to shake, the sweat pouring off again and his eyes blown back up like two large eggs floating in the darkness.

"JP, calm down," said Aziza. "You're waking up all the wildlife out there. We're not about to go throwing you to the crocodiles—I mean, what are you thinking, man? Why, you're an undersecretary to one of the most important departments in the country."

"Yes, my God, man," exclaimed Viper, "do you really think we would do something like that? Look, just climb down the ladder…here at the back of the boat. Hold on to the ladder and wash yourself. It's just the pussy, man. You stink like rotten fish. Come on, I'll help you. Aziza will get you a clean towel. You want some soap?"

Viper smiled and held out his hand. After a brief pause, Jean Paul reached up and Viper nodded at Denis then pulled Jean Paul out of the chair. Denis joined them, and together he and Viper guided the naked man over to the ladder, Jean Paul still holding the towel to his crotch. They carefully helped him as he dropped the towel, stepped onto the ladder and began to descend down into the dark water. As one foot entered the water he let out a short shout, "Waah! It's cold!"

"Here, take this with you." Aziza held out a bar of soap and as he reached for it, he lost his balance and slipped, dropping straight down into the water, his nose catching on one of the ladder rungs with a thud as his body shot downward. He thrashed about, hands grabbing wildly in the air. Finally, managing to gain a grip on the ladder he pulled himself back up, gasping and choking; blood now flowed freely from his nose, down his chin, and across his chest.

"What the hell are you doing, Jean Paul?" shouted Viper. "Trying to scare me? Here…dunk your head in again. Wipe yourself with your free hand and hold on with the other. That's it … that's it. The cold water will help stop the bleeding. You broke your nose, man. Ha … hard to imagine how you can break a nose like yours—wide and fat."

Jean Paul looked up at Viper, blood still running from his nose like a turned-on faucet. He coughed, spit, then settled back, immersing his head into the water. He blew water out of his mouth as he lifted his head back up again, then slapped his hand with frustration as a swarm of gnat-like insects discovered him. "Help me. Get me out of here."

He pulled himself up slowly and as his upper torso reached the deck railing Viper and Denis each grabbed him under the armpits and pulled him over the railing and onto the deck, where they continued to hold him. "Good man. That must feel much better," said Viper. "Now, why don't you go inside and get yourself dressed."

Jean Paul began to stagger toward the hatchway when Aziza stepped alongside him, placed one hand on his back, and stuck her foot between his feet and Jean Paul, like a large bale of flesh, fell face first onto the wooden deck where he lay unmoving as Aziza fastened his feet together with plastic handcuffs. With Viper's help they rolled him over, and then she secured his hands with his wrists in front of him. "Denis, help Viper, I'm going to start the boat up," she said as she started toward the cockpit.

"Wake up, Jean Paul," shouted viper. "You had a nasty fall, man. You gotta wake up."

Jean Paul moaned, his eyes began to flutter, then they rolled open. "What happened?" He looked around, tried to rise up, but lost his balance, falling helplessly back onto the deck. "My arms! What? I can't move my arms—my hands—you tied me up!"

"Don't worry, my friend. The boat's moving now, and we didn't want you to get hurt again or roll over board so we just secured you— for your own safety."

"Where are we going?"

"We're going back to Ouésso now. It's getting light, and we're going to drop your girlfriend off back where we found her. Then we're picking up a friend who's flying from Brazzaville later today. But first, we need to make a little side trip."

"Side trip?"

"Yes. Aziza and I, we got these friends we want you to meet."

Jean Paul rolled onto his side and attempted to lift his head. He could see the gray dimness of dawn just beginning to filter through the heavy haze that hung over the river. Then he rolled back in the opposite direction and could see Aziza, who was now up in the cockpit and driving the boat and Denis who was standing close by, just below Aziza. "Denis, what are you doing? Help me! Get these things off my hands and my feet!"

"Sorry, boss. You shouldn't have screwed with them. Aziza and Viper—they're the boss now."

"What? Viper! Get me out of these things. I'll give you back your money—I can give you back all the money, and you'll get the concession. You understand? You'll get the contracts—no cost to you. Where you taking me? Oh, fuck. What friends you talking about?"

"Aziza, he wants to know about our friends!" shouted Viper.

"I see them now!" Aziza shouted back. The boat was racing now at top speed, the bow slapping the surface of the water as it surged ahead. "Go ahead and stand him up so he can see—he needs to see them!"

Viper slipped a rope between Jean Paul's bound hands and nodded to Denis. "Here, let me help you, my friend." He pulled the rope taut, then tugged hard as Denis lifted Jean Paul from behind, and they shifted him into a standing position. Pulling on the rope, Viper led him over to the starboard side of the boat. With his feet still bound, Jean Paul couldn't maintain his balance, but Denis held him up as Viper continued pulling until they had him braced against the side railing. Viper then positioned a chair behind him. "Here you go, sit down my friend. Have a nice deck-side viewing seat so you can see my friends."

The boat rolled slightly as Aziza started into a turn. "Here they are!" she screamed out over the high-pitched wail of the boat's engine.

Viper then joined in with Aziza's screaming and yelled out,

"Look! Look at them—look, my friend!" He grabbed Jean Paul's ears from behind and forced him forward, leaning him out over the railing. Then, he twisted Jean Paul's head sideways so that he was focused toward the bow of the boat and in that instant, the boat rolled hard onto its side. Aziza's screaming had become almost hysterical, as though she were riding on the back of a wild, bucking horse, and Jean Paul found himself staring into the gaping mouth of a large bull hippopotamus, enraged and lunging with all its force directly at the speeding boat. They came so close to it that its huge head completely blocked out the sun that had just popped above the treeline on the shore beyond. It let out an enormous roar just as it snapped its jaws shut, missing the boat by no more than a yard or two.

Aziza steered the boat into a wide arching U-turn, still laughing and shouting, while Viper, also laughing now, slapped Jean Paul on the back. Viper recoiled immediately and shouted up to the cockpit, "Aziza, look! He shit in his pants—only he don't have his pants on! Oh my God, he completely lost it! Jean Paul, you bad boy—nobody ever potty-trained you!"

Aziza, continued laughing, paying no attention now to the others as, once again she accelerated the boat and began steering it back for another pass at the hippos. "Look!" she screamed, "there must be at least twenty of them!"

Like rapids, the water around the hippos was boiling now as the herd plowed its way back toward the shore, away from the approaching boat—with the exception of the huge alpha. This hippo did not retreat with the rest of the herd. This one moved forward toward the boat— its mouth snapping, a coughing roar belching from deep within. As the boat began to close with him, he broke into a full charge—head-on, jaws wide. Aziza swerved, again just in time and the mighty jaws clamped down onto nothing.

"No, no, no," screamed Jean Paul. "Please! You're going to kill us all! You're crazy!" His screams turned into sobs as the boat pulled away from the hippo. He coughed and sobbed and began to mumble unintelligibly. He made a sudden effort to break away from his bindings but only ended up slipping out of the chair, sliding in his own excrement as he frantically squirmed back and forth in an effort to pull himself away from the boat's edge, squirming like a worm dropped on a hot sidewalk.

Aziza's screeching surged once more as she again began to maneuver the boat for another round. Viper grabbed the rope that ran between Jean Paul's hands and pulled hard, sliding him back toward the boat's side rail. He looked around for Denis who had moved away from the stern, as if not sure he really wanted to be there. "Denis! Get over here," Viper yelled, as he grabbed Jean Paul once more, lifted him up, this time holding him in place with one arm while he braced himself by grabbing a hand-grip with the other. "Denis!" he shouted again, "Give me a hand." Then, looking at Jean Paul, "Come on, he wants to see you—one more time!"

As soon as the boat turned again, the hippo knew that it was coming back, and he started his charge immediately. Aziza had the boat running at full throttle, and the two massive opponents, like ancient jousters, flung themselves madly toward each other. The air was now electrified with the deafening roar of the massive river horse and the heightened electric scream of the boat's engine, overlaced with Aziza's hysterical shriek, as the two bodies rushed together on their cataclysmic convergence. Just as the pulverizing collision was about to reach the point of absolute certainty, Aziza, for the third time, turned the steering wheel sharply—and in that instant, Denis arrived behind Jean Paul, and with his eyes closed, and his face curled into a painful grimace, pushed ever so slightly while Viper gave a quick tug on the rope and with the centripetal force of the turning boat, Jean Paul was swept over the side and directly into the gaping mouth of the charging hippopotamus. In one crushing slam, the hippo's mouth sundered Jean Paul's body in two. It rose up off the bottom of the river as if standing on its hind legs and shook its head in a long arching movement, sending the upper half of Jean Paul flying into the air with a trail of his now-pulverized inner organs spraying out like a rainbow over the stern of the retreating boat.

"Yeow!" shouted Viper, looking at his hands. He had failed to release his grip in time and the rope had hissed through his hands, burning the skin of his palms raw. Oblivious to whatever pain might have been running through his hands, he placed both of them on the stern railing and leaned far out over the water, his eyes wide open, the whites now red with rage, a swollen vein running down the center of his forehead like a scar, and he screamed, "You don't fuck with me, you idiot—you don't fuck with the Viper!"

12 – THE FOREST PEOPLE

Ngiome liked it here where the forest opened up at this large grassy clearing, the place where the elephants came to drink and take salt. He loved the light. He also enjoyed being close to the *nyama* who came here—the animals. There were the *mokombosa*—the chimpanzees— and the big ones, the gorillas, and the many smaller ones that always stayed up high in the trees. There were the bongos, the buffalo, the red river hogs—some were hunted by his family, the *bisi ndima*, but not here. Many times he had seen a yellow-backed duiker drinking from the river and standing very close to it, a leopard, also drinking from the river. This place was special—this was the *bai*, the place where all shared and all were safe.

Now, none of their numbers were as great as they once had been, and many of them, particularly the elephants, spent most of their time hidden in the dense forest. The *bilo*, the ones who called themselves Bantus, had come one day, arriving from the sky on a giant flying pirogue from which they sprayed fire from their *bondoki*—guns—not like the guns the Bantus from the village people used for hunting, but guns like he had never seen before—guns that pained the ears with their loud rattling like a hard stick being dragged across a river bank full of small rocks, but louder—much louder. The *bilo* murdered the elephants—almost the entire herd.

Some of the buffalo and bongos were killed as well—only the gorillas managed to escape unharmed. The few elephants that did escape were resting in the shade along the *bai*'s edge—now they stayed hidden in the forest, returning to take their salt and bathe in the river only at night. His family had seen it all. They were lucky—they were deep in the forest collecting tara roots and mushrooms when the *bilo* arrived. When they heard the sound of the great flying pirogue, most in his family had run back to their camp where they cowered in their huts, but not Ngiome. He had gone to the *bai* and watched. He saw as it hovered like a giant dragonfly, spitting its fire out at the elephants below. Then it perched on the ground and the *bilo* came out with terrifying machetes that screamed with a sound like all the hornets of the forest gathered together at one time. And with their screaming machetes they cut the elephants. It was as if the entire world had gone upside down—as if the sky had become black and fallen into the earth and lightning had struck, burning everything it touched.

Nothing he had seen that day could he comprehend. When the *bilo* left they took only the tusks of the elephants. They seemed to have no interest in the meat. The Bantus his family knew—the masters from the river village that lay three days downstream—those people always ate the meat of the animals they killed. Meat was part of life; it allowed all to live—like forest roots, nuts, mushrooms, fruit, and honey. Those who came in the flying pirogue were not normal *bilo. Perhaps*, he thought, *they must live on death and nothing else— perhaps they had come from some foul hole in the earth that had opened up at night.* The forest was everything—how could something come that was not of the forest, and in one day—less than one day— obliterate with such totality? Could this be the beginning of the end— the end of everything?

Some of his family members travelled to the village to exchange bush meat and honey for metal tools, and they talked to the Bantus who lived there about what had happened, but although some of them had heard of flying pirogues that carried people, they had not heard anything about a flying pirogue that spit fire and brought death.

Time had passed, and the flying pirogue had not returned. Slowly some of the *nyama* began to return to the *bai*. The smaller ones came first—the little duiker, the possum, the porcupine, and the red river hog. Then the bongos came, the gorillas, and a few buffalo. The elephants were the last to return. Now their numbers were few. Where once there had been thirty or more on any given day, now they were only three or four at a time—sometimes only one appeared.

Then, one day the sound of the flying pirogue did come back. This time, however, it found the clearing empty. The horrible noise it made was now a warning to those few creatures that came to the *bai*. They were all hiding back in the forest by the time the thing had arrived. Ngiome had been hunting that day, far off from the *bai*, and most of his family had been with him.

Ngiome was not the oldest in the family, but it was he who was the *mangese*, the one the others turned to whenever important decisions had to be made. When they heard the flying pirogue that second time, he told the hunting party to split up with the women, children, and older members of the group going back to the camp. He and the men proceeded to a point near the *bai*, being careful not to get too close. They waited and listened, but the sound of the lightning guns and the hornet machetes never came, and so they moved closer. They stopped again and listened. They could hear the thundering roar of the flying pirogue, but still no sound of the lightning guns. Soon it became quiet. They could tell that it had not left, but the deafening noise had ceased, and in the quiet that followed, they heard the voices of *bilo*. Moving ever so slowly they crept to the edge of the *bai* and, keeping themselves concealed within the line of thickened vegetation that lined the meadow's edge, they peered out toward the center where the giant pirogue now rested in stillness. "It is not a pirogue," one of the hunters whispered. "It is a giant bird."

"Yes," another agreed. "It has a big eye, and the *bilo* spill out of its anus, like shit."

They were able to see eight *bilo* on the ground, walking about as if searching for something. The big bird's eyes were strange, linked together, and forming what looked like one long eye that wrapped around its head. The eyes were clear, and it was possible to see inside, where one more *bilo* remained. The large gaping hole in one side could, indeed have been the creature's anus—or perhaps it was the mouth. Ngiome remembered that it was from this hole that the *bilo* had cast out their bolts of lightning.

One of the *bilo* called out to the others. He spoke in a strange tongue—not Lingala, which the Bantu used in the village. The others began to gather bundles that they had thrown out of the bird, and they carried them over to the one who had called out. They began to open the bundles and spread them on the ground into large sheets of fabric. They then took metal sticks that appeared to grow in length and these they used like *fito* from the forest, pushing them into the ground and, then, stretching the fabric over them, forming huts, just as his people lay large leaves over bent *fito* to form their own huts.

Ngiome had been watching one of the *bilo* gathering wood and grass and then seemed to be starting a fire when he noticed another who was directing the others, like a chief from the *bilo* village. His heart jumped when he saw how strange looking this one was. He was completely different from all other *bilo*—in fact he was unlike any *bilo* that Ngiome had ever known. His skin was too light. He had seen an albino *bilo* at the village once when he was very young, but this one was not like that—this one was more of a light tan, as if his skin had been decorated with some form of dye—and his hair—it was smooth and colored more like the hair of some of the monkeys that lived in the upper canopy. The light skinned one's clothing was also different. They all had some kind of covering on their upper and lower bodies, head coverings and dried skins wrapped around their feet, as had those *bilo* who killed the *nyama*. Some of his people who had been to the river village had spoken of *bilos* who wore clothing, but not like this. These *bilo* all had clothing that looked the same—it was decorated to look like tree leaves. On the other hand, the light skinned *bilo*'s clothing was pale and without a pattern, like the belly of a crocodile.

Ngiome was not the only one who had noticed the strange man. All of his people were now staring in wonder, and then Sondu, one of the younger men, started walking out into the *bai*. He moved slowly, as though he were walking in his sleep. He walked straight toward the light skinned one and had gone almost three elephant lengths before any of the *bilo* noticed him.

The *bilo* who saw him shouted. The others stopped and looked toward him, including Ngiome and those who were still concealed along the edge of the forest. The *bilo* who shouted pointed toward Sondu and in perfect unison, everyone's head turned from the shouting *bilo* to Sondu who had now stopped and was standing perfectly still, staring at the light skinned one.

No one moved at first, then, the light skinned *bilo* said something to one of the other *bilo*, who spoke back to him, both looking at Sondu. Then the *bilo* walked toward him, but stopped when Ngiome's cousin turned and looked back toward his own people. He looked at Ngiome then back again toward the *bilo* and for several heartbeats they looked at each other in silence. When the *bilo* spoke, he used the words of the Bantu people—Lingala.

"*Bayaka,*" he said, using the name that some *bilo* call those *bisi ndima* who live far off, closer to the villages—the ones who have forgotten how to live in the forest. "*Bayaka,* we have come to trade with you. We have oil, cloth—and knives. Do you understand Lingala?"

The cousin laughed then turned his head back to Ngiome again. He didn't understand a word.

By this time all of the family members had stepped into the *bai* and all looked now at Ngiome, waiting to see what he would do. He nodded to each of them, then stepped out into the open and began to walk slowly into the *bai*. He approached the *bilo* who had been speaking, continued past him, and on, until he stood directly in front of the light-skinned one. Speaking in Lingala, he said, "My name is Ngiome, and I ask if that is also your name?"

The light skinned one looked at the *bilo* and spoke to him, using a language that was incomprehensible to Ngiome. The *bilo* quickly joined Ngiome and the light skinned one and said to Ngiome, "This is the boss man. He comes from far away—beyond where the sun sets at night. He is very strong and very wise, but he does not understand our language. You must talk with him through me."

"My grandfather told me of a man who looked like this light skinned *bilo*. That man knew many kinds of magic, and he stayed in the forest with our family for two seasons. He lived in the hut of my father until the people built him his own hut. He had a basket of metal that could repeat sounds our people made when they spoke and when they sang. This man came, he left, he never returned—all before I was born. His name was Ngiome. My father named me Ngiome. I ask if this light skinned *bilo* carries the name of Ngiome?"

By this time all of the *bisi ndima* had gathered in a semi-circle behind Ngiome, and the rest of the *bilo* gathered behind the light skinned *bilo*, everyone now looking at Ngiome and the light skinned one, who, like all of the *bilo*, was at least two heads taller than Ngiome. Speaking again in the strange tongue, the interpreter repeated to the light skinned *bilo* everything that Ngiome had said. The light skinned one responded, and the interpreter again spoke to Ngiome.

"The boss man said that his name is not Ngiome. He is much like the man you describe though. He comes from very far away, and he wants to trade with you and your people."

"We trade with *bilo* at the village—many days travel downriver. Why do you come here to trade in this great pirogue that flies?"

"The boss man searches for a special place in the forest. He asks that you and your people help him to find this place. He will give you metal, fabrics, and knives in exchange for your help."

"Other *bilo* came here before in a giant pirogue like your pirogue, but all black. They killed the *nyama* that come here to drink and take salt. Do you come to kill elephants?"

The two *bilo* exchanged words again, and then the interpreter responded, "We have heard about those *bilo* who kill the elephants. They take their tusks. Those are very bad *bilo*. We do not kill elephants—none of us kills elephants—no animals—we kill no *nyama*. We bring our own food. We only come to search for a special place—and we ask for your help. You can show us the trails, and your people can help us to carry our things."

"What do you need to carry?" asked Ngiome.

"Our huts, our food, and special things that the boss man needs to take with him."

Ngiome laughed and looked around at his family. Several of them laughed with him. Then he continued his conversation. "If you need food, you gather it as you walk through forest or you hunt if you want meat—and why do you carry your huts? You make huts from liana and leaves. The *bisi ndima* only carry nets and spears or bows when we go through forest. You come in great flying pirogue, but you are like the *bisi mboka*—you do not know how to live in the forest."

"Yes, that is correct. We do not know how to live in the forest. That is why we ask you, the *bayaka*, to help us."

"We are not *bayaka*. The *bisi mboka* in river village call us that— they also call us *baka*. We are *bisi ndima*—*bayaka* are those who leave the forest. They live near villages that lay beyond river."

At this point the light skinned *bilo* held up a machete and pulled it out of its sheath. He handed it to the translator as he spoke to him once again. The translator nodded his head, then turned back to Ngiome and with a smile, offered the machete to him. "This is one of the knives we have for you—take it—see how fine it is." He then looked at the other members of Ngiome's family and said, "We have one for each of you who can come with us to help carry our loads and to help us find the trail that will take us where the boss man needs to go."

Ngiome held the machete in one hand and ran the thumb of his other hand across the blade to test its sharpness. He then held it out to one of his cousins who took it and went through the same motion. He passed it on to another and gradually all of the family members drew closer together as discussion broke out among them.

Ngiome looked at the light skinned *bilo* and asked, "What is this place you want to find?"

The light skinned one and the translator exchanged several words, then the light skinned *bilo* pointed toward the direction of the sunsets and the translator said, "It is in that direction. The boss man thinks that it might be three or four days' walk there. He also said that he thinks the ground drops down in the place he seeks, and the trees grow very tall."

Ngiome's expression changed. His eyes narrowed, creases formed in his forehead between his eyes, and he stared sharply at the two *bilo*. He said nothing at first, then he spoke, the tone of his voice now very distinct and direct, "The place you speak of does not exist—no person can go there—not the *bisi ndima*—not the *bilo*—it is not possible to go there."

The two conversed with one another again, then the translator said to Ngiome, "The boss man knows this place does exist, and he must go there. He also knows how to find this place by himself, but he offers many gifts to anyone who can help him. He wants your people to help carry things and to show him any trails that will make it easier for him to go there. He says there are big swamps that must be crossed, but he thinks that your people know the best way."

Ngiome turned, looked around at his family members then grabbed the machete away from the one who was holding it. He threw it on the ground in front of the two *bilo* and said, "Any who go to that place will never come back." He turned back to his own people and continued, now shouting, "You will no longer exist if you go. No one guides these *bilo* to that place!" He then turned his back on the *bilo* and walked quickly back across the bai and into the forest. The other *bisi ndima* watched, then, one after another, they followed.

The *bilo* translator picked up the machete, held it up, and called after them, "Here!" he shouted, "take your machete—this is our gift to you—it is yours!"

Ngiome and the other pygmies had not gone far when they stopped and began to speak to one another in whispered tones. Although several of them wanted to stay and take the gifts that were being offered, Ngiome was adamant in his insistence that leading the *bilo* to the place they asked about was not a possibility. Finally it was decided that some of them would stay at the edge of the bai to observe what the *bilo* were doing while Ngiome and the others returned to their camp.

The discussion continued as they made their way back to the camp and as evening approached it became more heated in tone as those who were already in the camp joined in. Only when the sound of wood popping in the campfire and the smell of smoke mixed with cooked meat filled the air, did the conversation slow down and everyone's attention shifted to the freshly prepared meal. But the calmness did not last as one of those who had stayed to observe the *bilo*, came running into the camp.

"You're late," someone said, "Where are others?"

"They went back into bai," he exclaimed, out of breath. "Kaki talked with the *bilo*, and now they're all eating at the *bilo* fire."

"But you came back alone."

"The *bilo* offered more gifts, and soon the others started talking. They decided to help the *bilo* go to the forbidden place. They intend to go when the sun comes back. I was afraid. I told them not to go—as Ngiome told them—as we always have known."

They all looked at Ngiome who was now standing with his back to the fire, looking into the forest, both hands grasping a round stone he had picked up, his thumbs slowly rubbing it, deep in thought.

◆ ◆

The following morning, nine of the *bisi ndima* left with the *bilo*. Eight of them helped carry bundles, and one led the way as their guide. They started out following one of the game trails that entered the bai from where the sun disappeared each night. Ngiome and several other family members went to the bai in the morning to try and stop them, but by the time they had arrived the open glade was empty. The had heard the loud noise of the great flying pirogue just as the sun came up, and now it was gone as well.

Several of them wanted to follow, but after some discussion it was agreed that they should not. Ngiome told them that the place they were going to could normally be reached in no more than two days if one knew how to get there. "With the *bilo*," he said, "it will take them five or six days. We should wait. If Sondu and Kaki and the others have enough sense to just lead them to the place where the ground drops, but not go on themselves, they should be back here in seven or eight days.

Eight days later all nine of the wayward *bisi ndima* came strolling back into the forest camp. At first no one would talk with them, then someone asked, "Where are *bilo*?"

"They went down into the darkness where the ground falls into the earth. We begged them not to go, but they did not listen so we dropped what we carried for them and we left."

"So why did you come back here?" one of the women asked.

"We came back to our home—to our people."

"We are not your people," said another woman. "We all know of the place you took the *bilo* to is forbidden and no one must ever go there—even *bilo*"

"Especially the *bilo*!" someone else exclaimed.

By now the entire group stood in a ring around the nine young men. Everyone was silent now, looking at each other. Finally one of the women said, "This no longer your home. You all leave—go to the village. You all can become *bisi mboka*. You must go live like *bayaka* now—like little leeches among *bilo*."

"Maybe you will find another *bisi ndima* family to take you in— beyond the river," muttered an older man.

The nine young men wandered around the camp for a while, but no one would talk to them. Everyone turned their backs whenever the men approached; they looked away, avoiding any eye contact—as if they were not there. Two of them had children, but the mothers took the children and pushed them into their huts as soon as the fathers attempted to talk to them. One reached for some mushrooms that were piled on a large leaf, but the woman who had collected them stepped in front of him, cutting him off. Soon someone began to sing. She was joined by another and then another, until the entire family, with the exception of the nine outcasts, was singing. They began to cluster together, linking their arms—men, women, children, and elders—and as they sang, they began to weave back and forth as one elongated, interwoven body. They sang and danced, stomping their feet on the ground—back and forth, and now rotating, first in one direction, then in the other. This sudden, spontaneous ceremony continued on and on until gradually, all nine of the banished men drifted slowly out and away from the camp, finally disappearing back into the forest, exiled from their own families as if they had never existed.

The next morning, just as the *bisi ndima* were preparing their morning meal, one of the banished men called to his wife from the forest. "We're taking one pirogue. We're going to the *bilo* village. The *bilo* will give us machetes, and now life will be easy. You can join us there. Let Ngiome stay here alone. We will wait for you at village."

Many more dawns came and went, but none of the wayward *bisi ndima* came back—nor did any of the *bilo*. After seven moons had passed the great flying pirogue returned, but it did not set down in the bai. They could hear it far above the tops of the trees. It came and flew back and forth, its sound disappeared toward the direction of the forbidden place, then returned for a short time, circled around once, and disappeared again. Two dawns later it returned, flew back and forth, then left again. The *bisi ndima* knew that it must have been looking for the *bilo*, but they knew the *bilo* would not be back. No one who went into the forbidden place ever came back.

♦ ♦

Many more dawns had passed since the last time a great flying pirogue had flown above their heads when the sound of its approach returned. This time it was different though. Ngiome had noticed before that each of the previous giant pirogues, or birds, made sounds that were distinctively its own. The rhythm differed just as the grunt of a red river hog differs from that of a giant black forest hog. It was the noise of another giant priogue—one that had not been to the bai before.

13 – BIENVENUE

"Bad ju-ju. That's what we call it where I come from," shouted Prince, trying to make himself heard over the thumping roar of the helicopter as it hurtled rapidly along a low chain of forested mountains, cloaked in dark clouds that glowed off and on in random patterns like a deep slate-gray fog filled with fireflies. "First we get up here and find the copter's broken down—lose another day getting it fixed— just in time for these storms. Man, I hate flying in these storms!" He looked around and realized he was just talking to himself, but continued on anyway. "Carver, you're looking a little green, man; I thought you were ex-military. You've flown through this kind of shit before, haven't you?"

Carver, sitting stiff as a board, one hand gripping a grab bar and the other clenching the edge of his seat, his face pale with beads of sweat rolling down his forehead, looked at Prince while Zora answered for him, "He might have been a jock back in the day, but I don't think he's ever seen any military duty." The helicopter suddenly dropped, as if in a state of free-fall, then leveled off for a second or two, rose upward, rolled to one side, then the other. "Even if he had been," she continued, "this is no joy ride. How 'bout you, Prince— you enjoying it?"

"Yes, I guess I do enjoy it. I look at it like a wild carnival ride so you might say I trick myself into enjoying it. Ha!" Prince laughed, then added, "My way of coping."

There were seven of them in the Eurocopter; it was filled to capacity. In addition to Carver, Zora, Prince, Lucas, and the French pilot, two soldiers had been assigned to them as escorts in accordance with a government mandate. The soldiers were both in the same condition as Carver, one of them in the process of losing his breakfast in an airsick bag while the other clutched a bag in his hands in anticipation. Lucas sat with his head tilted back and his eyes closed.

"We'll be past these mountains in just another minute," yelled the pilot. "Should calm down a lot then. The air conditioning hasn't worked for months now so we're forced to fly with the windows open—otherwise it wouldn't be so noisy."

"How far out are we?" Zora yelled up to him.

"Fifteen minutes—should be there in fifteen minutes." He looked over his shoulder at Carver and added, "If there's no more bags, you can puke out the window—just make sure you lean out far enough or it'll just blow back in!"

The mountains along with the storms that clung to them began to recede into the distance now and with their departure, the turbulence shifted from violent thrashing into a slower choppiness. "Almost there now," the pilot yelled out.

The sky lightened as the clouds broke apart, and as the chopper began to descend, bright streaks of sunlight broke through, one ray at a time, and danced across the sponge-textured canopy that now came into clear focus as it raced beneath them. One of the sick soldiers could be heard dry-heaving, and the other was moaning when Carver stood, leaned out the open window and regurgitated, unfortunately facing into the wind. Lucas turned his head in time to avoid a direct hit, but the two soldiers who were just beginning to manage their own queasiness, took the full brunt. They both began vomiting into their bags while Lucas, eyes open now, wiped his arm across his face and just looked at Carver. "*Merde*," he mumbled.

"What the hell!" the pilot suddenly shouted out as he put the helicopter into a breaking motion, quickly slowing down while banking slightly to one side. "What the hell is this? Look—over there!" He pointed at something straight ahead of them.

Prince and Zora both stood and grabbing hold of the ribs of the helicopter's framing, leaned forward and looked out through the cockpit window. "That's another helicopter!" Prince blurted out.

Zora leaned forward a little further. "Kamov Ka-62," she said, "Russian."

"SBP," the pilot yelled back. "French company, but the owner's Russian. It's the only copter like that around here, but what the hell are they doing here? All their concessions are up north—they're way out of their territory!"

Lucas, who had now squeezed himself in between Prince and Zora, craned his neck into the cockpit to get a better look. "That guy at Le Croco Fou—the smooth-talking Russian—we know they've been spying on us—but, *merde*—they know the exact location," then almost muttering to himself, "How? How did they know where to come?"

The Russian Kamov had also spotted them, and now the two helicopters began to glide carefully toward one another until they faced each other like a pair of large dragonflies checking each other out. The Kamov was larger than the Eurocopter with a little over three additional meters in length. The two vehicles were now close enough that each pilot could see the other. Almost simultaneously they grabbed their radio mics. "*Mbote na yo*, Rodrigue," the pilot spoke into his radio. The pilot of the Russian helicopter was a Bantu; the two knew each other, and they spoke in Lingala.

"What are you doing out here, Rodrigue? You're way out of your territory."

"Lionel, *c'est toi*? You're a little out of your zone too, little brother. This pretty scary place, man. You should not be out here in that little toy."

"We got some missing people out here somewhere. This is a search-and-rescue mission. But you—what are you doing here with that oversized bug?"

"We just dropped off the big boss with some other people. They going hunting, man—crazy white people!"

"Hunting. What the hell for? Since when do rich white men hunt bush meat? I might not be as smart as you, Rodrigue, but I'm not that dumb. What are they really hunting?"

"No, serious man—they're hunting—the *zabolo-yindo*—that's probably where your missing friends are too! Hey—"

"That's the clearing—over there!" Lucas shouted, drowning out the two pilots' conversation. "God damn! Prince, you see that?"

"Yes, I see." Prince grabbed the pilot by the shoulder and shouted, "Ask him who that is—Carver, you better look at this—stop pukin', man. There's a whole camp set up down there."

By this time everyone seemed to be talking at the same time. As the two pilots continued on in Lingala, Lucas was trying to give orders to his pilot in French, the soldiers were moaning and Prince and Zora were trying to calm Carver down. They both reached back to help him, his face pale and clammy, drained of all color, as they pulled him up into a standing position. He took one step toward the forward cockpit, almost lost his balance, but Zora and Prince grabbed him by the arms and pulled him forward so that he could hang on to the metal cockpit frame. As Carver began to drag his legs back up under himself, the Eurocopter suddenly dropped and rotated with its nose pointing almost straight downward causing everyone to lose balance, falling together in a heap. The pilot yelled out, "Back in your seats! You're throwing us off balance—this is a small boat, you guys!"

"Who are those people?" Prince shouted again to the pilot as they all groped their way back to their seats. "Where'd they go? Where'd that copter go?"

"They're gone," the pilot repeated Prince's observation. "He just cut me off, turned, and left."

"He was talking about *zabolo-yindo*," Prince said, "What's he talking about?"

"He said they just dropped off a hunting party. Said it was the big boss and that they were hunting *zabolo-yindo*. The black devil—that stupid myth Lucas mentioned the other day.

The helicopter was moving again, zeroing in quickly on the large clearing from which Hoyt and his party had launched their expedition, the place where no one had ever been—or so everyone had thought.

"I see six large field tents down there," said Lucas.

No one spoke. The cabin had fallen silent for a moment—just the humming throb of the propeller whisking the air over their heads. Everyone's head was twisted toward the windows or bent forward so they could get a glimpse through the cockpit bubble. As they got closer it became apparent that a waterway of some sort cut across one side of the clearing. Reflections sparkled like a swarm of fireflies across most of the open clearing, revealing little rivulets that coated the area like a network of veins. The six tents were clustered together along the tree line on the side furthest away from the main waterway. As the distance closed, people could be seen scurrying about, then coming together, looking up at the approaching helicopter.

The pilot slowed their descent and began to hover in place as he scanned beneath for options.

"Over by the tents—just this side," said Zora. "You can see where the other copter was parked—grass is all flattened out. Should be pretty dry there."

Without answering, the pilot eased the machine forward and settled it down. He switched the motor off, looked back at his passengers, and announced, "This is it."

Lucas was out first, followed by Prince and then Zora, who reached back to grab Carver's hand. "You'll have to get used to being on firm ground again." She continued holding him, now with both hands, and looked into his eyes. "How you feeling?"

"Better—much better."

"You still look pretty drained. We need to move out quickly, but you should rest up first—get something back into your belly—get some electrolytes into you."

"We gotta see what these people are doing here," he gasped. "I want to know how they found out about this place."

"Well, well, well," came a voice from the group that was now gathering about them. "They say this is a small world, but this—this takes that cliché to a new level—unbelievable."

A tall figure stepped out from the group and stood immediately in front of Zora, arms outstretched. *"Bienvenue!"* greeted the seemingly delighted Russian.

14 – A MISSING TRIBE

Carver was seated, slouched forward on an upended wooden crate, slowly sipping an energy drink from a metal mess cup. A small tent had been set up behind him, and a larger field tent was in the process of being erected next to it by Lucas and one of the soldiers. The other soldier and the pilot were carrying supplies from the helicopter and stacking them up next to the larger of the tents. The Russian and his entourage were scattered about, most of them just loafing, chatting in small groups, some napping in the shade. Half of them were hooked up to iPods—their heads slowly bobbing up and down or back and forth.

"Where's Prince?" Carver jumped upright at the sudden sound of Zora's voice. She had just walked up behind him and was now standing at his side, looking toward the Russian compound.

"He's talking with the Ruskies—there's two others. We didn't see them when we landed—must have been hiding out somewhere. I was about to go join them—feeling back to normal now, I guess. I've done a lot of flying but never got sick. Guess I've never had a ride quite like that one, though." He let out a little burp, followed by a sigh. "Where've you been?"

"Looking around. Wanted to confirm the game trail where Hoyt and his party stepped into the woods."

"Did you find it?"

"Oh, yeah. Found some other interesting things as well."

"Like what?"

"Poachers came through here—maybe a year ago. I mean big-time poachers—organized, mechanized—what you might call industrial-scale poachers. The whole area along where the river runs through here is lined with elephant remains—just bones now—along with a few other creatures too. Buffalo ... whatever happened to be there at the wrong time. Complete slaughter. They came in helicopters and sprayed the herds with AK-47s. I dug slugs out of some of the bones. They killed everything—cut their tusks off. Looked like they used chain saws—even babies—they couldn't have had more than a few inches of tusk." Her tone of voice dropped and had a slight quiver to it, as she continued, almost talking to herself now. "Killed everything. Cut them up like garbage, then flew off. If someone paid them enough they'd kill people—probably have. God, it makes me sick—so upset. Makes me want to scream. I hate them—if ever..."

"If ever, what?"

She looked at Carver, her eyes narrowed and focused on him with an intensity he had not seen in her before. She spoke softly. "I swore on my mother's grave that I would never take another life. But—if I ever catch one of those ..." she paused for a second, "those monsters—they'll wish they'd never been born. What I'd really like is to catch the soulless creeps who buy the stuff—the ones who send them out here with their big guns. There's serious money behind these bastards—helicopters? You think maybe our friend, Oleg? Lucas sort of suggested that they were pretty ruthless," she continued but her voice seemed to drift off, "I can smell it on him—and you say there's two more of them?"

"Yeah. A man and a woman—both kinda weird-looking. Guy's tall, looks fit, long dark beard and shaved head makes him look like one of those Cossacks—maybe just because he's associated with Oleg I think of a Cossack—hah!" Carver chuckled to himself. "The guy's half covered in tattoos but the odd part is that he's literally cut in two—one side of his face, one arm—totally tattooed, the other side's normal. The woman looks small next to him but she's probably about your height—short hair, big nose—kind of butch looking."

Zora sighed, let out a long slow breath, then sat down on the ground next to Carver. They sat in silence, her chin resting on her knees, her eyes staring into the forest beyond, Carver trying to digest what she had just been saying, looking back toward the other camp. He shook as a subtle spasm ran through his body followed by a nervous twitch and dropped his cup. "Shit!" he said to himself as the remains of the drink soaked into his lap.

Zora glanced at him briefly then, staring back into the forest she began to speak again, her voice now calm. "So, Carver, did you see what was in Oleg's helicopter when it flew off?"

"No—we were five hundred feet above the trees, rocking back and forth, and I'd just been puking out the window. Should I have seen something?"

"It had passengers—lots of them. I wasn't a hundred percent sure at first but now … you could see the silhouettes of what looked like several heads bobbing about behind the pilot. The Kamov Ka-62 they were flying? It carries up to fifteen passengers and two crew. They had just dropped off this bunch here. I counted nine—Oleg and eight soldiers. Now you say there are two others—that makes eleven, plus the pilot, add in all the supplies and there's no room left for anyone else." Zora looked at Carver, "So who was that in the back of their copter? They dropped off their party of eleven, plus a ton of supplies, then flew off with the cabin full of passengers they must have picked up here."

She slowly stood and looked over toward the Russian camp. "Have you seen any pygmies running around here?"

"Pygmies? No."

"That Kamov was filled with them. That's what I think. The whole cabin was filled with pygmies—and, in spite of the fact that dozens of people have been traipsing back and forth across just about every square foot of this side of the glade here, I was able to sort out a number of prints from fairly small people. I would estimate anywhere from fifteen to twenty of them—some were probably children. So, look around. Where are they now? We're looking at a missing tribe, Carver? What in God's name do you think that Russian sleaze wants with a helicopter full of pygmies?"

"I haven't a clue," responded Carver as he stood up, both of them now staring out toward the Russian camp. "Lucas and the pilot both said Hoyt was greeted by a bunch of them shortly after they'd landed. A small hunting tribe—extended family or something—some went along with Hoyt, some stayed behind. The satellite photos we saw suggested a small hunting camp nearby."

"That's where I'm going now—must be close. I should be able to find it without too much trouble. Their footprints all came in from the northwest side of the glade—one of the game trails should take me right to it." She looked around, then up at the sky, at the dull glow beyond the haze, making a mental calculation on how much daylight she had left, then looking back at Carver, "We've got about two hours before dark. Have these guys get some dinner started as soon as they're through unloading, then go over and hang out with Prince and the Russians. Don't say anything about the pygmies yet—except maybe ask if they've seen any. Just don't let them know that we suspect they're trafficking pygmies—or whatever they're doing." She ducked into the small tent for a second then came back out with a headlamp. "Well, you know what to say and what not."

"OK. You want to take some kind of protection with you?" He nodded his head toward the soldiers' two semi-automatic weapons that were leaning against a box next to the large tent.

"What would I need one of those for? The only danger out here is right over there," she motioned her head toward the other camp. "These people cannot be trusted, Carver. Hunting for a black lion, my ass. Somebody's tipped them off about what you and Hoyt are looking for."

She turned and started toward the tree line, hesitated briefly, turned back to him and said, "I'm going to find the pygmy camp, but—Carver?"

"Yeah?"

"Don't let him know that I speak Russian."

"You do?"

She smiled, turned her back to him, and quietly disappeared into the jungle.

15 – OLEG'S GUIDE

The sky over the *bai* had just lost its last streak of orangey-gray and the dark shadows of the forest had begun to seep out into the lonely opening in the jungle. The constant background music of birds and monkeys began to downshift, and a large hornbill sent out its final call of the day. A campfire had been lit and Viper was opening a case of beer and had begun to distribute bottles to Lucas, Lionel, and the Bantu soldiers. Oleg was pouring wine for Aziza, Prince, and, Carver, who had joined them shortly after Zora's departure to find the pygmy hunting camp. They were in that brief interlude between day and night where the forest fell silent, when, with no forewarning, the ear-piercing crackling of some unseen insect rudely interrupted the quietude—its opening sound, like a clap of thunder—unexpected, and right in the midst of the group.

They all froze in place for an instant, then Lucas let out a laugh, followed by one of the Bantus. Someone blurted out, "Fuck! That scared the shit out of me!"

"Where is that motherfucker?" another asked.

"Over here," one soldier called out, and they all looked toward a clump of tall marsh grass, lighting it up as the converging light shafts from their headlamps zeroed in. One of the soldiers approached the clump and poked around in it with a machete as the others watched. Meanwhile, more locusts joined in, along with an accompaniment of crickets, beetles, and the intermittent croaks of frogs or toads; all those who had lain dormant during the day, waiting for that initial call, announcing the great drama that played out each night.

"Better watch out for mambas, man," someone warned. A small generator kicked on and several lights that had been strung up cast off a low arch of illumination that encircled the group.

They all laughed again then stopped, abruptly. Zora was standing at the edge of the lit-up area. She had just drifted into the camp without a sound—one minute she was not there, then, she was—a specter, slipped in from nowhere.

One of the Bantus jumped, then mumbled something to himself; another let out a nervous laugh. A short silence followed, then Oleg stepped toward Zora, holding his glass out to her. "Zora! Great entry—an exotic aftershock to that giant cricket—completely dramatic, I must say. You're just in time for a glass of wine."

Zora took the glass as Aziza moved up next to Oleg. "So this is the young lady we've been hearing about." Aziza, not a French speaker, had switched the conversation to English.

"I see I'm not the only female camping out in the *bai* tonight—and you are?"

"Zora, this is Aziza Meyer, a close business associate of mine from New York and also a good friend whose own interests in exotic hunting happen to coincide quite nicely with my own—and here ..." Oleg turned and held his arm out toward Viper who had been lurking in the background, "Another good friend you must meet—Seryoga Ivanov."

Viper stepped up to join them, switched the beer to his left hand and held out his right, which Zora took and shook, with a polite nod of her head and a smile. "*Enchantée*, Monsieur Ivanov."

"Pleasure to meet you, mademoiselle, and the name is Viper. My friends call me Viper."

Carver, Prince, and Lucas were now standing with Zora who glanced quickly at Carver, then bowed slightly to Oleg as she held up her glass and toasted in French, "*A votre santé.*"

They all raised their glasses and responded. "Here, Zora, please take a seat—by the fire—keeps the mosquitos away. We were about to dine and talk about our amazingly coincidental plans when you came walking out of the bush."

Prince, placing one hand on Zora's shoulder, guided her to a fold-up director's chair, one of several that had been spread about. As she sat he whispered to her, "Carver told me you had gone off on a little foray of some sort. We were starting to worry about where you were."

Prince, Lucas, Carver, and Zora sat in a semi-circle around one side of the fire, their backs toward the forest while Oleg, Aziza, and Viper placed themselves together, continuing the arc so that each group faced the other at a slight angle. One of the Bantu soldiers moved to join them just behind Viper when Oleg turned to him and said, speaking again in French, "We're going to be talking in English, Denis. Go keep an eye on the soldiers over there, and have someone bring us some food."

"Oleg," interjected Aziza, "He speaks pretty decent English—he should join us here."

Oleg looked at her, then said, "Yes, of course he should." Then, calling out to Denis, "Denis, just tell the cook to bring the food. You dine here with us."

Turning back to the others, he continued, "Denis is a major in the Brazzaville army. He's been assigned to us at my request. He's a good friend and has been indispensable to our company—we never have delays because of some moronic red tape you know, that kind of thing. He is officially in charge of our mandatory military escort, and luckily, since there are no locals out here to hire as porters, he has worked things out with these soldiers so that they will double as porters for the expedition. They'll all get very nice bonuses of course."

"Like your uniform, major," Zora said as he returned.

Carver, Lucas, and Prince all looked at Zora, then at Denis, who was wearing a light blue soccer jersey with the name, "Razak" printed on the back. "Manchester City," said Carver. Realizing the others were staring at him, he added with a somewhat apologetic expression, "He's a soccer fan." Then smiling at Denis, he added, "I like Barcelona myself." Denis returned his smile and sat down between Aziza and Zora, closing one of the gaps between the two groups.

108

"There was a small hunting tribe of pygmies nearby," said Zora as she looked directly at Oleg. "It's my understanding that several of them had joined Dr. Hoyt's expedition as hired-on porters and guides." She looked at Prince, and asked, "You have told them about Hoyt?"

"Yes," said Oleg. "Prince has informed me of Dr. Hoyt's most unfortunate disappearance. In fact, we have both been filling each other in on the fascinatingly diverse attractions that have brought us all out here together. The odds of such a coincidental meeting ever happening in the first place are certainly deserving of some kind of celebration, I would say. But, I also ask myself: Is it really that coincidental? Could it be that your man's disappearance is in some way related to the prey that has drawn us into this expedition?" Oleg's eyes shifted back and forth from Prince to Carver, then to Zora, where he held his gaze and continued to speak. "Ah, yes, the pygmies. Tell us about the pygmies, Viper."

"Huh? Ah, yeah. There was a small group when we got here. Since we got the Bantus here for porters we decided we didn't need the little jungle bunnies. What we do need is intelligence. You know, someone who knows the jungle—a local who knows the trails." Looking at Lucas, he continued, "Oleg told you that we are searching for this black lion—information we received has convinced us that this creature is not just some jungle myth."

"*Zabolo-yindo,*" Prince interjected, "It's Lingala—means black devil. That's what the tribes east and north of here call it. The Mbendjele Yaka, pygmies up north who still hunt—they come out of the forest and tell tall tales to Bongili and the Bodingo—those pygmies who have turned to farming—the ones you see in the villages. The Bodingo then pass it on to the Bantus and eventually, the stories work their way into the bigger towns and finally down to Brazzaville and Kinshasa. This is the common path that stories like this take."

"Except in this case," Viper cut back in, "our people up in Cameroon have reported the same story, but a few months ago a more detailed accounting from a bushmeat hunter who drifted down from southern Sudan—makes his living selling meat to the timber crews.

This guy claims to have actually seen it. He'd gone south, further than bushmeat hunters usually go. He was with two others—all three were brothers. This guy was up on a ridge and his two brothers had gone down into a ravine chasing some small antelope, when he heard a loud roar—big cat. Then he heard a scream—gun fired. He started into the ravine, then saw one of his brothers. His head torn entirely from his body, blood everywhere. He saw something in the brush and then saw his other brother being carried off by a large, black lion. They don't have lions in Brazza-Congo. Most people, especially the natives in the bush—have no idea what a lion is. This guy was from Sudan—he'd seen lions before. He not only said that it was black, but that it was the biggest lion he'd ever seen in his life. He did return without his two brothers and he had obviously seen something that had scared the hell out of him—he was a complete wreck—shaking constantly."

"You add that to the other stories that we've been hearing," Oleg continued. "There are multiple accounts now of bushmeat hunters going into that area but then never being heard from again. This Sudanese hunter is the only firsthand eyewitness account we've received. Viper went up with Denis to interview the guy—along with Aziza."

"Assuming this thing does exist, why didn't you start your hunting expedition from the north?" asked Carver.

"My guess is, for the same reason you came this way. We looked for the best possible place to get in close by helicopter. Like I'm sure you do, we have access to pretty high-tech GPS maps. We blew the entire area up as big as we could get it and looked for landing spots. Starting in the area where we thought the Sudanese had gone, we moved outward in expanding circles. This was the closest place that looked half useable as a landing site. We estimate that we're now about fifty-five miles south of the place where we think the hunter lost his brothers. Since there are no known sightings north of that point, we assume that he saw the cat at the northernmost reach of its range. That would make us somewhere south of its range—or maybe even into it. How far though, no one knows, but many big cats can cover fifty miles easily, sometimes more."

Several heads turned toward the Bantus, and the conversation stopped temporarily as three of the soldiers approached carrying dinner. Utensils were handed out along with bowls of some form of stew. "Goulash," said Aziza. "Whenever you go camping out with Oleg you get served spicy goulash. There must be fifty cans of this shit piled up in the mess tent over there."

"I get it from Croatia. It reminds me of this stuff we always ate on camping trips when I was a kid in the Boy Scouts—the Russian Boy Scouts. You probably thought that was just a British or American thing."

"I always assumed it was international," said Zora, "but, you—I can't quite picture you as a Boy Scout. Do the Russians have a merit badge for shooting lions?"

Oleg stared at Zora for a second, slapped at a mosquito that had landed on his forehead, then yelled out, "*Merde, putin*—mosquitos! Denis, get me some of that repellent!" Then, looking back at Zora, he added, "I don't know how we got on the topic of Boy Scouts, but you should know, the man who originally started Boy Scouts in Russia was named Oleg."

Lucas moved his chair in closer to the fire and said, "Get closer to the smoke, Oleg."

Oleg moved in toward the fire and the others followed. "OK," he said, "enough Boy Scouts." Then, turning his attention to Carver, he continued, "I know you people are here to find your missing colleague. I have two questions: one, do you agree with my hypothesis that perhaps he and his companions have also become victims of this mythical black lion? And two, what was he doing here in the first place? Where was he going?"

Carver looked directly at Prince, then back to Oleg, but before he could respond, Prince interrupted. "I think I can answer that for you, Oleg. Dr. Hoyt was in the employment of Central African Timber International, which you probably know as CATI. He worked as a botanist, doing various kinds of research for the company. He also had a medical background and a number of personal scientific interests that would often spin him off into areas that had nothing to do with CATI. He failed to share with anyone exactly what it was that had drawn him out here, but I have a theory."

"Which is?"

"Ebola—or I should say, some Ebola-like virus. I think he suspected that there was some highly toxic and deadly virus that was floating around out here somewhere." He glanced briefly at Carver, then Zora, and Lucas, and finally back to Oleg as he continued, "Oleg, if Dr. Hoyt's hypothesis was correct, then I would go on to suggest that this black lion might in fact be real, but it's not really a lion— it's some highly devastating disease that can kill anyone who gets within close contact. That would certainly help to explain the human population density in this area. It appears to be something like zero humans per square mile across an area of almost one thousand square miles. That's like the middle of the Sahara or the arctic, only here, there's no shortage of food and water and you certainly won't freeze to death. People have been asking this question for years now, but no one has come up with a reasonable hypothesis and then tested it out."

No one spoke. The lowered voices of the Bantus interspersed with the hum of insects now occupied the vacuum left by their silence. A full moon suddenly popped up from behind the forest canopy on the far side of the *bai*. The air was remarkably clear and the temperature had dropped. A swamp fog began to lift off the wet side of the glade and crawl toward the camp. A diving mosquito could be heard and Carver, clearing his throat, started to speak, was cut-off by Zora.

"So, if what Prince says about Hoyt's motivation for being here is correct, then that would reinforce my proposal that we minimize our exposure." She looked straight at Prince, "I will repeat what I have been urging to each of you these past few days. Carver's the only one who really has to go in there," she pointed back to the dark forest behind them, "to try and find Hoyt—and I am the only one who is qualified to guide him. We need to leave here as quickly as we can after daybreak and the rest of you need to climb back on that helicopter and get out of here before the next rainstorm floods this place."

She looked back at Oleg, Viper, and Aziza. "You and your little entourage here, you might want to call in your own helicopter and get out too. But that's just my advice—you can do whatever you want—which I'm sure you will." Zora stood and looked out at the moon. "Don't let that moon fool you. Those storms we flew through late this morning were moving in this direction. It's going to rain tonight—possibly a lot."

After another minute of silence, Oleg spoke again. "Zora, that's a clever little theory you have there, but I have to say, we are pretty well convinced that our lion does exist and—I must confess to you also that big game hunting is my passion. Hunting big cats is my deepest, most sacred personal passion. We will be going hunting tomorrow."

Thunder rumbled somewhere in the distance. Zora seemed to notice it and looked toward Lucas, but his attention was on the Russian. "Oleg," he said, "you mentioned something earlier about needing a guide or tracker. Is one of these Bantu soldiers here going to be guiding you?"

Oleg laughed, then, looking at Denis, said, "Get the pygmy. Bring him over here."

Zora, Carver, Prince and Lucas all looked at one another. Lucas stood up, looking at Oleg, "Pygmy? I thought they were all gone."

"There's one left," said Oleg, and then they all stood up as Denis came walking back toward them with a short man, no more than four feet tall, close behind. The man was clothed only with a loincloth, something that looked like a rat's tail hanging from the back and an animal skin hat on his head. "I would like to introduce you all to our guide. He calls himself Ngiome."

No one spoke at first. Then Zora repeated the name, "Ngiome."

The pygmy looked at her, smiled, and walked directly up to her until the two stood no more than a foot apart. Zora, who was the shortest person in the camp, towered over him. He continued smiling, then reached up and touched her hair. She smiled back and he began to stroke her hair. She stood perfectly still as he continued. The others just watched, casually glancing back and forth at one another. The pygmy stopped, took a short step back and said something that none of them could understand.

"He's speaking his own tongue," said Denis. "He understands enough Lingala that we can talk, but mostly he speaks pygmy. In fact, he speaks a different pygmy—it's not like the Mbenzele up north or the Aka's."

Zora looked at Ngiome and spoke something to him in Lingala. He cocked his head slightly and smiled, then looked at Denis.

"You speak Lingala like people from DRC. He doesn't understand," said Denis.

Zora tried again. This time Ngiome laughed, then spoke back to Zora. The two then proceeded to talk, slowly, each laughing between exchanges.

Viper took Denis by the arm and asked quietly, "Does he understand her?"

"Yes—not too well, but they seem to be understanding each other some."

Viper then leaned toward Oleg and said in Russian, "I don't like her talking to him. Maybe we should get him out of here."

"Don't worry, Viper," he answered, then, switching back to French and addressing Denis, "What are they talking about now, Denis?"

Denis laughed. "He's never seen a white woman." He laughed again, "I guess you call her a white woman." He laughed again, "He wants to know where she comes from. She's having trouble because he uses lots of pygmy words—I don't understand so good either."

"He's seen me," said Aziza. "Aren't I a white woman?"

"He thought you were a man," said Denis.

Aziza's eyes narrowed, her face tightened up like a screw and she took a step backward. Viper put a hand on her shoulder and whispered in her ear. She glared at Zora and lipped the word, "bitch."

Everyone was gathered around now, including Lionel and the Bantus. Ngiome suddenly stooped down into a squatting position and Zora joined him. As they continued to talk, Denis translated into French and Lucas into English for Carver and Aziza, although Aziza didn't appear to be paying much attention. She continued to glare at Zora.

The conversation carried on for some time. Someone stoked the fire at one point; someone else sprayed himself with repellent. An owl hooted across the *bai*, then suddenly, without any warning, Denis reached down and picked Ngiome up by the armpits, saying to him, "That's enough. We go out tomorrow. You sleep now." Then, looking around at the others, "We all sleep now. *Excusez-moi*, Madame, but we have very big trip tomorrow. I need to sleep now and so does our guide. He is my responsibility."

Zora stood and, speaking to Denis, said, "That was a bit abrupt wouldn't you say, Denis?"

She glanced at Carver. "Interesting. I was trying to tell Ngiome that I had found his camp a couple of hours ago and that it was empty." Turning her gaze toward Oleg, she continued, "Is there something I should know about the pygmy camp, Oleg?"

"What do you mean?"

"I mean, where did everyone go? There's a whole camp out there and its empty. Was this guy the only one you found here when you landed?"

Thunder sounded again—this time it was louder and was followed by a sudden gust of wind, then the smell of rain swept across the *bai*. "Here it comes," said Zora. She looked toward her companions and shouted, "It's a big one! Back to the tents! Make sure everything's secured—the helicopter too!"

16 – FLASH FLOOD

"They're leaving!" Denis shouted, as he stood at the dark entrance to Oleg's tent, a lantern in one hand and dripping water.

"Who's leaving?" Oleg asked. He was wide-awake. He'd been awake ever since the second barrage of thunder and lightning that had hit sometime in the middle of the night. The thunder had stopped an hour earlier, but it had been pouring rain ever since.

"The Americans. They been loading stuff in their helicopter for the past thirty minutes. Now I just saw them climb in—listen."

The whine of a helicopter engine could just barely be detected through the pounding roar of rain. Oleg swung his legs off his cot and onto the ground. "Shit!" he said. The floor of the tent had at least three or four inches of water on it. His feet recoiled, and he held them for a minute suspended above the ground. "It's flooding in here!"

"You should see outside," said Denis. "Viper told me to come get you. Everything's full of water—turning into a swamp—and fast."

"Just what that bitch said," Oleg mumbled to himself. "It's a big one."

The helicopter made a coughing sound then the whine picked up speed and turned into a hum, getting louder, faster and finally accelerating into a deafening roar. Several voices could be heard yelling. The roar accelerated again and this time a light flashed across the tent's opening. "There they go!" yelled Denis.

"Get Viper and Aziza in here. I gotta find my shoes—shit! They're soaked!" He shook his boots, then started putting them on as Denis disappeared through the door. He reached over to a makeshift table he had set up next to his cot, grabbed his headlamp, flipped it on, then followed Denis. Two seconds later he was back, now looking for his hat.

Oleg could barely see the light of the helicopter as it quickly rose up and out of his field of vision. The rain was coming down in sheets—constant and steady. "Never seen rain like this," he mumbled to himself. There were shouts coming from the direction of the main supply tent which appeared to be lit from inside. He ran as best he could in that direction, his boots, thoroughly saturated, sloshing through the water that was everywhere—and continuing to rise.

He ran into Viper and Denis almost immediately. "*Il pleut des cordes*," he yelled.

Viper grabbed him by the arm and turned him back toward his tent. "We got everything under control over there. We gotta get your stuff up above water right away. Denis and I'll help."

"What about the Americans? Are they really gone?"

"No, their tents are still there and I saw Carver and the girl on the ground watching as they took off. I think it's just them though. Aziza went over—said they needed to get their ship off the ground before the water got too deep. Said she saw the others get on the copter—that guy Prince, the Belgian, and the soldiers."

They piled into Oleg's tent. Oleg pulled his hat off and shook the water off while Viper and Denis began picking up anything that was on the ground, stacking it on Oleg's makeshift table. Denis opened a crate to see what was inside, then closed it and started piling other things on top.

Viper looked at Denis and then at the crate and laughed. "That's the rest of your wine, Oleg. Little water shouldn't hurt it too much— make a good base to hold up the stuff we need. Where's your gun and ammo?"

"I already had it in that sling there—the gun. Shit—the ammo! No—it's ok. It's on top of that box full of shit we brought to trade with the pygmies. Don't need that shit now."

Within minutes they were through. The three of them stood still

117

for a minute, looking at one another. "All the tents got water like this?" Oleg asked.

"Yeah," Viper answered. "Some worse than others, but most about like this. This shit better stop soon though or we're going to be shit up the creek. Guess this is what they call a flash flood—ha!" he laughed.

"More like a hundred-year flood," said Denis. "My guys say they never seen rain like this before. Probably been raining like this a long time upstream. That's why the level went up so fast. It was going up while we were sitting around eating dinner. We never noticed."

"I'll bet that girl noticed," said Viper. "She gives me the fucking creeps, Oleg. I've never seen a bitch like that before—she's not normal … fucking freak."

Oleg looked at Viper, then stepped over to the tent flap and looked out. "Viper—you say they left the American and the girl? Just the two of them?"

"That's what Aziza said."

Oleg stepped back out into the rain and looked over toward the other camp. He smiled, rain running down his face. "No shit."

17 – CONVERSATION ON A LOG

The rain had finally stopped and the entire surface of the *bai* was covered in water. A heavy mist hung suspended above as the first dim light of dawn began to appear. Zora de Ryken sat up on the makeshift bed she had thrown together from plastic storage bins. She put on her jungle boots and stepped out of her tent. She had heard something. People from the Russian's expedition were still murmuring and fussing about in their camp but it was something else; something that came from the far end of the *bai*, just inside the tree line. She cocked her head and listened. At first it seemed it could have been an owl—a deep-throated owl. But then it migrated into something else. It began to sound human, then animal, then human again. She glanced over at the other tents, then turned and began to walk toward the sound.

Five forest elephants had emerged from the jungle and were mining for salt at the narrow upstream opening where the river flowed into the *bai*, while several gorillas foraged about just beyond. Thirty yards downstream, Ngiome stood, perched on a large log. He was singing into one end of a long wooden shaft. It was some form of primitive forest trumpet.

When Zora saw that it was Ngiome, she stopped. He hadn't heard her approach so she remained still, now knee deep in water, and watched him.

Ngiome gradually lowered his shaft, then, sensing the presence of something behind, he turned, looked at Zora, smiled, and motioned for her to approach. Zora returned his smile and quickly joined him on the log. He settled into a deep squat and she sat next to him. A smaller log just in front of them was lined with mud turtles and the air above was thick with birds. The heavy rain and flooding had caused a microburst in the mosquito population. The birds were feasting, and they watched.

One of the first things a young child learns to say is "What's that?" And so it was with Zora. "What's that?" she asked Ngiome in Lingala, as she pointed at another mud turtle that had just climbed onto the small log in front of them. He answered in his language, then she repeated the word. She had come in contact with pygmies two years earlier when she was in the eastern Congo, but they were Mbuti, and Ngiome was either an Aka or Baka—or possibly some mélange of the two. She wanted to learn his language but would have to start at the beginning. "What's that?" she asked, this time pointing at Ngiome.

"*Bisi ndima,*" he answered. Then, pointing at her he said, "*bisi,*" then repeated it again, pointing back at himself.

"Human—person," Zora said.

He then waved his hand toward the forest and said, "*ndima*".

"Forest," Zora said. "*Bisi ndima,*" she said, pointing at Ngiome. "Forest people."

Again, she asked, "What's that?" pointing at his wooden trumpet.

"*Molimo,*" he answered.

They continued on as the morning light increased. She asked about the insects, beginning with the most obvious and plentiful—butterflies, dragonflies, beetles, gnats, fruit flies, and mosquitos. She could tell he enjoyed teaching her the names of the wild things that were so important in his world. The lesson went on—yellow warblers, swamp warblers, fly catchers, sunbirds, weavers, tits, sparrows, canaries—birds that were familiar, but different, many distant cousins to those she had known in her past.

They were starting in on the frogs and turtles when a sloshing noise of something large and slow, approached through the water behind them. They both turned. It was Carver, cautiously working his way across the flooded plain. He waved and held up a pair of binoculars. "They're all freaking out back there," He shouted, as he got closer.

The elephants froze dead still and looked toward him. Zora held her finger up to her lips, motioned downward with her other hand spread flat, then pointed toward the animals. He didn't understand and yelled again, "They think the pygmy bolted on them."

One of the elephants, a small bull, took several steps toward Carver, raised his trunk and let out a loud honking sound—a warning. The other elephants quickly disappeared back into the trees, as the bull began to back up, his head swaying nervously back and forth. When he reached the tree line he turned and quietly melted back into the foliage. The gorillas that had been foraging nearby followed suit and faded discretely into the tangled growth. A chain reaction had begun—an entire row of turtles, in a series of rapid splashes, dropped into the muddy water followed by several small crocodiles. A tiger heron flew off in one direction, his wings hitting the water as he lifted off and several egrets took flight in the opposite direction. The river martins and swallows seemed unfazed by the sudden intrusion. They continued their rapid zigzagging flight patterns, engorging themselves on the mosquitos that seemed to multiply faster than the birds could consume them.

"Good job, Carver. You really know how to announce yourself," said Zora as he got closer.

"Sorry—didn't even see the elephants. I was focusing on you two."

"You also managed to chase off some gorillas, some turtles and God knows what else." She held out her hand and helped him climb onto the log. "Have a seat. I'm learning how to communicate with Ngiome."

Ngiome smiled at the sound of his name. Zora pointed at Carver and carefully spoke his name to Ngiome who nodded and said, "*Bilo.*"

The two of them continued with a few more exchanges, then Carver, getting impatient, interrupted. "Oleg and his sidekicks are raising hell with one of the soldiers. Apparently one of them was responsible for keeping an eye on Ngiome. They think he flew the coop."

"Hmm, Ngiome," she looked at him and now spoke in Lingala. She spoke slowly, repeating words, trying alternate words, using gestures at times. "Why were you staying in the tent with the soldiers back there? Why were you not in your own camp?"

"I went to my camp last night," he answered, "after the rain started. The *bilo* make their camp where the water always comes when it rains big. Your camp too. *Bisi ndima* always make shelters where ground stays dry."

Zora translated for Carver, then continued, "Ngiome, where did all of the *bisi ndima* go—your people?"

"The *bilo* took them away in their great dragonfly to big village far away."

"Yes, they told us that and I saw them flying away. Why did they take them away?"

"They want Ngiome to take them to forbidden place. They take my people away so that I take them to forbidden place. They tell me they bring my people back if I take them."

Zora translated again, then Carver said, "That confirms what we both thought about the bullshit story Oleg told us last night—just after everything almost went to hell. Coercion, Russian mafia style. After you left he told Prince and me that they took the pygmies to the village in exchange for Ngiome's guiding services. He suggested that it was a big favor to take them. Hell, there's no place to land a helicopter at the village—not the one downstream from here."

"They probably took them all the way to Ouésso," Zora added.

"He made it sound like a jungle version of one of those charter bus tours to the big discount retail centers—like they all couldn't wait to get there."

"How did Prince react to that? He would know better. He told me that taking pygmies to a big village is a sure way to destroy them— culturally, socially, spiritually—they give machetes to the men and colorful cloth to the women. The men end up as lackeys to Bantus, doing peon work for nothing—hunting bush meat. The women get forced into prostitution."

"That's when the rain really started. We broke off the conversation before Prince could react. Actually that was when you came back and told us to start putting stuff into the helicopter."

"Hmm," Zora seemed to be thinking of something, then turned back to Ngiome. They talked for several more minutes, then she turned again to Carver. "Lucas was on the helicopter that came back to look for Hoyt. I started asking Ngiome if he recognized Lucas, but when he came out with Denis last night, I don't think he even noticed him. I also asked him where Oleg told him he wanted to go. They are, in fact, going to the exact place we intend to go to—what his people refer to as a forbidden place. I didn't really understand it all, but Ngiome seemed to be saying there's some kind of dark animal that lives out there. He said he saw it when he was very young, but only from a distance. He was with his grandfather and remembers seeing the eyes of something looking out from a thick forest. His grandfather told him it was the guardian of the forbidden place. Apparently, Denis told him the tall white man is here to hunt this dark creature, and he, in turn, told Denis that the creature does, indeed exist. So sounds like Oleg really is going hunting."

She spoke again to Ngiome, then back to Carver, "I asked him some more about Hoyt. He said that nine of his people accompanied Hoyt, which we know, of course, but also that his people all came back. They abandoned Hoyt and his party as soon as they got to the edge of the so-called *forbidden place*. They had gone against the will of the rest of the tribe so when they got back, the entire lot were banished."

"Where'd they go?"

"To a village. They went downriver—he said it's a five-day trip by dugout. He actually used the French word, *pirogue*. I'm sure it's the village we identified when looking at the satellite views of the area. What do you make of that? They banished almost a third of their tribe because they went against the will of the others."

"I don't know—don't know what to make of it. Did he say how long it takes to get to this forbidden place?"

"He said it took him and his grandfather two days to get there and two to get back. He claims that only he and his grandfather have ever been to this place, so his people took longer to get there when they went with Hoyt—they were gone for almost eight days. That would suggest that it took them five or six days out, travelling with Hoyt and his party, then two to get back."

The three of them turned as a man's scream could be heard coming from the direction of the camp, then Zora stood up. "Sounded like Viper—let's go. I've got an idea on how we should proceed. We can discuss it on the way over to the camp."

As they started wading back across the flooded *bai*, Zora, stopped and turned to Ngiome. "Ngiome, do not come back with Carter and me. Go back into the forest and return to the camp from the other direction. It might be best if Denis and the others do not know that we have talked." He understood and nodded, then Zora continued, "My friend, Carver and I are going to the same place that the tall white man wants to go. We need to find our friend who has disappeared— the one I asked you about."

Ngiome became agitated and blurted out, "No—you cannot go there. It is forbidden and no person who goes there ever comes back. You will not find them—your friends no longer exist!"

He spoke quickly, and Zora had trouble understanding but she did seem to get the gist of it. "Ngiome—we will all go there together. I will find what happened to our friend. If it is forbidden to go to this place, then you must only take us to the edge. You will go back to your village after that. If the tall white man does not come back, it does not matter. I will come back. And Ngiome, I will find your people who were taken in the *bilo*'s flying pirogue and bring them back to their home."

Ngiome smiled and changed his direction, walking toward the forest, the long wooden shaft resting across one shoulder. As Zora and Carver continued toward the camp, Carver asked, "How did you two find each other so early in the morning?"

"I was awakened by an unusual sound. It was Ngiome. He was down where you found us, standing on that log and singing through that hollowed-out shaft of wood."

124

"Looked like a primitive flute of some kind."

"Exactly, but it's not really a flute. He doesn't blow through it. He sings through it."

"Singing to himself, huh?"

"No—to the forest."

18 – DEPARTURE

"Was that Viper I heard screaming?" asked Zora, as she and Carver came splashing into Oleg's camp.

Aziza looked over her shoulder at the two arrivals and responded, "leeches—Viper has a problem with slimy things. His legs were covered." She looked at her companions and laughed. "We're all covered with them. But I like slimy things! I like to squish them. Sit still, already, if you want me to do this," she said to Viper. She was in the process of shaving his head.

"Viper, I had the same reaction," Carver said. "Caught one on my leg last night, then this morning there were a dozen more—I haven't stopped picking."

Viper didn't respond. He looked at them, a line of tension running through his face, highlighted by a swollen vein running down his forehead; a ridge, that further accentuated the tattooed side of his head. He was sitting on a crate, shoes off, his feet pulled up, heels resting on the edge of the crate and he was rubbing them with a blackened towel as Aziza ran a straight-blade razor across the top of his head.

One soldier was cleaning his AK-47, another was moving crates around outside the main supply tent, but most of them were eating or swatting at insects. There was no fire this morning; not after all the rain and flooding. One of the soldiers was heating an open can of spam over a portable gas stove while the others were just eating their food cold—all from cans—Vienna sausages, beans ... lots of beans. Several empty cans littered the area, along with fragments from opened wood crates and other random sorts of human-generated debris.

Zora muttered to Carver under her breath as the two of them moved beyond Aziza and Viper. "First they come here and kill all the animals, now they're spreading their garbage. Next phase should be to cut the trees; level the forest. You realize that before those elephants were slaughtered down there, the only human beings who had probably ever seen this place were Ngiome's people. You and I, we may be witnessing the beginning of the end for one of the last truly wild places on the planet."

"And this forbidden place," he responded, "it sounds like not even the pygmies have been there."

"That's about to change. Carver, I'm assuming that Hoyt and everyone in his expedition are dead. Are you sure you really want to go on? Maybe we should just stay here—what do you think?"

"I need to go, Zora. Hoyt was my friend, but also, my company..."

"Your company, right—of course, the company." she said, "They smell something big here, don't they? They want to be the ones who get to cut it all down. They want it all—and I guarantee you Oleg's company wants it too. Where do you stand, Carver? You're not really one of them—I can tell."

"OK, Zora, I'm not one of them, but I need closure on Russell. And this crew here—" He threw his eyes toward the other camp. "We can't blame them on these animals getting slaughtered here—there's no indication it was them. I know they're in the timbering business but, in fact, we do know they came here to hunt a lion and not to look for logging sites. Did you see Oleg's hunting rifle?"

"No, I didn't."

"I saw it while you were out looking for the pygmy camp yesterday. He was zipping it up into a special carrying bag. It's big—not something you'd just go lugging around in the jungle unless you had a special use for it. I would guess that it is something you'd use for really big game. So I'm thinking his motive for being here is legit."

"He's a snake, Carver. And those other two are even worse. I can smell them a mile away. We can't trust them but—they are here, and we all seem to be going in the same direction. Just be careful what you say."

"So what's our game plan, Zora?"

"I can move fast in the jungle, so I'll go ahead of everyone else. If there is even the remotest chance that Hoyt might be alive, I'll need to get to him as quickly as possible. That was your original plan in the first place. You travel with them. I'll leave trail-markers as I go, and I will keep in constant touch. I'll return to camp with you at night. By going ahead and leaving markers, you and those people should be able to make much better time than Hoyt did.

"Do you think you can deal with going along with Oleg and his crew?"

"No problem," said Carver. Then he looked past Zora and pointed. "There he is." Ngiome had just stepped out and was heading toward Denis. He no longer carried his *molimo*, but carried a short spear and a large net strung across his shoulder.

"He's back!" one of the soldiers shouted. They all stopped eating, some stood up and slowly started toward Ngiome and Denis. Oleg stepped out of his tent and joined them, but his eye caught Zora and Carver. A slight smile crossed his face. He gave them a short bow before continuing on to Ngiome and Denis.

"He said he left when the water started coming in the tent," Denis interpreted. "He went back to his hunting camp to sleep. Ha! Now he says we should have put our tents up at his camp. He says it stays dry there."

"We shouldn't underestimate the pygmy, Denis," said Oleg. "He was certainly right about that, and he's back now. Tell him we want to get going." He looked at his watch, then waved at Aziza and Viper. "Tell everyone we need to be on the road in two hours—they need to finish eating and get ready. Everyone knows what he's supposed to be carrying—just make sure they get rid of anything that got wet last night and replace it. The two who stay behind can straighten out this mess after we've left."

Denis shouted out a few orders, and immediately everyone was in motion—empty and half-full cans were tossed randomly off, and then the soldiers started taking down the smaller two-person tents that had been strung up to dry out along with an array of clothing items. Oleg pointed at Ngiome and said something else to Denis, then walked over to join Carver and Zora. Aziza flipped her blade closed, and followed Oleg.

"So you two got left behind," said Oleg. "Where did your two colleagues go? And your military escorts?"

Carver smiled at Oleg and responded, "I was told that there is no law that dictates how many military escorts you need to have so—as far as Brazzaville is concerned we are operating out here under the escort of your soldiers. We hope you don't mind." He paused for a second, then continued, "As it appears, we are all going in the same general direction."

"How do you know what direction we're taking?" asked Viper. He had put his boots back on and, along with Aziza, had now joined the others.

"Last night when I was talking to Ngiome," said Zora, "I asked him where he was going to be taking you to hunt this black lion. It's the same direction our colleague took when he disappeared." She looked at Oleg, then, and continued, "Oleg, I guess I should apologize to you. We both got off to a bad start and now—now, here we are—in the middle of nowhere, and we need to get to the same place."

"Ah, I accept your apology, Zora." He looked at each of his two companions and asked, "We would all gain now from some cooperation, don't you agree?" Then, speaking in Russian to Viper, "How convenient—and we were just talking about what they are really doing out here."

Carver gave him an inquisitive look, and he quickly switched back to English. "Excuse us, we often slip off into our mother tongue. I just reminded him that we thought we'd lost our guide this morning and," looking at Zora, "your colleagues—the ones who seem to have deserted you, Prince and Lucas—they told me that you are an excellent tracker and a guide."

"What they told you is correct," said Carver, "and, they did not really desert us—it was us, in fact, who insisted that they leave. Oleg, let's sit down. Zora and I have discussed this, and we have a proposal to suggest that I believe would be beneficial to all of us."

Oleg led them over to the previous night's campfire where several of the folding chairs were still set up and they all sat. "OK," Oleg said to Carver, "What do you have in mind?"

"Our missing expedition was headed to an area that's about a five-day hike from here. It's when they got to that area that they disappeared. If Zora understood Ngiome correctly, it sounds like the same area where you might be most likely to find your black lion, assuming it does exist. Dr. Hoyt's expedition called in at a set time each day using a JTRS."

"What's that?" asked Aziza.

"Joint tactical radio system. It can work off a satellite, but it can also bounce transmissions off the ionosphere when there's no satellite available. I assume you probably have a similar system."

"That we do," said Oleg.

"As you know, these communications devices depend on a battery and in order to keep it from getting run down they had to follow a very precise schedule. Their communications relayed directly to our offices in Brazzaville—to Prince and Lucas and, at the same time to our headquarters in Seattle. Based on Dr. Hoyt's communications, we know exactly where they set up their camps each night. Our plan is for Zora to guide us to those exact coordinates. She already knows where they started so the process of following in their tracks should be doable."

"So are you suggesting that we just follow along with you?" asked Viper, "What are you getting out of this?"

"Yeah," said Aziza, "Why don't you two just take off now? Wait for us and you lose another two hours, or do you really think you need to share our military escort?"

"It's now three weeks since they disappeared," said Zora. "Personally, I don't think they're still alive, but if they are, we know that their pygmy escorts left them about the time that we lost communications with them. So let's say they lost the use of their satellite radio and lost their way on top of that. If they are still alive and they are lost, we need to find them as soon as possible. I move quickly through the forest—Carver cannot. He's strong, he's in good shape, maybe better than you people, but this is such a foreign environment to him—to all of you, and—its potentially dangerous. Deadly dangerous for someone who doesn't know it very well."

"And you think you can move through this jungle that much faster than us?" asked Oleg.

"Yes," Zora affirmed.

"I told you she was a fucking freak," said Viper, speaking in Russian. "Cocky freak!"

"Enough, Viper," Oleg snapped back at him.

Zora looked back to Carver, and he continued.

"This is our proposal. Zora takes the lead—in fact, she'll leave now, as soon as we're through talking. She'll pick up the route following Hoyt's coordinates. I'll travel with your group. Zora will leave markers and your guide, Ngiome, will lead the rest of us at a slower pace, following Zora's trail. Zora will be carrying a hand held— call it a cell phone—that has limited range, but can communicate back to me. I'll be carrying the satellite radio. She'll check in on a regular basis with me, up until she gets out of range. Hopefully that will help us stay on her track. She'll get as far as she can, then will come back and camp with us at night. If she can get to the place where we lost Hoyt in just two days, that alone will give both of us a lot of potential intelligence that would be really nice to have and maybe she'll actually find Hoyt."

"Then," Zora cut back in, "if I can pick up Hoyt's trail from that point, assuming you'll be able to keep within radio range, I'll be able to get reconnaissance data back to you as I proceed, and if I see any signs of a lion, you'll be the first to know."

"I like it," said Oleg. "Not a bad plan." He looked at both Aziza and Viper and they both nodded back in agreement. "But what about your concern with us finding out what Hoyt's secret mission was? We all know that we're competitors and—"

"Carver saw you zipping your gun up in that bag yesterday," said Zora.

"Yes, my MKII," said Oleg with a proud smile. "Browning Mark II Safari—.338 magnum."

Zora looked at Carver, then back to Oleg. "That would be the choice for hunting large, dangerous game. If you were only carrying a Kalashnikov, like the rest of your crew, I wouldn't believe your hunting story in a million years. Carver and I both feel pretty confident your mission here is, in fact, what you claim it to be. Spying on Carver's mission as a competitor is, as of now, a secondary concern. In other words, I think we can trust you enough to allow for some cooperation, assuming we are going in the same direction, one way or another.

"Oleg," she continued, "I overheard you talking to Denis over there, and it sounds like you plan on leaving a couple of the soldiers here. Is that right?"

"Yes, they will stay here to manage this as our base camp. Also, we have a satellite communication system set up—probably a lot like yours, but we also have two phone sets. One stays here at the base camp, the other comes with us. If you have one also, that makes three. That would give us a triple redundancy, which might not be a bad thing to have. We plan to talk daily with our support team in Ouésso—that's where our helicopter waits for us, as does yours, I would assume."

"Just a suggestion," she said, "but I heard what Denis said Ngiome had told him about drier ground conditions at his village site. You might want to have your team move the camp over there. That's where I was late yesterday. It's the same general direction we'll be taking and no more than a half hour hike from here. The pygmies had all the game and water they could ever need right here, but now we see why they didn't build their huts here."

"Good point," said Oleg. "You have lots of useful suggestions, Zora—any more?"

"No, that's it. I assume you know enough not to lug a bunch of canned food out there." She pointed at the empty cans lying about.

"No, no. That's just for the base camp—like the wine and beer and," he paused and looked at Aziza, "maybe even a box of cigars. No, we will be very lightweight."

"I want to talk to Ngiome before I take off," said Zora. "I see him over there following Denis around. Let me see if I can explain our plan to him and make sure he's OK with it. I have trail signs I like to use for anyone following and need to make sure he knows what to look for. Carver, why don't you give them Hoyt's final campsite coordinates and go over any other details you can think of. I'll be right back."

Carver pulled out a small notebook and started reading off numbers to Viper who was recording them while Zora spoke with Ngiome and Denis. Several minutes later she was adjusting her backpack, checked some items in it, picked up a machete, then spent a couple of minutes with Carver testing their hand phones. She went back to Ngiome again, and the two of them, with Denis, walked to the edge of the forest where she cut several vines and small-caliper trees, demonstrating to both of them how she intended to mark her trail.

Carver, Aziza and the two Russians joined them. "OK," she said, "I think we're all on the same program now." She looked at her watch. "I have 9:14 on my watch. Carver, I'll call you at noon. If for any reason you don't hear from me, turn your radio on every fifteen minutes until you do. We'll talk again at three, then, I'll try and get back with you before sunset. I have my headlamp, but still … I prefer not to be looking for you after dark. If you can get your group moving here you might make it to Hoyt's first camp site before nightfall."

"All you have is that machete?" asked Viper. "No gun?"

"She reached behind her back and pulled out an eight-inch long knife—it looked razor sharp. "Swedish Morakniv Bushcraft tactical knife—the machete stays here." She slid it back into the sheath which hung from her belt. "I've got all I need," she said, looking at Viper, then at Carver. "Let Prince know what we're doing," she said, then she was gone.

19 – COUSCOUS AND DRIED NYAMA

Like the forest hawk that flies through the jungle, quietly and with precision, Zora traveled through the tangled landscape without changing speed. Seeing, hearing, smelling everything—she moved without hesitation. Her eyes constantly scanning, she read the landscape like a speed reader reads a page—she could see it all and comprehend it all—instantaneously. Time and the constant rain had washed away most signs of Hoyt's passage, so she kept to the game trails that led in the direction she knew to follow. She paused on occasion to use her GPS, but her inner compass was her main guiding system, and she steered her course accordingly.

Two hours had gone by when she arrived at the campsite where Dr. Russell Hoyt and his expedition party had spent their first night after having traveled for a full day. She went over the ground, carefully putting together the picture in her head of what they had done, how the camp had been set up. The campfire was obvious, and she could see where several tents had been pitched. The pygmies had constructed temporary shelters for themselves by bending over saplings and fastening large leaves across with vines. They were still intact and could be re-used, she noted. Near the fire pit, she found several chairs the pygmies had made from sections of small tree limbs they had cut. The chairs had been fashioned from sections of wood by cutting one end and spreading the cut ends outward like an upside-down umbrella, then planting the other end in the ground allowing the user to sit into the splayed end—a primitive version of a director's chair. *Clever*, she thought. She found everything—the stream where they took water, where they had wandered to collect fuel for their fire and where they had defecated. She noted that they hadn't left any trash. "Hmm," she mumbled to herself, then speaking to a small gecko that was carefully working its way across the clearing, she said, "that's an uplifting sign—not that it matters, I guess." She looked at her watch—too early to call Carver so she tried out one of the pygmy chairs, drank some water and ate an energy bar. As she stood up she smiled at the familiar cooing sound of a turtledove near the stream where Hoyt's people had most likely taken water. She looked at her watch again and then she moved on.

◆ ◆

Eight hours later Aziza was leaning against a tree, covered in sweat, her face drained. "I need another break," she said, exhausted and speaking to no one in particular. She reached for the water tube that projected from the right side of her backpack and was about to start drinking but paused, lifted her head slightly and sniffed the air. "I smell smoke. Do you smell that? Hey Viper—you smell smoke?"

"Yeah." He had stopped as well, which brought the others who were behind him to a halt. "Oleg," he yelled out, then stepping past Aziza, continued on toward Oleg and Carver who had just disappeared further up the trail. "Smoke," he yelled out.

"Must be Zora," said Carver as Viper caught up to him. "The smoke ... she said she'd meet us at the first camp site—must have beat us to it."

"*Merde!*" they heard Denis yell out. Denis had positioned himself just behind Ngiome for the march as he was the only one who could communicate with him. He looked back at Oleg. "The pygmy said something I didn't understand, then took off."

"It's OK," said Oleg. "We all smell the smoke—just a couple minutes."

Five minutes later the party began to meander into the campsite, one after another. Ngiome was already there, smiling at Zora who stood facing him with her hands gripping his shoulders. She nodded to Denis, then, speaking to Oleg who came in just behind him,

"Welcome—it may not look like much, but it should be a lot drier than last night."

Carver arrived, not too far behind Oleg. He smiled at Zora but said nothing. "You all right?" she asked him.

"I'm fine," he answered. "Just glad to see that you're OK."

A fire was going, and a rope had been strung across it with some of Zora's cloths hanging above—wet clothes, dripping slowly down into the fire which hissed back at each drop that fell. Zora was wearing only a pair of men's quick-dry hiking briefs and a wet mesh bra camisole of the same material. Both pieces of clothing were light tan in color, which on first glance created the impression that she was naked.

Oleg stared at her for a few seconds, then said, "You do know how to make a man feel welcome after a long sweaty march, don't you, my dear."

She looked at him questioningly, shrugged and replied, "Never seen a woman's legs before, Oleg?"

"You might want to put something more on before the rest of them show up. They're already a bit provoked just by having to follow after a woman guide."

One after another the others filed slowly into the campsite. The soldiers carried much heavier loads, and most of them had fallen behind during the march. By the time the last came shuffling in, the sound of his heavy breathing followed by the impact of his backpack hitting the ground was all that broke the silence. They all stared at Zora.

Aziza stepped up close to her and said in a low tone, "You might want to listen to Oleg and get some clothes on, Zora."

"I just washed my stuff, and it's drying out," she responded. "I've lived with soldiers before, you know, and most of them were a hell of lot rougher than these guys. They can deal with it." Then, speaking to the entire group, she pointed to the former tent sites that encircled the fire. "These cleared-off spots are where Hoyt's people had their tents. The ground is good here, so you might want to pick a spot and get yourselves set up."

She watched as each of them slid out of their backpacks, but still not moving from where they stood. They leaned their weapons against their packs and, then, one after another, dropped to the ground. They were obviously exhausted, some more than others—a few sat leaning against their packs, others were bent over, arms gripping their knees to their chests. The soldier who had been assigned to bear Oleg's hunting rifle consulted briefly with him before setting it down. As tired as they were, they all continued to steal glances at Zora.

Only Carver, Oleg and Aziza remained standing. "Ok, show us the tent sites," said Oleg. "Which is the best one?"

"Here—they're all pretty good—they appear to be level and clear of roots and stones—I just finished checking them for vermin when you showed up. I'll be staying over there," she pointed to an open area between two large trees, "that's where Ngiome's people slept—looks like four mounds of large leaves, but they're nice little shelters. Similar to the ones back at their hunting camp, but smaller. They're pretty much intact and I checked them out, too." She placed her hand on Carver's shoulder as if to usher him toward the leaf huts. "You should stay in one of those and save yourself the time of setting up the tent—I'm staying in that one," she motioned with her head toward one of the huts where her backpack sat in the opening. Ngiome's head popped out of one of the huts. He smiled at Zora and planted a machete in the ground in front of the opening, then picked up one of the pygmy chairs she had discovered earlier and set it next to the machete.

"I see you guys gave him a machete," she said, looking at Denis. "Did you give it to him, or is it a loaner?"

"Oleg said if he's a good boy, he gets to keep it."

Carver and Denis took the other two pygmy huts and dumped their gear inside the openings as the others started setting up their tents. Zora pointed two of the soldiers to the creek nearby, and as they left to get water she stuck her head inside Carver's hut. "Can I give you a hand?"

"No, but thanks. Not much to do—just roll out the sleeping bag and then figure out which of these dried food packages to try out tonight."

Zora glanced around the campsite, then stooping in the opening to Carver's hut, she spoke again, lowering her voice. "How did it go—with them?"

"Not bad—actually, not bad, at all. Didn't really talk with the other two that much, but Oleg and I walked together the entire day. He was really pretty good company—well educated. I certainly feel a little more at ease having them as travel companions for the next couple of days. Interesting, though ... neither of us ever talked shop—timber business that is. It was like we both satisfied one another's suspicions about the other so we talked personal stuff."

"Personal stuff?"

"Well, not completely. He did ask a lot of questions about you."

"Doesn't surprise me—he's a creep. That was my initial take on him, and I've seen nothing that would suggest I change it."

"I'm sure you're right, but Zora, you got to admit—you're not the typical female—I mean, come on—he is a man." He smiled at her, and added, "And so am I."

"God, Carver! Don't ever put yourself on the same level with him—in any way!" She frowned and shifted away from him, then asked, "So what did he ask about me?"

"He was particularly interested in your military background."

"What'd you tell him?"

"I told him what I know. None of what you told me at the hotel, but the kind of things Billy told me when he was building you up as some kind of super-guide. Ha, I did tell him how I first saw you—my surprise. I told him you'd been in Special Forces, a top-secret op in the Congo, and all that. The Special Forces bit got a reaction out of Oleg."

"What kind of reaction?"

"He seems to have an interest in military-related topics, especially U.S. military. He insisted that they don't take women in Special Forces."

"He's right about that. They don't—or at least they didn't when I went through."

"So you weren't in Special Forces?"

"I was attached to them as a specialist. Of course, since I was a specialist attached to a Special Ops unit I was required to do their training. I did the entire Special Forces training program—including some joint training with the Seals. I lived with them, I was stationed with them, and I did two special ops with them. I even married one of them—but I was there as a specialist. Officially the military was able to say that no woman had ever been a Special Forces member and of course there is no record anywhere that has me connected to an ODA."

"ODA?"

"Operational Detachment Alpha Team."

"And you were a specialist at what?"

"Languages—translator. In fact, all Delta Force members are supposed to be skilled at some language. I'm a polyglot, as you may have figured out. I'm proficient at several languages and I can learn a new language quickly. That, was my specialty."

"Not tracker or guide?"

"I know they have that buried somewhere in their records, but the official documents always had me down as Captain Zora de Rycken, Translator. Somewhere, probably, another document exists that has me down as a guide and tracker."

"Hey, Denis," Carver suddenly said in a louder tone, looking over Zora's shoulder.

"Time to eat, Monsieur Carver, Mademoiselle." Denis was standing just behind Zora. He was shirtless and had his automatic weapon hanging by its strap around his neck, a water proof bag in one hand. "Oleg told the cook to include you two."

Zora turned to look at him. "That was thoughtful of him. Who's cooking tonight?"

"Kiho," answered Denis as he moved toward the campfire, "He likes to cook. The others elected him chef."

Five minutes, later everyone gathered around the fire, watching, as Zora pulled her smoked, but dried-out cargo pants and shirt off the fire while one of the soldiers set up a large pot full of water to boil.

"They hanging up high enough not in my way," he said to her

as he stared at her legs, then turned with a little smile to two of his comrades who were settling down across from him.

"No. Time to get them down—almost too dry now. Lucky they didn't start to melt." She pulled the shirt on, stepped into the pants, then picked up one of the pygmy chairs, steadied the blunt end on the ground, fanned out the splayed top and sat down on it next to the fire. The others were all sitting on the ground, several with their backs resting against a log that had probably been placed there by Hoyt's party.

"What the hell's that thing?" asked Aziza.

"So me kind of chair the pygmies must have made. There are several scattered around. They're quite brilliant, really—fairly comfortable, keeps you off the damp ground, and makes it harder for ants and chiggers to get to you." Zora pointed toward several more that were lying on the ground near-by.

Aziza picked one up, examined it, then dropped it and sat on the log. "This is more my speed," she said.

As the others joined them, Zora noticed Denis had opened the bag he was carrying and had begun to clean his weapon. "Denis, you got yourself a real gun I see—not one of those cheap Kalashnikovs. I take it the AK-47 is standard army issue in Brazzaville."

"You know what this is, Zora?"

"Looks like a Swiss SIG 550—fine weapon. French commandos use it a lot."

"You seem to know your hardware pretty good," said Oleg.

"You could say that," she responded, looking at Oleg, "It was a requirement in a previous job." Turning back to Denis, she continued, "Were you Foreign Legion, Denis?"

"Yes." He stopped what he was doing and looked at Zora as he spoke. "I went to France to work when I was young but joined the Foreign Legion when I couldn't find work. I trained in Guyana—saw some action in Mali. I came back here when my contract was up. They were reorganizing the army here, and I walked right in as an officer— and I kept my SIG 550. Like you say, it's a nice weapon." He smiled at her and added, "You keep surprising me, Mademoiselle."

"What do you consider the best automatic weapon, Zora?" asked Oleg.

"I like the M16—that's what I was trained on."

"American shit!" exclaimed Viper. "If it's so great, how come three quarters of the world is using the AK?"

"Cause its one-fifth the cost of an M16—or a SIG 550 or even a French FAMAS. In fact, you can get them on the black market for one-tenth the cost. The Russians mass produce the AK-47—they're cheap, poor accuracy over longer range, hard to reload. I'd take an M-16 any day over a Kalashnikov."

"You know so much about automatic weapons, but you go running around this jungle with nothing," said Viper. "How do you explain that? You think you got some kind of magic protection—or are you just crazy?"

"The question, Viper, should really be to your group here, what the hell do you need all this firepower for? Oleg's got his big lever-action gun for the mythical lion, but all these AK47's, the Swiss gun, that would all be great if we were expecting to run into some bands of guerillas, but I don't think you're going to find anything like that out here. All this hardware is just extra weight that you end up wasting your energy on. Trying to keep it dry for one, but mainly carrying it—and carrying all the ammo when you and these soldier escorts could be carrying something you could eat. To answer your question though, I have my knife, my legs, my senses, and my wits—that's what you need to survive out here. That and a little luck, maybe."

"Good point, my dear," said Oleg, "but if I told these brave soldiers to stack their weapons here and pick them up again on the way back, they would think I was crazy. I think that having them gives them comfort—a little security. I actually think that secretly, these men are scared half to death out here."

"You're probably right. This might even be the furthest into the bush that any of them have ever been. I'll bet they're all city boys from Brazzaville or Pointe Noire—the only jungle they get into is when

141

they drop into some river town up near the north borders, looking for poachers or illegal immigrants."

"Not to change the subject or anything," said Viper, "but what's on the menu for tonight? I'm fucking starved."

"Couscous and dried *nyama*," said Aziza, "interesting combination."

"What's *nyama*?" Carver asked.

"Meat," answered Aziza. "No fucking idea what kind—just meat. Could be goat, beef, even pork, *oy-vey*, God forbid. Why is it, everyone's carrying his own food supply yet we all end up eating the same shit? Is it going to be this shit for the next two weeks?" she asked, addressing no one in particular.

"Ngiome's not eating it," said Viper. "What's he eating there? And look at that—he's using a big leaf for a plate."

"Looks like mushrooms to me," said Carver. "Hey, Ngiome, want to share? Zora, tell him I'll trade half my couscous for half his mushrooms."

Zora translated and Ngiome stood up, carried his mushrooms over to Carver and each of them scraped half his food onto the other's plate. Carver immediately mixed everything together while Ngiome watched. Ngiome then picked up some of the couscous with his fingers and tasted it. He smiled and said something to Carver that sounded like a sign of approval.

"Zora," Oleg said, "I listened to the one communication you got off to Carver—so it sounds like you made it to the second campsite."

"Third," she responded. "I called in from the second site, but managed to get to the third before I turned back. Their trail was pretty easy to follow."

"You must have been running though—even on a straight line with no jungle that looked like a long way to me," said Viper. "How the hell can you get through this place that fast? Even Ngiome— he told Denis it took him two days to get to the edge of that forbidden place."

"I have longer legs than Ngiome."

142

"Ha, you can say that again—and nice legs," added Aziza.

"OK, OK," said Oleg, "Zora—tell us what you've found so far."

Zora took a swig of water, stood up and adjusted her seat, then began to speak, "The next two campsites are not much different from this. If you get started early enough tomorrow, you should be able to make it to camp three—maybe take a short break at number two, refill your water bags. You know the route and I'll add more signs tomorrow." She hesitated for a second, then continued. "There's a swamp between here and number two and I think it probably slowed Hoyt's group down. It's actually pretty easy to get through—just go straight into it—I'll have markers set out for you.

"I crossed through the main part of the swamp in about thirty minutes … maybe twenty-five on the way back. There's half a dozen smaller swamp areas after the big one—just keep going—none of those are as deep. You'll probably find it a little threatening with all the roots and vines you have to pick your way through. I saw a couple water snakes but they didn't look like poisonous varieties. Ngiome will keep you clear of anything like that anyway. In any case, like I said, Hoyt was probably slowed down a lot by the swamp. If you cut through fast, you can get to camp three by tomorrow night. Carver, you and I can use the same check-in times for our calls tomorrow."

"Zora," said Viper, "this is good reconnaissance work and we all really appreciate it—but, I want to return to the question I asked earlier, how the hell can you go that fast through this jungle? I know you got longer legs than Ngiome, but, I wanna know how you do it."

"Viper, if I tell you my secret, maybe you can tell me why everyone calls you Viper."

"Aha-ha-ha!" Aziza burst out laughing. "Maybe you'll get lucky Zora, and he'll show you—but you might be sorry. Go ahead and answer his question!" She looked at Viper, a big grin on her face.

"You keep your fucking mouth shut, Aziza."

"What are you worried about, little brother? We're out in the middle of nowhere. We might never get back out of here based on what we keep finding—who gives a shit what I say or to whom?"

"I think this conversation has strayed a bit off topic," said Carver, looking at Zora.

"Right," she said, "Maybe it's time we call it a day."

The low rumble of distant thunder interrupted their conversation at that point, followed by a brief silence, then Oleg, looking at Denis, said, "Ask the pygmy if it's going to rain again. If it is we need to get ready for tomorrow—no more horsing around for tonight." Then, looking at Zora, he asked, "How far do you think you can get tomorrow?"

"I'll get to where Hoyt was when we lost contact with him. I expect to be there before my midday call in to Carver. Depending on what I find, I'll probably go beyond that."

Like a guillotine slamming shut, night dropped abruptly onto the exhausted travelers. As each began shifting in closer to the campfire, an owl hooted somewhere and the thunder sounded again, this time closer. High above, the sound of wind rushing across the tree tops began to filter its way down, a branch could be heard breaking, then the smell of rain followed, but it had not started to fall.

"The pygmy says it's already raining," said Denis.

20 – NZOI

"They think it looks like a spider robot," Viper said to Carver, translating the comments that were coming from the soldiers who had gathered around as Carver set up the satellite radio. The legs unfolded and extended out, supporting the main body of the system while the body itself simultaneously opened as the antennae slid upward. In less than sixty seconds, it was open and connected to the battery. Carver looked at his watch.

They still had a minute before Zora's call was expected. Everyone grouped silently around Carver, waiting, anticipating. One of the soldiers belched as he swallowed a mouthful of Spam. The sound of the empty can landing in a puddle off to one side followed, then Viper sprayed himself with Deet and the constant hum of the jungle around them filled the air.

Oleg crouched next to Carver as he looked at his watch again then flipped a switch. A soft hissing could be heard coming from the radio, followed by Zora's voice, "Carver, you there?"

"Yeah, Zora, I'm here." He glanced around, "We're all here."

"I passed through their last known campsite about an hour ago. Now I'm standing at the edge of the rim—I guess we can call it the rim. The ground drops off here in what looks like about a 30 to 40 percent slope. I have to tell you, this place is weird—never seen anything quite like it. Hoyt was right about the trees. They get bigger as the ground drops away. I can't tell how big really from here, but they are big—and it's dark down there. Like there's no bottom. "

"Have you seen any signs of Hoyt and his group?"

"They stopped here for a while. When you see it you'll understand. I don't think anyone would just go plunging straight down into this place. Looks like they took a lunch break—probably sat around arguing with the pygmies who, as we know, refused to go on. Believe it or not, I found footprints. Feint, but still here."

Carver looked at his watch again. "OK, Zora. The day's half shot. Are you heading back now?"

"No. I should be able to get to their next campsite before I have to turn back. Hopefully I'll find something that will answer a few questions."

"You sure you want to do that?"

"Look, I'll call you again at exactly sixteen hundred hours. Keep your people moving. See you at dinnertime. Oh, wait ... better give you a heads-up."

"For what?"

"You're not allergic to bees are you?"

"No, why."

You're probably going to run into some—soon, if you're making the kind of progress I assume you're making. You're going to hit an area that's inundated with them. Probably not enough flowers in bloom right now so they're looking for something sweet. They'll be all over you, trying to drink your sweat. They won't sting if you can just ignore them—warn the others. If anyone freaks out, they're going to get stung. You'll have them with you until you get to the next swamp—it's a small one, but once you get submerged into the water the bees will fade out and go their own way. Tell Oleg to warn his people—it's likely going to be tough on them."

"Thank you, Zora. This is Oleg. We'll be OK."

"OK, Oleg. Good luck. I'm signing off now—gonna take a look down into this hole. Talk to you all at sixteen hundred hours."

"Good for her," said Aziza. "Let's hope she's able to join us for dinner."

Viper looked at her and, speaking in Russian, said, "Didn't think you cared."

146

"I just don't want our black lion eating her up, my sweet. I'm expecting you to do that." Then, turning to Carver as he folded up his radio, she asked, "What's this about bees?"

A sudden smacking sound, followed by a short scream drew their attention to one of the soldiers. "*Nzoi!*" he yelled out as he slapped the back of his neck.

Oleg never had time to caution his men. The bees arrived. At first there were just a few, and as Zora had cautioned, they did not sting unless provoked. Fear and the panic it induced, however, resulted in uncontrolled efforts to slap the bees away, and to the bees, that was provocation.

Ngiome, who was accustomed to bees, began to yell at the men who were beginning to swat. Unfortunately, no one understood him. Those who had overheard the communication with Zora, understood the situation and were able to maintain some control. Denis tried to order the other men to stop slapping the bees, but it was too late as their panic seemed to act as an invitation, and bees began to arrive in rapidly increasing numbers.

"Denis!" yelled Oleg, "Tell the pygmy to get us to the swamp! Do it now!"

Denis shouted his orders to Ngiome, who understood immediately, and took off at a rapid pace. "Take your gear!" yelled Oleg, as two of the men began to follow, leaving their weapons and backpacks, but the panic that had begun with one man, now spread like a blanket that enveloped them all. "Your gear!" he shouted again. He pulled out his pistol and fired it into the air, but the panic had begun and they continued on, screaming and slapping.

Fortunately, the swamp was not far, and at a running pace, which quickly turned into an all-out sprint, they arrived within minutes. At Dennis's orders, most threw their gear on fallen trees, branches, or roots that cluttered the swamp before they attempted to submerge themselves into the murky water. One soldier dove for the water as soon as he arrived at its edge, only to find it not deep enough. He rose up to his hands and knees, his face now coated in muck, and he scrambled on in a blind frenzy, entangling himself in a mass of roots. He lost a boot before he was finally able to find refuge in the greater depths of the mire.

The bees quickly lost interest as the water and mud washed away their sweet sweat. Oleg and Denis were the first to stand upright. Both quickly looked around to assess the situation. Denis began calling out to his men.

"Mashaka," he shouted. One of the men did not seem to be there. "Where's Mashaka?" he asked the others. "Did anyone see him?"

No one had seen him. "We're missing one man," he said to Oleg. "I'll go back and look for him. I'll take the pygmy." He paused as he looked around.

"He's over there," said Aziza, pointing back in the direction from which they had come. "The pygmy."

Ngiome was squatting on a long limb that swept down close to the ground, looking at them as if he had been patiently awaiting their emergence. When he heard his name, he hopped off, and waded through the water toward Denis, and began to talk. After a brief discussion, Denis turned to Oleg, and conveyed the gist of the discussion. "He said Mashaka ran off the wrong way. The pygmy followed him. He says the *bilo*'s dead—stung to death.

"Tell him to go back and find his gear," said Oleg, "Take one of the others with him—that other guy who left his stuff behind. We'll continue through this mess and wait for them on the other side." Then, looking around at the others, "Get your stuff and let's get out of here."

It took them a while. Their sweat-drenched backpacks were still covered in bees.

21 – AN UNFORTUNATE LOSS

"Kiho! *Lamuka*—wake up!"

Kiho, the soldier who liked to cook, was seated on the ground in front of a fading fire, slumped against his backpack, sound asleep. His eyes snapped open wide, his body twitched as if reacting to an electrical shock, and he let out a short cry at the sudden sound of Zora's voice. He rotated his head slightly to one side and squinted, trying to avoid the light from her headlamp.

"What are you doing out here? You're going to get eaten alive by mosquitoes. Denis put you on night watch or something?"

"Zora!" he blurted out, "They worried about you. Where you been?"

"Don't worry about where I've been. Looks like everyone's asleep around here. You need to be in your tent, man—and your face! Oh, no! You got stung, didn't you?"

"We all got stung … and I'm supposed to wake the boss when you come back."

"Let them sleep—and get in your tent before the bugs suck all your blood out." She looked around, then added, "I need to sleep. I marked one of those huts for myself when I came through here this morning."

Kiho started to get up. "Sefu!" he yelled out.

"Shhh! I said, let them sleep!" she whispered. She put her hand on his back and applied a light shove in the direction of the tents.

"Carver," she whispered, as she leaned into his tent. She reached in, touched him, and repeated, this time a little louder, "Carver." He groaned and shifted slightly, but did not wake up. "I'm back, Carver." She shook him, but he still did not respond. "OK. We'll talk in the morning. Have a lot to tell you but I'm wiped out—need to get some rest now."

She found her own shelter and scanned it with her headlamp as she poked about with her knife before crawling in. The camp was quiet, with just the usual nighttime mix of creaking, buzzing, and an occasional faraway shriek. Ngiome's face was just discernible, peering out from one of the small shelters. She nodded at him, then ducked into her own hut. She continued poking her knife about once she was inside. Something slithered out the back, and she shined her headlamp toward it just in time to see the tail of a small lizard disappear … then she collapsed onto the ground and fell into a deep sleep.

◆ ◆

"What happened to you? You didn't radio in—then you show up in the middle of the night. Didn't bother to tell anyone you were back." Oleg was bent over looking into Zora's hut.

"Oleg," she said as she slowly raised her head. She took a long drink of water, then looked at him. "OK, I'm up—just need to take care of my bladder, if you don't mind."

"Everyone's up. We have a fire going—hot tea. Ngiome found some roots of some kind last night, and Kiho's frying them up."

"Be right there."

Zora crawled out of her shelter, relieved herself nearby, then slowly made her way over to the campfire. Everyone was talking at once—Lingala, Russian, French, and English. Only Ngiome was silent, sitting on one of the pygmy chairs, alone just beyond the ring that had begun to form around Zora. She leaned toward him and asked, "Did you sing to the forest this morning, Ngiome?"

He smiled at her and nodded with an affirmative, yes.

"I didn't hear you—slept right through it," she teased.

She squatted down next to the fire. One by one, the others sat down with her, Oleg on one side, Carver on the other. Viper, Aziza, and Denis were clustered together across from her and the soldiers

150

were tucked into the group at each side. Ngiome got up, took his chair with him and drew closer, stabbing his chair into the ground next to Carver. Everyone had stopped talking, and now they all looked at Zora, waiting for her to speak.

"Here, have some tea," Carver said as he handed her a steaming cup.

"Thank you," she said. "You got some nasty red welts on your face, Carver. Guess you got to meet those bees yesterday." She looked around. "All of you."

"Did you go into forbidden place?" Ngiome asked. All heads turned to him—no one understood him but Zora. She had not spoken with him since the previous morning, yet her comprehension seemed to have improved, almost overnight—as if the language sector of her brain had continued processing while the rest had been busy responding to more immediate issues.

"Yes, Ngiome, I did," she answered.

Ngiome stood up from his chair, stepped between Carver and one of the soldiers, squatted down on the ground, and looked up at Zora. "I am glad you are here."

"So am I," she said. Then, looking at Carver and switching to English, she said, "I tried to call in at sixteen hundred hours. The connection didn't seem to want to work. Couldn't have been the distance. Maybe the drop in elevation put me in a black-out zone—it's a pretty deep depression."

"You should have come straight back when you couldn't get through," said Carver. "You gave us a scare."

Zora didn't respond immediately. Her eyes still scanned the group. She looked back toward the tents. "Who's not here?" she asked, then, answering her own question, "Mashaka." She looked at the soldiers and asked in French, "Où est Mashaka?"

The soldiers' eyes widened at her question. They looked nervously at one another. "Denis, what happened to Mashaka?" she asked.

"He panicked when we got into the bees. It was bad—very bad—he panicked. Started running blindly—ran off the wrong way.

151

Everyone else was dealing with the bees so no one noticed, except the pygmy."

"We finally got to the swamp and just submerged ourselves," said Aziza. The little fuckers still wouldn't leave us alone. You'd duck your head under the water, then come up for air and wham, one of them would hit you in the head like a kamikaze. Like they knew you went under the water, so they just hung out waiting for you to pop up—fucking nightmare.

"We must have stayed in the water for … seemed like an hour," said Carver, "When they finally backed off, we went to pick up our equipment and some of them were still crawling on the backpacks."

"What about Mashaka?" Zora looked back at Denis.

"He's dead. The pygmy took me to where he'd last seen him. The pygmy followed him, I think." Denis looked at Ngiome and speaking in Lingala, said, "Tell us—tell the brown girl. What happened to soldier who run off when *nzoi* attack?"

"*Bilo* run; Ngiome go after. He fall, so Ngiome cover with big leaves to keep *nzoi* off. Soon he stop moving. When Ngiome look under leaf he all blown up like big frog. *Bilo* dead."

"He's probably being eaten by hyenas or something by now," said Viper, with a smirk on his face.

"You're his commanding officer, Denis," said Zora. "Don't you need to at least get his dog tags or something? Anyone retrieve his gear?"

"Dog tags?" asked Denis, "What's that? Insects should have him half stripped to the bone by now. No one will ever see him again."

"Ha!" Viper laughed, "You gotta watch every step out here. One minute you're walking along and the next, the bugs and worms are turning you into fucking fertilizer!"

"Not to be laughed at, Viper," said Oleg. "The poor man is dead now, and we still got a way to go." Then, looking at Zora, he added, "Yes, we did retrieve his equipment."

"Huh?" Viper responded. "I thought his load was lost. He dropped it the minute the fucking bees went after him."

"No, the pygmy got it," said Denis. "I carried it across the swamp. We dumped the pack, but split everything up between the boys. I think we got everything."

"Nevertheless," said Oleg. "We've suffered an unfortunate loss."

"Agreed," said Carver, "but now, I hate to change the subject. Zora," he turned to look at her, "I need to know what you found."

The group quieted again, and all eyes were back on Zora.

She looked at Carver, then Oleg, then back to Carver. "I found Hoyt."

22 – PANTHERA LEO – PARDUS

"Hoyt's dead."

"Jesus," Carver muttered to himself, looking down at the ground. "Oh God, no … that's not what I wanted to hear." He shook his head. "Russell."

Zora looked at the others and said, "They're all dead."

"Poachers," said Denis. "They must have run into poachers."

"Not poachers," said Zora, "In fact, I wish it had been."

"What do you mean?" asked Carver. He grabbed her by the arm, his face pale. "Tell me what happened?"

The soldiers, who didn't understand English watched, whispering among themselves except for one who was spraying himself with insect repellent. Those who understood shifted in closer. Ngiome remained perched on one of the pygmy chairs just outside the group and watched, listening intently but understanding nothing.

"Go on," said Oleg."

She looked at him and continued, "You might be hunting for something more than just a wild myth, Oleg. They were killed by some kind of very large predator—or predators—the signs I saw suggest there could have been three of them, maybe more."

Oleg grinned and looked at Viper, then Aziza. "My lion!"

"Lions don't live in the rain forest," said Denis. "I said this before. There are no lions in the Congo—there never have been." He looked around at the others, an expression of angered frustration on his face. "People here don't even know what a lion is."

"I know, I know," said Oleg, "we all know that. The nearest lion to this place is over five hundred miles away. But this one is here. I can feel it in my blood. Now she says there might be three or more. That's how lions hunt—it's a family event. There *is* a lion—a black lion. And we are going to find him!"

"Whatever it is," continued Zora, "it is, in fact, black. I found black animal hairs all over the place. Also footprints—rub marks on trees."

"My God, Zora!" exclaimed Carver. "But there were eight of them, more than that even. Hoyt had one of our senior managers with him and six soldiers, plus the pygmies they took on back at the landing spot. And they had weapons; at least the soldiers did!"

"Don't forget, Carver, the pygmies turned back when they reached the rim. In any case, it started getting dark just after I found them. I wasn't able to make a full assessment." She paused then started up again, speaking in a lower tone. "Whatever got them, it came at night. I could see where two of the soldiers were dragged from their tents while they were sleeping. There were clear signs of panic. At least one of the men ran off, deeper into the forest. The tents are shredded, equipment broken and strewn all over the place. Three of the AK-47's had been fired—the magazines, empty. My guess is, the guns that hadn't been fired belonged to the two who got dragged from their tents. They were sleeping two per tent, just like Denis's guys here. The cats got one from each tent. Looked like one struggled, the other didn't. Probably grabbed by the head or neck when he was dragged out—died immediately. Those who fired their guns must have done it in total panic. Probably couldn't see what they were shooting at. At least there were no signs of any dead or wounded animals."

"What about Russell?" asked Carver. "Maybe he was the one who ran off."

"I couldn't tell who was who because—odd detail—all the remains I found were missing their heads. I looked at clothing fragments to try and identify individuals. The soldiers wore jungle camouflage fatigues, and based on that, it looked like one was missing, plus the footprints I found of whoever ran off were from the same army boots

155

the soldiers wear. Then …" She reached into her backpack, pulled out an item and dropped it onto the ground in front of Carver. "I found this." It was Hoyt's passport. "The pouch I found this in was ripped apart and splattered in dried blood stains."

Carver took the passport, opened it and shook his head, moaning. He looked at Zora and she could see the deep sadness in his eyes.

"I'm so sorry," she said. She put her hand on his shoulder, said nothing for a minute then continued, "Their satellite radio looked like it might have been operable. The legs were broken off, but it looked OK. I tried it out—totally dead … could be the battery was just shot."

"Shit," said Viper, looking at Aziza and speaking in Russian, "this is just fucking fantastic!"

"Easy!" said Oleg as he cast a warning look at Viper. Then, looking back to Zora, he asked, "Tell me more about the lions, Zora. You said you found black hairs. Was there anything to confirm they might have been lions?"

At first she didn't answer. "I came to find Dr. Hoyt, not a black lion," she finally responded, her voice deflated. Then she added, "I need to drink something." Aziza filled a cup with tea from a pot that sat on a piece of stone next to the fire. Zora gulped some down then, looking back at Oleg, said, "Lots of prints. I have to admit, though, I've never seen a lion print before—just jaguar, puma … smaller cats. I've seen some leopard prints since we left the base camp. They looked a lot like the leopard prints but were huge—bigger than a jaguar—lot bigger. I'm not a cat expert, but I would guess we're looking at a cat that weighs in at four hundred pounds, maybe more."

"Only a lion or tiger can be that big," said Oleg.

Zora nodded. "We can rule out jaguars and tigers. Now lions, we all know they hunt in family groups. There've been documented cases of man eaters operating in pairs, and I'm pretty sure I was able to identify the prints of at least two separate cats—could have been three."

"So you agree: they're lions," said Oleg.

She looked at him intently and responded, "Panthera Leo."

"Pardus," added Oleg with a smile of satisfaction, "black."

Carver stood up suddenly. "We gotta get going," he uttered, looking back and forth."

Zora grabbed him by his belt and pulled him back down. "Sit down, Carver. We're not going anywhere."

"Zora, you and Carver can go on and discuss your plans for the day," said Oleg, "We're not wasting any more time here. We have a long trek today." He stood up and started toward the tents; Aziza and Viper followed.

"You're right, Zora," said Carver. "We don't need to rush now. One of my best friends is dead and nothing I do now can change that. I do need to go on, though. I need to see for myself what he found."

"To see what he found? Carver, you paid me to find him and that's it. I found him. He's dead, his whole crew is dead, and there's nothing left to bring back—just that passport. You have no reason to go out there now—not unless you want to end up like him."

"Zora, the company is paying you and me not just to find Hoyt, but also to complete his mission, if we don't find him. I need to get out there and see what he saw, collect some data."

"The company?" she replied, her voice becoming increasingly agitated. "Carver, if the company knew what was going on here, they would never expect you to go out there and risk your life just to gather some information. As much as I don't care for big corporations, I do know they're not that reckless. When they find out their entire expedition is dead, my guess is, they wouldn't try to return until the Congo army has declared the area safe."

They both paused and looked toward the others as they heard Oleg shouting, "Denis, tell those guys we leave as soon as they can get packed up." Oleg glanced in their direction then began walking back toward them.

"You're not going out there, Oleg," Zora said, as he approached.

He chuckled, shook his head, then looked at her and said, "You, my dear, are not about to tell me where I can or cannot go."

Carver stood. He shifted toward Oleg and looked down at Zora.

"At this point, Zora, the danger means nothing to me. You're probably right about the company, so I'll say right out, it's no longer about the company—it's about me. This forest you've seen; it's my life! This is what my entire life has come to. I didn't even realize it until now. I'm at the pinnacle of my life—my future. I'm about to experience what it's like to be the first—the first to walk on the moon—to do.... I have to go on."

"OK Carver," said Zora, "You personally need to see this place. That I understand. But you need to do it carefully, and in a well thought-out way. There might be research to do, but this is no longer just some unexplored region in the middle of nowhere. This is a totally unique site. Hoyt was right. As soon as the world finds out about it, the whole area will be cordoned off—as it should be," she added with emphasis. "No one should ever be allowed to cut any of the trees in this place, and whatever those felines turn out to be, no one should ever be permitted to hunt them. It's a treasure—a treasure that no one has the right to take or destroy."

She stood up and facing them, added, "None of you has any business being out here. You're all a bunch of lizard-brained..." she paused and looking at Oleg, continued, "narcissistic ignoramouses. You're spoilers—all you want is to kill, exploit, and destroy. This is just one more invisible world to you. You come here, kill the animals, cut down the trees—turn the whole place into a massive moonscape! And Carver—didn't you look down at the ground as we flew out of Ouésso? We didn't see it when we flew in because it was too dark. The rivers all had nice green strips running along their banks and on the other side of those green strips—devastation—all grey and brown with pools of mud—an entire world of dead emptiness. It looked like an aerial view of a strip-mining site multiplied to a power of a hundred." She stopped talking—took in a deep breath, and then added, "And I'm not going to help you." She then looked at Carver and added, "That includes you. Let them go, if they want, but you and I start back—today!"

By this time, Aziza and Viper had joined the discussion. "Hey, Carver," said Viper. "If she don't want to take you, you can come with us."

"Of course, he can come with us," said Oleg. Then, addressing Zora, "You had a difficult day yesterday. I can tell. It must not have been easy. Relax for a minute and think about what you're saying. No one here is about to cut any trees down," and looking at Carver, "Hoyt's life can't be written off for nothing either. I empathize with you, Carver. You do need to go down there. You need to do whatever you do—finish Hoyt's mission, man."

Zora was about to speak again when she felt something touching her arm. It was Ngiome. He was standing next to her. She began to translate for him, but realized as she looked in his eyes that he seemed to have caught the gist of the conversation.

"Denis!" Oleg shouted out, then, turning to Viper and speaking in a low tone and in Russian, said, "Tell Denis to come get the pygmy and tell him we go now. I don't want her talking to him." He cast his eyes toward Zora, and added, "I'll shoot her outright if I have to. " Viper shook his head in the affirmative and slipped off to where Denis and the soldiers were folding up their tents.

Zora turned from Ngiome, looked at Oleg and put her hands up to her face, pressed her palms against her eyes, then ran her fingers up through her hair. Carver stepped over next to her and put an arm around her, which she immediately shook off. She picked up her teacup from the ground where she had left it, drank what remained, then went over and sat down on the log next to the campfire. "She glared back at the others but said nothing.

Carver followed her to the log and sat down next to her. "I don't want to go without you," he said, "But if you don't want to continue on, I understand. I *have* to go now, and I'll go with them if I have to. I guess Ngiome will take us. You will get paid the balance of what you're owed for getting me this far ... and for finding Russell."

"Carver, you're not getting it. Ngiome is right. Anyone who goes to the forbidden place, does not return. I'm afraid for you. Them, I could care less," she said as she thrust her chin toward Oleg and his companions.

Carver reached out, grasped her arm, and looked at her with an intensity she had not seen in him before. "This might not be a rescue mission any more but it is still a research mission. It's my research mission now—mine, and Russell's. We're one day's march out and there's no way I'm turning around. I need to see with my own eyes what's out there. I need to find out what Russell died for. He put his life into this, and now he's lost it for this. I need to follow up—there needs to be some kind of closure for him—and for me."

Zora slowly pushed his hands away. She looked at him and said, "Carver, I'm sorry—very sorry. I'm not going on. You go with them. It's not easy for me to say this but, you'll have to go without me, so—just go."

♦ ♦

An hour later, Ngiome was picking his way carefully through the forest, following the trail that Zora had left the day before—the trail that Hoyt's expedition had taken a month earlier; Denis was directly behind, followed closely by Carver. Aziza and Viper were several meters back from Carver and the small squad of soldier escorts—minus one—followed. Oleg took up the rear position. Zora was not with them.

23 – THE WORLD ACCORDING TO OLEG

The expedition had not gone far when Oleg slowed his pace. He glanced back over his shoulder. Finally he stopped, looked back again, then ahead just in time to see the last of the soldiers disappear. He remained motionless for a moment, then stepped to one side and leaned against a large tree root that ran parallel to the path. He continued to wait. Minutes passed. A rat scurried across the trail and then a small snake slithered across in the opposite direction. He saw neither. Finally he stood upright and grunted, "Hmm." He stepped out into the middle of the path, squinted and scanned the area again in both directions. He saw nothing—heard nothing. He sighed, muttered under his breath, swatted at some flies, shrugged his shoulders, turned and started walking.

"You better hurry up."

He jumped at the sound of the voice that seemed to have come from nowhere but in fact came from directly behind him. "Zora!" he said.

"Yeah, it's me. You're fucking lucky it's me. Otherwise they would have had to stop and send Ngiome back to find you when they realized you'd gotten your dumb ass lost. Could have cost you half a day's march."

"I don't get lost. I was simply waiting to see how long it would take you to come along."

"Look at that large tree straight ahead of us with the palm growing out of its base. Did they go to the right of it or the left? Do you have any idea which way they went, Oleg?"

She walked past him and kept on without hesitating. She ducked under a low-hanging palm branch and passed to the left of the big tree. He stared at her for a second or two, then began to follow.

"You were pretty confident that I'd be coming, weren't you?" she asked, as she continued to walk, her back to him.

"I don't even need to answer that, now do I?" he responded. He followed in silence for several more minutes then added, "The only thing I'm not completely sure about is why you changed your mind and decided to stay with us. Either you really do feel responsible for Carver, or, based on your ranting back there, you want to make sure I don't get to shoot my lion."

"Both," she replied. "What I want to know though, is why you waited for me. If I were going to continue after you, I would have caught up with the lot of you whether you were waiting or not. By waiting, you really did take a chance on getting yourself lost."

"Ah, but there you're wrong. I did know."

"There you go again—arrogant know-it-all. By the way, were you aware that I very rarely express myself with expletives? *Asshole* and *fuck* are not part of my active vocabulary, but, you are an asshole. And now, I think … just today … I'm suddenly talking like my mouth were a flowing sewer, like your slimy sidekick, Viper—not that Aziza's much better. Do you have that effect on everyone?"

"You're confusing me, Zora. What is it you really want to know? You ask why I waited for you then you want to know if I have somehow influenced your use of expletive language. Which do you want to know?"

"It seems like you can't wait to tell me, Oleg. Go ahead."

"Gladly, my dear. I'll start with your language. The language you use is of your own choice. You can blame someone else, but when it really comes down to it, the words are your own and they come from you. It's really a matter of your own loss of self-control. I do get a small touch of satisfaction though when I hear you say 'fuck.'"

"I'll bet you do. There goes that lizard brain of yours. You might be real clever at manipulating stock markets or whatever the hell you do, but you have the brain of a reptile—and no soul."

162

"Soul is a human invention—or should I say fantasy. I have no idea what it means. All I know is that people constantly use it as an excuse for their failures—failures to focus on what really does matter. It's a pathetic fallback for all their weaknesses, their inabilities to really see and understand what life is about."

Zora stopped abruptly, turned and looked at Oleg causing him to almost run into her. "You have got to be fucking kidding me! What life is about? I don't think there's any big secret as to what it's all about for you! Fill your pockets, feed your face, feed your ego, ejaculate a few times, maybe kill someone, then back and start all over again. Not an uncommon trait in many men but, then, in your case, highly extreme." She turned and continued walking.

"Excellent! You managed to sum it up perfectly. Basically that is what it's all about and I'm quite pleased to see that you actually understand. And I must say that for me to hear you say that has justified my waiting for you."

"I assumed it was so you would be able to hear me put you down—or put you in your place. That's got to be a new experience for you. Does it get you off in some way?"

"Zora, I will admit, I do like your exuberance—and I like the fact that you are less predictable than most. You have great potential."

"Sadly, Oleg, I have to assume that you did too at some point in your life. Whatever happened?"

"Whatever happened? Are you trying to get me to talk about myself? Because if you are, you must know that I do, in fact, enjoy talking about myself—especially to such an intriguing young woman and in the middle of a remote rain forest."

She didn't respond at first. *Narcissist*, she thought to herself, *always need to be the center of everything—love to talk about themselves.* "Well," she finally said, "you know Carver told me the other night that you spent half the day prying him with questions about me so I have to assume that you've already heard enough from my end—and since I know so little about you ... please, do talk to me and tell me about you. I'll make every effort not to get bored. But ..." She hesitated as a small snake wriggled across the path. A leopard coughed somewhere. She looked back at Oleg as he smacked at a mosquito, then she completed her thought. "We do need to catch up to the others before they realize they've lost you, so make it short … if you can."

"Now Zora, I believe that I was only able to scratch the surface with what I got out of Carver. I think you have a lot more you could tell me. Like I said, you intrigue me. You're smart but, like so many intelligent young people—naive."

"Naïve! Isn't that what conservative-leaning people always fall back on when trying to explain why an educated person with a different point of view, in fact, has a different point of view? But you're not at all what I would consider conservative, Oleg. So coming from you, I will assume that you consider me naïve simply because I refuse to accept your deranged point of view."

"Oh, but I do understand you. I know exactly where you're coming from. It's you who does not understand where I'm coming from."

"Then tell me."

"You see, we're all born and we all die, as you well know. People talk about history—what went on in the past, how the human race got to where it is now. But history really does not matter other than as a tool to be used today, in the present, for the manipulation and control of others and the environment to best suit your own life. History is a movie, you see. We all have only one life. You're not a Hindu or a Buddhist or one of those New Age American morons are you?"

Zora didn't reply.

"Whatever happened before my birth, or yours—and whatever is going to happen afterwards, are of no consequence. All that matters is what you do during your own life because that is the only reality—the beginning and the end of everything. Reality is now. It's me, and in your case—reality is you. Once you thoroughly come to understand and accept that, everything else you ever do will fall right into place, just as you want it to, with no baggage attached. No more religious hocus pocus stuck in the back of your brain, grinding at your unconscious self, feeding you with guilt—a witless subservient to humanity's fantasies that have grown out of a thousand years of mass hysteria and fear."

"I are quite self-centered, Oleg. I wish I had a recorder now—but keep going."

"Do you know how I became so wealthy, Zora?"

"Well I'm sure you didn't create or invent anything. If I had to guess, I would say that from the very start, your modus operandi has involved deception, exploitation, coercion, maybe some good old-fashioned brute force, but, please, go on, Oleg."

"Yes, yes, of course, those have always been useful tools, and I would never hesitate to make use of them when necessary. The ends always justify the means, as you must know. In my more youthful days I did take more chances than I do now, but those early endeavors did result in quite substantial sums of money for me, so I certainly have no regrets. And wealth begets wealth, and when you know how to delegate, it grows ever so much greater. Viper and Martel—Martel's a colleague back in Nice—I've brought them along nicely and even allowed them to take over some of our peripheral enterprises. Viper has done quite well. I generally tell people he's my bodyguard, but in fact, he's done quite well as a manager. He's expanded what he started with and has even branched out into new avenues. I get a piece of everything, and I always look to expand into everything. This timber company you've heard references to is nothing. I've always loved commodities, and I love banking even more. You might say I have become a true and enthusiastic proponent of the capitalist system."

Oleg stopped and took a drink of water, wiped the sweat off his forehead, then offered a drink to Zora who had stopped to wait for him.

"No, thank you," she said, then, smiling, added, "just in case whatever you're suffering from is contagious."

"Oh, it is contagious, and that's why I'm telling you about it."

"You think you're going to convert me? Do you wow people with all your wealth, power, and machiavelic cleverness?"

He put his water bottle away and they both continued walking.

165

"As you well know, once a critical mass of wealth has been obtained, more becomes easier. I invested, I diversified … I always researched whatever I got into. I've never made a blind or foolish investment. I saw the 2008 collapse coming and I placed myself accordingly. When the whole world was reeling, I was feeding off of their blunders. Whatever I did, I always invested with the intent to own and control.

"Now Viper … what I can do that most of your market and banking big shots fail to do is, every now and then, call upon Viper and his network of resources to assist in the persuasion department. This timber company I have. I was able to pick it up by manipulating the market from the receiving end, driving them to the verge of bankruptcy. Then, I quietly bought up a controlling share of their stock, took over the company, and finally turned it back into a major player in the international market. Of course, any good entrepreneur who's worth his salt does that on a regular basis. So I buy companies cheap, sell some of them for huge profits when they're not worth anything, keep the ones that are worth something, and basically, I have built up my assets from just over a billion euros to twenty times that in a five-year period. Having Viper in the shadows has pretty much guaranteed success with every transaction."

"So what are you trying to tell me, Oleg? No, don't answer that— you're such a bore. So what's your goal? Do you have a goal?"

"Well, you know what selling short is, don't you?"

"Yes, I do."

"Well, my ultimate life goal—it's all geared toward shorting— the biggest short of all. I plan on shorting the human race. You see, going back to where we started, it is my life and my life *only* that matters. Nothing else in the universe has any validity whatsoever. You were practically crying back there about forests being exploited and destroyed. What you fail to see is that no matter what you do, say, or think, you are not going to change anything. Humans are stupid, short-sighted, and greedy—and that's at every level of the social and educational ladder. These forests are already gone as far as I'm concerned. I've carefully collected all the data out there—and I mean all of it. Natural resources, environmental depredation, financial, political, demographics—and water—that's a big one! The bottom line is, no matter where the human race thinks it's going, I know exactly where it is going. Now there are others out there who know this as well, but they're stuck in a state of denial. And, that's the beauty of my life. I've very quickly been able to enrich myself to the point where I have total control over my own life and everyone else's. I know it's all going to come to a very ugly ending, and I know when that's going to happen. The timing couldn't be more perfect, you see. About the time I hit what would be considered old age, the entire planet is going to be in total meltdown, and that's the last thing I'll get to see before I die and, oh God … what a sight it should be!"

"Wow, Oleg, you're really starting to scare me."

"I'm not through."

"Oh, no?"

"No. This whole planet, you see, is going to just continue to sink deeper and deeper in the hell of its own making—until you all just disappear as a species. And all of this," he stopped and waved his hand out along the trail, pointing to the forest, "all of this is just here for us to take and turn into mud, and that's exactly what's happening now and will continue to happen. And do you know what I intend to do about it—me, an individual with almost unlimited power? I will do everything in my power to make sure that when the game is over, I have the best seat in the house, because I will watch it all come crashing in on itself and it will be the greatest send-off I can imagine for the end of my life. For you see, Zora, after I am gone, life will no longer matter. It will no longer be."

He paused, waiting for her to react, but she just kept walking. He cleared his throat, spit, took a quick swig of water, then continued. "Now that goes for you, too, of course. After you're gone, it's all going to go to shit no matter what you do in your life. So why worry about it? You've got the brains to make yourself so rich you could never spend it all if you lived another three hundred years. You could have anything and everything you ever wanted, and you would have no need to worry about a thing. And when you're gone, all that exists will no longer be and, therefore, should be of no significance to you. Life will cease to have any meaning or value."

She stopped again and looked at him. He winked at her, smiled, and added, "Just a little advice from someone who's been around a bit."

Zora turned and continued walking, shaking her head as she walked.

"I don't share my deepest insights like this with everyone, you know. You're special, Zora. You may be rejecting everything I'm saying, but I've planted the seed. It's with you now, and it will keep coming back to you, and maybe, just maybe, you'll wake up one morning, and realize that it all makes sense, and your friend and admirer, Olegushka Levkov will be there waiting for you—just like I waited for you today."

"Oleg, you really know how to give a woman the creeps."

"Ah, ha, ha, ha!" he laughed and as he did, he tripped over a root and stumbled forward into Zora.

"What are you trying to do?" she snapped as she pulled away from him. She turned and stared at him as he regained his balance. "Come on," she said. "I hear someone up ahead. Looks like we've caught up to the others. Maybe you better shut it down for now. I think I've heard all I can take on life according to Oleg."

"Zora, I assure you, anything I drive you to do, you will never be sorry for. In fact, you will thank me. And I look forward to that day."

There was a movement ahead, and she didn't seem to have heard Oleg's last remark. She quickened her pace and a minute later, Carver appeared, coming toward her. "Thank God!" he cried out.

24 – A CASE OF OPHIDIOPHOBIA

"I see the pygmy didn't take off in the middle of the night," Viper said to Oleg, speaking in Russian.

Oleg, Viper, and Aziza stood at the edge of the rim, gazing into the dark foreboding unknown they were preparing to enter. They had camped at the same spot where the Hoyt expedition had spent their last night, where they were last heard from before they disappeared and where their pygmy guide and porters had turned back. A light rain was falling.

"I was sure he was gone," said Aziza. "I didn't hear him yodeling at the trees this morning."

"Yeah," said Viper. "We weren't wakened by the little jungle bunny this morning—I was actually getting used to it."

"Zora asked him to keep quiet this morning." They turned to see Carver standing behind them. "She seems to think that whatever it is down there didn't come after her because it might not have been aware of her presence. She asked me to spread the word to everyone to keep real quiet as we go. Don't know how easy that's gonna be," he added as he stood next to Oleg and gazed downward.

"Right," said Aziza. "Can't hurt. We should take every precaution possible now."

"Russell's camp was attacked at night while they were asleep," said Carver. "They probably had no idea there might have been something like that down there. You might want to get Denis to make sure his people understand."

"What's she doing?" asked Viper, gesturing toward Zora.

"Talking to Ngiome," said Carver. "Filling him in on what she saw and trying to calm him a bit. He's not too eager to go down there, you know."

"Viper, tell Denis to keep the imp away from her," Oleg said in Russian, then switching back to English. "Tell Denis to get ready to go and tell him to go easy on the pygmy. We all know he's not looking forward to this but we need to get moving." Then, in a lower tone, as if speaking to himself, he added, "This slope looks like it's going to be a little challenging."

"Hey Carver," Oleg called out as Carver started back toward his shelter. "I saw you on your radio a few minutes ago. Anything interesting?"

"Nope, just checking in with Prince—he's back in Brazzaville. Lucas is staying up in Ouésso with the helicopter. They want a check-in three times a day now. How 'bout you? You said your guys back at the clearing weren't answering their radio."

"Yeah. Our helicopter went back there yesterday to check on them. Apparently they couldn't land—too much water. Said it was flooded like a lake and all our stuff looked like it had been washed away. Also said they saw what looked like a torn up tent tangled up in the bush downstream and no sign of Denis's boys."

"That's not good. I suppose that means our supplies are washed away too—not a big deal for us—just a spare battery, couple cases of meds and food. Hopefully your soldiers just moved to higher ground."

"Yes, but the fools should have at least taken their radio with them." Oleg then reached out and, placing his hand on Carver's shoulder, asked, "She talking to you this morning?"

"Not really," he answered, "Been giving me the cold shoulder ever since you caught up with us yesterday."

Thirty minutes later, they began their descent. They didn't plunge straight downward, but followed a game trail that had been carved into the side of the steep sloping wall; the same route that the doomed Hoyt party had followed. Although the trail showed evidence that it had been used by forest elephants, it was steep and slippery. A thin rivulet had formed in the middle of the path as water descended in thin trickling threads; the path was slippery. Zora led the way followed by Ngiome who carried only his hunting net and machete which he tied to himself using the rat tail that hung off the back of his loin cloth, his spear balanced on one shoulder. Spread out in a line behind them came Carver, Oleg, Aziza, Viper, and finally the five soldiers, with Denis taking up the rear. All but Ngiome and Zora were loaded down like pack mules.

"Where the hell's the bottom of this shithole?" Viper called out to no one in particular.

Zora looked back and held her finger up to her lips. "Shhh! Keep it down. We need to go slow here—it's slippery. Maybe another twenty minutes, and it should start to level off."

"That rotten egg smell seems to keep getting worse as we go down," remarked Aziza as she placed a hand on Viper as if to calm him. "Carver said it was sulfur."

As the trail took them deeper, the faint light within the forest slowly diminished, like the dimming lights in a theatrical production, it dropped and dropped to ever lower levels. It was mid-morning, but the illumination from above was gradually fading as if the sun were setting, and as the light continued to fade, so did the constant hum and chatter that drifted down from the arboreal fauna that inhabited the canopy above. Their world was becoming quieter as it became darker—quieter to the point that now their own breathing and the intermittent sucking of someone's foot being extracted from the mud had become the predominant sounds, set against a backdrop of constant dripping.

With his mouth open in wonderment, Carver was completely lost in the immensity of the trees that seemed to grow larger and taller the deeper their descent took them. Indeed, as he and Hoyt had predicted, the forest canopy remained level with that of the forest they had just passed through, yet, where the ground fell away, the trees just seemed to have extended their trunks downward, and the longer the trunks became, the wider they grew in diameter, and the further the ground

171

dropped, the darker and heavier the air became. Most of these trees seemed to be supported on buttress root systems and often those roots wound along the edge of the path like walls, starting thirty or more feet above where they would shoot off from the main trunk like a giant fin, tapering downward and running as far as forty or fifty feet before they finally veered off course somewhere or disappeared into the earth below. "These are as big as anything I've ever seen," he whispered to himself as he walked along one long buttress, patting it with his hand. A spasm of excitement ran down his spine as he imagined how Russell must have felt.

Several times they stopped as one or another of them would slip, falling, grabbing onto vines or young saplings. Each time someone fell, the entire party stopped, and everyone would use the pause to rest, take a drink, secure their gear. The tension that resulted from attempting to maintain their balance only added to their fatigue and the more exhausted they became, the harder it was to control their descent. Finally, someone fell hard; one of the soldiers. A scream pierced the air, and everyone froze in place. "Shit!" said Zora. She took off her backpack, balanced it against a small tree then started back up the trail. "What now?"

The scream was followed by several short groans, then the whimpering cries of someone in pain. Denis had come down from his rear-guard position and was bent over one of the men. "It's Mo," said Kiho, his eyes wide with fright. "He started going too fast and was grabbing onto the vines and small trees and...."

"I see," said Zora as she squatted, facing the moaning soldier. Mo was sitting on the ground, his head rocking back and forth in pain, tears in his eyes. Two of the other men, Nabu and Reth, were on each side of him. Denis had grabbed his arm and was holding it up, examining it. A long thorn, thin and sharp, like a hypodermic needle, had pierced his hand when he had grabbed one of the small trees to slow his descent. It had broken off from the tree when he fell and was now sticking out each side of his hand. Blood ran down his arm.

"Hold his arm still," Denis said. Reth secured Mo's arm with both of his hands as Denis braced the pierced hand with his own left hand. He carefully grasped the thick end of the thorn and in one swift movement, extracted it from the man's hand. Another scream followed. "Nabu! First aid kit! Now!" he commanded.

"OK," said Zora, looking back down the trail, "Let's take a little water break."

The man's cries had slowed to whimpers and finally, taking slow, deep breaths, he quieted down, then gradually raised himself up onto his feet with the help of his two comrades. Denis looped the soldier's AK-47 over his own head and handed one of the others his backpack. "Here, get this on his back. We'll go slower 'til we get to the bottom. Keep a close eye on him. OK," he called toward the front of the column, "Ready to go."

They all began to stand up again, slinging their loads onto their backs when, suddenly, there came another scream, this time followed immediately by a burst of automatic weapon fire, and then Viper, shouting hysterically in Russian, "Motherfucker—motherfucker!"

Carver and Aziza were the only ones standing. The others had flung themselves to the ground the instant the gun fired. Zora lifted her head, looking in Viper's direction, then jumped up and ran to him. "Are you out of your mind?" she shouted, standing over Viper who was writhing on the ground, pushing himself up against a large vine, his finger still squeezing the trigger of his gun which was now empty. He was white as a ghost, trembling, his feet pedaling against the ground as he attempted to push himself backward, away from the source of his hysteria.

"You shot a snake. God knows what kind—it's torn to shreds now." She grabbed the weapon away from him and threw it on the ground. "You moron! Whatever it is down there that stalked and killed Hoyt—whatever it is—it now knows that we're here!"

Aziza had knelt down next to Viper and held him by the shoulders. "Calm down, baby—it's OK. You got it—you fucking blew it apart. Come on—get up now—get up." She looked at Zora and said, "He's afraid of snakes—ophidiophobia."

173

"Christ! What next?" She looked at the scattered pieces of snake again, and added, "What's left of it—doesn't even look like a poisonous variety," then speaking to Ngiome, asked, "What kind of snake was that?"

Ngiome's name for the serpent didn't mean much to any of them, but Denis, who was now looking at its remains, laughed and said, "Brown snake. Brown house snake. City people use them for pets."

Oleg had picked Viper's gun up from the ground and, handing it to him, said, under his breath and in Russian, "Don't ever let anyone take that away from you like that again. Get up and get your shit together. Fucking little harmless snake! Let's go. Let's get down this hill for God's sake!"

"I don't get it," Carver said to Oleg, as he started back down the path. "He calls himself Viper and he's covered in tattoos that make him look like some kind of snake worshiper."

"Long story," said Oleg. "He doesn't like to talk about it." Oleg gave him a pat on the shoulder then turned to look back toward Viper and Aziza.

Viper slung the weapon over his head as he stood back up. He was staring at Zora, who was talking with Ngiome further down the trail, and, speaking in Russian, mumbled in a low tone to Aziza, "She's never leaving this place. Cunt's dead meat—fucking dead meat."

"Yeah, yeah, OK. We'll deal with that later. We gotta keep going now. Come on, baby—let's go. You wasted the snake real good."

"You can have that faggot she's leading around—I'm getting her," he continued on, under his breath.

"Come on, you two," said Oleg, "and Viper, don't forget to reload. Took you a whole magazine to kill one little garter snake. I hate to think what you're gonna do when you run into the lion."

25 – THE SUNKEN FOREST

"Filter it before you drink," warned Oleg. The trail had just taken them under a waterfall that gushed off an outward-extending precipice, creating an archway of water across the path. Viper ignored Oleg's warning as he stood beneath one of several smaller chutes, tilted his head back, mouth agape. The soldiers quickly followed his lead while Carver and Aziza adhered to Oleg's advice. Zora and Ngiome stood further down the path watching, and Mo sat slumped against the pile of backpacks, grimacing at his injured hand.

The shouting and laughter of the men as they began to play in the waterfall was a sudden contrast to the morose mood that had hung over them since their start that morning.

"That racket's going to get our lion all stirred up," said Aziza under her breath as she edged closer to Oleg.

"Like Zora said, Viper's gun has probably already alerted the lion. Let them have their five minutes—if their frolicking lures the cat to us, so much the better."

Eventually, the raucousness began to settle down and, as each of them came out from under the water, a calmness settled over the group. "Don't smell that rotten egg stink here," said Viper as he noticed several of the soldiers breathing deeply and smelling the air.

"Negative ions produced by the waterfall," said Carver. "They attract and bind together with the positively charged particles of dust, pollen, and hydrogen sulfide that create that unpleasant sulfur smell. Increases the weight of the particles causing them to fall to the ground—clears the air. The increased oxygen level makes everyone feel lighter."

"Thanks for the science lesson, Carver." Then, calling out to Zora, he asked, "Hey—how do we get beyond that thing?" Viper pointed ahead to a large downed tree that blocked the trail just beyond the falls.

Zora walked up to the fallen tree and without saying anything, squatted low to the ground and quickly scurried into a dark gap between the tree and the ground. Ngiome followed, and then, one after another, each member of the party crawled through, grunting and complaining, pushing and pulling their gear as they went. Emerging on the other side, they stumbled away from the tree, chattering between themselves as they reloaded their gear onto their backs—then a hush fell across the group.

They had arrived at the base of the steep incline the trail had been clinging to all morning. The ground leveled off here and appeared to roll out before them into a misty, cavernous space—a space of massive proportions. The buttress roots of two huge trees plunged downward from heights of thirty or more feet and swooped, crisscrossing over the trail ahead like a succession of layered walls. The vista beyond was obscured by mist that rose up from the rushing stream as it cascaded from the waterfall behind and zigzagged its way between the trees.

The forest was very old here, and the trees were enormous with trunks reaching upward like sentient giants to support a continuous canopy of interlacing green foliage. "Only when lightning or high wind from a passing storm manages to strike in just the right place does the canopy open up," Carver said as he stood in a trance-like state, his mouth half open, staring in wonderment. "It might open just enough to allow a rare sliver of direct sunlight to penetrate to the ground below. Without that sliver of light, the forest floor remains in near perpetual darkness—darkness so complete that the formation of new plant forms is limited to ferns, fungus, mushrooms, and the dangling shoots from plant life…" He waved his arm up to the canopy above. "Plants formed from seeds that sprout in the crotches of mid-level branches, so high up, we can't even see where they start. It drops its shoots—you can't tell them from the vines ... and there," he pointed to something lower down. "That narrow-crowned younger tree—desperately in search of a way to the light above."

In sharp contrast to the canopy's density, the understory stood open—an openness broken only by the massive trunks and wriggling strings of descending vines. The vast sense of space was deceiving, for at ground level, the forest floor was littered with fallen trees, branches, and roots. The winding buttresses that fanned out from each of the trees with their sinuous curves created a living maze of roots that sprung away from the main trunks like green serpentine walls, winding their way downward in wriggling snake-like patterns, overlapping one another, shooting off smaller roots which in turn generated additional sets of roots, all wandering and spreading until finally swallowed up by the moldy earth below. Their continued passage would not be easy.

Oleg stood frozen in place. His gaze rotated slowly as he took in the extent and immensity of the trees. "My God," he gasped, "Like the groined vault in some surreal cathedral—this is—"

"They—they could easily be as tall as redwoods," said Carver. "Russell knew we'd find big trees here, but, this… If it weren't so dark, you could see—God knows how far."

A magical stillness hung over the group; only the sound of the rushing water could be heard. Someone swatted at an insect, then Carver exhaled and whispered to himself, "Look at that…" as his eyes tracked a pair of yellow birds that had suddenly appeared from above. The birds swooped along for several hundred feet just below the bottom of the canopy, disappeared behind a trunk, then some vines. They reappeared briefly like stars, twinkling on and off until finally they faded from view.

Carver breathed deeply, then continued. "The size of everything is—it—it throws me off." He stopped again and took a drink of water, but his excitement was too much; he choked and half of what he took in ran down his chin. He turned around, looking in the opposite direction. "I can't even tell what kind of trees I'm looking at. And the ground—everything's encased in moss or fungi of some sort. Look!" He pointed to the ground and swept his arm around and upward.

"Everything's covered with it—ha!" he laughed.

Viper, speaking in Russian, mumbled to Aziza, "Look at that faggot—wouldn't be surprised if he's got a hard-on over the trees."

"Yeah," she mumbled back to him, "and Oleg's getting one over the thought of setting up a sawmill down here."

"After he gets his lion...." Then noticing Oleg staring at him, he continued on in English, "Huh—yeah. Hey Carver, what do you call this place?"

"Zora said Ngiome refers to it as *the place where the forest came out of the earth*. Hoyt called it *the sunken forest*."

26 – BUILDING A PYGMY HUT

It was mid-afternoon by the time they reached Hoyt's final campsite. Not wanting to stay where their predecessors had met their demise, they decided to skirt the site and establish their own camp further into the forest and close to a stream. There were no ready-built pygmy huts to be found this time, so Zora asked Ngiome if they could construct new shelters for themselves. She sensed anxiety building in him since they had left the rim of the caldera, and she hoped the process of working together might help ease his tension. The scarcity of saplings and smaller trees in the sunken forest made the task a little more time consuming than it would have been elsewhere, but they were able to use thick vines for the framework. These they bent over to form overlapping arches, which they lashed together with smaller vines, then overlaid the frame with large leaves that became the roof. Working together, the second shelter was completed in half the time it took to do the first. When they were through, Ngiome walked carefully around each hut, inspecting the roof systems, then took a deep breath and smiled at Zora—the deep furrows that delineated his forehead had softened. She placed her hand on his shoulder and the two wandered over to where the others were setting up their tents.

Zora sat down on one of the long buttress roots that wound its way around one side of the campsite while Ngiome fashioned himself a chair out of a short piece of wood he was able to scavenge up. "You were right to set up away from Hoyt's site," said Carver as he joined them. "Hmm, nice natural bench here." He sat down next to Zora. "We just need to set the fire up over here. I'm tired of squatting or sitting on the wet ground. It's always damp, if not saturated."

She didn't respond at first. Then looking at him, said, "I'm not happy with you, Carver. I don't like being backed into doing something I know I shouldn't be doing."

"I told you, you were off the hook, Zora. I didn't make you come with us. I'm doing what I need to do—whether you come with us or not. I just have to do it. But, you're here now, and I'm very happy about that."

"Did you really think I was going to let you come down here alone—and with these psychos?"

"I wouldn't have been alone. We have Ngiome guiding us and them." He looked toward Oleg's tent, "Viper—he's unstable, that's for sure, but Oleg's been pretty decent. He's obviously competent, and the lot of them—they do have experience in places like this..."

"Carver..." She paused and ran her hand through her hair. "You should have heard Oleg when he and I were walking together. I think he's more of a psycho than Viper. And Ngiome—have you looked at him? He's scared half to death. This is his worst nightmare. And you ... you're so lost in your own world, you've become blind to everything else. I tried to convince myself that you were just another corporate predator, but I know that's not true. You do work for them, and you came here partially because they told you to, but you really are a scientist. You came here to find your friend, but you also came for the curiosity and the thrill of possibly finding something. This place is a potential game changer to your career, and ... you've allowed your mission to blind you."

"You're right. But I'm not blind. I know I'm walking into a potential fire. And, I'll admit I'm scared. In fact, I'm scared half to death, but I can't, *not* do it. When I thought you had turned back, I went on, but I felt like one of those World War One movie characters, who at the sound of the whistle, goes charging out of a trench into the face of almost certain death. I felt numb as I hiked along, thinking you were going the other way. When I saw you, it was like I had just awakened from a bad dream."

"It is a bad dream, Carver, and the bad part hasn't even started yet. If you want to stay alive, you're going to need to stay awake. And Carver?"

"Yes?"

"You're more than just my client now. You're a real person. That's right—a real person. And in spite of your little oddities—your inability to make rational decisions—I realize that I care for you. You are my responsibility, and I intend to make sure that you leave this place alive."

They stared at each other intently for a moment then Zora cleared her throat and looked toward Ngiome, who had been listening, but had not understood a word. "And Ngiome," she said. "I intend to make sure he leaves here alive as well."

27 – HOYT'S LAST CAMP

"I only got a quick glimpse of Russell's campsite when we passed through it," said Carver, speaking to Zora. "Since we're all set up here, can we take a walk back there? We still have a good amount of daylight left, and I'd like to start going through whatever we can find. It'll give us a chance to talk on the way over without having to worry about them listening in."

"OK, Carver, I guess we can do that. I'll tell Ngiome where we're going."

Zora translated for Ngiome, then added, "Don't let them leave the hurt man here alone," He nodded, and as Zora and Carver quietly slipped away, Ngiome made his way over to Denis's tent.

"I feel like we've been trudging through this jungle for a month now, but in fact, it's not even been a week," said Carver after they'd been walking for several minutes. "I always thought I was in great shape, but I'm really starting to feel it. I'm not used to the relentless weight of this heavy warm air—sucks my energy away."

"Don't worry, we should be out of here tomorrow and on our way back." She stopped suddenly and held her hand to Carver's chest and put a finger up to her lips. They both stood in silence while she carefully looked around; listening.

"Hear something?"

"Yeah—I still hear them fussing around at the campsite—but ... something moving." She pointed upward, "In the trees—close—group of monkeys or something, but too far to be sure. Nothing to worry about." She took her hand off his chest, turned, and continued walking.

"So I agree with you on Viper—sociopath's a good tag for him, although my background in psychology is pretty limited, and I'm not that sure what a sociopath really is versus a psychopath, but either word fits him as far as I'm concerned, and I sure as hell don't want to get in a scrap with him. I mean, he's obviously in really good shape, and so am I, but if the guy wanted to fight me, I don't want to have to find out what it's like fighting a psycho, you know—I don't want a knife in my gut. I don't think he'd hesitate."

"Viper's a dangerous human being—if you want to classify him as human," she said with a chuckle. "All three of them are dangerous though. Oleg doesn't like to get his hands dirty, but he's the puppetmaster when it comes to Viper. I'm sure he has some control over Aziza as well but she's the biggest mystery to me right now.

"Yeah, she is a weird one," said Carver. "Each day when you were scouting ahead, Oleg and I walked together—we talked a lot, and I asked about the two of them. He always seemed to end up being the one getting information out me though—he has a knack for that."

"You like to talk about yourself, Carver—most people do. Oleg knows that, and he's a master at allowing people to talk while he listens—and learns. You said that you two hardly spoke about the lumber business, but I guarantee he's learned a lot about your business over these past few days, and you probably don't know any more now than you did a week ago about his."

"The guy's a billionaire," said Carver. "He's involved in just about every commodity you can think of, including timber. In fact, from what I understand, timber is a minor enterprise for him."

"Money-wise, it is minor, but he seems to have a special interest for it. He wants this place. You know that, don't you?"

"He really left me believing that he wants the lion. I'm sure he wants the timber rights to this place, but that's secondary—he needs to get his lion first and foremost."

"He lives to accumulate—everything and anything. Did you see him as we started down into this place? Every time we went by a particularly large tree, I could almost see dollar signs popping up in his eyes—like an old-fashioned cash register. This place is without question the most unique place—or I should call it the most unique secret? It could be one of the biggest secrets left on earth, and for that alone—he wants it. And—that brings us to the most interesting part of my conversation with him. Once you do get him talking—it's all about himself and his take on the world. He's a narcissist—probably what they call extreme—an extreme, malignant narcissist. And he's brilliant. You add a little bit of intelligence to his kind of narcissism, and you have a potentially dangerous individual. Every other human on the planet is here to serve his needs. And now, in addition to the uniqueness of this place, he knows that you're here to confirm what this place is and then to secure it as an asset for your company. The very fact that you or your company might want this place just makes it that much more appealing to him. I wouldn't be surprised if his possession of this forest hasn't already taken precedence over shooting his mythical lion."

They both stopped as they arrived at an open area and there, in front of them stood a two-person tent, intact except for a tear in one side of it. Just beyond were strewn the remains of several other tents, backpacks, and gear of various sorts. "Not sure what's going to be left of their bodies," said Zora, "The heads are all gone, like I told you, but the rest won't be around for long. Beetles and worms were carting them off at a pretty rapid pace and it won't be long until the mold and moss covers up what's left."

"Jesus," Carver uttered in a depressed tone. "This isn't easy for me, Zora. It's like a part of me has been cut out."

"I know, Carver, but you need to separate the scientist from the friend now. There's got to be a lot here for you to see."

She held his hand for a minute then led him around the site, quickly finding Hoyt's climbing gear, including two bundles of 150-foot lightweight rope. Carver found Hoyt's iPad and a waterproof case that included a journal and a book full of technical notes.

Suddenly Zora noticed that Carver was staring at her. "Carver... Are you all right?"

"Zora, don't we need to be worried about the lions coming after us now? I mean—we don't even have a gun with us or anything."

"Not now, but probably tonight. They attacked Hoyt at night. In general, big cats like to hunt at night. My concern is that these cats are now acclimated to dining on humans. Most big cats, even when they may never have clashed with humans, will shy away from us— they always seem to understand that we're potentially dangerous. But these seem to have no fear, and I'm asking myself why they attacked the way they did. Have they possibly had prior contact with humans and have they developed an appetite for us? We need to be wary, but mainly late at night."

As they continued searching through the scattered remains of the campsite, Zora kept all of her senses on high alert. When Carver started toward a duffel bag that was lodged between some vines she reminded him to approach with care as she had found a snake in one on her earlier visit to the site. After half an hour of scavenging, Carver looked over to her and noticed that she was standing still, looking up toward the lower canopy. "See something?" he asked.

"The noise I heard earlier. Looks like a troupe of chimpanzees up there."

"I don't see anything."

"About a hundred feet up—right there," she pointed as she spoke.

"OK. Yeah, I saw something move."

"They're watching us—at least twelve of them."

"You see twelve of them and I can barely see anything moving— you gotta be kidding me."

Suddenly one of the chimps began to descend down a vine, followed by several others. The first chimp landed on the ground, looked at Zora and Carver, then began to walk toward them, taking a diagonal approach, knuckle walking on all fours.

"Don't move," cautioned Zora.

"I'm not about to. I've heard that chimpanzees can be aggressive and dangerous." He stepped closer to Zora and whispered, "What do you think?"

"From what I've read about them, they're dangerous when threatened or when a competing group encroaches into their territory. I think they would be raising hell if they felt threatened. They're coming slowly but seem to be curious. Stay calm."

By now most of the others had joined the first chimp on the ground, and they all began to approach—slowly and with a sense of caution. The first chimp, a large male, paused, then came straight at them, now walking upright. It got to within ten feet of Carver, stopped, and turned its head away, but kept its eyes focused on him. Slowly it rotated its head back toward Carver, stooped downward slightly, then suddenly jumped, landing directly in front of him. Carver reached out and grabbed Zora by the arm as he stepped back, almost stumbling. The chimp opened its mouth wide, revealing a set of large teeth, accentuated by two long, sharp fangs. It cocked its head back and forth several times, wrapped its arms around itself, patted himself on the top of its head with one hand, and let out a short grunt. It sounded like a question.

"Zora," whispered Carver, nervously, "these chimps have never seen humans before. I'm sure of it!" He cast a quick glance at her and noticed she was smiling.

The large male then stooped over to scoop up a chunk of the dense mossy turf. He tossed it aside, then reached down into the opening and pulled up a handful of dripping wet moss, lifted it up over his head, opened his mouth and, squeezing it, lapped at the water that ran out. He stooped again, pulled up another handful and stretched his arm out, offering it to Carver.

Carver very cautiously took a step toward the chimp, reached out, and took the offering. Imitating the chimp, he lifted it above his head, opened his mouth wide and squeezed water into his mouth. He turned to Zora and said, "Hasn't been boiled—think I'm gonna get sick?"

"Too late to worry about that now," she answered.

The chimp then thumped the ground with one of his hands and made several stuttering grunts.

Carver laughed and imitated him. Immediately the entire

troupe started chattering and showing their teeth in wide grimacing expressions.

The large male moved closer to Carver, carefully reached out and gently touched his shoulder. Carver responded by touching the big ape's shoulder. The chimp responded by pinching the fabric of Carver's shirt between his fingers and pulling on it.

"He's never seen clothing," said Zora.

Carver smiled at her, slowly removed his shirt, took something out of the pocket and stuck it in one of the pockets in his cargo pants, then handed the shirt to the chimp. "Take it," he said. "I've been asking myself why I don't just take it off anyway and go around bare-chested."

The chimp took his shirt, smelled it, then started pulling on it with both hands. He lifted his head and started into a series of high hooting sounds, then dropped the shirt, reached out and touched Carver again, this time on his bare chest.

"That you can't have!" said Carver with a laugh.

Suddenly several of the chimps started chattering—louder and faster, looking around and beginning to act agitated.

"What's going on?" asked Carver.

"They heard something—so did I—gunshots."

The large male turned toward the rest of his troupe and started grunting, took a few jumps back to the others, then turned back to Carver and Zora and repeated the same, slightly more nervous grunting sounds.

Zora waved her arm in the direction from which the sounds had come and said, "No!" She shook her head and waved her arm past the group of chimpanzee—twice—as if pushing them to stay away. "Don't go there—no!"

Carver followed Zora's lead and went through the same motions.

The chimpanzees looked at them for a few seconds, and then the male pounced forward, picked up Carver's shirt and quickly scurried over to a vine, which he began to climb. The others followed and as they looked up, Zora and Carver noticed several more that had remained above, silently witnessing the strange drama below.

"Consider them our lookouts. As long as they're up there, not too far away, any predator comes around—they'll start making a fuss."

One of the chimps let out a low scratchy noise, then began repeating it faster and faster, quickly building it up into a scream as the group slowly worked their way further upward, gradually disappearing.

"Did we just chase them away or do you think they were responding to the gunshots?" Carver asked.

"Seemed to me like it was the gunshots. They're probably like most animals and have much better hearing than we do. Those gunshots, though, were not from the camp. They were much further off and in the wrong direction. Maybe we should head back and see what they're up to."

"You sure you even want to know?" asked Carver, "As long as they're back there somewhere and we're here, they're no threat to us."

"They have Ngiome with them. I am concerned for him—at least while he's in their company. Let's go."

Carver quickly gathered up the climbing gear and Hoyt's notebooks and stuffed them into a backpack they had retrieved from the one standing tent. As he lifted it onto his back, Zora called out to him from the other side of the compound, "Here you go, take this— maybe this will put you at ease." She held an AK-47 out to him.

28 – BUSH MEAT

"Where're they going?" Aziza asked Denis as she noticed two of the soldiers, Kiho and Reth, disappearing behind the buttresses of a nearby tree, carrying only their AK-47's and ammo belts.

"Hunting," he answered. "Everyone's tired of eating that dried *merde*. I told them to go get us some fresh meat."

"Oleg OK with that?"

"Yeah. He said to have them do a little scouting around while they're out there—keep their eyes open for lion tracks—or any signs of lion—like fresh kill."

"Hope they don't get lost."

"They been in the jungle before. They know how to use a compass."

In addition to the natural obstacle course defined by the massive root systems, general visibility was poor, in any case, as so little sunlight ever made it down to the forest floor. The random scribble of buttress roots made walking in a straight line an absolute impossibility, and any creature not adapted to such an ecosystem would be hard-pressed to be able to detect visual references that would allow them to navigate through such a world without becoming lost. Aziza's comment was well founded, as the two soldiers wandered off in a state of absolute ignorance as to their own severely limited awareness of orientation, for this was not like the forests they knew and their compass would offer little help.

The men wandered almost aimlessly for thirty minutes, but saw practically nothing. Several times they were able to catch a glimpse of something small and rodent-like that would quietly dart between roots or slip into a cluster of vines, but nothing that even came close to what might qualify as edible game. They knew there was life out there somewhere, for they could hear the faint echoing sounds of the myriad fauna that occupied the thick canopy, 150 feet above their heads.

"I think maybe we're wasting our time," said Kiho.

"You wanna go back?"

They had both stopped and were looking around as they talked.

"Hey," said Reth. He pointed to an area off to one side. "Light. May be an open space where the light's getting through." He looked at his companion and smiled. "Where there's light, there's new growth and where there's new growth, there's bush meat."

"Let's check it."

They unslung their weapons and started toward the soft glow of light that seemed to be leaking out from between a grouping of large trees.

"Up there," said Kiho, pointing upward. "Big branch probably broke off in a storm and opened up—like a window."

"It's bright, ha," Reth laughed. "We've been in this jungle so long we forget what the sun looks like." Placing his forearm across his eyes, he added. "Need my shades, man!"

"Shh!" Kiho put his finger up to his lips. "Listen—what's that?"

They both stopped. A feint scratching sound could be heard.

"Coming from over there," said Kiho, pointing toward the middle of an area that was highlighted by a series of long descending light rays.

What looked like an entire tree lay shattered into multiple pieces across an area half the length of a soccer field. It was, in fact, but one branch from a tree. It had opened up the forest ceiling just long enough for the light to allow several dozen new trees to take root and start their rapid race upward. A large bulging termite nest had engulfed the trunk of one of the trees about fifteen feet up from the ground and that appeared to be the source of the scratching.

Readying their weapons, the two soldiers fanned out around the tree, one in each direction. Looking up they could both see movement now coming from one side of the mold-covered nest. A dark shape which at first appeared to be a rounded growth coming off of the nest, made a short shuddering movement. It stopped, then repeated the action. As their eyes became accustomed to the light, both soldiers were able to see that some creature had attached itself to the termite nest. Its head was completely buried inside. A rounded back and tail were just barely discernible, the back undulating ever so slightly as the head stretched deeper into the nest.

"Bush meat!" shouted Kiho. It was a tree pangolin, what some describe as a walking pine cone with four feet—an odd little creature whose back is covered with protective plates, a bit like an armadillo, but with an overall shape more like that of an anteater. "We gonna eat you tonight, baby!" He raised his AK-47, took aim and let off a quick burst.

The nest blew apart with chunks of debris exploding out from it in every direction. Both men stood, patiently watching—waiting. Finally something seemed to slip loose from the greenish brown blob of growth that remained attached to the tree. It slipped slowly at first, then quickly for just an instant, before finally dropping to the ground with a light crash. Kiho ran into the dense new growth that shrouded the base of the tree, he slung his gun over his head, then bent down. When he came back up he raised his right arm up into the air, grasping the dead prehistoric-looking anteater by the end of its tail and turned to his partner. "Fresh meat tonight brother!" he said with a big grin.

"You think there's enough here to feed everyone?" Reth asked.

"It's gonna have to be. It was hard enough just finding this—and we need to get back." Kiho flung the dead pangolin up around the back of his neck, wearing it like a heavy scarf.

The two started walking back in the direction from which they had come, but then, as they left the sunlit area behind, they stopped.

"Is this right?" asked Kiho.

"Yeah, man. Remember—we saw the light to our right side, then walked toward it. So we walk away from the light, like we're doing, then we turn left." He looked back toward the light. "We need to go further this way—till we just barely see the light—then turn left."

"Right," said Kiho. "That big tree there. We came from behind that."

Fifteen minutes later they had left the window of light far behind them—and they were completely lost.

"Kiho, stop, man. This isn't the way. I don't recognize anything."

"Neither do I," said Kiho who was looking at his compass. "Shit, man—we went north when we left the camp. We went west to get around that one big tree root, then we went east cause we were still blocked to the north. Now we gotta go south again to get around this mess and I don't know where the fuck we're going. Everywhere I look, everything looks the same and this compass … I don't know."

"We gotta think about this, man. What the fuck do we do now, huh?"

"Let's listen, maybe we can hear them." Kiho sniffed a couple of times. "Don't smell the campfire."

"Look, maybe we send them a signal—shoot our guns."

"Good idea. You go first. A couple rounds—wait a minute—do it again. If we do a few like that, they won't just think we're shooting at something—make it sound like a signal."

Reth nodded, flipped the safety on his weapon, put it on single-shot mode, pointed it into the air and fired three evenly spaced shots.

"OK, good," said Kiho. "We wait a few minutes then do it again—keep going, though."

"Keep going, but which way?"

"We both agree this isn't right—so we go that way."

They veered off the course they had been taking, zigzagged between two walls of buttresses that projected out from two separate trees, then between two more, sometimes finding themselves completely boxed in, changed directions each time, wandered aimlessly, then stopped and discharged one of their weapons. Three more shots—but nothing.

Reth and Kiho continued on and considerable time began to pass. Kiho looked at his watch. "Shit! It's getting late. We been gone over two hours—three more hours and it's gonna be dark. They must know we're lost by now."

"What if we're just getting further and further away? Maybe we should just stop now and wait—keep shooting, but wait."

"Hold it," said Kiho. "Look at the ground here. It's worn away— this is a game trail. It could be the trail we took coming down here with the pygmy and the jungle girl."

"Yeah, you might be right, man."

"Let's see if we can follow it."

The two began to follow what they thought to be a trail. The sudden discovery had given them hope, and they now moved ahead with Reth in the lead, driven now by a newborn sense of enthusiasm.

Suddenly he came to a stop, Kiho almost running into him. "Something moved up there."

"Where?"

"Right there." He pointed straight ahead at a mass of vines that, at first looked like vines growing up or down the face of an enormous tree. There was no tree. The vines were simply suspended from above and stretched across their path like an enormous crocheted blanket. From one end to the other they might have measured thirty to forty feet across, and in the middle they were so dense they completely blocked any visibility to what lay beyond.

Reth checked his gun, then took a few steps forward, carefully. "I heard something in there—maybe more meat."

"Careful, man—go slow."

"Think it might be the *zabolo-yindo*?"

"Could be, man, but I don't believe in that shit. If it's a lion, I can kill it. I killed a leopard once and I can kill a lion." Reth took several more steps and Kiho followed close behind, then they both stopped again.

They scanned the mass of vines carefully—looking and listening. They could hear one another's breathing, but nothing else other than the constant dull hum of the jungle. Reth lowered his gun and turned toward his companion, wiped the sweat from his face with one arm, and said, "Maybe we should just unload a clip into this shithole." And in that instant, as he spoke—as he looked at his companion—the wall of vines erupted, and the silence was shattered with a devastating roar as a towering dark mass of terror came charging onto them. It came with such suddenness that neither man was able to register in his mind what it was. The fear that surged through Reth froze every bodily function in that instant—including his heart. Kiho turned and ran as fast as he could, tripping over a root, his head smashing into the hard ridge of one of the tree buttresses that confined the two men, like two domestic beasts in a narrow corral. The forest elephant that came charging through the vines toward the two men trampled them both before either was able to identify what it was that had delivered the blow that terminated their lives. It was a painless death for the two soldiers—one minute they were alive and breathing, the next they were not. The elephant's calf stood quietly watching, eyes wide and quivering—quivering from a fear its mother had transferred to it—a memory that had driven her here from the *bai* where so many of her kind had been mercilessly slaughtered not so long ago. The mother made a 180-degree turn with one foot on Kiho's head, grinding it flat into the muddy earth, along with the carcass of the pangolin, both pulverized now into an unrecognizable batter of human brain and bush meat.

29 – A BAITED TRAP

"Mo, wake up!" Zora stood over Mokonzi, the soldier who had run a thorn through his hand. Mo was lying on his back in one of the tents, his head sticking out through the flap that was tied open. He moaned, opened his eyes halfway then closed them again. Zora crouched down next to him and gave him a light tap on the cheek. "Mo, wake up. Where is everyone?"

"There's Aziza," said Carver who was standing behind her. "Aziza," he called out, waving.

Aziza looked toward them, nodded her head and started over.

"Zora said she thought she heard gunshots."

"We didn't hear anything, but two of Denis's boy scouts went out to shoot some fresh meat for dinner—maybe you heard them."

"Where's everyone else?" Zora asked as she stood up.

"We're in Oleg's tent—Viper, Oleg, and me, that is. The two that went hunting have been gone a long time, so Oleg sent Denis and the pygmy out to find them."

"Anybody been keeping an eye on Mo? He's not looking so good."

"He kept whining from the pain so Denis gave him something to knock him out."

"You said two of the soldiers went out—which ones?"

"Reth and Kiho."

"So where's Nabu?"

"He's around somewhere—supposed to be getting wood for the fire—maybe sleeping in his tent over there," she motioned toward two other tents that were pitched close together, but far from Mo's.

"Look who's back, boss." Viper had just come out of Oleg's tent and was looking at them, a twisted smile on his face. Oleg's head popped out, then the two of them walked over to join the others.

"We better watch out now," Viper was speaking in Russian. "Look at the *pédik*, boss, the faggot got himself a Kalashnikov—and he's gone stud on us—strutting around with no shirt. Maybe he finally got it up enough to stick to the bitch there."

Carver, with Hoyt's rope slung over his head and one shoulder and a duffel bag over the other, was still holding onto the AK-47. He noticed that Oleg and Viper were looking at it and assumed correctly that their exchange in Russian had to do with the weapon. He held it up, and smiling at Viper, said, "Found this in Hoyt's camp—guess I'm going to have to learn how to use it."

"Yes, my good friend." Viper reached out for the gun and continued, "Don't want you to hurt yourself. Maybe you should let me keep that for you, Carver, I can hang onto it for you and tomorrow you and I—we go out in the woods a little ways, and I'll teach you how to shoot."

"That's all right, Viper. I think I can manage it, although I appreciate the offer."

"But I thought you didn't need a gun. You got your *meuf* there to protect you." Viper looked at Zora with a lewd smile, then pursed his lips and mouthed a kiss toward her.

"Find anything interesting at the other camp?" Oleg asked.

"Got what looks like all of Hoyt's climbing gear, his iPad, and some notebooks—their satellite seems dead—damaged pretty bad, but got the battery—might come in handy as a backup for ours."

"What about the big cat?" Oleg asked, looking at Zora.

"It's cats, with an *s*, Oleg—at least two of them. You might want to remember that when and if you run into one."

"Oh, I'll be running into them all right and—the sooner the better. What about tracks though? Did you find anything that might give us an idea of where they went or where their lair might be?"

"Looked like they went northwest when they left Hoyt's camp.

May have passed a little to the north of here. Otherwise, nothing to add to what I already told you."

Mo moaned then, and Zora squatted back down next to him. "You awake, Mo?" He moaned again but didn't wake up.

Zora leaned into the tent and took Mo's hand, then looked back out to the others. "Carver, pull the other flap back so I can get some more light in here. I want to check his hand." Looking at Aziza, she asked, "Any of you been keeping an eye on him?"

Carver reached down and pulled the second tent flap aside, then squatted next to Zora.

"Not good," she said, then, standing again, "You people have some more antibiotics you can give him? It's getting infected—starting to put out a little pus."

"Denis'll give him something when he gets back," said Oleg.

"He gets gangrene out here, he's a dead man," Zora said.

Viper, speaking again in Russian, mumbled under his breath, "There she goes again, the *súka*'s talking like she's in charge. We'll tell Denis alright—give the dumb nigger another pain killer to shut him up maybe, but we don't waste antibiotics on that—he's a dead man."

Zora glared at Viper, this time holding her gaze on him. He looked back, and the two stood locked in a quiet stare-down. The tattoo-free side of his head appeared to become even whiter than it already was—a cadaverously cold, dry white. Aziza put her hand on his arm and gently urged him away from Zora.

Zora's eyes moved to Aziza, then to Oleg. She stepped away from them and nodded toward the other tents. "You got Mo's tent set up all alone here—while yours are all over there."

"He was making a lot of noise," said Oleg.

"And you like that, don't you?" She stared at them briefly, then continued, "You have all of your tents over there, backed up to those two big trees, each of them facing toward Mo from different angles— and Mo—he's isolated and wide open here—easy pickin' for some night-prowling predator." She gave them a light but sarcastic smile.

"You assholes planning on using this poor guy as bait?"

Oleg, Viper, and Aziza each took a step back from Zora, as a sudden tension ran through their bodies. Her question was a clear accusation.

Once again, Oleg diffused the situation. "*Ostýn'*," he said to Viper, speaking in Russian, "not now—we need to keep her alive for now, you understand?" Then, speaking in English, "That's completely unfair, Zora. It's untrue, and as much as I respect you, you're sounding a bit paranoid."

"You won't mind then if I move him over next to the campfire?"

"Be my guest—you can move him anywhere you want. It was Denis's guys set him up here anyway."

Zora squatted down and examined Mo again, then stood up and looked around. "How long since Ngiome and Denis went out?"

"Hour and a half," said Oleg, "Maybe two hours now."

"It's going to be dark soon and none of them are back yet. I'm going to go find them." She turned to Carver and said, "You stay here. I'm getting my headlamp. It'll be dark in half an hour. Maybe you can help me move Mo when I get back."

"Zora," he said, "you might want to take that gun we brought back."

"No, I'll be all right, but," she looked at all of them, "Get the fire going—bigger than it is now—and stay together. No one should stay alone when it gets dark, and that includes Mo."

She started toward her shelter, but stopped. Her body straightened, and she shifted her head slightly to one side, holding it, then, looking back to the others, "You hear that?"

"What?" asked Aziza.

"Listen."

Just barely audible over the unremitting buzz of the jungle, a new sound could be detected. It was distinguished by a repetitive series of panting grunts that seemed to accelerate, level off, then, fade.

"Chimpanzees," said Carver. "Damn—they must have followed us back here—we saw them earlier."

"*Kruto*," said Viper. "They sound far away. Where are they?" he asked, looking at Zora.

The sound started to build again, this time closer and overlaced with jabbering and short bursts of hysterical screams. The noise built up, then settled down again and finally leveled off into a low mix of grunts. Now the sound of movement through the trees could be heard as well.

"They're here," said Zora. "Someone's coming in from over there," she pointed beyond the tent area. "The chimps heard them and are going over to investigate."

Without a word, Oleg, Aziza, and Viper started off in the direction she pointed to. Carver started to follow, then stopped, looked at Zora, then back at Mo. "I'll stay with him."

30 – THE NEXT VICTIM

The doleful cry of some nocturnal bird slipped from out of the indigo void that defined the shafts of giant trees and resounded through the encampment of disparate souls, seven of whom remained of the ten who had been there less than a day before. One of those seven had not many hours left, as life was silently taking leave of his rotting shell. The narcotic pain reliever that had been administered to Mo in ever-increasing quantities had now worn off, and the suffering soldier had begun once again to moan like a lost and hungry cow. Much to the chagrin of at least three of those campers, his tent had been relocated closer in.

"I'm ready to shoot that useless *dúra*," Viper muttered in disgust.

"Not yet, my little *chuvák*, he can still serve a purpose."

Viper, Oleg, and Carver were seated around the campfire, their backs resting against two of the massive root bastions that served as a de facto fortification to the camp; Oleg and Viper on one side, Carver on the other. Carver was slowly feeding pieces of wood into the fire from one of several piles that lined the pit. His mind was elsewhere, thinking about what he had read in Hoyt's notes. The other two were speaking in Russian.

"Hah!" Viper chuckled to himself, "I keep thinking of that pig when we got the big tiger—damn, it was fucking cold—at least we had brandy. Here all we got is powdered energy shit we gotta mix with water and now all these fucking niggers have gone off and got themselves killed. Now we're gonna have to fetch our own water, and purify it ourselves."

"Yes, my Viper, life is a bitch, but now we have the opportunity to use human bait instead of a pig. We just have to put up with the moaning. If you think about it, the pig's squealing in that old armored car was considerably worse than that useless thing over there—besides, I thought the sound of a human in pain gave you a sort of pleasure."

"Just when it's a young virgin." Viper smiled and glanced at Carver as he prodded the coals with a stick, sparks scattering. "When do we get rid of this one and his whore? After we bag the lion, I would think, huh?"

"Correct," answered Oleg. "Right now we only have her and the pygmy who can track. We need to keep all options alive for the time being. I'm worried the pygmy might take off—especially after those two cretins got themselves crushed by an elephant. He and Denis both looked shook up when they came in last night. The girl's already tried to talk this guy into leaving." He nodded toward Carver. "They'd be gone now if he wasn't so delirious over these giant trees. We can't afford to get rid of either one—yet. You've got to try and control yourself around her. I know she irritates you. Just don't blow it."

Mo, who'd begun to quiet down, suddenly cried out. "Carver," Viper said, now speaking in English, "how about you and me drag Mo off a ways so no one can hear, and we slit his throat—put the dumb fucker out of his misery?"

Carver looked at Viper but said nothing.

"Just kidding, dude! I know you wouldn't do nothing like that—at least not with your little *détka* sleeping just over there."

"What's *détka* mean? I can guess, but you know, I wouldn't mind learning some Russian—especially if it might be useful."

"Baby," said Oleg. "Baby, like you would refer to your woman as opposed to a child. It's a term of endearment." He dragged out the word *endearment*, emphasizing it.

"*Détka*," Carver repeated. "Humph," he shrugged and went back to poking the fire.

Suddenly a bird chirped somewhere far above. They all looked up, then Oleg glanced at his watch. "Five a.m.—we've been on watch for two hours now. Viper, how'd you like to boil up some water so we can enjoy some of that gourmet coffee?"

"Good idea," said Carver, looking at Viper.

Viper shot a stern look at Carver, then glanced toward Oleg, stood, and slowly walked over to one of the empty soldiers' tents.

"He means well, Carver," said Oleg, "He's actually a really good guy once you get to know him—and loyal—I can trust him with almost anything, and ... you may not have sensed this, but, I feel he's really taking a liking to you."

"Yeah—I grew up hanging out with jocks who were a little like him. One or two would always have that negative macho way of trying to bond. But—Oleg, I often ask myself how you two—actually all three of you—how did you three end up together?"

"We've known each other a long time, especially those two. You know they were both orphans—they came out of the same orphanage."

"Really? But she's from New York—Brooklyn, I thought. And Viper—he's French or Russian or a combination maybe?"

By this time Viper had come back with the coffee and started boiling water.

"Viper," said Oleg, "I was telling Carver here about your early years with Aziza."

Viper looked up at Carver. "Yeah—Aziza and I were together in the orphanage—in Poland. I'm not Polish, but I was in this orphanage. The Russians set up orphanages in East Europe 'cause they didn't want to admit that orphans existed in Russia. Everyone there spoke Russian. Aziza wasn't Russian, but she was like my sister—we were together since maybe five or six years old. By the time we were thirteen, it was obvious no one would ever adopt us, when, bang—out of the blue, this Jew couple shows up from the States. They were told Aziza's mother had been a Jew. Next thing you know—they take her—just like that. One day she's there—next day she's gone. She was my sister—sister," he repeated as his voice droned off.

"So Viper runs away," said Oleg. "Made his way to Marseille—got picked up as an errand boy by the Mafia. Then, maybe ten years later, he and I crossed paths and next thing you know, he switched allegiances. I saw that he possessed a unique intelligence that those back-street thugs never understood—probably because he was smarter than most of them to begin with. Anyway, I saved him from a life of petty crime and—here we are."

"So how did he get back with Aziza?"

"I'd like to say it was Facebook," said Viper. "But it was before that bullshit was even invented. I tracked her down the old-fashioned way—with a little help from my old contacts in Marseille. A little cash into the right hands at the old orphanage got me the IDs for the old goats who adopted her—next thing you know, I showed up at her place in Brooklyn."

By now the early-morning sounds of life had begun to filter down from the canopy—day was on the verge of breaking but the light hadn't begun to filter through yet. Ngiome could be heard singing to the jungle somewhere not far off. A movement near the tents caught their attention, and Zora came crawling out of one of the small single-person tents. She had decided to move in closer to the other tents after Ngiome and Denis's return for security reasons. She looked toward the fire and waved her hand, but didn't come over.

"What's she doing?" Viper asked, addressing no one in particular.

"Looks like she's going to find the pygmy," said Oleg.

"Ah—is she shacking up with him now? You bein' left out in the cold there, Carver? The little jungle bunny gettin' your pussy, man?"

"It's not mine, Viper, you can be sure of that."

"Right—you two are just business. Bullshit—you can't tell me you're not getting some of that tight little pussy, man."

Viper's train of conversation was put on hold as Zora and Ngiome came over to the fire.

"It's starting to get light now. We're going out to look for signs of Nobu. Be back in an hour if we don't find anything by then."

"Where would you even start?" asked Carver.

"He had no reason to have gone anywhere unless he was collecting firewood or going to get water. After Ngiome and Denis came in last night, we found signs that he might have gone toward the stream. We'll start there." She put her headlamp on, said something to Ngiome and the two of them started off.

"Want to take that with you?" asked Carver, pointing to an AK-47 that was propped-up nearby.

"No, thanks though," and without a sound, the two of them quickly disappeared.

"Gives me the creeps the way she shifts around in the jungle like that," said Viper. "I really wonder where that dumb nigger disappeared to. If he did just go over to get water though, we would have heard something if the lion had jumped him."

"He had his weapon with him," added Oleg. "It's not in his tent, we know that much."

"Maybe he decided to go out and join his two buddies—help with the hunting," said Carver.

"Not likely," came Denis's voice from out of the dark.

They hadn't heard him approaching and jumped at the unexpected sound of his voice.

"More likely that he just deserted—ran off—trying to make his way back to the base camp."

"What are you doing up so early?" asked Viper. "Still dark as shit around here. I sure as hell wouldn't get out of my bag this early if I didn't have to."

"Couldn't sleep," Denis responded, "I had five soldiers I was responsible for just three days ago, and now I got only one and he don't look like he's gonna make it another day. The pygmies call this place the forbidden forest, and they warned us about the black devil that stays down here. I'm starting to believe their talk. This place is bad, man—it's bad." He squatted down next to Viper. "You got some of that coffee shit for me, man?"

"Here!" Carver tossed the bag of instant coffee.

Denis poured the coffee into a cup, added hot water, and took a sip. "Ahh, never thought I would actually want to drink this shit." He rolled back onto his buttocks, stretched his legs out, and leaned back against the tree buttress next to Viper and Oleg. "Three fucking guys gone in one day—four if you count Mo—he may not be dead yet—but he's sure as hell useless now."

"Oh, he'll be dead soon," said Viper.

"Amazing," added Carver, "the government requires us to come out here in the company of a military escort and here we are, we're all just fine and the entire escort is dead—except you, of course, Denis—and maybe Nobu."

"That's cause I'm not like them."

"Yeah," said Viper, "you're an officer, you have experience."

"I consider myself European. I was French Foreign Legion. I lived in France—Toulon. I speak proper French—not Brazza-French like those peasants."

"Where'd you learn English, Denis?" asked Carver, "Your English is pretty good."

"Thanks, man. I learned English when I was a kid. I worked at the docks in Pointe Noire. My father—he worked there—then, later, I worked on some of the oil rigs. Met lots of English—not Americans but, English—*les Anglais*. They played *fut* with us—you call it soccer. Anyway ..."

"Can I get in here?" Aziza was slowly moving toward them. "You *schmuckums* making all this noise over here, you not only scare the lion away, but you keep me from getting my beauty sleep."

"Welcome to the survivors' club," said Carver, "and please do have a seat. Here—you got the whole rest of this bench."

"Carver, you don't know what you're in for," she said as she sat down on the ground next to him and slapped him on the thigh as she settled back against the buttress. "Where's your girlfriend?"

Before Carver could answer, Zora and Ngiome reappeared.

"Any luck?" Oleg asked.

"Depends on what you consider luck," answered Zora. "We found these." She dropped Nabu's weapon on the ground then held out his iPod, dangling from its wire. "Good reason not to use one of these things when you're out in the jungle. With those little plugs you stick

205

in your ears, you can't hear what's sneaking up behind you."

"Was it the lion?" asked Aziza.

"Yes—it was the lion. We found tracks where it came right up behind him. He probably never heard a thing—looked like he was bent over filling his water bag—signs of some minor thrashing about, but not much—it just dragged him off."

"Did you try and follow the tracks?" asked Oleg.

"A bit. It dragged him maybe two hundred yards, stopped in the crux of tree buttresses where it appears to have devoured his midsection. It might have stayed there for a while then took off with his head and upper torso, leaving his legs behind. Not a pretty sight. We followed the tracks for about ten minutes, then decided to come back."

"Well, Denis," said Viper, "another confirmed kill for you. Now it's just you and Mo."

"Just Mo," said Aziza. "Remember, Denis is not really one of them—he's one of us."

"Well," said Oleg, "why don't you sit down and join us, Zora. And tell him he can join us." He pointed at Ngiome. "We're about to have some breakfast while we wait for a little more light. After that, maybe you two can take us down and put us on the track of this lion. If it has just eaten and is still carrying half of Nabu with him, we might be able to catch up to him—after all—we are here to go hunting now, aren't we?"

"You might be, Oleg but not Carver and me. I think Carver has his own agenda. He needs to finish up some of Hoyt's research, and I need to make sure he gets it done so the two of us can get out of here and back to where we belong."

"Where you belong?" asked Oleg. "Why, I just assumed that you of all people, belong right here. I would even go so far as to say, that you, Zora de Rycken, are as at home here as is that black devil of a lion." He waved the back of his hand outward. "Somewhere in that rotting wilderness—just waiting for," he looked around at his companions, "it's next victim."

Zora stood staring at each member of the group, then said,

"Do any of you give even the slightest damn that you've managed to lose three of your people in one day? And you're all just sitting around, sucking up that shit coffee and talking like you're discussing yesterday's soccer scores."

31 – PUGMARKS

"Here you go—check this out." Zora and Ngiome were crouched on the ground not far from the top of the bank of a narrow stream.

Oleg, Viper, and Carver quickly approached and stooped down opposite Zora.

"These are the pugmarks of your lion. Ever seen anything like this before, Oleg?"

"Wow! That is a big one!" he exclaimed. "I'm not sure I can really tell one species from another though—just know that big cat prints don't show the claws. They walk with their claws retracted. I do have a sense for size though—like this one is the size of a tiger I once tracked. I've seen several lion tracks—some might have been about this size."

"Well," said Zora, "Until our descent into this forest, I'd only seen jaguar and puma tracks—I actually saw a leopard after we left base camp, but he was up in a tree and I never noticed any pugmarks. Ngiome said he's only seen leopard prints, and he says that's what these look like, but these are way too big—then again, he's never seen a lion in his life—apparently never heard of a lion until you people came along.

"A mature male jaguar's print is about four inches long and maybe five inches wide; puma tracks are smaller and I assume that leopards are somewhere between the two. Like you said, Oleg, this thing is really big—bigger than anything I've tracked."

Zora stood and walked several paces closer to the stream's edge. "Now look at this one," she squatted down again and pointed to the left, "another just like it over there. You can see that the toes are splayed out here when compared to the other print. This is where it sprung from. Fifteen feet away is where it hit Nabu." She stood and walked downstream, but away from the edge. "The cat's prints coming in this direction show a zigzag gait. That would suggest that it was just on a casual morning walk. It seemed to have come on Nabu as he was on his way down to the stream. It sidetracked him, then stalked up behind. Didn't waste any time—the minute Nabu bent over, it pounced. You can see where it dragged its prey away here—problem from here on, the ground is covered with that moss, so no pugmarks to follow—just a few drops of blood and fragments of human flesh, which the worms and bugs are cleaning up as we speak." She raised her voice and stared at Oleg who was looking at his reflection in the stream, "This is the direction you're going to take if Ngiome agrees to track him for you."

"Huh? Oh, he'll be taking us," said Viper.

Zora gave Viper a sobering look, then continued, "Well, I've gone over every detail I can think of with him, including precautions he might want to take, just based on my own big cat experience. He seems to know leopards pretty well so I think, as long as you do what he says, your chances of coming back for dinner tonight shouldn't be too bad."

Oleg stepped back from the stream, took one more look at his reflection, then cleared his throat and said, "You mentioned earlier that you both tracked him a bit."

"Yes—you should be able to fast-track what we already covered in short time and get caught up to where we broke off. The cat was carrying what was left of its kill and was probably taking it somewhere to cache, so not a high chance of it doubling back to stalk you—at least not unless it thinks you're stalking him. Now, on the other hand, we know there's more than one."

"Any guess as to how far he might go before he caches his leftovers?" asked Oleg.

"Could be no more than a few hundred yards beyond where we gave up. I have no idea, but maybe not much further than that. It also might be that he's taken it back to share. It might be a female we're looking at. He might be a she and the other prints I found at Hoyt's camp could be offspring—some of those prints were smaller than these. Since lions live in extended families—prides—there could be a whole den full of them. Just take caution before you start shooting. If they are living in a den you might want to figure out where it is. I'm just suggesting you work up a game plan today and do your hunting tomorrow—carefully and with intelligence, but Oleg—I'm preaching to the choir, aren't I? We all know you're an old pro at this."

"I appreciate your advice, Zora—and you are right, I have done this before. I've shot four lions, but I must admit—none were in a jungle like this. OK," he said, looking at Viper, "let's go back, get our firepower, some water, and whatever else we need, and get going."

"Who's staying with Mo?" Zora asked.

"Aziza," said Viper. "We need Denis with us. He's the only one who can talk to the pygmy."

"She won't be happy about that," said Viper.

"She'll be just fine," said Oleg. Then, nodding toward Zora and Carver he added, "Tell Aziza they'll be close by. She can arrange a signal in case she has a problem."

"Her only problem will be Mo," said Viper. "Maybe she can just put him out of his misery while we're gone—that would be nice.

32 – THEY'RE ALL DEAD

"What's that smell?" Carver asked.

"They're cooking meat," said Zora. "Denis must have shot something—hard to tell what but, definitely meat."

"Let's hope they'll be willing to share. I'm starving."

"Me too," she said as she looked up into the trees.

"Still looking for the chimps?"

"Yeah, I'm just wondering where they went—I half expected to see them again, especially after they followed us back from Hoyt's camp yesterday. Probably way up there, foraging."

They could see smoke from the fire filtering through the trees when they heard a bird sound from off to their right. It was a soft melancholic whistle that had an echoing effect toward the end. They both stopped, and Carver remarked, "That's the first bird I've heard that close since we left the rim."

"Sounded like some kind of a thrush, but it's not a bird," said Zora. "Look," she motioned in the direction of the sound with her chin. Ngiome stood, not far off, smiling at them.

"Zora," he called out as he held up his small net. It contained several fan shaped brownish mushrooms.

"Ganoderma," said Carver as Ngiome approached.

"What's that?" asked Zora.

"Looks like what some people call a shelf mushroom. They grow on trees. May I?" he asked Ngiome.

Ngiome understood his gesture and held up the net.

Carver took one and peeling back an outer layer, commented,

"Double-walled, truncated spores. Look at the brown and yellowish inner layers. Definitely some form of Ganoderma."

"So you know your mushrooms. You impress me, Carver."

"Always had a fascination for fungi," he said. "Took a few mycology courses back in my college days." He handed the net back to Ngiome.

"More *bilo* vines?" Ngiome asked, looking at the climbing rope that both Carver and Zora were carrying.

"Yes, *bilo* vines. Carver will use these tomorrow to climb trees."

Ngiome gave her a questioning look. "Why does Carver not just climb trees—vines are already there?"

"Good question. I'll ask him."

"He wants to know why you need all these ropes to climb trees," she translated to Carver.

"Tell him I'm much bigger than he is—too heavy to climb the way I imagine he does."

She translated back to Ngiome, he responded, they exchanged words back and forth then she translated back to Carver. "I asked what they found today. He said no lion but they found the rest of Nebu's corpse. I'm not sure I understood him fully but I think he purposely misled them while tracking the lion. He's scared."

"I can tell," said Carver. "I could see his expression change as he was talking."

"You climb your tree tomorrow, Carver, then we get the hell out of here … and we're taking him with us. Are you with me on that?"

"Yes. Yes, of course," said Carver as he shifted his shoulder and adjusted the ropes. "Look, let's get back to camp, OK? I want to unload this and get ready for tomorrow." He looked at Ngiome, the two traded smiles then he added, "While you think up how you're going to get him away from those people."

"We're taking Carver's vines to the camp, Ngiome," said Zora. "After, you can take me to find more mushrooms. We'll talk about tomorrow while we hunt mushrooms." Ngiome nodded and the three proceeded on toward the scent of cooking game.

"Ah, the *shagetz* and his *meschugena* are back," mumbled Aziza under her breath, but loud enough to be heard by Zora and Carver. She was sitting on the ground with her back resting against a tree buttress, watching Viper who was squatting on his heels next to the fire, roasting a large bird on a makeshift spit. Oleg sat on the ground nearby, cleaning his hunting rifle.

"I see your friends came back to relieve you, Aziza," said Zora. "You should be in a better mood now."

"Yeah, they're back. Good news is they haven't shot the lion yet. Means I get to be in on it."

"How's Mo doing?"

"He decided he'd had enough—not long after you left. I had to hang around here half the day talking to a dead man."

"Yes," added Oleg. "Apparently the poor fellow expired while we were out tracking the lion. Quite tragic, really—and just from one little thorn."

"Where is he?" asked Carver, looking into Mo's tent.

"Denis and Viper dragged him off somewhere."

"We took him down past the stream where Nebu bought it," said Viper, "but further downstream so the stink don't get us when we go for water."

Carver sent a worrisome glance toward Zora and said, "I didn't think he was that far gone."

"Oh, he went fast," said Aziza. "Quiet for a while and finally I went over and looked in on him—dead as a log." Then, pointing at Viper's spit she added, changing the subject, "See what we got cooking?"

"Some kind of guinea fowl," said Viper. "The pygmy nailed it for us," he gave Ngiome a thumbs-up sign, "Pretty handy little guy, huh. We were on our way back here when he held up his hand for us to stop. We stopped—he darts off, disappears into nowhere, we hear a gobbling noise—a squawk—then back he comes holding up that little spear of his and he's got this bird stuck on the end of it."

"That's great, Viper," said Zora. She turned away from him and looking at Carver, said, "I'm dumping your rope here—Ngiome and

213

I are going to collect mushrooms. Maybe you should come with us."

"They're all dead," said Carver. His voice level began to drop as he continued. "All those poor soldiers are dead. I'm too tired to go anywhere." He took a deep breath, and then, raising his voice, said, "I think I'm going to stay here—in my tent. Want to look over the notes we found. See what else he wrote about that tree. You and Ngiome go. Just don't take too long."

"Right," interjected Aziza, "you two disappear on us, we're fucked." She looked over to Carver and asked, "Think any of us can find our way back alone, Carver?"

"All we gotta do is backtrack up to edge of this place with a little help from my compass," said Viper. "Once we get out of this hole our SAT radio should start working again—just a matter of using the GPS and working our way back to base camp again. Easier than shit."

"Yeah, real easy," said Carver. "Just like those two who got crushed by the elephant. Denis was sure they'd gotten lost and they had a compass."

"Huh," grunted Viper, "They were just dumb shits."

Carver threw him a stern glance, started toward his tent then realized that Zora and Ngiome had gone to Mo's empty tent. He changed his course and joined her as she squatted down and looked inside. "They killed him, didn't they?" he whispered.

"I think so," she answered. "Can't tell for sure though. They could have suffocated him. He was weak enough, there wouldn't have been a struggle." She stood up and continued in a normal tone, "Sure you don't want to come with us now? You can arrange your gear after dark."

"No, no, I really want to look at those notes." He glanced back toward the three at the campfire and added, lowering his voice again, "I'll be OK. They're focused on their lion right now, but you're right. We need to put some distance between them and us as soon as we can." Then Carver reached out and gently gripped Zora's arm. "I'm really sorry I dragged you down into this mess."

"It's too late to be sorry, Carver," she said. "It's time to decide how and when we get out of here, but you stay here for now. You'll be

OK. I want to get Ngiome away from them so I can talk to him." She turned to Ngiome, touched his net and pointed into the forest beyond the camp. "We're going after more mushrooms," she announced. "Be back before it gets dark."

Zora and Ngiome had walked no more than a few paces when she stopped, abruptly, and turned back to the others. "Where's Denis?"

"Went to get more meat," said Viper. "This thing's not gonna go far." With both hands gripping the spit he lifted the cooking bird up and held it out toward Zora, then returned it to the fire.

"We saw several of those small antelope," added Oleg, "the ones they call duikers—not far back. He'll be alright."

"Hope you're right," said Zora. "We have about two hours before it gets dark and there is more than just one lion out there." She turned her back on them and continued after Ngiome who had just disappeared from view.

33 – MOKOMBOSA

"Here," said Ngiome, "Good—Zora try."

Zora carefully pulled one of the brown mushrooms from the thick green coat of moss that covered the base of the tree and everything else around it—the ground, the vines, the giant buttress roots; everything up to some point well above their heads. Only the scattered clusters of round, brown mushroom heads broke the monotony of the ubiquitous sea of damp emerald greenness, popping through like large tumorous moles. She lifted it to her mouth and without hesitating, took a bite. She chewed, swallowed, then smiling at Ngiome, nodded her head in approval.

Working together, they began filling his net. Ngiome concentrated on those mushrooms close to the ground while Zora gathered those that grew higher up. They cleaned up the base of one tree then moved onto the next. Within half an hour the net was full so Ngiome took off his hat and started to fill it as well.

"Delicious," she said in English, then repeated it in Ngiome's language. "If they haven't already eaten all of the guinea fowl, this might be good cooked with it. We can add in some couscous and we'll eat well tonight. Do you ever cook mushrooms with meat, Ngiome?"

"No, we never cook mushrooms."

"Then tonight maybe you can have your first stew—mushroom-guinea fowl stew."

Ngiome took the net and slung it over his head and shoulder, then balanced his short spear on his shoulder. Zora carried his hat and as they began walking he looked at Zora with a smile and said, "coooscoos is a very funny name—funny food."

"You said you liked it."

"Yes—I like very much, coos-coos. It looks like tiny grubs but tastes different. Zora can show me where it grows someday."

"I would love to," she answered.

Then Ngiome stopped and, cocking his head to one side, asked, "Hear that?"

"Yes."

They both stood still, listening, and then the sound came again—the staccato hooting of a chimpanzee, echoing its way through the winding tree-formed alleys. "*Mokombosas*," said Ngiome, using the Lingala word for chimpanzee rather than his own expression which would have translated into "hairy forest people."

"Yes," said Zora. "Let's go see them. They might be the same ones that followed Carver and me from the other campsite."

"Ha," chuckled Ngiome. "While we go see the *mokombosas*, your friend and the white *bilos* will eat all the guinea fowl before we get back."

"That's all right. We'll have the mushrooms."

"*Bisi ndima* always share food. The white *bilos* are just like the *bisi mboka*—they don't share anything. If the guinea fowl is all gone, we'll find some nice big grubs."

"Grubs huh? That would be a first time for me."

As they drew near to the chimpanzees, Ngiome stopped. He set his net between his feet, placed both hands next to his mouth, and let out his own version of a chimpanzee hoot. The chimpanzees immediately stopped their chattering. Ngiome repeated the sound and was answered by one long drawn out grunting noise followed by the sound of movement through the trees. Within seconds the silhouettes of several chimps appeared along the lower branches above.

Ngiome laughed, then let out one of his yodeling calls—like the calls he made each morning when singing to the forest. The chimpanzees recommenced their hooting; looking down, then back in the direction from which they had just come. Some began patting themselves while others were pointing down toward the two humans, their mouths opened wide, exposing their teeth—a form of smile.

"I count eight of them," said Zora as she flashed her fingers to signify the number to Ngiome. "Same group. I recognize the big male there—and look—ha!" she laughed. "He still has Carver's shirt!"

The alpha male grabbed onto a vine and began to descend. Arriving at the offshoot of a buttress, he released the vine and walked upright along the top of the elongated fin-shaped root, his arms held upward and bent at the elbows and stretching Carvers shirt out over his head, swinging it back and forth as he walked. He reached a point just above Zora's head and about ten feet out in front of the two humans and there, he stopped, wrapped the shirt around his neck, bent over and placed his two hands on the buttress so that he stood on all fours with his body facing them sideways, his head turned directly toward them. Slowly, the others worked their way down until all eight stood or sat along the buttress; curious observers, looking down at Zora and Ngiome.

"Here—let me have the mushrooms—I'll offer them one."

Zora set Ngiome's hat on the ground and selected two large mushrooms. She held them up to the chimps, then took a bite out of one, and started chewing it. Two smaller chimps showed their teeth again and several of them let out little grunts. Zora held out the remaining mushroom again as she finished off the first.

The alpha male suddenly jumped off the buttress. Landing directly in front of them, he reached out, took the mushroom from Zora and took a bite. He turned and grunted back to his group, and then a medium-sized chimp, a female, dropped down next to him. She opened one of her hands and held it out to the male, presenting some kind of fruit. The male took it from her and held it out to Zora.

"Fig," she said as she took it. She bit away half of it, then handed the rest to Ngiome who stuck it straight in his mouth and began chewing, a big smile on his face.

A young male then joined the alpha and the female. It stepped out toward Ngiome and opened its hand up to reveal something he had been carrying. Ngiome laughed and looked over to Zora. "Look, Zora. *Mokombosa* collect mushrooms too!" Indeed, the chimpanzee had been collecting mushrooms.

The male then took a step toward Ngiome and pointed at the hunting net. Ngiome opened the net and took out another mushroom, offering it to the chimp, but the chimp ignored the mushroom and pointed at the net again.

"The net!" said Zora excitedly, "he's interested in the net, not the mushrooms." She looked at Ngiome and went on, "Go ahead and give it to him. Let's see what he does with it."

Ngiome dumped a small pile of mushrooms onto the ground then handed the net to the chimp. The big male took it in both hands, began to pull at the webbing, then turned it upside down and scattered the remaining contents on the ground. He shook the net gently, then with both hands stretched it across his face, which he pressed into it while he made small probing movements with his tongue. He stood up straight, then arched his back and held the net out toward the rest of his group. He was quite large and standing just in front of Ngiome, it became evident that the chimpanzee was taller than the human. He placed the net on top of his head and opened his mouth wide to let out a stuttering laugh, then turned his head from side to side, looking around at the other chimps. The female next to him reached up and took the net from his head and started examining it herself then she sat on the ground and started placing the mushrooms back into the net.

Zora stooped down and helped her as the entire group began to chatter, each of them starting with slow hooting sounds, then building up into faster rhythms. Zora lowered herself into a squatting position and as she did, the female reached out and patted her on the head. Zora responded with a stroke along the chimp's arm and the hooting from the rest of the troop continued to build—the faster they went, the louder they became. Zora and Ngiome were both laughing.

It was in that instant, when the cacophony seemed to have reached its pinnacle, that Denis's gun cracked out like a bolt of thunder whose lightning shot out with a malignancy that in that single instant shattered the heart of one two-year-old chimpanzee and ended the communal innocence of seven hominid creatures whose only mistake had been an acquitted curiosity.

Complete silence hung over this innocent encounter of not so different species. Facing each other, they stood frozen, as time ceased to move for one final beat of their communal heart. Then, the stillness broke as the lifeless body of that child—that embodiment of primeval innocence—collided with the ground at the feet of the bewildered four who stood, mouths agape. And then, all hell broke loose.

The collective scream that ensued split the air—an equipoising echo to the gun's rude invasion into their moment of poignant subliminal peace and joy. The seven remaining chimpanzees and their two human companions stood riveted in horror and disbelief, unable to move. Then the five that had remained perched along the giant buttress root scattered, each flying over Zora and Ngiome's heads like large dark birds. The female dropped the net and bent over the dead yearling while the alpha male screamed and jumped back and forth, touching the lifeless chimp. Ngiome crouched next to the female who looked up, fear in her eyes as she began to let out a long, drawn out moan.

Zora stood still, stunned, unable to move at first, unable to accept what she was witnessing, then she screamed, "Nooo!" as she saw him—Denis—rushing toward them from the other side of the buttress, gun in hand. As he hurdled over the lower end of the root, he looked up and, seeing Zora, stopped.

"You!" he shouted out, "What the—what the hell you doing here?"

The expression of distress and disbelief On Zora's face, the horror and disbelief became rage, and she flew at him. Speechless, he realized she was coming at him. He tried to raise his gun, but her hands were already on it and in one motion, she twirled around like an ice skater in a spin, and swung the barrel back into Denis's face, splitting his nose open. Blood gushed out as he staggered backward, tripped over a root and landed on his back. He thrashed about briefly, disoriented.

Zora stood over him holding his gun and screamed at him, "You stupid fucking motherfucker!" She took the gun and smashed it as hard as she could against the top of the buttress root. "Murderer!" She smashed the gun down again and then again. At first the magazine snapped away and then with the next blow, the entire weapon broke into two pieces. She flung the part that remained in her hand off, high into the air where it bounced off the trunk of a tree.

By this time Denis had managed to get back onto his feet. He staggered back a step, then reached down to his belt and pulled out a large knife. His eyes had narrowed into dark slits—blood smeared his face, his teeth were clenched tight and he snarled like an animal, "I'll kill you!" He started toward her but lost his balance. He climbed back over the buttress root and staggered, reeling back and forth, toward Zora. "The crazy Russian said he was going to get you, but now—I am the one who is going to cut you to pieces you fucking bi—"

Before Denis could get the next word out of his mouth, the alpha chimp dropped down behind him—and as he came down, he swung a large branch, like a club, from high over his own head and brought it down directly on top of Denis's skull, which cracked open like a large egg. His eyes wide open and white as his pupils rolled upward, Denis dropped to his knees. His mouth gaped open, but not a sound came out.

The chimpanzee lifted the branch again, screamed, and brought it down, cleaving what was left of Denis's head into two pieces, the branch now sticking out where his nose once had been.

Zora stepped back, staring, dazed, as the alpha brought his club down for the third time. Another chimp arrived carrying the barrel of Denis's Swiss SIG 550 and the two pounded Denis's body flat onto the ground where it quickly transformed into a mass of unrecognizable, fragmented organic matter that seemed to disappear as if it were being soaked into the sponginess of the moss-covered ground.

Zora became aware of something squeezing her hand. Looking down, her gaze was met by Ngiome's face staring up at her. "Come," he said, "we go."

She took a step back from the nightmare that continued to play out before them. Several more chimps had joined the fray, jumping

221

up and down, dancing back and forth, grunting hysterically and throwing objects—sticks, clumps of turf—at what once had been Denis Mikonga, former French Foreign Legionnaire, corrupt officer in the armed forces of the People's Republic of the Congo, and bush-meat hunter. A line of ants had already formed, as the forest began the process of reallocating the now inanimate corpse.

Still holding onto her hand, Ngiome pulled again, and the two carefully withdrew. They backed under a curtain of dangling vines, hopped onto a winding buttress root, climbed upward toward the tree's trunk, and jumped off onto another root which stretched down in the opposite direction—travelling quickly along the network of roots as if on an elevated highway.

When they finally stopped, the scene of the slaughter was well out of sight, but they could still hear the frenzied chimpanzees. Ngiome pointed up toward the lower canopy and they could see more chimpanzees moving through the trees, heading toward the uproar. "Big family," he said. "*Mokombosa* like *bisi ndima*—big family, but hunt in small group."

They continued to walk, now on the ground. It was growing dark and they could hear distant thuds of thunder far above, muted by the dense layers of canopy. "I don't have my headlamp with me—can you find your way back to the camp in the dark, Ngiome?"

"Yes," he replied, "but difficult in this forest—need to watch out for snakes, leopard—and the black devil."

"Maybe we stay here," she said. She looked upward. "We can climb a tree and sleep up high. Cover ourselves with big leaves like you use to make your huts.

"I can't deal with those other assholes right now anyway," she said, speaking in English and under her breath.

34 – THE TREE HOUSE

The night air arrived with a chill but that was not what caused Zora to shiver.

"Denis was a bad *bilo*," said Ngiome.

"I still see Denis inside my head," she responded. "The *Mokombosas* came to Ngiome and Zora like friends."

"Denis is dead because he come into the forbidden place."

Zora reached over, gripped Ngiome's arm, and looking into his eyes, said, "Ngiome, Zora will leave this place. Carver will climb a very large tree tomorrow and after he has found what he is looking for, he and I will leave. You will come with us, do you understand? We will leave very early the day after tomorrow, and we will take you with us."

They were about seventy-five feet above the ground, nestled into the crotch of a large tree where one massive branch took off from the main trunk at an almost perfect right angle. Vines, which continued upward on each side of the branch, were thick enough on one side to form a screened wall. They had woven several liana leaves between the vines to completely block off that side, then managed to attach several more overhead to create a roof. Once their shelter had been secured, Zora had cut through one of the vines to see if it contained water in its tubular interior. It didn't, so Ngiome set a plate-sized leaf out in the open just beyond their feet to collect rainwater.

A light groaning sound rose up from Zora's stomach. "Now I'm hungry," she said. "We left the mushrooms with the *mokombosas*—and your hunting net."

"Ngiome still has mushrooms," he said. He took off his hat and inside there remained half a dozen.

"Ah, you are so smart, my friend," she said as she selected one and popped it into her mouth.

"I think the *bisi ndima-yindo* wondered how the net was made," he said as the two of them quickly emptied the hat.

"Yes, I think so."

Zora's ability to understand Ngiome's language had been improving dramatically on a daily basis. Both of them continued to mix Lingala with Ngiome's BaKaya. Neither of them was even close to fluency in Lingala, but it was a workable common ground. Still in shock from their disastrous encounter with the chimpanzees, they just sat, side by side in silence, listening to the rain, occasionally exchanging a random thought.

Zora took a deep breath, which came back out as a long quivering sigh. Ngiome looked at her and said, "*Mokombosa* is the name *bilo* people, like Denis use. My people call them *bisi ndima-yindo*." He repeated, "*Bisi ndima*," and thumped himself on the forehead, then he said, "*yindo*" and pulled at the small tuft of hair on his chest, then rubbed his hands across his shoulders and upper torso.

"*Bisi ndima-yindo*," said Zora. She nodded and smiled as she thought to herself, *hairy forest people*.

They remained quiet again for several minutes until Ngiome spoke again. "*Bilo* use fire machetes to kill everything. They killed elephant the first time they came. They killed buffalo, then they killed *bisi ndima*, and now they kill *bisi ndima-yindo*."

"Ngiome," said Zora. "You say that the *bilo* killed *bisi ndima* (your people)?"

"Yes."

"Which *bilo*? Denis and his soldiers, or the white *bilo*?"

"The white *bilo*. The *Bilo* with long hair on his chin and snake drawings on his face."

"Viper?"

"Yes, Viper." Ngiome pronounced his name perfectly.

"Tell me what happened?"

"When the white *bilo* first came—with black *bilo*—they asked Ngiome to take them to the place which is forbidden. They said they searche for the black devil. When Ngiome told them no one can go to the forbidden place—no *bilo*, no *bisi ndima*—soldiers took my people and bound them with long *bilo* vines—vines like Carver wants to climb trees with. They told Ngiome that if no one takes them to find the black devil, they would kill people with their fire machete—then when no one talked to them, the white *bilo*—Viper—he took a fire machete and killed Pico—Ngiome's nephew. He killed him in front of everyone. Then the big white *bilo* and Denis talked and the soldiers put my people in the flying pirogue. Denis told me they would go to the *bilo* village in the flying pirogue and if Ngiome helped catch the black devil, they would bring my people back."

"The one who calls himself Oleg told me they took your people to the village because the *bisi ndima* wanted to go to the village and they did this to please you so that you would help them. Now Ngiome tells a different story. Now that I know the tall white *bilo* and Viper—and the white *bilo* woman, Ngiome's story makes much sense to Zora."

"The *Bilo* say things that are not true. Ngiome does not understand."

"There is a word in my language for people who do not tell the truth. The word is *liar*. If I say he lies, it means that he does not tell the truth. What is your people's word for people who do not tell the truth?"

"No word. Ngiome never met a person who did not talk the truth."

"Ngiome," she placed her hand on his forearm, "you do not have to do what the white *bilo* has told you to do. Zora will help get your people back—and Zora will make sure that the white *bilo* does not hurt any more of your people with fire machetes."

"My people are gone. The *bilo* took them to a big village very far away, not to the village where the *bisi ndima* go to trade with the *bilo*. When the *bisi ndima* go to the big village, they do not come back."

"No Ngiome, I will take the flying pirogue that I came in and go to big village and bring your people back."

225

"Ngiome is scared for Zora. The Viper-*bilo* wants to kill Zora like he killed Pico."

"You are right to be scared, Ngiome. The white *bilo* is very bad and Viper-*bilo* is the worst of all, but now it is the white *bilo* who will be scared. Denis and all the soldiers are dead now. Only you, Carver, and I are left. Oleg, the woman *bilo*, and Viper need us to find the black devil and then to lead them away from the forbidden place—back to *bai*."

"They cannot leave," said Ngiome. "All who come here never go back—never leave. The white *bilo* cannot leave."

"That would probably be a good thing, but we must leave and we must take Carver back with us."

"No, Zora does not understand—no person—no white *bilo*, no Carver *bilo*, no Zora, no Ngiome—we will never leave—we cannot leave."

"Why do you say we cannot leave?"

"It is told in the stories of our people." He closed his eyes and continued. "The grandfather of Ngiome carried stories for our people. The grandfather also carried the *molimo*."

"*Molimo*—the long shaft of wood you sang into?"

"Yes, when my father was gone, my grandfather told me I was to carry the stories after he was gone."

"And the *molimo*, is that part of the storytelling?"

"The *molimo* is for singing to the forest. All of our people sing to the forest—every day. The *molimo* allows us to reach deep into the forest. We sing to the forest and the forest sings back to us and we are all one. We are the forest—the forest is the *bisi ndima*."

"But the forbidden place—what is the story of the forbidden place?"

"Long ago—before the *bisi ndima* existed and before the forest existed—there was nothing. Just mud. *Ndura*—the world—was dark. There was no light—only brown mud. Then, one day, there was a loud noise. Louder than any noise that has ever come since or ever will come. The ground broke apart, a big hole appeared and fire came out of the hole. The fire became the first lightning and the great noise became the first thunder and together they caused the sky to drop the first rain. The rain put out the fire that was coming out of the hole and it filled with water, and out of the water came the forest, and from the sky came the light, and the forest spread out to cover all the land and the mud turned green and the *bisi ndima* who are part of the forest were there and so were all of the *nyama*."

"This place where we are now—this forbidden place—is this where the big hole appeared?"

"Yes, it was here. This was the first forest. All the *bisi ndima* and the *nyama* lived here together. The *bisi ndima* would hunt some of the *nyama* and some of the *nyama* would hunt others and sometimes *nkoi*, the leopard, the greatest of hunters—he would hunt the *bisi ndima*. But we only hunted when we needed to eat and no one ever took more than was needed and the *nyama* always did the same and when we did hunt, we always shared what we caught or what we found. When we found honey, mushrooms, yams, we always shared, until one day when one man killed an elephant. It was big enough to feed all the *bisi ndima* who lived at that time—but he hid the elephant and kept it for himself and his family and he did not share it. When the others found out, instead of telling him he had to leave and live alone outside the forest like we do today, the others started doing the same thing. Soon the forest would no longer listen when the *bisi ndima* tried to sing to it and then the forest stopped singing to the *bisi ndima* and the *bisi ndima* could not find food when they needed it and then the water in the river where they bathed became hot and burned them and they became sick and started to die and finally the light stopped coming and it became night in the middle of the day and while it was dark the forest spoke out and told the *bisi ndima* that they had to leave, they were no longer welcome in the forest. The *bisi ndima* were frightened and they fled. They climbed up the steep slopes that led to the outside world and they fled and when they stood at the top they cried and called back into the forest and asked to be forgiven and begged the forest to allow them to return but the forest refused. They stayed there and sang for many days and each day the forest refused them. Finally they sang one more time and this time the forest answered and told them that if they could go back to living the way they had lived at the beginning, they would be allowed to take some of the forest and some of the *nyama* with them but they would have to live beyond the edge of the first forest and any who tried to return would be destroyed completely as if they had never existed. They would be turned into black nothingness. The *bisi ndima* left. Each family went in different ways. It was decided that my family would stay close to the first forest and would become the guardians. It has always been our family that has kept the story and it has always been our responsibility to make sure that no one—not *bisi ndima*, not *bilo*—ever go back into the first forest, for it is forbidden."

"What about the *bilo*, Ngiome? Did they also come out of this first forest?"

"No, the *bilo* grew out of the mud that lay beyond the forest. They are not *bisi ndima*. They do not understand the forest—they fear the forest, they harm it—they want to destroy it"

"But you don't fear the forest do you?"

"To fear the forest would be to fear myself. How could I fear the forest? The trees are my own arms, the ground my own feet, the water—my tears and my sweat."

"So now that we are in this first forest, the forbidden place that is partially submerged into the earth from which it came, have you no fear of this forest either?"

"No, this forest is where my family first came from, but we have been banished, and to return is to no longer exist. If I were to die back in the forest where my family now lives, I would die, but I would not stop existing. Because I am part of the forest, I will always exist as long as the forest exists. By coming here, Ngiome will no longer exist."

"But you came here."

"Ngiome brought the white *bilo* here. They are the enemies of the forest. If Ngiome brought them here and they turn into blackness and no longer exist, Ngiome will not mind so much if Ngiome no longer exists as well, for Ngiome has taken them out of the forest and the forest will be happier. If Ngiome's family cannot return, some other family of *bisi ndima* will still be there, somewhere and part of the forest."

"Ngiome, have you asked yourself why I came here? I am not a white *bilo*. I am not a black *bilo* but, I am some kind of *bilo* and I came here with the white *bilo*, Carver. I am not happy that Carver came here but maybe Carver is not such a bad person."

Ngiome laughed.

"Why do you laugh?"

"Zora is not a *bilo*. You just said you were some kind of *bilo*. You are *bisi ndima*." He laughed again. "You are just very funny-looking!"

Zora laughed and then they both laughed together. Finally she stopped and looking at him, said, "Listen, Ngiome—tomorrow you take the white *bilo* to look for the black devil. If you find tracks of the black devil, you take them the wrong way—do not let them find black devil. While you take them to hunt the black devil, I will take Carver to climb one of the big trees. Tomorrow night when we all return we will wait until the white *bilo* sleep. When they sleep, Ngiome, Carver and Zora will leave. We will leave the forbidden place and the white *bilo*. They can hunt black devil by themselves—without Ngiome. You understand?"

"Yes," he answered. "And I will sing to the forest tomorrow—and maybe the forest can make the white *bilo* disappear and maybe the forest will allow us to leave."

35 – EARLY MORNING RISE

"Trouble sleeping?" asked Viper as Carver appeared, shuffling like a somnambulant through the early-morning mist, his headlamp sweeping slowly back and forth across the ground. The rain had stopped earlier, but now the air was heavy with moisture that floated above the ground in the form of a dense cloud. Visibility at this early pre-dawn hour was practically nonexistent.

"You too?" he mumbled as he flipped off his lamp and sat down in front of the fire that Viper was stoking.

"Huh? This is fucked-up, man—where the fuck are they? I mean, the only three people who can get us the fuck out of here—I mean, everyone's getting knocked off. The soldiers I don't give a fuck about, but—this is fucked—even the midget—where is that little fuck? The bitch get killed and he run off, you think?"

"Common, Viper—you don't need to dis her like that—just 'cause she gave you shit for shooting your gun off at that little snake."

"You kidding me? She's your bitch man—I notice how you look at her. How come you're not knocking the bottom out of her every night? Here—" Viper poured some of the stale coffee he'd been reheating into a cup and held it up to Carver, "have some—tastes like total shit, but I'm actually getting used to it. Can you believe that?"

"Thanks," said Carver, "I appreciate your generosity—especially this early." He looked at his watch. "Five a.m.—another hour before it even gets light enough to see your dick when you take a piss. Oh—almost forgot," he put his cup down and stood up again, "that's what I came out here for—got sidetracked when I saw the fire going." He flipped his headlamp back on and faded into the dark, his gait a little smoother now.

Viper took a sip of his coffee and followed with an acidic belch. "Fucking coffee," he muttered.

"Ahhh!" Carver screamed suddenly, "Shit—oh—fucking shit!" his panic-ridden voice sounding louder as he came stumbling back into view.

"*Merde!*" exclaimed Viper as he jumped up, dropping his cup. "Now what—trying to scare the shit out of me?"

"What's going on?" Aziza's voice croaked out from the darkness of her tent.

"Who was that?" asked Oleg as he appeared, pistol in hand.

Carver, his fly down, tripped over a low root and plunged back into view, landing on his chest, arms and legs spread-eagled.

"It's Carver," said Viper, "must have caught his dick in his zipper."

Carver raised himself up onto his hands and knees. He was shaking. "Oh Jesus," he said in a broken voice and looking at Viper. "You of all people don't want to know."

Oleg reached down and helped him back up onto his feet. "What was it?"

"Snake," Carver was still shaking. He groped his way toward the campfire, reached out to the buttress to catch his balance, and then lowered himself onto the ground, hugging both arms around his knees as he leaned in close to the fire. "Huge—it's huge! I was standing right next to it! I started to piss and—oh shit—I must have pissed right on it—it suddenly just lifted its head up—high as me! Two round shiny eyes—red eyes! Looked me right in the face!" He pushed his hands up the side of his face, into his hair and shook. "It looked right at me." He leaned his head forward, burying the lower part of his face between his knees and arms, then lifted it again, and stared into the fire as he continued to tremble. "My head lamp—must have blinded it." He looked at the others, "Otherwise I'd be dead!"

Kneeling next to Viper, Aziza had one hand on his back and was rubbing it, her head next to his, she whispered in his ear. Viper was shaking, his eyes quickly shifting back and forth. Abruptly, he pushed her away and leaned out to grab his AK-47 and clutched it tightly to himself.

"Give me your gun," Oleg said to Viper, "I'll go check it out." He handed his pistol to Aziza as Viper reluctantly passed his semi-automatic over. Oleg checked the safety, which was already off, then patted Carver on the back. "Come on, show me where it is."

Carver lifted his head, looked briefly at each of the others, then up at Oleg. He took a long deep breath. "OK," he said—his voice still unsteady. He started to stand, lost his balance, caught himself with one hand, and then carefully raised himself onto his feet.

Oleg placed a hand on Carver's shoulder and the two men walked back to where Carver had seen the giant serpent. "Right there," said Carver in a hushed voice. He pointed but there was nothing. They scanned the area with their headlamps then Oleg unleashed the AK-47, emptying the magazine into the darkness.

"It's gone," said Oleg as they returned to the camp fire. "I sprayed the area just in case."

"You didn't see it?" asked Viper.

"No—like I said, nothing there—must have taken off as soon as Carver scared the shit out of it. Probably just trying to digest his dinner." Then, looking at Carver, "That would explain why it didn't strike out at you."

There was prob'ly nothing there to begin with," said Viper. "The pussy's just so afraid of the dark, he sees shit."

"Well, I guess we're all wide awake now," said Oleg, changing the subject. "We might as well have some breakfast. We go hunting today everybody. If the pygmy doesn't come back, we go without him. I'll track the cat myself, if I have to. What about you, Carver? Think your girl left you?"

"She'll be back."

"Yeah, but if she isn't—you come with us," said Viper. "We'll teach you how to hunt big cats. How about that? I can hunt while you tell me all about these big trees."

"Sounds like a plan to me," said Aziza. "You're with us now Carver—otherwise maybe you'll end up cat food."

"Let's get some carbs into our bodies, people, and get our lovely asses moving," said Oleg. "Come along, Viper. Couscous anyone?"

Within minutes, the four of them were huddled around the fire, quietly spooning couscous and dried carrot shreds into their mouths, the light clinking of metal spoons against metal cups the only sound.

"That's a familiar smell—can you spare any of that?"

All four choked on their food at the sudden sound of Zora's voice. They looked up but didn't see her at first. It was still dark and the ground was shrouded in mist. Carver and Oleg stood up as all four looked back and forth until, finally, out of the gloom, emerged the forms of Zora and Ngiome.

"We got caught-up in something I don't want to think about right now. Decided it would be safer to sleep up in a tree for the night."

"So you didn't get eaten by lions after all. I guess the four of us are quite happy to see you this gray and dreary morning," said Oleg as he set down his cup and stepped forward to meet them with just the hint of a smile on his face.

Zora passed Oleg and continued straight to Carver. "You all right?" she asked.

"Now I am—yeah."

"I'm really sorry—I know we probably caused a little anxiety with our unannounced absence. We had a pretty rough time."

"You didn't cross paths with Denis by any chance, did you?" asked Oleg. "He also failed to appear last night."

"We've got some unfortunate news about Denis, I'm afraid to say."

"What happened?" asked Aziza.

"He's gone off to join the rest of his squad—got himself killed."

"Huh? You gotta be fuckin kidding me," blurted-out Viper as he dropped his cup.

"What happened?" asked Oleg.

"He must have been hunting or something, but he shot a chimpanzee. When he went to check out his kill the other chimps attacked him. I guess he wasn't prepared and when they hit him—well—they beat him to death. We heard the gunshot, and by the time we got there it was over. We were both pretty upset. It was getting dark, then the rain started and we couldn't see anything—even with my headlamp. We just climbed up a tree and made ourselves a shelter."

Ngiome said something that no one could understand. They looked at him, then at Zora.

"He said we lost all the mushrooms we'd collected—and his net." She said something back to Ngiome then turned to the others. "How about some of that delicacy you people are eating—can you spare a little?"

"Get yourselves some spoons and just finish off what's in the pot," said Aziza.

"Fuckin' little jungle bunny don't want a spoon," said Viper, "he just eats with his hands—like a chimpanzee—huh-huh," he chuckled to himself.

"Carver," Oleg said, "while they're eating why don't you and I get our maps out and have a look at where we want to go today? I know you and Zora know where you're going, but we only have a rough idea and that map of yours has more useful detail on it. If you don't mind sharing, that is."

"Sure," said Carver, "why not?"

Zora and Ngiome quickly finished what was in the pot while Carver and Oleg convened over their maps. By cross-referencing the GPS coordinates and compass readings they had established before descending into the caldera with current compass readings, they were able to make an educated guess as to where they were on the printed copy of the satellite map. The map covered an area of nine hundred square miles, and having known the coordinates of Hoyt's last communication, they were able to estimate their current location within what they assumed to be a one-mile radius.

"Any luck?" asked Zora as she came up behind Carver and, leaning on his shoulder, looked over at the map.

"I'd say we're about here, said Carver pointing at an area that looked exactly like everything else around it. The map included the entire perimeter of the ancient caldron they had identified and the rim had been highlighted with a yellow marker. The location on the eastern edge of the rim where Hoyt's last communication had been sent out had a small red square drawn around it. "This is about a day's march from the rim, and taking into account we did a lot of switch-backing as we came down, I put us here."

"As the crow flies," said Oleg, smiling at Carver, "as you Americans would say, that looks to be about seven miles from our starting point at the rim—like you said—a lot of switch-backing—I would agree with you."

"What do you think, Zora?"

"I'd say that's pretty close. I would guess that the topography information your satellite data was able to produce is pretty much on target, as well." She pointed at another spot close to the spot they had identified as their current position. "That's probably where Hoyt's last camp is—maybe three quarters of a mile closer toward the center of the depression. These two small rivers look like they converge near the center—here. Then it flows out to the south where the topo shows the rim dropping in elevation—looks really steep along the banks here—cuts through what looks like a narrow but very deep gorge. This is where the river must carry the drainage for this entire area—heavy rapids here. One more road block that's discouraged any wanderers from exploring beyond that point."

"So this is the approximate route we took tracking the lion yesterday." Oleg slowly traced his finger across part of the map. "It doesn't show any small streams anywhere, but our track followed the stream for most of the way and you can be guaranteed that the stream is headed toward this river, the one that has formed toward the northeastern area of the rim. Predators like to follow waterways when looking for prey—that makes sense—so it also might make sense that the lion's den is close to the center where the two rivers converge."

"If this is where Hoyt's last camp is, then, according to his notes, there's a monster tree another three quarters to a mile west of there, maybe somewhere around here," said Carver. "This is where we need to go, Zora. I want to see that tree, maybe climb it, take a few samples—then we can get out of here."

"Let's move our camp now and get a little closer to the center," said Oleg. "Your tree seems to be in the same direction we're looking at so I suggest we all follow the same route 'til we get there. We can set up a new camp, maybe where your tree is, then while you play in your tree, Carver, we'll go see if we can pick up the lion's track. We'll go as far as this first river this afternoon and make it back to the new camp by sunset." Oleg looked at Carver and touched him gently on the forearm. "You don't need to terminate your trip right away though. I feel like we've all been together now for weeks—even though it's still only a little over a week. Carver, we would be greatly disappointed if you just climbed your tree then walked away and left us behind. You should take your time—do your research. When we bag the lion, we can all leave together. What they say about safety in numbers is true, you know. Every time someone goes out on their own or in pairs, they don't seem to come back. You two need to stick around until we're all ready to leave. What do you say?"

By now Aziza and Viper had joined them and were standing behind Oleg, listening. "Yeah, Carver," Viper interjected, "last night you showed me how you use your ropes and those sharp things you put on your feet—tomorrow I'll show you how to shoot. Stay with us, man."

"Alright," Zora interjected, "we'll all go to Hoyt's big tree. I'll explain to Ngiome where to take you from there," she looked at Viper and smiling, continued, "and not get lost. When you get back tonight, we can talk about tomorrow. It's three quarters of an hour to Hoyt's last camp, maybe two hours to his big tree." She looked at Carver, took his map, folded it and handed it to him. "Let's pack up and get going. I'll tell Ngiome what's going on." Then, as she and Carver moved away from the others, she said, speaking under her breath, "Ngiome knows we're leaving after you climb the tree. He's coming with us." She looked toward his shelter and added, "We didn't sleep too well last night, I think he's over there taking a short nap."

36 – BIG TREE

The tree was big; bigger than anything Carver had imagined—even after having seen Hoyt's notes. No one moved. They just stood in a line, staring, their heads sweeping back and forth, then up and down. Finally, Carver said, "The actual base, if you don't take the root system into account, measures thirty-one feet and four inches in diameter. The circumference measures ninety-six feet. That's according to Hoyt's notes."

"The root system—is that what you call that shit all around it?" asked Aziza.

The root system was not made up of the thin, long-reaching fin-like lateral formations that so many of the trees had. These roots were massive and tangled; tangled like an enormous pile of giant octopuses that oozed out from below the huge bole of the tree. At the same time, they were in fact buttresses because of their size and their spread from the main trunk, which was impressive, and they did serve as the tree's foundation. There were seven large primary roots that sprung out at twenty to thirty feet above the ground, according to Hoyt's notes. Those primary roots measured from nine to nineteen feet across where they rolled out from the trunk—the growth patterns were nervous and abrupt as each root twisted, turning back on itself while dozens of sub-roots shot out on each side, winding around themselves, disappearing under and over one another, resulting in a massive coiled entanglement that covered the ground up to a distance of sixty feet from the face of the trunk. Vines dangling from above became mixed up in the roots, and the whole mass was littered in ferns and several varieties of large-leaved plants.

"Can you tell what species it is?" asked Oleg.

"Not really. The trunk looks a lot like *Eucalyptus regnans*—also known as a mountain ash, although it's a type of eucalyptus and has nothing to do with an ash. 'Centurion' is the name given to one in Tasmania. That one's considered the second-tallest tree in the world. Anyway, the root system's all wrong here and this one, is maybe two and half times as big in circumference as Centurion—plus, the climate here doesn't really jive. In other words, I have no idea. It appears that Hoyt discovered a whole new species."

"What's that?" asked Viper, pointing at what looked like a duffel bag propped up in the crux of a large split in the root system, about halfway up and into the root mass.

"Ah-ha," said Carver, "let's hope that's the rest of Hoyt's gear." Carver dropped his backpack on the ground and quickly started climbing his way into the root mass and up to the bag. He slung it over his shoulder and came back to a level place on the ground where he held it up, brushed away some of the green growth that had begun to attach itself, opened it and emptied the contents. He spread everything out, looking each item over carefully and smiling, obviously pleased with the discovery.

"That what you wanted?" asked Zora.

"Yes, this is good."

"Looks interesting," said Viper as he stooped and picked up what looked like a miniature crossbow.

"It is what it looks like," said Carver, "a bow. It's used to launch the throw line up over one of the lower branches. We fasten one of the climbing ropes to the end and once we get the weighted end up and over the branch, we pull the climbing rope up, looping it over. The lower trunk is usually difficult to free climb and this one looks like at least a hundred feet until we get to a branch we can use as an anchor."

"Come on, Viper," shouted Oleg. "We need to get our tents up and get on our way—we've wasted enough time already."

"I'll be going up in maybe fifteen minutes—I'll give you a shout when I'm ready and you can see how it works before you take off."

Viper acknowledged Carver's offer with a light grunt as he sauntered off toward his companions who were already erecting their tents with some assistance from Ngiome.

"Looks like you've got a harness, some spurs, a helmet—even gloves," noted Zora as she squatted down next to Carver.

"Hoyt came prepared," said Carver, I just wonder why the ropes were back in his camp but all this stuff was over here."

"I think what we just carted over here might have been extra rope. Look over there." Zora pointed over Carver's shoulder. Both ends of a rope were hanging down along one side of the trunk, partially obscured from view by a mass of vines. It was looped over a large stump that jutted off from the trunk about eighty feet above. "Looks like you won't need to demonstrate the crossbow to Viper. He's going to be disappointed," she said with a note of sarcasm in her voice.

"He probably got himself set up here," said Carver as they both climbed up through the roots to where the rope hung. "He set this rope using the stump up there as his anchor. I would guess he climbed up to that level at least just for a look around. He must have gone back to the camp when he realized he'd need the rest of the rope and spent the night there, planning to come back the next day. The lions got them that night." Carver pulled on the short end, looked up, then back down at the long end, which was coiled on the ground along with another section. "Two-hundred-foot rope—like the others. It didn't take much to figure that these two weren't going to do the job—in fact, they were probably only intending to do preliminary surveys the day they came out here and only carried enough rope to get up to about two hundred feet. And this monster disappears into the canopy, which is … I would guess just under two hundred feet."

For a few seconds, they both stared up then Carver reached for the rope end. "Look how it's totally coated in mold—the part that's on the ground. Wouldn't take much longer for it to have just disappeared from view."

"You'd still see the coiled form for a while," said Zora, "synthetic

239

material—probably doesn't break down very quickly. "

"Polyester-Dacron—not the same stuff you use going up Denali."

"Right—look Carver, let's get your tent set up—our tents. Looks like I'll have to use one tonight." She looked over toward Oleg's party then went on, "Tomorrow we get out of here. You better get all the climbing and exploring in that you want today—we've got about six hours of day light left so I hope that's going to be enough."

"You're kidding. It could easily take several hours just to get up there and start to settle in. Tomorrow's too soon. I could use a week just to break the surface on what we've got here."

"You've already learned a lot more than you must have expected, so we need to quit while we're ahead. You might be the client, but out here I'm the captain and I'm not giving you a choice. We leave tomorrow."

He looked at her for a second, then asked, "You more afraid of the black beasts or them?"

"Both," she said, then nodded her chin toward the others, "but mostly them."

"Do you think they suspect we're planning to leave?"

"Well, they have overheard us discussing it. They may not expect it to happen tomorrow. They have no idea we're taking Ngiome with us. We're going to have to slip out quietly—maybe we take the early morning watch shift and do it then."

"That's not going to go over too well. You think ..."

"Careful, here comes Oleg."

"We're about to leave, you two," yelled Oleg as he approached several yards into the root system. "Can I get you to talk to the pygmy for me one more time?"

"Sure—be right over."

"Thanks—it's going to be sign language for us until we get back."

"I understand." Zora finished unfolding her tent frame, then followed Oleg over to where Aziza and Viper were fitting water bottles and AK-47 magazines into their daypacks. Ngiome was watching, his short spear in one hand and the machete that Viper had given him, strung around his waist. "What would you like me to tell him?"

"Tell him we go west from here until we run into the stream the lion followed. We want to pick up its tracks and see if they take us to where the stream joins a bigger river. Most important—if we do find its tracks, we follow them. If we don't find the lion or its den in three hours, we come back here and continue tomorrow."

Zora translated Oleg's instructions for Ngiome, then added, "If you feel you are close to the black devil, change direction and do not let the white *bilo* find it—come back here. We leave after the white *bilo* sleeps."

"That sounded like a pretty long translation," said Oleg. "What else did you tell him?"

"I told him I would build a shelter for him for tonight."

"Good—good idea—very thoughtful of you." He continued looking at Zora for a few seconds, then abruptly grabbed his daypack, looked inside, zipped it closed and slipped his arms through the straps. "You two ready?" he asked Aziza and Viper as he walked over to his tent.

"Ready," answered Aziza. Viper opened and shut the chamber to his AK-47, but said nothing.

Oleg picked up his rifle, pulled it out of its case, which he shoved into his tent with his foot, then zipped the tent shut. He looked at Ngiome and pointed in the direction they had planned to take and said, "Alright, let's go." Then looking to Carver and Zora he added, "We'll be back before the light goes out. Maybe we'll have our lion, but I'm guessing we'll just confirm where he is and then get him tomorrow— or the next day. You two be careful up there." He motioned up into the tree with his head and then started off, gesturing to Ngiome to take the lead. Viper turned once and stared at Zora until she caught his gaze. He then reached down and adjusted his crotch, winked, and followed behind the others. The four of them quickly disappeared.

As soon as they were out of sight Zora turned to Carver and said, "Let's get our tents set up before we climb."

"I've only got equipment for one—if you want to go, I'll have to go up first, then drop the harness and spurs down to you. This is not the same as mountain climbing you know."

Zora laughed. "Carver, where do you think Ngiome and I slept when we didn't come back last night?"

"You said you slept in a tree but I figured it was lot lower than this."

"It wasn't as high as this, but we had no trouble going up the vines. We probably got up to maybe seventy feet and even managed to build a really decent shelter for ourselves once there—ha!" she laughed, "You didn't think I was going to let you climb up there alone did you?"

"I had no reason to believe you would be going up there with me—no."

"Let's get going. By the time you get your harness and spurs on, I'll be up there waiting for you—in fact, I want to check on how secure the rope is before you start."

37 – THE ASCENT

Like a mountain goat, Zora danced lightly across the root mass and upward until she reached the dangling line that Hoyt had put in place. Carver was not far behind. Vines of varying sizes had grown down from the tree above and into the crevices of the root system just beyond the rope. Zora took hold of one, looked back to Carver who was now adjusting his harness, and said, "I'm going up to check the anchorage on this before we start hauling gear."

"What?" he said in a distracted tone as he looked up at her.

"See you up there."

Zora started with a short jump, grabbing onto the vine with both hands, and within seconds was on her way. Carver stood watching, as she climbed the eighty feet like a trapeze artist—quickly and effortlessly. He looked at his watch and shook his head. "I would have timed her if I'd known she was going to do that," he murmured to himself.

The rope began to shake slightly. "It's good up here," she called down to him. "Tie your stuff on. I'll pull it up; it'll be quicker than you trying to tow it up from there."

"OK," he yelled.

She hauled up the extra rope coils first, followed by two bags of gear, then called down to him, "I'm going up to set the next rope—not enough room here for the two of us plus the gear. Once you get here we'll keep going in stages. Nice hefty-looking branches up there—looks like canopy trees running right across the main trunk. Should make for a good staging area."

"OK," he yelled again, as he started up.

It took Carver fifteen minutes to reach the first staging area. The going was slow, compared to Zora's free climb. Because the tree trunk was so massive and long, there was nothing for him to hold onto other than his own gear. He wore a climbing harness or saddle and had attached a foot loop to the rope. He climbed by pulling down on one side of the rope, sliding a friction hitch knot up, then applying his weight into the foot loop. The process was repeated again and then again, allowing him to slowly ascend the tree, one foot at a time.

By the time Carver reached the first staging area, Zora had already secured the next lift of rope. The gear she had pulled up was tied onto a spike that Hoyt had driven into the tree. He quickly transferred a load onto the second-stage rope and signaled to Zora. As she hauled it up, he took a long drink, wiped the sweat from his face, and looked around. When the rope dropped again, he sent up a second coil of rope, followed by the duffel bag. *I'll measure this on the return trip*, he thought to himself as he began the slow climbing process again.

"Wow—this is really nice," he said as he arrived at the next level. "Damn, we lucked out here. Looks like these branches just scissor across two sides like roadways—perfect access into the canopy. We could easily set up here and spend a day just taking side trips into these lower trees."

"We did luck out. With all these branches coming across you can't see too far in any direction, but while you were coming up, I climbed enough to get beyond all this growth. Our big tree goes at least another fifty feet beyond where we are now before it finally branches out."

"That would make the main trunk about 220, maybe 230 or 40 feet long before it branches." He looked at her, smiling, "Might not be as tall as Hyperion, but this is by far the tallest and biggest tree ever seen in this part of the world—or in any tropical forest! Nobody's going to believe this!"

"Hyperion?"

"California redwood. Tallest tree in the world."

"Right." She reached her arms up, stretched and let out a long exhalation. "Let's keep going."

"Give me a minute—I need to take this in." He took another swig from his bottle, sat down on one of the passing branches, leaned back against another, and then offered the bottle to Zora.

"No thanks. I've been getting water from these vines—one less item to carry."

"Maybe I should just leave mine here then—it's a lot of weight."

"No—keep the bottles for when we get up toward the top. Smaller vines up there—might not carry any water. In fact, you might want to refill it here."

She sat down next to him, resting both arms out on the branch behind her as if relaxing on a park bench. "Listen to the noise up here—monkeys, birds—we're right in the middle of it. From down there, these sounds might as well be a mile away."

"It's like the Grand Central of the rain forest—and the light level's gone up several notches—actually uplifting for a change."

"And the smells; flowers, fruit—a freshness I'd almost forgotten existed. Look ..." she pointed at a cluster of red orchids clinging to the side of a nearby branch. "Ripe figs somewhere up above us— source of that fruity smell—and just as I was getting used to the scent of perpetual rot. Ahhh, yes." Zora smiled as she arched her head back and ran her hands through her hair.

They rested for a few more minutes, then Carver took a deep breath, let it out slowly, pulled himself up, and said, "I'm ready."

It took longer to navigate their way through the entanglement of canopy branches than it took to climb straight up the naked trunk, but they made their way carefully upward until they finally emerged above the densest of the growth.

"Wow!" exclaimed Carver as he poked his head through the last layer of leaves, "not only do I see the sky, but the sun's actually out! I don't know when I last saw the sun—might have been when we flew out of D.C."

"We should probably hold up here for a couple of minutes 'til our eyes get adjusted," said Zora. They both squinted, blinked, and smiled.

Finally Zora grabbed a vine and started up to where the giant emergent branched out. Following their established routine, they towed their loads up to the next level with Carver following, using the rope and his harness, crawling slowly up like a cautious spider. It was a difficult and slow climb for him, and he was beginning to tire even though the load they were hauling had decreased as the rope coils got left in place at each pitch.

"I had to chase a couple of snakes out," said Zora, as Carver finally pulled himself up in to the cluster of branches.

"Wow! Jesus, look at this! It's like a whole other world. My God, you could set up a six-person tent and camp out for a week!" He looked around and counted, "One, two—five major boughs. After shooting straight up for some two hundred feet, the trunk just explodes outward into five huge branches—and in the middle is this—this garden!" He dropped his backpack and pointed at one of the large off-shooting branches. "Look at them—each one's as big as a full-grown tree. And this!" He swept his arm out. The five large boughs were separated from each other by a pair of elliptical spaces, the smaller of which measured approximately four feet in the short dimension and six in the long. The larger space, where they stood, had a more oblong shape and was at least twice as large. The two spaces were connected by a narrow gap between two of the boughs and the larger area had a slightly depressed, bowl-like form to it with standing water on one side. The entire "garden" was completely filled with a deep green carpet of ferns, lianas, bromeliads, moss, various forms of forb, and a multitude of vines and assorted branches, some of which grew straight upward, while others grew out between the main boughs, dropping off into the air below.

"Here, look at this," Zora said as she wrapped both hands around one of the branches that grew straight up and into the foliage of the crown above. "A completely different species of tree. Birds must have dropped the seeds. This is a garden—a secret refuge hidden away up in the sky!"

"Looks like an African mahogany—maybe three years old," said Carver as he dumped the contents of his bag and grabbed his camera. "Need to record all this—need to measure." He paused, looked upward, then continued, "But let's go to the top first—at least as far as we can. I'll measure on the way down. Only another sixty feet to go."

"Slow down, Carver—stop chattering and put your camera down for a minute. We're above most of the foliage now. Let's see if we can get the SAT phone to work—and while you're setting that up, give me your GPS. I'll see if I can get a reading on our location."

Zora clicked on Carver's GPS while he set up the satellite phone. "We've hardly used this thing and the battery's almost finished—still—there we go."

"It's working!" said Carver as he flipped on the switch. "Ouésso this is Carver, are you there?" He waited, then repeated his message, waited, and repeated it again.

Finally a voice came through. It was unfamiliar and had a thick accent. "Ouésso, I'm receiving you—this is Carver, can you hear me?"

"He's speaking in French, Carver—let me talk to him." Zora moved up next to the radio and spoke, in French at first, then she switched to Lingala. She spoke for several minutes, stopping once to look at the GPS. She read off their exact coordinates, then, cut off the communication.

"Prince and Lucas are both back in Brazzaville. Apparently they've made three flights back to base and circled this general area too. I told him Hoyt and his entire crew had perished, but that we were OK and we would be back to base in four days. The copter will be waiting for us, assuming they can land. He said last time they flew out the area was flooded again."

"Did you tell them how Hoyt died?"

"Yes, but I lied." She hesitated then went on, "I said they'd all died from some disease—looked like Ebola, but different."

"What the hell did you tell him that for?"

"We need to think this through, Carver—we need to discourage anyone else from coming out here 'til we can come up with a reasonable game plan."

They looked at each other, then Carver asked, "And what about the Russian and his goons? He seems pretty sure that he's going to be walking back out of here with the head of his black lion. Did you tell them the Russians were OK?"

"Yeah, he's going to relay that to their people and he's probably calling Prince now."

"I want at least one more day here, Zora—and how are we going to get back to the landing base in four days?"

"If it's just you, Ngiome, and me, we should be able to make good time, plus we know the route now. Anyway, I just committed to being there in four days. It's too dangerous here. I want us to be on our way by daybreak. We can work here until just before sunset—going down should be a piece of cake for you." She looked at her watch. "We made it up this far in almost two hours. If we both belay our way down we can descend in twenty minutes. It's only 250 feet from here.

38 – STALKERS

Ngiome stopped to let the others catch up. He sniffed the air. Something dead—it wasn't very strong, but he could detect the scent of a decomposing corpse. *The bilo that zabolo-yindo killed,* he thought to himself, *very close now.*

"*Ebembe,*" he said to Oleg as he stretched both arms outward and pointed his spear toward a dark gap between the trees ahead. "*Ebembe,*" he repeated. He used the Lingala word for corpse, even though the white *bilo* didn't seem to understand Lingala. *They don't even try to understand,* he thought to himself. "So-der," he said, now attempting to use the white *bilo*'s words.

"What?" asked Oleg.

"I think he tried to say 'soldier,'" said Aziza. "Maybe Denis's guy."

"Good—could be the cache—I don't recognize any of this though," said Oleg. "Ahh—wait—let me retract that. We came in from that side yesterday—there it is."

"Whoa," said Viper as the three of them joined Ngiome who was looking down at what remained of Nobu. "Looks like our lion came back to finish his meal."

"Not much left," said Aziza.

Viper clutched his AK-47 in closer to himself and looked around, peering into the dark shadows in nervous anticipation. "He probably won't be back then. We should have set up a blind and waited for him last night. Now our bait's gone."

"That's alright," said Aziza, "we still got a few candidates around."

She smiled and patted Ngiome on the back. "You'd make good bait, wouldn't you, my little one?" She looked at Oleg and continued, "Live human bait, Oleg. That would make this the perfect hunt."

"I say we use all three of them," added Viper. "The first two we just set up and watch—let the lion make a meal of them, get him used to it, then—we nail him when he comes back for desert—the bitch."

"Didn't you want to finish off the little bitch yourself, my Viper?" asked Aziza.

"My, my you two—behave yourselves," said Oleg. "I might have plans of my own for her."

"Interesting idea, but not likely to happen," said Viper.

"What do you mean?" asked Aziza.

Viper's eyes clouded over slightly and a subtle smile crossed his face. "Just a hunch I have. Maybe we won't be seeing those two again."

"You better not have some little scheme of your own cooking—not without me knowing about it," said Oleg with a scowl.

"Oh no, nothing—just a feeling."

Oleg kept looking at Viper, then reached over and grasping the flesh above his collarbone, squeezed him and said, "Don't make any moves without checking with me first. You know that—right?"

"Right—I always tell you first, Oleg."

Oleg let go of Viper and turned to Ngiome and said, "Find tracks." He squatted, pulled out his knife and sketched what looked like a large cat's pawprint. He stood and pointed down at it, then at the scattering of Nobu's broken bones. He sheathed his knife and made a walking motion with his fingers, pointed at his sketch again and then into the forest. "Find tracks."

Ngiome walked around the bones looking down at the ground, then turned back in the opposite direction, moving fern fronds, vines, and leaves with the end of his spear—squatting a couple of times to examine the ground closely. "*Zabolo-yindo*," he said as he pointed his spear at the ground.

Oleg squatted next to him. "What do you see here? Tracks?" He waved his hand around the ground just below the point of the spear. "I

250

don't see anything." He glared suspiciously at Ngiome. "What are you pointing at little man?"

Ngiome squatted, put his spear down, and with his forefinger, traced an outline in a large, almost circular pattern. The ground was covered with a thin layer of moss where he pointed.

"Are you taking me for a fool, you little shit? There's nothing here."

Aziza now stooped down and looked. "Huh," she grunted, "maybe there is. There's a really slight depression in the moss here. Could be an impression from the lion's foot."

"Let me see," said Viper.

Oleg quickly turned to him. "Stay there. Keep your eyes open. If that cat's around and sees all of us stooped down on the ground, he could attack."

Viper stood back and turned, waving the barrel of his weapon back and forth.

Ngiome had moved away from them and was now stooping again. He looked up and whistled, like a bird. When they all looked at him, he stood again, pointed his spear toward the ground, then, pointed his other hand ahead and motioned up and down. He turned and started walking, slowly at first and then more quickly. The others looked at one another, then followed, Oleg first, then Aziza and Viper at the rear, turning from side to side and back, waving and pointing his weapon as if expecting an attack at any moment.

"This looks like a game trail," Oleg said after they had been moving for several minutes.

"Yeah," said Viper. "It's definitely some kind of trail—and we must be near the stream again. I hear water running."

When they got to the stream, they stopped and Oleg opened his map, laid it on the ground, pulled his compass out and squatted over the map. "According to my readings we're here and this is probably the same stream that ran by our campsite yesterday."

"It's about three times as wide here," commented Aziza.

"Yeah—it should qualify now as a small river now—and we should

251

be getting close to where it runs into this bigger river." He pointed at the map then stood up looking at Ngiome who was examining the ground again.

Oleg joined him, looked down and smiled. "Oh, yeah—that's him. Just like the ones we saw the other day. And here." He had shifted closer to the water's edge. "This is a regular watering place— some kind of deer prints or something. The lion's prints are pointed downstream. Let's keep moving, that's the way—he's got his lair down here somewhere. Hunt's up one stream one day, then the other one—maybe downstream—no shortage of game here."

They continued on, always moving slowly and with caution until they came to a place where a large tree had gone down over the river, creating a natural bridge. Ngiome was stopped next to it. When the others caught up to him, he pointed to the ground with his spear, tapped the tree with his machete then pointed across the river. He nodded to the others, stuck his spear in the ground, grabbed one of the many vines that had gone down with the tree, pulled himself up onto the tree, then bent over and retrieved his spear. He beckoned to the others and they quickly crossed, Viper still taking up the rear position.

"Look at these tracks now," said Oleg as he crouched down to examine the ground again with Ngiome. "This looks like two lions here—these tracks are coming from the tree and then this seems to be a separate set coming from downstream. Looks like they might have walked around in a circle here, then—" he looked at Ngiome who had moved in a new direction, now heading back upstream. "They went that way."

They continued on as the trail eventually meandered away from the river. They walked in silence, following Ngiome, and when another hour had passed, they stopped to drink, and Aziza passed everyone an energy bar. She didn't offer one to Ngiome, but when he saw them eating, he disappeared for several minutes, then came back with some kind of root that he peeled with his machete and began to eat, looking up occasionally and smiling at the others.

They finished their break and continued on for several more

minutes until they found themselves back on the bank of the river. "I always thought that lions didn't like to go in the water," Oleg remarked as he looked at the two sets of prints that appeared to have gone straight into the river.

Ngiome patted himself on the chest with his spear and pointed across the river. He then pointed at the others and motioned for them to stay where they were.

"All right," said Oleg and he pointed at Ngiome and across the river, then back at Ngiome again and finally to his own eyes. "Ngiome go see."

The pygmy nodded, turned, and waded out into the river. It was about thirty feet in width where he crossed, and the water level got to just below his chin before he started to climb out on the opposite bank. He wandered around for a minute then squatted to examine the ground. When he stood up again, he looked at the others, motioned for them to stay put, and slipped into the thick vegetation that grew along that side of the river.

"So what's our game plan, Oleg?" asked Aziza. "We gonna keep tracking these cats and hope to get a shot at one?'

"We'll go back to the camp when he gets back. We don't really need to find the actual lair. I feel pretty confident that we know their range. We need to get down to the confluence of the two rivers, find a nice opening where there's signs of game, set up a blind, put out our bait, then wait."

"What are you thinking of for bait?" asked Viper with a slight smile beginning to crack his lips.

"After we've about finished dinner, you get up like you need to go take a piss. Go off somewhere behind the little harlot, wait a couple minutes—like you're relieving yourself, then, when you come back you whack her behind the head as you go by."

"So—you do want the bitch for bait—ha—but, Oleg—I want to rip her open real good first."

"She won't be the bait, Viper—we'll use Carver. We just need to get the jump on her and get her secured before we move on Carver. As soon as Viper whacks the girl, I'll stick my gun in Carver's face, and Aziza—you can whack him on the side of the head."

"Sounds like a plan," said Aziza.

"Here he comes," said Viper, pointing to the other side of the river.

"All right," said Oleg. "We all know what to do then—and—let's not discuss this anymore until the deed has been done—that includes not talking about it in Russian in front of Zora. I've been getting this uneasy feeling that she might understand us."

"Really?" asked Aziza.

"Just a suspicion—I thought she looked like she was listening a couple of times, but trying to act like she wasn't—not sure—but we shouldn't take any unnecessary chances."

Oleg greeted Ngiome with a smile as he came dripping out of the river and pointed in the direction of the camp. "Back to camp now, Ngiome—we find lions tomorrow." He pointed up toward the canopy above, then made an eating sign with his hand to his mouth, followed by a sleeping sign by pressing his hands together against his cheek with his eyes closed

"Think your sign language means anything to him?" asked Aziza.

Ngiome seemed to understand, shook his head, and started walking along the riverbank, heading upstream. He stopped after several paces and looked back at Viper.

"What do you want?" Viper asked.

Ngiome held his hands up to mimic a gun and pointed into the jungle behind them. A worried look spread across Viper's face, then he turned and went back to his sweeping motion with the AK-47.

White bilo does not understand, Ngiome thought to himself. *White bilo thinks he's stalking zabolo-yindo, but now zabolo-yindo is stalking the white bilo.*

39 – IN THE SECLUDED GARDEN

"Hyperion is 379.3 feet high—Centurion's 327 feet," said Carver as he plopped himself down on one edge of the open space between the boughs. They had returned to the secluded garden within the tree's boughs and both were exhausted. Carver drained his water bottle.

"So, you're telling me that this is not the tallest tree in the world?"

"Hate to disappoint you, but, no, not the tallest." He looked in his notebook and jotted down a few figures. If you add in the distance from the ground to the top of the root mass where we started, take our GPS measurement and the measurements we just took from the high point on the crown, this tree is 304 feet tall. That would put us near the top—not sure what place though—let's see." He continued scribbling notes in his book.

"Thing is—this is Africa, and Africa doesn't have anything that even comes close to what we're looking at here. The climate's all wrong, soil's not right—this tree, in fact this whole forest, is going to blow the lid off everything when this gets out. The whole science community will be falling all over themselves to get out here."

"Does that bother you, Carver—knowing that not just the science community, but every timber company in the world is going to be foaming at the mouth to get their greedy little hands on this place? In fact, that is why your company sent Hoyt here—and now you—isn't it?"

"True—your skepticism has been well-founded from the beginning, Zora." He reached out and touched her arm. "You might be the only sane person I know, and I feel like I'm beginning to appreciate that. You were right when you said we need to think this through." He looked up into the sunlight, squinted his eyes and smiled. "I gotta get my heart to slow down first though."

"Don't forget Ngiome," she said. "He's sane."

"Yeah, probably the most sane of us all." Carver tried to drink again but his bottle was empty. He got up and stepped toward the small pool that sat across from them. "Think this is safe to drink?"

"Full of tadpoles. Here," Zora took out her knife and sliced through a vine that dropped just within her reach. As water started dripping out, she leaned up to it and allowed the cool liquid to flow into her mouth, then holding her thumb over the open end, reached her other hand out to Carver. "Here, give me your bottle."

Carver handed her his bottle and she filled it from the vine, took another sip herself then lifted the vine above her head, allowing it to trickle onto her face. She opened her mouth, spit the water back out, then smiling at Carver, waved the end of the vine around and asked, "What do you call something like this?"

"Like what?"

"This place—here at the top of the tree trunk—this little garden we're sitting in now." She looked at him as he seemed to ponder her question. "I mean this part of the tree, where it suddenly shoots out—where these branches come off from the trunk to form the crown."

"This is the top of the trunk where it branches off."

"But isn't there a specific word for that?"

"Not really—should there be?"

"In French you might call this *une ramure*. It's an assemblage of branches on a tree, where they branch off. I assumed there was an English translation, but just didn't know what it was—same with Spanish. I thought maybe there was something in technical botany or forestry vocab. It's interesting that your profession doesn't have a specific word for it."

"I'll include that in my notes then—*ramure*. It is a specific condition that does exist in nature, especially in tall tropical trees like this one, so maybe it does deserve a word to define it. This one is quite unique though with this self-contained garden perched on the top of the bole. There are some big redwoods that have something like this, but not this extensive."

"*La ramure*," she repeated. "I think I'm going to lie down in it and take a short nap while you collect your data." Zora sat down and ran her fingers through the thick moss, then stretched her legs out, leaned back on her elbows for a second, then lay herself out flat, reaching up over her head, then out to the sides. She took a deep breath, sighed, then folded her hands under her head and looked at Carver. "We should just spend the night up here—except," then in a lower tone as if addressing herself, "we can't leave Ngiome down there with them."

"So go get him and bring him up—I like the idea of camping out here a while. In fact, it makes sense. We're safe up here—from the lions—the two-legged monsters—and the radio works here. I could take the time to gather all the information I need."

"I don't think we've got more than three or four more calls on the SAT phone before the battery's gone. We need one call for when we get back up to the rim and another for when we get to the base camp—just in case they're not there waiting."

"You come up with an interesting idea, then you immediately talk yourself out of it. You do that often?"

When she didn't respond, Carver looked at her and saw that her eyes were closed. He sat down next to her and resumed writing. He continued for several minutes, then looked away from the pad and put it down. He rotated his head in a circular motion for a minute, then gripped his neck with one hand and stretched it. Looking at Zora again, he mumbled, "I'm the one who needs a nap. I'm wiped out. Starting to tighten up."

"Take a nap then," said Zora, now with her eyes open and looking at him. She checked her watch. "We'll stay here a couple hours before we start down. You want more photos? I'll take a few if you want. Should have a couple with you in the shot to give a sense of scale."

"Thanks for the offer, but it would probably be best to have

257

you as the scale figure. I'll bet you're pretty photogenic—especially compared to me."

Zora sat up and looked at him. "Compared to you? What are you talking about? Am I getting a little peek here at some neurotic self-doubt? Or are you looking for me to tell you how attractive you really are?" She propped herself up onto one elbow, her chin resting in her hand, looking at Carver as a slight smile formed across her lips.

"Sorry—didn't really mean it that way. Yeah, you can take some pictures, I would appreciate that." He looked around and pointed at the gap between the two branches that led to the smaller open area. "You can do one of me standing just beyond the gap there," he waved his hand toward the pond, "and there—I can crouch down with the pond in front of me."

"You're blushing, Carver. Quit waving your hands around like a scarecrow and," she paused for a second, "tell me about yourself. Between you and Oleg—the ogre—you two have been asking me about myself. The flight down to Bellingham, the flight to D.C., then Brazzaville—you had to know all about me. Costa Rica, West Point, Special Forces, becoming a widow at the age of twenty-six, seeing a shrink for the last two years so that I wouldn't shrivel up and die—like you couldn't believe you were putting your life in the hands of a female who's been a borderline mental case. Then you've talked about your company, Hoyt, the mission. But I don't know the first thing about you—other than that you played football in college with Billy, you worshipped your friend Hoyt—Russell. I guess he was a mentor to you."

"There's not much to tell you, Zora. I mean, what do you want to hear"

"I want to hear about the real Carver. Who are your parents—are you like them? Where did you grow up? Were you afraid of girls when you were a kid? Define yourself for me—in ten minutes."

"I guess I was pretty straight arrow as a kid."

"Not surprising. You're a real good company man—good team player—a jock."

"Both my parents were teachers. My mother taught elementary school, and my father was a high school math teacher—he was also the assistant football coach. In fact, he was a Scout Master too—Boy Scouts. I had both of them as teachers plus my father as coach. I had to play it pretty straight. I probably drank a total of one case of beer throughout my entire high school career and didn't smoke my first joint until college. I didn't lose my virginity 'til I was nineteen, almost made it to twenty. I was always able to focus pretty well, so I did well academically and in sports. They always told me I didn't have the size or speed you need to play at a top Division I school, so it became a mission for me. I worked my butt off and ended up with a football scholarship to Washington. Billy and I both played defense— we were roommates. He was a much better ballplayer than me. He could have gone pro. I realized in my second year that I was never going to see much action so I transferred to Western Washington for my last two years."

"So, you're from that part of the country—Washington?"

"Suburb, north of Seattle. I grew up in walking distance from the university campus so transferring to Western was actually a way of breaking away. Western seemed to attract a lot of kids who were into outdoor sports; climbing, skiing. Not a great football school, which was good for me. I no longer had the kind of pressure I was getting at Washington. So, I concentrated on studies, played football, got introduced to climbing by some buddies. I always kept close contact with Billy. It was me who turned him on to climbing.

"You said you went to Cornell for grad school—forestry, right?"

"Yeah."

"But, Carver, tell me about those inner cravings and fantasies everyone carries around with them. What kind of things did you have—or do you have now, that lurk deep down inside—fears, cravings—things you would never talk about?"

"God, Zora. That's getting a bit personal, isn't it?"

"No, not at all."

"What about you, then?"

"Me? I didn't lead the kind of life most young American women lead. I spent half my growing-up years in a completely different culture. I've never been able to relate to the social mores of American women. I say exactly what I think, when I think it."

"That I've figured out. Tell me what I don't know."

"I lost my mother when I was three, then I lost the first and only man I ever loved. My great fear is that I'll always lose anyone I love—I fear being alone for the rest of my life." She sat up straight and looked at Carver. "So, what do you fear, Carver?"

"Right now—just you."

"Me?"

"I fear that if I told you I might be falling in love with you, you would reject me."

40 – INTERLUDE

Zora sat up straight, her eyes locked on Carver, and he was looking back at her. Neither of them spoke, and for Carver the entire world around them seemed to have stopped—the pair of yellow flycatchers that had been frolicking in the small pool seemed to just fade into silence. He heard nothing but the pounding of his own heart as it beat louder and louder.

Suddenly Zora let out a small gasp and in one quick move leapt over onto Carver's lap, straddling him as she knelt over him. She took his glasses off, tossed them aside, and then grabbed his head in her hands. His hands came up to her forearms, then slowly slid up onto her back where they tightened into a hard embrace, pulling her toward him until their lips joined together. She let out a small cry— he moaned, and their mouths moved hungrily across one another's face—kissing, sucking, biting, tasting. Her hands now worked their way back and forth across his head, feeling his hair as it slid between her fingers. His hands pressed and massaged her back and then her head, where his fingers ran through her hair. He gripped and pulled her head aside as he pressed his cheek into hers. They each gasped for air, then she grabbed at his belt and attempted to unbuckle it. "Help me," she pleaded.

Frantically, they pulled and squirmed until she had one leg free from her shorts and they both managed to open his pants and shove them down to his knees. Again, he took her head in his hands and pressed his mouth into hers and she pressed her mouth into his, and they made love with a desperate and maddening fury that built and built until, in one simultaneous explosion, all of their combined angst flooded out, and a calmness that neither of them had felt before, swept over them and both fell into a deep sleep.

"Carver," she whispered as her hands slowly felt their way up and down his back.

"Hmm?" He stirred slightly at the sound of her voice.

"Carver," she repeated his name.

He lifted his head and looked down at her. They were still locked into one another's embrace. He pulled one arm out from behind her and shook it lightly. "My arm's fallen asleep."

"I think you're crushing me."

He rolled over to one side, propped himself up on one arm and looked at her with his other arm still under her head. He began moving his fingers through her hair, leaned down and kissed her. It was a long, slow kiss and when he pulled back he looked down at her body, his eyes moving up and down. "We were in such a rush, we didn't bother to get undressed."

"You can finish undressing me now, if you want," she said.

He smiled and sitting up straight, pulled her shirt off as she assisted, then together they removed his shirt. Looking down at his bulky cargo pants and underwear that were still tangled around one ankle, they both laughed. Now, lying side by side, they began to caress one another—slowly—softly.

They made love again, only this time it was slower—the frantic desperation gone. Their bodies joined with a gentle smoothness, melting together into one. They enjoyed each other, they loved each other, and again, they fell asleep into one another's arms.

This time when they woke, it was dark.

"Is that smoke?" Carver asked, whispering into Zora's ear.

"They must be back from the hunt," she whispered back to him as she pressed her head into his neck and slowly ran her hand across his chest. "I like hairy chests, you know."

"Really?"

"Yes, I do."

262

"I feel as if we've been marooned on a desert island. I've been thrown together with you, Ngiome, those others—for what? And, how long has it been? I've lost track. I feel like I've been with you for a year—might as well have been a lifetime. We're in a different world. We've become isolated in this strange world and the reality is, we may never get out of here. We could both be dead tomorrow and nobody would know, nobody would care, but we are here now, you and me. And we're in this garden—this magic garden on top of the biggest tree in the universe and you have your arms around me and I have my arms around you and … I feel good here. Those people down there—they're on hold for a while, and … "

"And what?"

"I don't want this moment to end."

"Neither do I," he said as he tightened his embrace. He kissed her, and she kissed him and again, they made love, and, when they had finally sated themselves, they fell asleep in each other's arms one more time.

41 – A QUICK DESCENT

The sounds of night had begun to die down, and the air was still when a lone bird interrupted the quiet with a brief chirp. The first light of dawn had just begun to reach down through the crown of the giant emergent and into the hidden garden, barely illuminating the slumbering form of Carver Hayden, lying on his side in a fetal position, one arm folded up under his head and the other tucked between his thighs. He quivered slightly from the pre-dawn coolness and pressed himself against the warmth that radiated from Zora deRycken who sat with her legs folded and her back gently maintaining contact with her lover. Her hands rested, one on each knee, and were open but cupped with only the forefingers and thumbs connecting to each other. She sat straight, her eyes closed. Her soft face projected a tranquility that radiated outward like a veil that fell across the small hidden garden.

A long mellow cry rose up from the darkness below. It started as a dove-like cooing, but lingered on and gradually transmuted into the sad howl of a lonely canine. "What's that?" asked Carver as he slowly sat up rubbing his eyes.

Zora took in a long deep breath, exhaled and opened her eyes. She smiled. "Ngiome," she said. "That's not his normal morning song though—he's calling to us."

She rolled forward onto her hands and knees and crawled over to a V-shaped opening between two large boughs. She pulled herself up and cupping her hands to her mouth, attempted to imitate Ngiome's call. Several birds that shared this garden with them reacted simultaneously, and then with a rippling effect, others joined in from beyond, followed by some monkeys.

"That should wake everyone up," said Carver.

"Just want him to know we're all right."

Ngiome responded with a yodeling sound to which Zora answered with a poor imitation of a howling wolf. "OK," she said, and she crawled back and curled up beside Carver.

They lay quietly together, listening, as the bird and monkey sounds tapered off.

"I love the softness of your skin," Carver whispered as he slowly ran his hand along the deep curve above her hip.

"And I love your caress." They kissed as they slowly caressed one another. She closed her eyes, pressed her face against his and began to gently move her cheek along his, feeling his beard. She rotated her face and nibbled at him with her lips. "Are you going to make love to me one more time—before we climb down from here?"

"I wish I could make love to you and never go back down there. I could just stay here and love you, and love you, and never stop—but—I think I need to recharge."

"You mean I wore you out," she laughed.

"Let's just say you've taken me to my limit. We do have tonight, you know—and tomorrow, and—you're not leaving here without me, you know."

She laughed again, then pushed him over and rolled on top of him. The morning light had illuminated the whiteness of his body and she looked at him, up and down. Her hand slowly moved across his jaw, then her finger across his lips. "You are a handsome man, you know." She stroked his face again. "I'm trying to picture what you looked like when I first met you—you haven't shaved since we left Brazzaville have you?"

"You're right—you could say that my attention to personal hygiene has all but disappeared since we've been in the jungle."

"That goes for both of us. We've gone back to our natural state—to being the savages we once were—the *noble* savages. I like your

265

personal hygiene, by the way." She pressed her face against his abdomen and took a deep breath, "I like the way you smell."

He pushed her over and touching her belly with his forehead and the ridge of his nose, began stroking it. "And your scent makes me crazy." Then laughing, he said, "Look at this place! It truly is paradise. We're birds up here. There's a lightness I never knew could exist. Peace, freedom, joy, security…" He paused, and his eyes dropped for a brief second. "I worry that I don't really deserve this—this Eden."

"Garden of Eden," Zora repeated. "Do you think Adam and Eve felt like this? I mean, Adam and Even—that's just a story—but it was based on people—their longings, what they wanted, what they needed—what they felt they'd lost. It gets down to the basics of who we are. Last night—I screamed, didn't I? I can still feel it. It was like all the tension that had accumulated in me—the phantoms, the horrors, the sadness—like it got released in one massive geyser and I was Eve and, you and I and this place—we're all the same thing," She stopped, looked at him, and took a deep breath, "… and—I think I like you with a beard."

He laughed and grabbing her arms, rolled himself over, now straddling her.

"If I sound like I'm jabbering a bunch of gibberish it's," she paused for a second, "it's because I wasn't ready for this. I mean—what I'm feeling for you now—it's caught me off guard."

Carver pressed himself down on top of her and they held each other. Finally he relaxed his arms and rolled to one side and the two of them lay in silence as they watched the streaks of sunlight expanding across the boughs and foliage above.

Suddenly Zora sat up. "Look," she said.

Carver followed her gaze and there, no more than ten feet across from them, sat a white-faced monkey, a guenon, perched on the horizontal bend in a large vine. He was staring directly at them and when they looked at him, he cocked his head to one side, blinked, and rolled his lips slightly.

Carver rummaged around for a minute looking for his glasses. As he put them on he looked back at the monkey. "How long do you think he's been sitting there?"

"Probably all night, wouldn't you think?"

"Yeah—right."

"You made as much noise as I did—hey, look—by the pool—he didn't come alone."

Another monkey had just dropped onto the moss bed next to the pool. Soon another appeared, and then the first monkey left his position above and scampered down to the pool. He hopped into the water and splashed water into his face and, drawn by the sound of the water, several more arrived, as if by magic, from the vines above. An entire extended family—adults, juveniles, and females with infants clinging to their backs. Most of them plunged directly into the water while a few lingered along the edge, watching or drinking.

"They must come here every day," said Zora. "It's such a long way down to the ground and probably safer up here. A bathing hole in the sky—I love it."

"They have no fear of us. Like the chimps when we first encountered them."

They watched as the monkeys bathed, and when they were finished and started to wander away from the pool, Zora and Carver took their turn. They immersed themselves slowly, finally sitting in the center of the pond where the water arrived just below their waistlines. Carver, carefully shooing away tadpoles, stretched himself out on his back with his head leaning against the mossy bank. Zora plucked up a handful of moss and began using it like a sponge, first on herself and then on him. She started at his chest and then with slow, sensual movements, she ran it gently down his torso, into his groin and down his legs to his feet. He rolled over, moaning his approval as she continued up his back, to his head. She tossed the moss aside, plucked up a fresh handful, handed it to him then lay down in the water as he bathed her.

"When we get back to Seattle I need to put you on a serious feeding program. You're starting to waste away to nothing. It's no wonder you're able to climb up these vines as if you were a monkey."

"Climbing Denali takes every carb you have in your body. When you found me coming down the mountain that day—so long ago, it now seems—that was my second-consecutive expedition of the season. I was already at my lowest body fat level then. I don't think I'm really wasting away though, I'm at a level that was once considered normal—when our ancestors spent their entire lives running across the plains or through the jungles—like Ngiome. He never left that state."

"In any case, when we get back to Seattle, I intend to fatten you up—a little. I want to be able to sit down at a fine restaurant with a candle between us, a bottle of wine, and a big fat juicy steak."

"You wouldn't be insulted if I took rock fish in cream sauce, would you?"

He laughed and she smiled as she glanced over his shoulder. "Look," she said. They're still here."

Carver turned to see the entire troop of white face guenons perched in a single row on a large branch just beyond the pool. There were sixteen of them now, all quietly sitting and watching. Occasionally a mother would caress her baby while another picked carefully through the head of a sibling. "Have they been watching us this whole time?" Carver asked.

"Probably—wouldn't surprise me if tomorrow they don't start bathing each other with handfuls of moss."

Humans and monkeys sat quietly for several minutes, looking back at each other. Finally Zora stood up, stretched and speaking to the monkeys, said, "If you'll excuse us, we really need to get going."

"Wow, we should have washed these when we washed ourselves," said Carver as he pulled his shirt on.

"Yuck, you're not kidding. Guess we can wash them out tonight but, in fact, it really won't make much difference by then—we'll be used to it again in no time."

Carver wandered about the garden, taking pictures, then Zora helped him stretch his tape around the major boughs, and finally they measured the main trunk just below. The monkeys followed and watched, occasionally making small chirping sounds. Zora and

Carver would stop and make hand gestures to them, then attempt to imitate their sounds. When they were through, Carver opened up his satellite radio again and this time they were able to talk to Prince who had flown back to Ouésso where he said he would remain until he got confirmation that they had returned to the landing base.

"All right," said Zora, "have everything you need?"

"I'm ready," he answered. "Let's get going—but, one last thing." He took her in his arms and they kissed, embracing each other, neither wanting to let go. "Now I'm ready. Let's go see if Oleg got his lion."

Carver looked around, sighed, then climbed into his harness, put his helmet on and picked up one of the rope loops.

They had used three of the ropes to ascend the tree and only one remained unused. "I'd like to leave these other ropes in place for future use by whoever might come after us. I'll use this one for my descent. When I get to the next belaying station, you can lower the duffel bag. Now," he paused and looked at her. "I'll detach myself when I get there and send the harness up to you—I'd feel a lot more comfortable if you'd use the harness and rappel down. I get a sick feeling in my gut when I see you just dangling from these vines."

"I'll be OK. If you've been watching me, I always wrap a leg around another vine. If one were to break, I'm already half on the other one, and then, look—I've at least half a dozen vines always within reach. I worry more about you."

"OK."

He attached one end of the rope to his harness, wrapped it around one of the smaller boughs, and then attached it to a friction hitch on his harness. I'll be waiting for you."

She kissed him and said, "I'll be right behind you."

Carver stepped through the vee groove between the two boughs and pushed himself off, lightly at first, getting the feel for the rope. He swung outward and down, then back into the tree, gracefully meeting the massive trunk with his feet, and then pushing off again. Zora took hold of one of the vines and leaned out to watch as Carver repeated his rappel.

He looked up, they smiled at each other, and then suddenly, she noticed something out of the corner of her eye. She turned quickly. It was the rope. As it slid across the bough, there was a snapping sound and as she watched, a second snap split the air, this time louder, and the rope ripped apart. The two loose ends flailed wildly into the air, then disappeared like a shot into the depths below. Her heart exploded in panic as she reached out to grab one end, but her grasp felt only the air.

42 – RAGE

Zora froze. She stopped breathing; her eyes stared into nothingness, and her heart skipped a beat. For a split second, the entire world stopped, and then the sound of something crashing into the foliage below brought her back.

Zora looked down to where Carver should have been and there was no one; there was nothing, or almost nothing. She could see one of the rope ends draped across the canopy foliage below and she could see where Carver had passed through the upper layers. Several branches had been broken away and there was an opening but, she couldn't see into the opening. The original rope they had used to ascend the tree was still in place and without thinking she flung herself into the open air, grabbed the rope with one hand, pulled herself back against the trunk, bounced off with her feet and started sliding down at almost a free-fall speed, slowing herself as she grabbed the rope with her second hand and finally wrapping her legs, the skin on both hands and her thighs burning as she plunged.

She tried to call out to him, but the sound that rose out of her was but a whimper; a desperate, fearful whimper, "Carver … Carver." He wasn't answering.

Her descent didn't take her into the canopy at the exact place where he had gone through so, as soon as she penetrated the outer foliage, she released the rope and began to clamber through the cobweb of branches. Now she began thinking to herself, *he's OK—the branches stopped him. He's OK—he's OK.*

As soon as she reached a point where the interlacing branches

271

opened up she stopped. Holding her breath, her eyes began to search. It took several seconds to adjust to the darkness. "Carver!" she finally screamed his name out, "Carver! Say something—Carver! Ahhh!" she cried out, and then she caught a movement.

Burning sweat entered her eyes. She wiped it away, then pushed a branch aside so that she could get a clearer view. Carver was lying face up about ten yards below her and off to one side. His face was expressionless, but he was looking at her. One of his hands was moving, just slightly, motioning to her. "I'm coming!" she screamed. "Don't move—I'm coming."

She rushed to him, moving from branch to branch, jumping, swinging on a vine, then another branch, moving fearlessly. She arrived next to him and saw that he was alive. He continued looking at her, but said nothing. She took his hand and placed hers on his cheek. "Oh Carver," she whispered, her face now wet with tears. She knew by his position that his spine was damaged, and then she saw it—a branch, the end broken off and bloodied was protruding from his rib cage on his right side, the blood bubbling as he attempted to breath. He would be dead within minutes.

She pressed her face against his and started to cry, "Carver, Carver—my darling—no, please!" She looked at him and said, "I'm going with you. I won't let you die alone."

"No," he managed to whisper back to her. His eyes pleaded to her, "No." He clutched her arm with his loose hand and attempted to pull her. She looked him in the eyes and he tried saying something but she couldn't hear him. "Please—tell you," he whispered.

"Yes," she said, wiping the tears and snot that smeared her face now. "Tell me, my darling, tell me," and she place her head against his again and listened as he painfully gasped for air.

"Listen," he said, "go—for me—must go on."

"I know, I know."

"No—listen—listen." He choked; a spot of blood appeared between his lips then slid slowly down his chin. "My belt," he managed to say.

"Your belt?"

"Key—in my belt—sec—sec—pouch. Take it. Box—Brazza." He choked again, and she lifted her head to look at him. He smiled then the smile left, his eyes glazed over and he became still.

Zora cried. She cried loud and hard as she held Carver in her arms and she begged, not addressing anyone in particular. All the creatures in the surrounding trees had gone silent as if they knew and understood. Some hovered about, partially hidden in the surrounding shade; they listened and watched as she went on crying. Time passed, and she remained, holding him; her crying eventually tapered off into a low whimpering moan. The monkeys that had amused them earlier that morning, had come down and were gathered nearby—all remained silent.

Suddenly Zora felt something on her shoulder. It was soft and warm. At first she imagined that her mother had come to comfort her. But no, it was not her imagination; it was not the ghost of her mother. She felt it move, a slow calming caress. She lifted her head and turned and there, sitting on the branch behind her was Ngiome. When she looked at him, he took her head in his hands and leaned forward, gently touching his forehead to hers. Then he wrapped his arms around her as she quivered uncontrollably. Gradually the warmth of his touch began to exorcise the pain of her despair. Her breathing slowed, and she was able to release her mind—she began to drift off. Her body went limp, and she collapsed onto the little man.

The day was more than half gone by the time Zora began to repossess some sense of self-awareness. "Ngiome," she said, sitting upright and looking at him. "Carver can't stay here. We have to take care of him."

"Take him down?"

"Yes. We can use the *bilo* vine. Attach him to it, then lower him to the ground." She thought to herself for a minute, then said, "We'll make big fire—burn Carver—bury his ashes next to the tree. This is Carver's tree. He must rest here."

Zora climbed back up through the foliage and found the rope she had used. She pulled it down, rolled it up and looped it over her head and shoulder, then carried it down to where Ngiome had remained with Carver's body. Ngiome had used his machete to clear branches away below, creating an opening through which they could lower Carver.

She unhitched the torn rope from Carver's harness and replaced it with one end of the good rope. She looped the rope over a solid branch just over their heads, then over a second branch. She then unhitched the other end of the torn rope and pulled it away from the harness, coiling it up as she pulled it in. When she got to the end of the rope, she held it in her hand and stared at it—at the place where it had snapped apart.

She kept looking, as if in a trance until Ngiome asked, "Why are you looking like that at the *bilo* vine?"

She held it out to him and said, "Look, Ngiome. It was cut. Someone cut it—with a sharp knife." The rope end dangling in her hand, Zora's body shook, only now it was not from despair. She looked at Ngiome, and he recoiled. It was no longer Zora who looked at him. Her dark brown eyes had become red—red with the flames of absolute rage. Her gaze passed through him like the deranged stare of a rabid canine, and a shock of absolute fear stabbed into Ngiome.

43 – UN BOUQUET GARNI

"Do you see anything?" Aziza asked as Oleg scanned the understory above with his field glasses.

"Nothing."

"I know he went up there—the little *drek*. He was up early, yodeling his cockamamie bird calls or whatever the fuck he does. And the bitch answered him. Viper heard it too. They're still up there."

"Oh, I don't dispute that—I know they're up there. I didn't really think they'd spend the night up there though. I just wonder why our Lilliputian disappeared on us. Undoubtedly, he's gone up now as well. I'm just wondering why. As far as he's concerned, we should have gone out again looking for the lion, and he should have gone with us—dereliction of duty—guess the little *nain* wouldn't understand that concept though."

"We should have tied his ass up and used him for the lure. Now we've blown a full day.

Oleg collapsed his glasses, stuck them back into the leather case, and placed it on the long section of root that they had adapted to serve as a table. "Where's Viper?" he asked.

"Napping, I guess."

"Get him."

"Viper!" she yelled.

There was a movement by the tents and Viper's head appeared. He looked at them.

"Over here," she called.

"You see that?" he yelled as he started toward them. He was pointing up, behind them.

Someone or something was coming down the tree. Oleg retrieved his field glasses, looked back up into the canopy and said, "Now, what do we have here?"

"Is that Carver?" asked Aziza.

"Yes, it would appear so," said Oleg, still looking through his binoculars. "He's all limp—head's down on one side—not doing too well. And there's Zora hoisting him down. I do not see the pygmy. She's alone up there—that would account for the slow descent."

"What'd he say?" Viper asked Aziza.

"Something's happened to Carver."

"Huh?" grunted Viper.

"That's why the little *drek* went up there. He must have heard something—hears shit we can't hear."

"Yes, and that's why we need him—at least a bit longer," said Oleg. "Come on, let's check this out."

The three of them climbed onto the root mass and started maneuvering their way up to the trunk, watching the slowly descending body of Carver Hayden.

Viper started giggling as they approached the trunk of the tree. "Carver's dead," he chuckled to himself.

"Yes," said Oleg as he stopped and looked up, a slight smile now crossing his face. "Yes, I would say it does look that way." He looked at his two companions and went on. "Not exactly according to plan, but certainly convenient."

As they arrived at the trunk, Oleg continued. "Nice of her to send him down for us—all trussed up and ready to go. *Un bouquet garni,* you might say. The question now is, do we take him to the lions or do we simply set him out here and wait for the lions to come to us?"

"Do we really want to carry his cadaver a mile and a half through this jungle just to set up our lure when we can just set it up here?" Aziza smiled and looked at the two men. "Remember, if he gets carried anywhere, our porters are all dead, so it'll be you two who do the carrying."

The three separated as Carter's body arrived in their midst. As it made contact it fell over and slid into a crevice. Viper jumped after it and pulled the body into a sitting position, then grabbed Carver's hair and lifted his limp head. "I didn't really expect much trouble from this jerk-off any way," he said as he opened one of Carver's eyes with his free hand. "Look at me when I'm talking to you—huh—did your rope just happen to break?"

Aziza looked at him, "You cut his fucking rope, didn't you?"

Viper stared at her but didn't say anything.

"We should probably just leave him here for now, wouldn't you say?" Aziza asked.

"I would say so," answered Oleg as he looked at Viper. "Get your hands off him, Viper. She'll be down here in a minute—and watch what you're saying. Sound travels up you know. We don't necessarily want her to hear some of your comments."

"So how do you want to handle her now?" asked Viper.

Oleg looked up toward Zora and waved at her, then back at Viper and speaking in a hushed tone, said, "Answer Aziza's question—did you cut his rope?"

"Huh—ah—yeah—of course I did—I mean, what did you expect? He was showing off to me how he did his climbing shit, and then he just left me alone with his stuff."

"Maybe you better get back over by the tents—keep close to your gun. If she's figured out that the rope got cut, she's going to go straight after you."

Viper started to laugh nervously, "Oh—OK—so, should I be scared? I want her, Oleg. If she comes for me I'll be there—ha, ha," he laughed again, "with my arms open."

"You keep underestimating her, Viper. We need to do this carefully. Get over by your tent—sit in front of it—take you gun apart and start cleaning it so she can see what you're doing. Go on—go now. I'll be waiting here when she comes down."

Viper looked at Oleg then turned and started back toward the tents. "Aziza, you go over to that large root there near the tents, over there," he pointed, "Squat down like you're relieving yourself. If she goes toward Viper, she'll have to go past you. Get one of the AK-47's, have it close by and when she passes you, stand up and club her on the head. That should at least stun her enough 'til Viper and I can get to her."

"And what if she's moving too fast and I miss her?"

"Just shoot her—go for the legs—try not to kill her." Oleg looked up again. "She's coming now! She sees both of us, so take your time. Get across the root mess here—just like you would if you needed to take a piss." He looked up once more. "Go," he commanded under his breath.

Oleg dropped down into the crevice next to Carver and carefully straightened his head back up. He pushed Carver's hair back and went through the motion of adjusting his body then he looked up again toward Zora. It was taking her a long time to descend.

"Your hands," he exclaimed as she drew closer. "You're bleeding."

She looked at him but said nothing. Her hands were raw and bleeding from rope burns, as were the insides of her thighs, but all he could see there were the hanging shreds of her pants where the rope had torn them before it had ripped a path through her flesh. When she was within six feet of the root mass, she dropped, landed in a crouch, and then sprung up and quickly hopped onto the root, near Oleg. They looked at each other but neither spoke. Oleg stepped back when her eyes made contact with his. He followed her gaze as it shifted toward the tents, landing on Viper.

"Zora," he said, "you need to tend to your hands…."

She ignored him and vaulted over one root, landed on another, then, moving like a lithe predator, she quickly skipped and hopped her way toward Viper.

"Zora!" Oleg called out but said nothing more. He stood and watched and as Zora began to close on Viper, he could see her reach back and pull a knife out from the sheath that hung from her belt. She never saw Aziza.

44 – A MOST UNPLEASANT IMPOSITION

Zora was trapped in a dark place; a deep chasm lined with shadowy walls that looked like flakes of dirt caked around squirming roots. There was no up, down, front, or back; no point of reference. She was lost in the universe of an earthworm. She had no sensation of touch, yet she could feel it pressing in around her. She gasped for air. Was she drowning? Had she stopped breathing?

Gradually, fragments of awareness began to seep into her mind. It was a dream; a recurring dream; one she had gone through some time long ago. She wanted her mother and tried to call out for her, but her call was blocked. She tried again. Her voice had no sound; she had become mute. Her mother didn't come. The dream shifted. Now she was in a hospital, but not a real hospital—a clinic—Golfito—her appendix had just been removed—the anesthesia was not the most up-to-date and she was waking up with some difficulty. But the pain; it wasn't right. It was in her head and it tore through in a pulsating rhythm and with each pulse it left an echo like the reverberations of a jackhammer pounding through chunks of concrete pavement. She gasped again for air and then heard something. She could hear. She heard herself, but now she wasn't calling for her mother, she was just crying out from the pain—the unbearable pain.

She knew she was dreaming, but she didn't seem to be able to break out of it. She wanted to open her eyes; to make the dream end, but her eyes refused to open. There was a break in the pain and she could hear voices, distant, but maybe not. She couldn't quite make out what they were saying. It was the doctor—no, a nurse. They were talking.

She had stopped breathing again; she gasped for air—had to remember to breath. She called out again, but the pain; now it was somewhere else. Her hands, her legs, they burned—and now her head again. She opened her mouth to suck the air in, but as her lungs filled, the pain split through her head.

She felt something wet on her forehead. It was cool—soothing— it felt good. Another voice drifted in—the doctor again? No, not the doctor, but a man—a familiar voice. "You're going to be all right," he said. "You just had a bad accident. We're going to take good care of you. You just need to rest now."

Zora's eyes cracked open. They were just slits and only a light blurriness managed to filter through. She sensed movement, but everything looked to her as though she were floating in a vat filled with some mucilaginous substance—a specimen in a lab, attempting to look out. Her eyes closed and she made an effort to open them again, wider, and finally—she could see a face hovering just above.

"My poor dear," a man's voice again. "You've had a little concussion."

Her eyes closed again, and again she tried to breath. She could feel her mouth as it opened; the air as it rushed desperately into her lungs. A gasping noise, almost a cough resounded as she exhaled. Again, she attempted to open her eyes. She forced her lids to fold back, and again, through the muted light, she could see a face. It was Oleg.

"There she is," he said. "What a bang you took. You've been out for some time now and we were starting to worry about you."

"She awake?" It was Viper's voice.

Zora tried to lift her head. It rose up an inch or two then flopped back down. "Ahhh," she winced as the aching pain shot back through her head.

"Don't try to get up," said Oleg. "You probably have a concussion. You've been out for at least an hour—maybe more—in fact, it's almost dinnertime. Aziza's cooking up something good. We'll just get a little warm food into you and that should help bring you around."

"Uhhh," she tried to speak, but only moaned again.

"Here," came Viper's voice, "let me give her some of this." His face appeared next to Oleg's. She could see something moving. He was lifting something up, and then water began to pour onto her face. At first it was refreshing, but he kept pouring. It got into her eyes and as she attempted to breathe in, she sucked the water into her bronchial tubes and coughed, resulting in another shock wave of pain.

"That's enough," said Oleg. "Let's give her some more time while we get some dinner."

Viper's face appeared again and he leaned in close; she could feel his breath. Oddly it had no odor; as if the olfactory compartment in her brain had shut down. She felt something metallic touching her lips and slide slowly across. "Recognize this?" he asked. His head receded and she could see him smile. He slowly lifted his hand away so that her eyes could focus on it. He was holding a knife. It was her knife. "This is what I'm going to use when I bleed you."

He knelt down next to her, leaned in close again and she followed his movement, turning her head. She realized now that she was lying on the ground. "Uhhh," she attempted to speak, but again, could only moan. She tried to move her hand. It refused to move. She tried her leg and couldn't move that either. "Uhhh," she groaned again as she attempted to lift her head. It rose a couple of inches and then flopped down onto the ground again. "Ahh," she cried.

Viper grabbed her by the hair and lifted her head. "Look—you see that? You're all tied up. Oleg was afraid you'd hurt yourself, so we tied you up."

"A most unpleasant imposition for you, I'm sure," said Oleg, his face now hovering with Viper's in front of her, "but necessary, as I'm sure you would agree. As Viper said, we certainly do not want you to hurt yourself."

She felt Oleg's hand as he reached down and gently placed it on her breast. He squeezed her nipple and a lascivious smile crept across his face. She was naked; the realization hit her like a slap. Her eyes twitched as a cold sinking sensation began to draw her back into unconsciousness.

45 – SOUND OF THE BEE

The pain had subsided, and Zora's mind had begun to clear. She could hear the others talking. Occasionally Viper would laugh; more of a snickering giggle, a trait she had become all too familiar with. She shivered.

She craned her neck from side to side, trying to get as full a view as possible of her circumstances. What she was able to see only confirmed what she had assumed. She was tied down at each ankle and wrist and then spread out like an emaciated starfish, the rope ends secured to separate anchoring points, her limbs stretched tight. She squirmed, but the only real movement she could manage was with her head. It was dark now and the evening coolness made her shiver again; she was naked—totally exposed. All she could do was wait; wait until one of them made a mistake. She breathed slowly, taking her breaths long and deep, holding them, then letting them out; concentrating on her rhythms—the beat of her heart, the flow of her blood. She didn't bother to ask herself what they were planning to do. She knew—and she knew there was nothing she could do to stop it. They might just kill her, but she didn't think so—at least not right away. They would need her to track. Thank God Ngiome had stayed up in the tree. Hopefully he was well on his way back to the *bai*.

"You missed a good meal," said Aziza as she leaned over Zora.

Zora looked her in the eyes and said nothing.

"A shame, what happened to your boyfriend," came Viper's voice from not far off. "Better him than you, though—he's gonna get used for lion bait but, you—we got plans for you. And I have a very special treat for you." He squatted down, squeezed her cheeks, roughly, in his hand, moved her head back and forth, and brought his face up close. His breath stunk of canned sardines. "Tonight you're going to find out why they really call me Viper," he whispered. He pinched her hard, shoved her head back onto the ground and stood up. She winced as the pain ricocheted through her head.

"Gently, Viper," came Oleg's voice.

She couldn't see him, but he was close, *and he is the key*, she thought to herself. Viper was dangerous, but Oleg controlled him; he controlled both of them. And he was arrogant. And arrogant narcissists—always so sure of themselves—they have blind spots, lots of blind spots.

"My dear, Zora," he said. The other two had stepped aside and now Oleg was squatting down at her head. He began to stroke her forehead and then ran his hand up and through her hair. "I am so, so sorry that you are being put through this. I truly hope that you understand it is not my doing. Sometimes things happen, and I simply am unable to control them—and this—the way this is going—I did not want to see you have to go through this, but now it's out of my control. You do understand that, don't you?"

They looked at each other, their eyes fixed. Neither one blinked as each seemed to be waiting for the other. Finally he cocked his head slightly, took his one hand out of her hair, and with the other, ran his fingers across her breasts, down to her navel, which he circled, then stuck his forefinger in his mouth, and reached down again. She shuddered as he violated her, then he stood and looked down on her with a smirk of self-satisfaction. "*The prurient ape's defiling touch*–a little quote from an English poet I liked back in my youth. Titillating, isn't it? Ah-ha, no comment? You must be famished. Can we get you something to eat?"

She remained silent but kept her eyes locked on his.

"Perhaps something to drink?"

Her throat was parched. "Yes," she answered, then, clearing her throat, "I could use some water." Her voice was scratchy. She cleared her throat again and coughed.

Oleg smiled and looked at Aziza. "Why don't you get her something to drink?"

"With pleasure," said Aziza. She laughed, "My pleasure. Now, if you'll bear with me here for a second." Aziza undid her pants, pulled them down and squatting over Zora, urinated in her face.

Viper began laughing, then said, "Don't do that—fuck, Aziza, now she's gonna stink."

"And that should worry you?" Aziza exclaimed as she refastened her pants. "She already stinks, and besides, you should like it better that way." She looked back down at Zora, then to Oleg who nodded his head and handed Aziza a flask.

She leaned back over Zora and poured some water over her face. "Here you go—here's your water." Zora's eyes had closed but she opened them again when she realized it was water this time. "Open your mouth you little cunt," Aziza said as she pinched the sides of Zora's mouth open with one hand and emptied the rest of the water into it. "There—that what you wanted?"

Zora coughed and lost half the water. Aziza set the flask aside, then grabbed Zora's head in both of her hands, leaned down and bit her on the lower lip. Zora tried to pull away, but Aziza held her head firmly and continued biting. Finally she stopped, made a sucking sound and let go, turned her head to one side and expectorated a wad of saliva, red with Zora's blood against one of the woody bastions of the big tree.

Oleg was suddenly standing above her. He was naked. "I'm going to be doing you a great service now, Zora. I know you won't fully understand at first but when you do, you will, or at least should, be grateful to me. It's only because of Viper that I'm doing this. He is going to have you whether any of us want him to or not, so—I am simply going to prepare you. He is so brutish you know; the pain can be quite excruciating."

Zora didn't make a sound. It had started. She was helpless—physically—but not in her mind. Her only resort was her mind. She had never done it before, but she knew that it could be done. She closed her eyes and began to focus her awareness on her breathing. She slowed it, leveling the pace, feeling the movement of her diaphragm as each breath came in and each was expelled. She filtered-out the external sounds about her, concentrating on the wind far above as it clipped across the crowns of the upper canopy; she listened to all the creatures of the night; an owl, night jars, bats, insects—the bee. She commanded her inner voice to make the sound of the bee, and as the bee began to hum, the human voices and grunts that emanated from close by began to fade and Zora's mind slipped ever so gently, inward. She fell into a dream state; away from the physical reality of the material world and deep into that essence of her own, that world that was nonphysical. She lost track of time as she continued to recede, until—she ceased to exist. Zora left her body. Lightness swam about her and she began to float. She floated upward; ever so slowly and, looking down, could see herself, her skin bright and clear in contrast to the dark forms that hovered around her, and then her own form became only light, no longer recognizable as a finite entity.

She began to feel a soft presence close by. She looked around and she was not alone; there was a woman. A green aura seemed to emanate from within the woman's form which now appeared, clothed in a long robe, a shawl wrapped about her head—like a nun or a Madonna. Zora wanted to see the woman and her wish seemed to propel her toward the glowing form. As she got closer she wanted to touch the woman, but somehow she knew that she couldn't. The woman's head, which had been slightly bent downward, rose up and began to turn toward her, she couldn't see her very clearly, but she knew who it was. There was a familiar scent that she recognized and as the woman's head turned, it never seemed to come all the way around. It kept turning and turning; slowly, but with only a slight outline of the woman's face visible. The woman spoke; in a soft voice, almost a whisper, *"Te amo—te amo tanto, queridita mía."* Zora became overwhelmed with an almost unbearable ecstasy as the power of her mother's words, long ago faded but never gone, filled her soul. And now, looking back toward her own form on the damp, cold ground below, she could see her own face— her eyes closed, her skin smooth. She was at peace—blissful peace.

46 – THE NIGHT VISITOR

It had been thundering for a while. As always, it had started from far off, gradually increasing in volume as it drew near, eventually arriving directly overhead and then starting to slip away again, an echo of its earlier announcement. Only after it had begun to recede into the distance did the rain finally make its way through the thick layers above and begin to fall to the ground, dripping at first, but quickly expanding into a more substantial and soaking deluge.

Zora lay alone, naked and staked out like a dead animal, waiting to be skinned. The cold wetness of the pouring rain began to draw her back, back into her own body. Her eyes opened, gently and blinked. She opened her mouth and her torso lurched as she inhaled. The physical present swept immediately back into her awareness. She tried to stretch, craned her neck, looked around and saw nothing but the shear blackness of night, then she arched her head back and opened her mouth, at first lapping her tongue at the rain drops, catching the drops, using her mouth like a vessel, allowing the water to accumulate, then swallowing in slow gulps, taking pleasure as the coolness passed through her dehydrated throat.

Although the thunder had passed, it had brought with it a cold front of saturated air that now settled in and became stationary. The rain continued on in a hard and steady pattern. Just as Zora had begun to rehydrate herself, the discomfort of the rising pool she was lying in replaced her ravenous craving for water. She also began to feel the aftershocks from the physical abuse that she had been subjected to. Her resistance was low; she was bordering on starvation, she was unable to move anything but her head, her fingers, and her toes, and now the rising water threatened her with hypothermia. She was sinking, and she felt that she was going to die. She had to do something; something to keep herself from just slipping away. She had to make herself warm, to move.

She began to pull at her bonds, tugging and jerking until her joints began to ache; she thrashed, arched herself, flung her head back and forth, splashing the water that was gathering around her, then she coughed, lay her head back and sobbed, "Why—why?"

In defiant response to her question, the sky opened up and the rain surged. She screamed, but her scream was muted by the pounding of the rain and the thrashing of the branches far above. She tightened every muscle, then tugged at her bonds, hoping that just maybe the saturation of the rope would cause it to loosen. With one gargantuan effort, she pulled, then stopped and carefully cupped her fingers together, narrowed her hands, then pulled, ever so slowly, praying that one hand could slip through the bonding and when it did not, she exploded again into a writhing rage of frustration.

The rain finally stopped. It slowed to a drizzle first, then stopped, only the constant dripping remained. Zora had exhausted herself. She was too sick and damaged to sleep, but she had fallen into a semi-sleep state, sleeping, but with a troubled awareness still lingering, refusing to let go. Her mind became fixed, at first on the sounds of the dripping, and then, gradually, the sounds of life—the night life of the jungle that had turned itself off to wait out the storm, and now began to creep back in, slowly at first; the peep of a frog—a single frog—and then another and another.

One of her hands began to twitch. The circulation had been cut off to her extremities and now the discomfort was turning into yet another deranging agony. She twitched and shook, attempting to flex her digits. The skin of her fingers had become drawn into long stringy lines, blue at the tips, but she couldn't see them; now she could barely feel them. She had to relieve herself and she did, shamelessly and without care, taking comfort from the warmth as it seeped out from under her.

With her eyes closed, her mind began to drift, fogging over, and now and then a new sound from beyond pulled her back. Random thoughts passed through her mind. *Perhaps*, she thought, *if I can make it until dawn, when the others awaken, maybe they will allow me to get up, to move."*

A new sound roused her. She wasn't sure what it was, but there was something—not far. She concentrated, listened, and then she heard it again. This sound was different. It was soft, very subtle—the movement of air—the sound of breathing. It drew closer—and then a wet coldness touched one of her legs. She froze, not daring to move. And there it was again; air moving—inhaling—an animal. Its nose had just touched her leg as it explored her scent. She opened her eyes, carefully. She didn't dare move her head, but she moved her eyes, straining them down toward her leg. Everything was pitch black; she could see nothing. She listened and now it moved; it touched the top of her head and she felt the air move across her hair as it sniffed. She could sense its size; it was large. It reminded her of her grandparents' dog that would touch her with its cold nose to wake her in the mornings. Now it sniffed again—this time the sounds were louder, it drew its breaths in deeply, analyzing her scent, trying to determine what to do next—and then, nothing. The silence returned—just the frogs and insects. It had come to examine her—it had smelled her, and then it had moved on. She remained still—only her eyes moved—roaming—straining to see. Finally she decided to move her head. She rolled her head slowly backward, her eyes straining in the same direction. She could see nothing, so she began to rotate in a circular motion, pushing to extend beyond the limits of her field of vision. She repeated the circular motion, stopped, looked, and then she saw something; two luminous objects, golden in color, appeared to be floating in the darkness. She couldn't tell how far off they were, but they resembled lights. They flickered off, then back on again, and then they disappeared and were gone.

47 – A CONVENIENT ARRANGEMENT

"She's still alive," shouted Viper, gleefully. He was bent over Zora, lifting her head up by the hair. "Why do you cut your hair so short, bitch? You make it hard to grab. I want to drag you around by the hair—like a caveman drags his bitch when he takes her back to the cave to fuck her brains out."

"Calm down, baby," came Aziza's voice as she arrived behind him, peering around at Zora. "Relax, you're gonna have all day. Let's see what kind of shape she's in first." She knelt down on the ground next to Zora briefly then stood up. "It's like a sponge out here for Christ sake. Get a little wet last night, honey?"

"She's awake, but she just stares at you like a zombie." He stepped over her and stooped again, now grabbing her by the buttocks and hefting her up and down. "She's all limp, like a ragdoll—and cold—I can't believe how cold she feels. Check her out, Azize."

"Yeah, Zora, you're cold. You shouldn't stay out all night in the rain." She looked up and called out to Oleg, "Hey O, I think your girlfriend's gonna go into shock here." Then, looking at Viper, "Get her something to eat, something hot. I'll get something to cover her with. We need to warm her up if we want to keep her alive."

"Huh," Viper grunted, "yeah, OK—but stop calling her 'his' girlfriend."

A minute later, all three of them stood over Zora. "Untie the ropes, and let's drag her over there," Oleg said, pointing toward the trunk where Carver's body was still sitting propped up. "Not all the way, just get her above this water."

They untied Zora and then stepped back to watch as she attempted to stand. Viper laughed as she fell.

"Just drag her," said Oleg, then looking at Viper, "unless you want to carry her."

Viper stooped in front of her and said, "I can carry you—unless you want to get dragged across these big hard roots." He laughed and then continued. "If I carry you, maybe you can be a little nicer next time—don't play dead on me." He grabbed her head and squeezed it, looking into her eyes. "Don't play dead on me, you hear—you'll be dead soon enough." He grabbed her arms together, pulled them up, and hoisted her across his shoulder. "God, she don't weigh any more than my backpack," he said as he climbed up into the root mass and propped her up in a seated position.

"Here," said Aziza, handing her the metal cook pot with a spoon sticking out of it. "Hot rice with some kind of disgusting dried fish—eat."

Zora slowly reached up to take the pot but couldn't hold it, the entire contents spilling.

"You're a pathetic mess," said Aziza as she picked up the spoon, scraped some of the food off of Zora and pushed her head back, "Open your mouth—here—eat this or you're gonna die on us."

Zora opened her mouth and Aziza shoved the spoon in. She held the food in her mouth for an instant then slowly started to chew. She swallowed and Aziza gave her more. "Viper—here—take over, you're the one who wants her alive—come feed her."

"Oh, I want her alive too," said Oleg. "We all want her alive. Go on, Viper, feed her."

Viper took over while the other two looked on. "That seems to be almost all I can scrape off," he said as ran the spoon down her belly and along a thigh. "If you can bend over maybe you can get more by licking it off your self—or maybe you'd like me to lick it off, huh?" He put his arm around her and placed his face next to hers. "I can lick it off, then you can open your mouth and I can let it slide, nice and warm from my mouth into yours—like from the papa bird to the baby bird—want to try that?"

She turned her head away and looking at Oleg, said in a low, almost inaudible voice, "Had a visitor last night."

"What's that?" asked Viper.

"Oleg—talking to Oleg."

"She wants to talk to you," he said, looking at Oleg.

Oleg approached Zora, stooped down and placed his ear close to her face. "Go ahead, my dear—what did you want to tell me?"

Zora tried to sit up a little straighter, then cleared her throat. "I said—I had a visitor last night."

He looked at her with an inquisitive smile. "I had a visitor last night? Is that what you said?" Oleg then sat down on the ground next to her and placed an arm around her shoulder. "You had a rough night last night, my dear. Did you have a little hallucination?"

"Back where you left me tied up. Look around—you might find some pugmarks."

Oleg stared at her for a minute—contemplating something—then he began to walk back to where Zora had been tied down. "Aziza, you said you were going to get something warm to cover her with. Why don't you do that now—and Viper—stay with her, we don't want to see her disappear on us."

Oleg sloshed around, looking at the ground where Zora had spent the night. "Too much water, there won't be any prints here."

"Tell him to look along the high area there—where it's not so wet."

Viper repeated her suggestion to Oleg and Oleg shifted his search to the drier high ground. Aziza returned with a man's shirt and threw it over Zora's shoulder while Oleg continued to search. Finally he stopped, knelt down on the ground, then looked up at Zora, stood and returned to join the others.

"See anything?" asked Viper.

"Yeah," he answered. "He was here." He glanced over to where Carver's corpse was still leaning up against the tree trunk and said to Viper, "Check him out—see if he's been tampered with in any way—make sure he's still all there."

"Who's 'he'?" asked Aziza, "The pygmy?"

"The lion."

"The lion?" repeated Viper as he started climbing across the root mass. "You said he wouldn't be out in the rain—we didn't need to worry about him."

"He doesn't need to look at Carver," said Zora.

"What do you know?" asked Viper, who had stopped, and was now balancing himself on one of the roots.

"Unless he's sick or starving, big cats like that don't eat carrion," said Zora. "And that includes human carrion." Addressing Oleg, she continued, "If you people are serious about hunting this lion, you're going about it all wrong. I know these cats killed and ate Hoyt and everyone in his party, but under normal circumstances, they probably prefer, what to them is a more standard fare—like forest buffalo, or a river pig. There've been signs of all of them around, especially along the stream where the lion took Nabu. The confluence of the two rivers we saw on the map—where you headed with Ngiome the other day—that's going to be a major watering hole—like the *bai*.

Viper had progressed about halfway to Carver's corpse but stopped again. "Listen to her!" he said, "Sounds like you're recovering pretty quickly. Oleg, I don't trust the bitch, she's playing us. I say we tie her up here again, fuck her real good, then string her up as bait for the cat."

"Viper, go check on Carver," Oleg ordered.

Viper stopped, looked at Oleg and without saying anything else, turned and continued on toward Carver.

"Zora," Oleg said, turning his attention back to her, "Where did the pygmy go? Don't bullshit me—I know you know. He heard you up there in the tree then he just disappeared. I know he went up there—he just hasn't come back. And, that little spear of his is still over there near the tents."

"I sent him home," said Zora. "He was convinced that he had some kind of obligation to you—to be exact, he had to guide you to the lion so that you would bring his people back. Well, I told him since Carver was dead, my mission here was finished, so I promised him

I would fulfill his part of your agreement—and I told him that when I get back to the *bai*, I will personally retrieve his people. Ngiome's a very honorable person. The concepts of lying and deceit are pretty much unknown to him. They're simply not a part of his culture. He took you for your word and he was committed to delivering on his side, in spite of the fact that Viper murdered his nephew—in front of him and the rest of his family."

"Now that was unfortunate," said Oleg. "You know that Viper is not easy to control, and as much as I hate to admit it, I lost control of him that day, but I fully intend to make good on my promise to the pygmy."

"And I fully expect you to do that, Oleg. And that's why I'm here now. I promised him that I would take you to the lion, and I intend to do that. But you're not ever going to find your cat, Oleg, if you keep me tied up, especially if you allow that animal of yours to do," she paused for a second, "whatever it is he thinks he's going to do."

"Oh, he already got a good start last night," said Aziza. "I'm sure when you stand up and try to walk, you're going to feel it. He's been known to break a girl's pelvic bone—my Viper, heh, heh," she chuckled to herself.

"Zora," said Oleg. "You, yourself, just pointed us to the lion's pugmarks over there. Why in God's name do we need you to lead us to the lion, when we know that he's right here? Why shouldn't we just string you up, like Viper keeps suggesting, and set you out as our decoy."

"That's what I say," added Aziza. "We can tie you up, hang you upside down next to your dead boyfriend over there, and just sit back and wait."

"If he'd wanted me, he would have taken me last night," said Zora. "Truthfully, I think he wants one of you. After all, according to Ngiome, he was stalking the three of you almost the entire time you thought you were tracking him."

"What's she talking about?" Viper asked as he came slipping and sliding back across the root mass.

"The *drek* seems to think the lion was stalking us."

"Well, it wasn't Carver or me. We were up in the tree all day while you three were following Ngiome around looking for your lion. Ngiome told me that after you'd all crossed a small river—on a downed tree—he found two sets of prints. He followed them to where they crossed the river again. Then the tracks doubled back on the other side of the river, crossed back again, and fell in behind your tracks. You had two lions tracking you." Zora looked at Oleg and went on. "I understand that you told them the lion wouldn't be out in the rainstorm last night. Normally I would have agreed with you, but the tracks over there say otherwise. He—or it could have been 'they'—came right up and sniffed me. I felt his nose touch my leg—I could see its eyes watching me—then they left. They didn't want me." She looked at Viper now. "I think they want one of you, that's what I think."

"She's fucking with our minds, Oleg! Don't listen to her!"

"I'm not trying to do anything with your minds, in fact, I question whether you even have one," said Zora, looking now at Viper. "I want to get out of here alive, just like you do—and I know you don't want to hear this, but I think you need me to find your lion because—as much as you seem to know about hunting, Oleg—this is not your territory—and you—you three—just might not get out of here alive. I know how to track it, I'll know when it's trying to stalk us, and I can find its lair. I can at least improve your odds."

Zora leaned forward and attempted to stand up but couldn't maintain her balance and slumped back down.

"Ho!" shouted Viper. "You don't look like you're going anywhere, bitch."

"He's right, Oleg," said Aziza. "She's not about to go tracking anything today. Are we willing to sit around another day and just wait for her?"

"Oleg," said Viper, "it's easy—we know the cat's nearby. Is it gonna go back to the river and catch himself a wild pig for dinner? Why would he do that if he knows his dinner's right here waiting for him? We set up a blind—up against the big tree over there. We set the bitch out here. Don't stake her out like last night. We bend her over one of these roots and secure her there—then just wait."

Oleg stared at Viper, then stooped over Zora, lifted her up and placed one of her arms around his neck. "Come on, love. Let's try and walk a little. We need to get you so you can move a little better."

"What are you doing, Oleg?" Aziza asked. "What's it gonna be? You trying to get her walking again or do we set her out tonight for the cat?"

"I don't think we're going to see the cat tonight, and we want her in shape to start tracking tomorrow. We stay here. We will set up a blind—as a security measure. Go ahead—you two get going on the blind while I give her a little physical therapy." He pointed toward the tree and added, "Against the tree, but not too close to Carver. He's already starting to decompose."

Looking back at Zora, he lowered his voice, speaking discretely. "OK, you see where this is going now? I'll be expecting you to help us tomorrow and the next day and the day after that and, you're going to do it because I'm going to keep Viper from further violating your sweet lovely self. You're not going to find a better deal—unless of course, your friend should come back and surprise us tonight. And besides, it will be a great relief to me to have a guide I can actually talk to. Carver's dead. You no longer have a client, so you can stop thinking about him. I see you looking over there with those sad eyes. Now the pygmy's gone, and I no longer have a tracker. A very convenient arrangement, I would say—for both of us.

48 – VIPER'S MALAISE

"Another day to look forward to," Viper said as he quietly slipped up behind Zora. "Wasted another day just for you. I think Oleg's starting to lose it. He told me to untie you and invite you over for breakfast. But first—hold still." He reached around and forced her head back against his chest, then slowly slid a knife across her throat. "I really want to thank you for this knife, Zora. I can't believe how sharp it is—makes my clumsy combat knife look like a Boy Scout tool. I actually threw it away when you gave me this one. It's in good hands now. I really wonder what you thought you were going to use it for—'cause I do know how to use it." He released his hold on her and whispered in her ear, "Know what a snuff movie is?"

"Come on, Viper," she said. "It's going to be a long day—do you have to start it like this?"

"You didn't know that I'm in the snuff movie business, did you? Huh? Did you?"

"No Viper, I didn't."

"Oh yes. Trafficking young girls is just the tip of the iceberg you know. Young girls—virgins—and snuff movies." Viper released Zora's head, ran his hand down the side of her body and grabbed the left leg of her cargo pants. He then took the knife and quickly sliced the pants leg off, exposing her leg entirely. "There," he said. "I want to see these legs." He sliced the other side off then hopped over to untie one of the rope ends that she was bound with. "Oleg wanted you dressed again but not me. I was hoping for a naked tracker today."

"Viper, you said that I was being invited to breakfast."

"You are, but I really want you to understand—I want you to really be able to appreciate what I have in store for you."

Viper continued talking as he reworked the ropes. He tethered her feet, allowing her to walk, but with strict limitations, then made a hangman's noose and slipped it over her head.

"So my plan, Zora, is to make a film star out of you. Aziza can catch it all on her iPhone. And, we'll do it in daylight—not like the other night. I don't want you falling asleep on me again. Do you know how big I am down there, Zora—do you? But, of course you do—you've felt it firsthand! You—"

"Viper, what the fuck are you doing?" It was Aziza's voice. She stood directly behind him. "You were asked to get her and bring her over to the blind. We want to eat and get going."

"Huh? Yeah, OK. We're coming, alright?"

He untied the end of the rope that secured Zora's hands, tightened the noose around her neck and yanked on it, choking her and pulled her in closer. "I fuck the little virgins so hard they scream—and they keep screaming—and just as I cum I pull their heads back by their hair and the camera zooms in real close—so you can see the terror in their eyes. And, we film it all." He grabbed her again, pulled her head back and ran the knife across—this time just under her chin and above the rope that had already begun to turn her throat red. He was breathing hard now, and fast. "And when I cum," he whispered, "I'll slice open your throat and all that blood will just gush straight out toward the camera." He turned her around roughly and looked at her. "I'm going to make you a star."

She started to gag. Her eyes began to bulge, the whites growing big and round, when suddenly she took one of her hands that was now loose and swung it in a knife-chopping motion, catching Viper unexpectedly on the side of his head. As he staggered backward from the blow, he thrust frantically at her with the knife, throwing himself completely off balance. Zora saw the knife drop from his hand. She quickly lunged for it, but her feet were still bound and attached to a root. She fell hard.

She cried out from the pain as her cheek smashed into another root, looked around for Viper, who was still stunned from the blow, then quickly reached for her feet and frantically began to untie them.

"How fucking stupid can you be?"

Zora stopped and looked up. It was Oleg. He took the rope that dangled from her neck and stood her up. "Not you—him." He bent over, picked up the knife and pointed it at Viper. "Why do I always have to clean up after you?" He sliced the remaining rope that held Zora's arm, then threw the knife into the woody wall next to Viper's head. He then pulled on the loose end of the noose and tugged her forward until their bodies were snuggly pressed together and whispered, "I told you—you cooperate with me and I'll keep him at bay." Then, handing Viper the end of the rope, he snapped, "Here—tie her hands and bring her over to the blind. We want to eat breakfast so we can leave. We need her—understand?"

49 – AZIZA

"I must say," Oleg began as Aziza scooped a hot wad of oatmeal and raisins into a cup for Zora. "I'm not disappointed that he didn't show up last night. In truth, it would have been too easy."

"I wouldn't have called it 'too easy,'" said Aziza. "Not if you consider all the shit we've had to put up with just to get to this shithole."

"Here, I'll have some more, too," said Oleg as he held his cup up.

"You sure you want more?" Aziza looked at Zora and smiled. "It makes him fart."

"This is the first and only black lion ever known to have existed. By right, it should require a little extra effort. And—the beauty of it all is—it's all going to be legal." He looked at Zora and continued, "Thanks to your friend Hoyt, this cat is a man eater, and it's legal, of course, to shoot a man eater."

"Ha," laughed Viper, "That'll be a first for you, won't it Oleg?"

"No, the leopard I shot in Assam was supposedly a man eater—at least that's what everyone thought." He leaned toward Zora and winked.

Oleg wolfed down his second serving of oatmeal then stood up. "Viper, come with me—Aziza, you stay here and get all this stuff together—keep an eye on her. She can help. We're going to pack up the tents."

As the two men left, Aziza took the cup from Zora and threw it off into the root field, then reached across the blind platform, grabbed a backpack and dropped it in front of Zora. "Here, fill this up with food—and ammo."

Zora got onto her knees and started picking up boxes of pre-loaded

AK-47 clips, placing them into the bottom of the backpack.

"Not so easy with your hands tied, is it?"

"Maybe you could untie me so I can work a little more efficiently."

"Oh, you'd like that, wouldn't you? Leave the heavy boxes—Oleg keeps his ammo separate—carries it himself, too."

"Aziza," said Zora as she continued to fill the pack, "I don't quite get you—I mean, how do you fit in with those two?"

Aziza, stopped and looking at Zora, said, "None of us had mothers—at least that's one commonality—Viper and Oleg never even knew their mothers. I knew mine. Oleg knew his father, but Viper and I didn't—in fact, our mothers didn't know them either—ha!" she laughed. "Oleg told me you lost your mother when you were just a baby."

"She died when I was three."

"Ha—she didn't die like mine did."

"How did yours die?"

"To fully appreciate how she died, you need to go back a little. My mother's mother was a Polish Jew. During the Second World War, her family managed to hide out on a small farm in the mountains. They made it almost all the way through the war when some Nazis who were fleeing the Russians found them. She was gang-raped, and my mother was thus brought into the world. Thirty-five years later my mother was raped. This time it was a small gang of East German soldiers who were hunting in Poland—and—that's how I came into the world. I guess you could say I was born out of carnage—carnage in the Carpathians. Ha!"

"Sad, if you ask me."

"Sad is what happened next. The Krauts made her their sex slave. They put her in the care of a local peasant who kept up the hunting lodge when they weren't there. They would only come around a few times a year, and when they did, my mother left me with the caretaker while she entertained her soldiers.

"One day, the caretaker was gone somewhere, and I was there with my mother when the soldiers arrived. I was only five, but I remember every detail of it to this day. They got drunk and started taking turns with her. One of them thought it was hysterical that I was there and insisted that I be made to watch. As soon as my mother realized they'd brought me into the room, she picked up a bottle and hit the guy who was holding me. I remember—he had blood all over his face. He dropped me and started to beat her. He dragged her by the hair to the door and shoved her out into the snow—she was naked. He then took a hunting rifle—I remember him loading it. He went outside and screamed at her to run. She ran, and he started counting. I don't know how far he counted—he just counted—then he aimed and he shot. He missed, and his comrades started to cheer. He hit her on his third shot. I remember seeing the red blood spray across the snow—it was bright red against the white. I screamed and ran out to her and then I heard the gun go off again. I fell onto my mother and heard several more rounds go off. They were too drunk to bother coming out to see whether we were dead or alive. I would have frozen to death, but the old caretaker came back sometime during the night. The next day he dropped me off at an orphanage. All he told them my mother had died and that I was a Jew. I met Viper at the orphanage."

Zora stared at Aziza. She was speechless at first, but finally, cleared her throat, wiped her bound hands across her face and said, "What an awful story—I—I don't know what to say. I am just so sorry—so sorry that you had to live through that. What a poor child you were." She wiped her face again.

They both turned as they heard Viper and Oleg climbing back across the root maze, then Zora looked at Aziza and asked, "After all of that, how can you possibly?" She didn't know how to finish her question; she just looked back and forth, from Aziza to the two men.

"Revenge," said Aziza. "These two taught me how to deliver and enjoy an ever-so-sweet life of revenge."

"What are you talking about, Aziza?" Oleg asked as he stepped onto the platform.

"I was just about to tell our new guide here about my hunting reserve in Poland."

"Tell her later—I want to get moving. Viper, lengthen the rope between her feet—otherwise we'll be all day getting anywhere."

With overloaded packs on their backs, the party of four started off, Oleg leading at first, trying to use his GPS, but also referring to his magnetic compass and Carver's map. Zora followed and Aziza stayed behind her, holding on to the choke rope that remained tightly bound to Zora's neck. Aziza had an AK-47 slung around her head, and Oleg carried his hunting rifle, still in its leather case, grasped in one hand and balanced across his shoulder. All, with the exception of Zora, carried holstered Glocks, skinning knives, water bottles, machetes and cartridge bags on their belts. Zora carried the largest and heaviest of the backpacks, a belt that was loaded with additional cartridge bags, and water bottles. Everyone, including Zora, had additional cartridges in the bands of their Boonie hats. They were so heavily loaded that they made a constant racket as they walked; metal clinking against metal, poorly secured containers rattling against one another in their backpacks, water sloshing about in their bottles, boots thumping into roots, and the occasional grunt or obscene outburst as one of them stumbled. Viper took up the rear position, constantly scanning back and to the sides, as if he expected a sneak attack to come bursting out from some hidden place. He was the only one who actually had his weapon ready to use, but the only living thing he saw was an occasional lizard.

"I'm going to get us back to the river where the pygmy found the two sets of lion tracks. According to poor Carver's map, all we need to do is follow the river downstream until we hit the confluence with the other river. Zora, you take the lead once we get to the river." He turned and glanced at her as he continued to walk. "You able to keep up with those constraints on your feet?"

"Nice to know you're concerned," she answered.

"You get me to the lion, and I'll make sure that you leave this place with us—and alive."

"Oh, I believe you, Oleg. We'll find your lion."

No one said anything for a while, and then Zora looked back at

302

Aziza and asked, "What was that about a hunting reserve in Poland?"

"Private reserve," Aziza answered. "I assembled it from multiple purchases over several years. I go there for a couple of weeks each year. Interesting thing—the little hunting cabin where those guys used to go with my mother—it's right in the middle."

"Hmm—not by coincidence, I'm sure."

"Nope—not by coincidence."

They walked on in silence for several more minutes, then Aziza asked, "Zora, you like movies?"

"Don't see them too often, but I do."

"Ever seen *The Naked Prey*? Made back in the mid-1960s."

"No, can't say I ever heard of it."

"Great movie—Cornel Wilde. Supposedly inspired by the life of an American frontiersman named John Colter, but I always attributed its inspiration to the short story, *The Most Dangerous Game.*"

"Don't know that one either."

"They both involve hunting—human beings are the prey."

Zora didn't respond.

"That's what I do on my reserve. I get some fucking German asshole—one who's in uniform—cop or soldier—doesn't matter to me. I keep him tied up for a week, feed him gruel and stale bread, then I turn him loose—naked, of course. I give him a thirty-minute head start then I go hunting. One of them managed to evade me for four hours." She gave Zora a light jerk on her leash, as if to make sure she was listening. "I've been doing it for the last eight years—and this just happens to be the week I usually do it in. What do you think of that, hmm? This being my anniversary week."

"It's a long way from Poland, Aziza—and it's a lot harder to track. Who were you going to use as your naked prey here?"

"The pygmy—the fucking pygmy—and you told him to run off." Aziza's voice was getting loud and she was starting to spit as she talked, but Zora didn't see that since Aziza was behind her. "And you know what?"

Zora didn't respond.

"I asked, do you know what?"

Again, Zora didn't respond. Aziza pulled on the rope, jerking her back hard, almost knocking her to the ground. "When Oleg gets his lion—I'm gonna watch as Viper tears you up with his big cock. I'm gonna make sure he does it right and hurts you so you can hardly walk. But you don't need to worry about him slitting your throat, cause I'm gonna give you five minutes—just five minutes—and then I'm gonna hunt you like an animal—and then your head is gonna go up on my wall. You'll be the first bitch to go into my collection. I was hoping for a pygmy—now it's gonna be a fucking Latina bitch."

"Shut up, Aziza," came Oleg's voice from several yards ahead. "You're starting to sound like Viper."

50 – THE SOUND OF A SQUEALING PIG

"The river goes that way," said Viper as he yanked back on the rope, causing Zora to gag. "Where do you think you're going?"

Zora winced then bent over, coughing. She spit, then stood upright, inhaled deeply, and glaring at Viper sideways, replied, "The river makes a hairpin turn just beyond those fallen trees ahead. This is the way most of the game goes—look."

"Is he mistreating you again?" Oleg asked as he and Aziza came up behind Viper.

Zora pointed with her bound hands. "The trail goes this way. If you look carefully you can see it's littered with prints—including the lion's." Oleg stooped down to examine the ground. "And if you close your eyes and concentrate for just a minute you can feel the cooler air from the river. It's settled in along the trail. Smelling the water and feeling the coolness is what draws the animals this way. If you listen, you can hear the faint sound of rushing water. We're about to arrive at the confluence."

Oleg stood and gave Viper a stern look. "Stop jerking her leash like that."

Twelve minutes later, they were standing back on the riverbank. Just as Zora had told them, the river followed a sharply winding course and the small game trail was, indeed a shortcut, bringing them directly to the outer bank of yet another bend. The sudden squawking of a hornbill shattered the silence of the forest and drew their attention to a stout bongo standing on the far bank. The giant forest antelope lifted its head from the water and stood motionless, returning their

305

gaze—a magnificent sight with its spiraling horns and white-yellow stripes, laid out in zigzagging rows across its reddish back. Its nostrils pulsated in a gentle flapping motion as it sniffed the air.

"Want me to take it out?" Viper asked. "We could use some fresh meat for a change."

"No, not yet," Oleg answered. "If we're close to the main watering area, I don't want to spook anything. Let's catch something we can use for bait—then we can think about dinner."

"The rivers converge just beyond there," said Zora. "Almost straight past the bongo." She looked at her three captors and added, "That animal's never seen a human before. Its looking at us and sniffing us, but shows no signs of bolting. It doesn't know us as predators." She looked at Oleg and continued, "We're going to find that to be the case with all the wildlife here. If you have to kill something for meat, make it a forest hog if you can."

"You concerned about something, Zora?" Oleg asked.

Speaking in a low tone, she answered, "Please don't let them go on a killing rampage."

Oleg looked at her for a minute, then, turning to Viper, said, "Keep going. Remember, we're here for the lion. Let's get to the confluence and set up camp. We can decide what to do about dinner after we've scouted the area."

Within another half hour, they stood at the convergence of the two rivers. The fabric of forest was different here. The canopy was more open than it had been since they had entered the sunken forest. The light flooded in, and with it, the sounds of an intensity of life that had been absent throughout much of their trek. The second river was much wider than the one they had been following, and the canopy which leaned out and over it was broken in places where open gaps in the foliage allowed direct sunlight to plummet onto the water's surface, causing brilliant, blinding reflections. The remains of trees, broken and uprooted by past floods, lay helter-skelter like pick-up sticks along the banks, resulting in an impenetrable thickness of vegetation.

In contrast, the web of land between the two rivers was but a mud flat, barren of much growth. A rim of high grass separated it from the deeper forest and the overgrown riverbanks. It was here that Zora de Rycken and her three captors halted to survey their new surroundings.

They had become accustomed to the quiet within the cavernous understory of the giant trees, where all wildlife activity seemed to have been sequestered off to the far reaches of the canopy. Now the hum of life was suddenly everywhere. The air was alive with the sound of flapping wings, singing birds, and buzzing insects, and then there came a deep snorting sound.

Zora looked toward the source, smiled, and remarked, "Full of life."

"Only thing I've seen is that big antelope we just walked by," murmured Viper.

"Over there," she said, pointing across the flat to where the tall grass was growing. "Forest elephants." They could hear the sound of breaking wood and then movement—large dark forms swayed slowly, the tall grass around them waving as though a wind were blowing through. "And over there." she pointed further upstream. "I can just see a buffalo standing out in the water—you can see his head—between those fallen trees on the edge."

"And there," exclaimed Aziza. "I just saw something moving on the ground, just to our right."

"Chimpanzees," said Zora. "They've been following us half the day. This is the first time I've seen them come down to the ground though."

"They've been following us half the day, and this is the first time you say anything?" Viper glared at Zora.

"We're tracking a lion, not chimpanzees. If I stopped and pointed out everything I've seen on the trail, we'd never get to where you want to go."

"Where do you want to set up, Oleg?" asked Aziza.

"Let's dump our loads here for a few minutes and look around. Maybe upstream a little—on this side, but back, away from the water."

They spent almost an hour walking up and then back along the larger river. They finally found an area that was somewhat open and showed signs of heavy river hog traffic, so they decided to set their camp on the far side of the opening, away from the river and along the edge of the trees. "We set up against these big trees," said Oleg. "Gives us a solid back wall and a good, wide view of the area. We can do another platform like we had last night. What do you think, Aziza?"

"Makes good sense to me. Shall we go back and get our stuff?"

Oleg walked over to the larger of the trees and turned. With his back to the tree and looking toward the river, he took his rifle out of its case, placed the stock up to his shoulder and looking through the sight, swept the barrel slowly across the open area. "Yes, we set up here. Let us acquire our gear."

Within a half hour they had retrieved their gear and began setting up a camp. The only rope they had left was what was being used to keep Zora bound up, so they abandoned the idea of building a hunting platform and simply set their tents up on the ground, as close as they could get them to the large tree.

"Aziza," said Oleg, as he watched Zora attempting to pick up firewood, only to drop it each time the rope reached its limit. "Bring her over here. I'll put her to work starting the fire while you two gather wood."

"Oleg," said Viper, "How about if I go down by the river and wait for one of them pigs to come by. We need some meat in us—even her." He motioned toward Zora with his chin.

Oleg thought for a minute then replied, "All right—get us a pig and take Aziza with you. In fact, get us two pigs—one for dinner—one for bait. Shoot it in the leg—drag them both back here and we'll tie the wounded pig up out there." He pointed toward a dead limb sticking upright in the open area.

"Oleg, those things are heavy!" said Aziza. "How do you expect the two of us to drag two pigs back here? Especially one that's still alive—it'll be fighting us the whole way."

"One at a time—start with the bait. Take some of Zora's rope. We can take her neck rope off as long as I've got her. If you get another one for dinner tonight, you go back for it after you get the live one staked out."

"OK, we'll see what we can come up with. Maybe we find pigs, maybe something else. Maybe that buffalo's still down there. Aziza, you're a good shot—you go for the bait—I'll go for the dinner."

"How do you expect me to start a fire with my hands and feet all tied together like this?" Zora asked, as Viper and Aziza picked up their weapons and set off.

"I'll start it—you take a little break. Sit there and do nothing for a few minutes."

"Being tied up isn't much of a break. You know you really don't need to keep me bound up like this. I'm weak—I'm in pain—you think I could really run away from you at this point?"

"It's for your own good. You don't seem to want to believe me, but I am doing everything I can to keep you safe. They both would have killed you by now if I hadn't intervened."

"Just cut my ropes, Oleg, and cut the bullshit. You free me, and I'll lead you to your lion and as long as I'm free to move around, I can deal with your two psychopath companions." He didn't respond. She looked at him for a minute as he opened one of the packs, then she continued. "I really don't understand what you're doing with two people like that. With all you have to deal with. You're a very high-profile man—and those two don't make any sense—the liability—especially Viper. I can't believe that lunatic wasn't locked up years ago."

"Well," Oleg didn't finish what he was about to say; he was concentrating on getting the fire started. He had lit the gas stove and was using it to dry some of the damp wood they had collected.

"Want me to do that?"

"God, would you shut up for a minute?"

"No!" she snapped back at him. "Tell me—what are you doing with those two nutcases? They murder people, for God's sake. Do you murder people too?"

He finally had the fire started and began to add dry wood as she watched. Then, rising up, he stepped behind her, grasped her by the arms, rotated her to face the fire, and then sat on the ground behind her, still holding her arms.

"Come on, Oleg. What are you doing?"

Not answering, he wrapped his legs around her and slid forward until her back was snugly fit against his front. He then wrapped his arms around her, pressed his face against her neck and whispered in her ear, "No, I've never murdered anyone. Why would I? I've always had someone else to do it for me." He was quiet for a minute, listening to her breathing. "Personally, I don't particularly enjoy having people killed, but there are times when it makes sense—certainly you understand that. "

"Get off of me, Oleg—please."

"Ah, please." He relaxed his grip around her and lifted his head back, but did not shift his position. "Zora," he paused.

"Zora, what?"

"You are so young and I have a lot to teach you."

"Teach me?"

"Yes, you didn't think I was just going to leave you here, did you? I told you I was going to protect you from Viper—and Aziza. Yes— they both want to sink their venomous little teeth into you and just suck the life right out, but that's not going to happen. It's not going to happen because I have my own plans. The first thing I need to do is to begin the redirection or, might I say, the correction—of your education. Do you understand what that means?"

"What I understand, Oleg, is that my original assessment of you, although accurate, had completely missed the fact that you are as mentally unbalanced as Viper, if not even more so."

"Your assessment of me? How interesting. Did you, in your assessment, classify me as a narcissist?"

"I checked that box the instant I first saw you at that bar in Brazzaville—the way you looked at yourself in the mirror just screamed narcissist."

"Zora, every human has a little narcissism in him, and the more self-awareness you possess, the more narcissistic you are likely to be. It's only logical." He caressed her arms with his hands for an instant, and then reached around her and pulled her in close again. She squirmed in an attempt to shake him off, but he only tightened his hold. "Every human being, at birth, perceives himself as the center of everything. They very quickly discover the unknown—everything out there that they don't understand—and when that happens, most react with uncertainty and fear; their self-confidence ceases to evolve, they stop developing the creative sides of their brains, they evolve into passive beasts, like cattle, and their lack of curiosity leads them to lives of platitudinous boredom. They lack the energy to discover, choosing instead to languor along behind the dogmas of primitive religion. Religion—mankind's answer to anything and everything that he does not understand—mankind's greatest disaster—his ultimate downfall." He paused briefly, as if to recall where he was going with his tirade. "This is not what happens to me—and I understand that I have been tagged as a narcissist in the past—just another label from those who don't quite seem to be able to figure it all out. Now, lack of empathy is considered to be a predominant feature of the narcissist—and, thank God, I have absolutely no empathy for anyone. The mere concept of empathy eludes me. Like all human beings, I was born with the perception that I was the center of everything. Unlike most, however; I have been fortunate enough to have retained that realization. As I grew into adulthood and studied at the finest universities, I absorbed knowledge—I have made it my mission to comprehend the unknown. And with the knowledge I have obtained, has come power and—knowledge is power. Knowing one's self is power."

"That last statement makes sense, Oleg. I agree with you—knowing one's self is power. But the way you use that power is the key to life, Oleg—and look how you use your power."

"The secret to life, Zora, is knowing that you are the center of all that is. Before your birth there was nothing—and when you die, all will go back to nothingness. I think we discussed this once before. Since all of those outside of your own circle of perception are of no consequence, what happens to them after you die is also of no consequence, therefore, anything you do in your lifetime only makes logical sense if it is done on your own behalf, be that murdering another human being, or simply taking what you want out of life, regardless of how it might impact any other person—or the planet—for that matter. Hah!" he laughed, "The fools worry about overheating the planet! So what! If it ever does get so hot that humans can't live on it, so what! I will be gone by then, so it really doesn't matter, does it? But—if they want to worry about it, I can certainly find a way to profit from their fears. Hah! Fears again. All you need to do is keep the masses in a state of fear—they'll do anything you want. And the beauty—the beauty of all this knowledge, this awareness of one's own self, is that this one simple power is all you need to possess everything. Zora, I am the center of the universe and by right, anything and everything I desire or want, is and should be mine." He released her and pushed her over to where she was facing him. "And that includes you."

Zora was silent.

"You've gone quiet, Zora."

She remained mute.

"You must be thinking to yourself now, *Oleg thinks he is going to possess me*. Well, you are right. I told you that I have plans for you, and I do."

He grabbed the rope that ran from her hands to her feet and dragged her closer to the edge of one of the tree's roots, propped her up against it, then sat down looking at her. "I never knew my mother— did you know that? It was by design of course. My father was a powerful member of Moscow's most elite. He was one of those power figures who kept a low public profile, yet always lurked behind the scenes pulling the strings—of the economy, politics, the military— everything. He never married, but when he decided to produce an heir, he enlisted his experts who developed a list of potential mates based on intelligence exams, physical assets, and DNA. He made his final selection, impregnated her, and when I was born, he had me raised by a staff of hand-selected nurses, teachers, coaches. I never saw my real mother. I never suckled her breast. I have no idea whatever happened to her, and I never cared. He was in his early sixties when I was born. And you know what? There were two things he did that I intend to do differently." He pulled her head back to look at her, as if expecting a reaction to his last statement. She remained silent.

"One—I am going to produce my heir before I get into my sixties—and two—I'm not putting together a think tank of psycho-social morons to select the vessel that will carry my heir. I plan on making that selection myself."

"If you're the center of the universe, and no other human beings are of any consequence to you, what do you need an heir for? I sense a big contradiction here, Oleg."

Oleg sighed and then rolled Zora over again, now facing away from him. He placed his hands on her back and slowly started moving them. His movements were gentle. He slid his hands under her shirt and began to make circular stroking motions, reaching around to her breasts and then gradually exploring out to her rib cage, down along the curve that ran from her waist to her hips, across to her abdomen, and then downward again, stopping when he felt her thighs tighten.

"The other night you went catatonic on me," he said as he pulled his hands back. "Now I sense an effort at physical resistance. I like this better—I like it when you respond—I know you can feel me that way. You should make an effort to enjoy it, you know."

He released his grip on her, undid his belt, and reached under her clothing again. This time she reacted quickly. Arching away from him she began to thrash about and managed to break loose from his hold.

"I love this—it's like breaking a wild horse." He regained control of her, and this time attempted to pin her in place by wrapping his legs around her while he continued to grope and probe with both hands. She responded again; twisting, bucking; he regained control, only to lose it once more. They rolled and rocked across the ground like two wrestlers, where one dominated the other but simply could not subdue his stubborn opponent. They were both breathing hard now. "You can fight me all night if you want, Zora, but I outweigh you by at least eighty or ninety pounds. You know I'm going to win—why do you keep fighting? You know if I have to wait for Viper to get back and help, then I'll be forced to offer him seconds. You don't want that, do you?"

And then they heard something. It was a long whining grunting sound. Oleg released his hold, stood up, and looked around. It was getting dark, and across the open area that spread out toward the river, he could see the bent forms of Aziza and Viper. They were dragging something—something large and noisy. They stopped, and Viper's voice called out, "Can you get over here and give us a hand? This thing's fucking heavy."

Oleg turned back to Zora as he started out to help the others. "Sounds like they got a pig," he said. "God, how I love the sound of a squealing pig—almost as much as a squealing woman."

Lying on her side, Zora rolled slightly in one direction, then quickly reversed and rolled up into a sitting posture. With her hands tied to her feet, she had to stretch her head back in order to look out at the approaching hunters. Night had fallen, but the sky was clear, and the faint light of the moon was reflecting off the river's surface, backlighting Aziza, Viper, and the hog, and as she looked she caught a movement off to one side. *The chimps again*, she thought to herself. She adjusted her position and twisted her head to try and catch a better glimpse, but it was dark and she saw nothing. Then she detected another movement and could just barely make out a dark form slowly working its way through the dense growth. It moved quietly. It was coming in her direction and as it passed through the dull reflected light, she was able to see it. It was Ngiome.

314

51 – WHAT'S MY NAME

The staked-out hog's squealing gradually wound down and finally went quiet some time during the night. In spite of the hog's silence, the night had been long, but now nighttime was ending. As the early morning light was barely beginning to show itself, a flock of parrots landed in a tree on the far side of the river and proceeded to shatter the calmness of the moment, squawking over the rights to a cluster of fruit, overlooked by the previous day's foragers.

"Motherfuckers!" bellowed Viper as he scrambled out of his tent, his AK-47 in one hand. "Where the fuck are they?" He pointed his gun toward the trees across the river and emptied his clip. The parrots' squawking only intensified and as they flew off in a panic they were quickly joined by the residing birds, monkeys, and elephants, that had never heard the sound of a firearm.

"You happy now?" asked Aziza from her perch on the shooting platform, where she had spent the past three hours watching the red river hog while keeping an eye on Zora. You just woke up the whole fucking world—although I don't see Oleg sticking his head out here."

"Huh—yeah, Oleg. Guess he's too worn out—after fucking his brains out half the night," then lowering his voice, "Why are we getting cut out? He said she was mine."

"He wants to take her back to the Villa. She's become a challenge for him—like a wild stallion—he needs to break her."

"That's not gonna happen unless he gets her hooked. We'd all be a lot happier if he'd just concentrate on the lion and let me cut her fucking throat."

"Right, but speaking of the lion, our pig's been awfully quiet down there. How about running out and checking on it."

Viper looked over to where they had tied the river hog to the dead tree trunk in the mud. "Hmm—you're right." He went back to his tent and grabbed a new clip, ejected the spent one, and slid the new one into his gun as he started down toward the hog.

"Fuckin pig's dead," he yelled as he kicked at the inanimate carcass.

"What the hell," she said as he came back. "Shit, you only shot him once, and it was a clean shot—didn't even bleed that much."

"There's a hole in his neck—looks like he bled out from there. Weird—I know I didn't hit him there. You were with me. Single shot in the leg."

"What are you talking about?" It was Oleg. He had finally come crawling out of his tent.

"Pig's dead, but no lion. Something got him in the neck."

Oleg wiped some crust out of his eyes then looked toward the staked-out hog. "Show me."

"Aziza, you can pull Zora out of my tent and retie her while we look at the pig."

"If he's dead, cut off something to eat," she called out as the two men started out.

Aziza ducked into Oleg's tent where she found Zora huddled in the far end, her hands and feet tied together. "Relax," she said, "I'm going to get you out of here. She quickly redid her bindings to allow her to move about as she had the day before then led her out, pulling slightly on the neck binding. "Come on, eat something—you'll feel better."

"Some water," Zora said as she attempted to straighten up. Still partially hunched over, she shuffled toward the fire, her steps short and choppy from the tethering at her feet.

"Here," Aziza handed her a water bottle. "Sit over there."

Zora sat down, lost her balance, dropped the bottle, then rolled over to one side and using both hands, pushed herself up to a sitting position. She picked up the bottle, took a drink, and stared at Aziza.

316

"Ah—looks like my princess has arisen," said Oleg as he appeared behind her.

"I don't think she likes the way we've been treating her," said Aziza.

"She should be thrilled and grateful for the way I treated her last night." He stepped around and took her chin in one hand. "Eat up—then I'm taking you down to the river to get you cleaned up. You don't look so well, and we have a big day ahead." He released her chin and walked over to the fire, picked up a small pot, filled it with oatmeal, and sat down next to Aziza, the two of them facing Zora. "New plan. Viper's going to roast one of the hog's legs while Zora gets cleaned up, then after we get some fresh meat into our bellies, Zora's going to take us to the lion's den. He didn't come to us last night so we'll go to him." He shoveled several spoonsful into his mouth, then leaned over and handed it to Zora. "Here, quit daydreaming and finish this—then we go. I want you to give me your assessment of what happened to the hog, then we'll get cleaned up in the river."

Minutes later, Oleg and Zora started out toward the dead hog and the river. Oleg led slowly, his rifle balanced on his shoulder and the rope in his hand. He kept her moving with light tugs accompanied by soft words of encouragement.

"He impaled himself on a piece of wood or something," she said as she squatted over the remains of the red river hog. The striking red fur of his throat was matted with dark blood that was now almost black. Zora felt the neck, then slipped her finger into the hole, wiped it clean on the beast's back and pushed herself up. "Let's look around—see if the lion might have at least approached to check him out."

They both wandered back and forth around the dead animal for several minutes, then Zora said, "No lion."

"That's it? No signs of the lion anywhere?"

"No."

"OK, come on then, let's go—pestering flies so thick you can hardly see." Oleg swatted at the air then gave Zora a light shove, pushing her ahead now, as he followed, rope in hand.

Ngiome's spear, she thought to herself. He slipped in after the moon had gone down and put the poor thing out of his misery but the lions—he was here too.

They arrived at the water's edge to the sound of a splash nearby. Oleg started to take his rifle out of its case.

"You don't need to get that out," said Zora. "Just a couple of otters—look," she pointed downstream. "There they go."

"Sure that wasn't a croc?" He looked around, not sure that he could trust her, then he leaned his rifle against the sandy bank that ran along the river, reached into one of his cargo pockets and pulled out a bar of soap. "Come here. I'm going to loosen the rope on your hands so you can have a little more movement." He loosened the rope and extended the length that connected her hands. "There—now be so good as to remove your clothes, take this soap and go wash yourself."

Zora had been barefoot since she had gone up into the giant tree with Carver, and her clothing now consisted of nothing but a torn quick-dry T-shirt and battle pants, the legs of which had been cut off the day before by Viper.

She sneered at him and said, "My clothes need cleaning too—I'll just leave them on."

Oleg pulled on her neck rope, towing her to him, wrapped his arms around her and pressed his body into hers. "I said, 'take your clothes off'—are you hard at hearing?" He then loosened the neck binding and lifted it over her head. "This is the only shirt you have now. You want me to rip it off or take it off?"

She said nothing and tried to pull back, but he continued holding her. He gradually relaxed his grip, then reached out and lifted the shirt up and over her head. He paused for a brief second while the two looked at each other, then he grabbed her pants, unbuttoned them, and pulled them down to her ankles.

"Why don't you just kill me—or let your two friends do it?"

He pulled her back and pressed himself against her again, then grabbed her by the hair and held her head back, looking into her eyes. "I told you I was going to take care of you. I've already told them you're off limits—you belong to me now."

She pulled her head forward, trying to break his grip, her eyes drilled back at him, her dark brown irises dilated as anger spread across her face. "I don't belong to anyone, you sick piece of garbage."

The muscles in his face tightened. He pulled her head back again and leaned down and bit her on the neck. "For the rest of your life, you will be mine. You are now my property to do with what I wish. Before I'm through with you, you'll be crawling to me like a dog and you will beg—you will beg. Do you understand?" He pushed her away and then took her hands and placed the soap into them. "Now get in the water and wash yourself." He turned her around, slipped the rope back over her head, and shoved her into the river. With her feet still tethered, she lost her balance and fell face first into the water.

In spite of her bondings, the buoyancy of the water allowed her to regain her balance easily and she stood up. The water was waiste deep. She twisted halfway around to face him and cried out, her voice shaking, "Why don't you just kill me—what do you want?" She then flung herself into the water, submerged, resurfaced, and stood, her back to Oleg, and started to soap herself.

"Turn around so I can see you," ordered Oleg.

"I need to watch for crocodiles," she answered, her voice cracking.

"You said there were no crocodiles. If there are, I'll watch for them. I said turn around. I want to watch while you get soaped up."

She ignored him and submerged herself back into the water.

"Soap your crotch real good—that's going to be my lunch—but I don't need to tell you that—I'm sure you're already thinking about it." He smiled at her and raised his eyebrows.

Turning suddenly, she threw the soap bar at him. "Here, I'll rinse off, then you should go. You stink too, you know—but I don't need to tell you that." She turned away from him again and remained crouched in the water, her head above the surface. She dunked her head a couple of times and spit a stream of water out like a fountain. The cool water was bringing about a therapeutic calmness. In a semi-floating position, with her feet just barely touching the bottom, she took a several deep breaths, closed her eyes for a minute, then stood up and began to walk back to the shore.

"Stay in the water," Oleg ordered. "You think I'm going to let you sit out here alone with my rifle over there?" He had taken his clothes off and was stepping into the water, still holding the end of her neck leash. She backed away, keeping as much distance from him as she could, within the limitations of the rope that linked them. As she was watching him, she caught a slight movement in the tall grass that ran along the top of the bank and just above Oleg's rifle. She looked but saw nothing. A moment later she heard the sound of a bird—one of Ngiome's signals.

Oleg wrapped the end of the rope around his wrist several times, making sure that he was securely attached to her, then he dunked his head below the water, came back up and started soaping himself. "Don't move," he said and submerged himself again.

Zora took this opportunity to scan the tall grass beyond the bank, hoping to see Ngiome and perhaps send him a signal of some kind. She failed to notice that Oleg was swimming toward her under the water. When she did, she stepped back, but forgetting her foot tethering, lost her balance and fell. By the time she had regained her balance; Oleg had grabbed her by the arm and pulled her back. She could feel his erection as he pressed himself to her.

"Here," he said as he slowly slid the bar of soap across her chest, pushing it against her breast, "Take the soap and do my back." He turned her around then placed the bar into her hands.

With both hands grasping the soap, Zora began to rub his upper back with small circular motions. She worked her way upward to his shoulders and then suddenly lifted her hands straight up and came down as hard as she could, hitting the crown of his head with a corner of the soap bar. Because of his height, she was unable to get the leverage necessary to bring it down with the impact she had hoped for and the bar glanced off to one side. Before he had time to react, she jumped upward and looped her tied hands over his head, around his neck, and pulled back. At the same time she hopped off the muddy river bottom, planted her knees in the small of his back, and pushed into it while pulling against his neck. This was the opportunity that Zora had been patiently waiting for. It was now or never; she would not get another chance like this. She had to kill him, and she had to do it quickly.

Oleg's arms flailed out and back, groping blindly for her head. Zora pushed and she pulled, unloading every ounce of energy she had left. She knew that she was weak from three consecutive days of torture and overexposure, she no longer had the physical strength to overpower him without being able to use some form of surprise. Her blow with the soap bar had not hit its target, and even though she had successfully secured him in a deadly stranglehold, her strength was gone and she could feel that he was going to break the hold. Her strategy had to be modified, and fast. Taking a deep breath, she launched herself, with Oleg still tight in her grasp, over to one side and under the water. If she couldn't break his neck or strangle him, she would drown him.

Zora was able to hold her breath for a long time and she knew she could easily outlast someone like Oleg, but the water was too shallow. Managing to get his feet planted on the bottom, Oleg finally succeeded in grabbing her and with one massive effort, he thrust himself upward and flipped Zora over his head, breaking her grip on his neck, and plunging her down into the water in front of him.

Oleg bent over coughing and spitting, his hands on his knees, as Zora slowly rose back up out of the water. Physically spent and unable to stand, she knelt on the bottom, her head just above the water level. Without saying anything, Oleg waded over to her, grabbed her by the neck and slowly lifted her up. With his loose hand, he reached around, grabbed her by the hair, bent down and kissed her. He then threw her over his shoulder, carried her up onto the bank and slammed her down hard onto the ground.

"Do you realize that you just gave me the most exciting three minutes I've had in years?" he said as he straddled her, pinning her down with one hand while holding her tied hands over her head, he planted his knees on her thighs. He looked around and picked up a stone and threw it. "No more unexpected bumps on the head from you today—huh?" He tried to kiss her, but she turned her head so he went to her neck, kissing, biting, and licking. As he worked his way down to her breasts he released his hold on her hands and looked up. "I'm letting go of your hands. You can hit me if you want—it will only get me harder if you do. Now I'm going to loosen up the binding on your feet so you can spread your legs and then I am going to fill you once again with my God-seed."

He looked at her, and continued, "It truly is God-seed I give you, you know. The earth you all talk about saving is nothing more than an enormous chunk of rotting cabbage and the human race a mass of maggots that wriggle across it, mindlessly devouring. They devour the cabbage and every day we get closer and closer to the end. It's so clear—and I, Olegushka Levkov—I approve of it for as I have said to you before, when I am gone, everything will be gone. And you, my tender little dear should delight in the fact that I am so inclined as to plant into you, my glorious seed."

He shook her and she turned her head as tears began to roll down her cheeks. He shook her again and leaning his head down close to hers, he whispered, "I am God, Zora—I am God."

322

52 – BROWNING LEVER-ACTION BLR

Thirty minutes later Oleg was sitting with his back leaning against the bank. Zora was lying next to him in a fetal position, her back toward Oleg. They were both naked, and Oleg was gently stroking her hip. "My sweet Zora. This is going to work out for us, you know. In your own way, you're getting as much out of this as I am. The more you despise me, the more you enjoy having me." He rolled over, pressing his body to hers. "For three days now I've been planting my seed in you, and I want to tell you—I'm not like my father was. I'm going to keep you after you've given me a son—and—as long as you behave, I'll let you see him." He placed his mouth next to her ear. "Maybe you're already pregnant. Tell me—they say that often a woman can tell immediately. Zora, are you pregnant? Has one of my mighty sperms attached itself to your lovely egg?"

She squirmed away and twisted her head around to see his face. "If I'm pregnant," she said; her voice strained. "If I'm pregnant, it's certainly not from you. If I'm on cycle—and I always am, I would most likely have been ovulating when I was with Carver. What did you think Carver and I did all night up in that tree? Sorry to blow your pathetic fantasy—besides, you—ha," she half chuckled. "I'd bet money that you're sterile." She shook her shoulder, trying to break away from his grasp. "*Közel!*"

"*Közel!*" he repeated. "Ah-ha! So, you know a little Russian after all!"

"Ha!" she laughed, then switched to Russian. His eyes expanded when he realized that she was totally fluent. "Of course, I do—it was one of my majors in college. The army even sent me to Moscow on a three-month exchange program my last year in school and—I've been quietly listening in on every conversation you've had with those two *kakáshkas* of yours."

Oleg pulled back to his former position, with his back against the bank. "Hmm," he grunted. "This changes everything. Not the fact that you speak Russian, but the possibility that you could be with child—other than mine." He reached over, placed his hand back on her hip and resumed his stroking. "Our sexual relationship should not change—if anything, it should continue to get better." He leaned over, kissed her on the neck and whispered in her ear again. "You're no longer running off in your head into some kind of transcendental trance now are you? And, you almost came this time, didn't you?"

She bent away from him, deepening her fetal position.

"We may have to move to a new strategy. When the helicopter picks us up at base camp, they will be told to bring something special for you. I will, after all, have to put you on a diet of my own concoction. Ever try heroin, my dear? Hmmm? What do you think of that? Well let me tell you—it works wonders with people like you. By the time we get to Brazzaville, you will be a complete catatonic—and when I get you back to France, assuming you are pregnant, we will induce an abortion, and then—and only then, will I slowly bring you off the addiction and when you are perfectly clean again, I will impregnate you. Only this time it will be with my offspring—and if it's not a male, we will once again abort, and try again. And after the child is born, you will continue on as my sex slave—I should say—one of my sex slaves, for I already maintain a stable of up to a dozen at any given time. Most of them came to me on their own, however, and with very little, if any, coaxing. And when you learn to please me, I will keep you for a long time—and—you will live a life of luxury that will be beyond anything you ever imagined. If you don't, I'll give you to Viper, and he can make you a star in one of his awful little movies."

A splashing sound somewhere upstream, caused Oleg to look around. He saw nothing and turned his attention back to her. "Otters again?" He stopped stroking and started kneading her flesh with his fingers. "What do you say we get dressed and go eat some of that pork Viper's been cooking?"

Oleg stood, picked up Zora's clothes and held them out to her. "Time to get..." Stopping in mid sentence he began looking back and forth along the bank. "What the...?" he said. "My rifle! Where's my rifle?" He pushed her to one side and ran over to the bank where he had left it. "My rifle!" he screamed. "Where's my fucking rifle?"

53 – VIPER

"Chimpanzees?" remarked Viper, as he stared at Oleg, his eyes narrowed in an expression of disbelief. "Chimpanzees took your gun?"

"It's gone," said Oleg. He was clearly agitated; his voice breaking, face drawn and pale, his eyes twitching nervously.

"Your Browning," muttered Viper, shaking his head and looking down at the ground. "Oleg, you had that custom made. Solid stock, fucking Browning BLR 300, lever action—stainless steel—not to mention the case—handmade Italian leather." He looked up at Oleg, still shaking his head, then bent over and picked up two skewers of meat that were simmering next to the fire. "Fucking museum piece," he muttered.

"She didn't throw it in the river when you weren't looking, did she?" asked Aziza.

Oleg stopped blinking and stared at her. "If she had been able to get her hands on it, she would have tried to use it on me."

"Can I have some of that?" Zora asked, looking at the spits of meat Viper was holding.

"No—get that shit out of my sight," said Oleg. "How can you think about food now?" He jerked the leash sharply causing her to choke.

Viper lifted the meat to his nose and sniffed, waved the spits back and forth in front of Zora, smiling at her, and then tossed them off into a web of vines where one remained stuck. "Too bad. It was pretty damned good, but not for you."

"You gotta get your gun back, Oleg," said Aziza. "Does she know which way they went?"

326

"Yeah, straight up into the trees." Oleg paced back and forth, mumbling to himself. Several minutes passed, then he stopped, looked at the others, said, "Let's go—we go for the lion—now. Aziza, you and Viper take turns managing her—hour on, hour off. You start. I'll take your gun while you manage her. I can kill a lion with an AK just as easily as with the Browning. Just have to get closer—but in this jungle we're not about to get any long shots in anyway."

"How do we know where to find it?" asked Viper. "Our bait's dead and half-eaten now. Didn't do any good when it was alive anyway."

"Zora, we're going back along the river to where we saw lion spoor yesterday. Then you figure out which way it's going and see if you can follow it. Their den's gotta be around her somewhere." He reached down and picked up a water bottle. "You been filtering more water for us?" he asked Aziza.

"We have enough for today," she answered.

"OK, Aziza—you start with Zora. Loosen up her foot bindings—give her enough slack so she can take normal steps. Just don't give her enough to run—maybe tighten up the leash—no more than five or six feet between her and you. Everyone load up on ammo, water and energy bars. We'll come back here tonight so we travel light. Load Zora up too—dump whatever shit she has in her backpack out and fill it with water and ammo." He walked over to his tent, ducked in for a minute then came out holding a daypack. "I got the map, compass, first aid, and binoculars. Let's go—Aziza, give me your gun."

Fifteen minutes later, Zora stopped and squatted down to examine something on the ground. She looked up at Viper. "This is where the red hog was when you shot him."

"Yeah, looks about right."

She stood and continued on, Aziza close behind and the other two trailing by about ten to fifteen yards.

As they rounded a bend in the river, they startled a dozen large vultures, causing them to rise up from the ground, their massive wings pushing the air like windmills. They had been dining on something that was spread out over a wide area. One greedy bird was still busy tearing into whatever it was. When it saw them approach it lifted its bloodied head, let out a hissing sound and hopped backwards several feet before taking to the air to join its companions.

Zora approached the carcass, stopped, stooped down to examine part of the carcass, then stood and started forward but was stopped by the rope. She gagged, then, looking at Oleg, said, "Can you tell her to give me a little more slack? I need to check these prints, and she keeps jerking me back."

"Aziza, just keep up with her, would you—and Zora, if you don't want to get choked, tell her when you're changing direction—just communicate—you got all the slack you're going to get. So tell us, what was it?"

"Giant forest hog," said Zora. "See all the dark-black hair. The head's totally gone but there's a tusk—big one—big male." She stood upright again and looked at Oleg. "Lion got him—last night—so close to where we were—amazing nobody heard it."

"Nobody heard cause you and Oleg where making a racket of your own," commented Aziza.

Oleg gave her a dirty look then turned to Zora. "So which way?"

"Away from the river—into the forest—that way," she pointed. "Tracks are recent and clear—two of them and they're probably really full. Looks like they polished off almost half the hog before turning it over to the vultures. These are very big cats. This hog was probably more than twice the size of the red river hog you shot, Viper. There's no way to tell how much the vultures have eaten, but the two lions could have consumed as much as 150 pounds each." She stopped and pointed at the ground. "Different cat here—now there's three of them."

"Shit, Oleg," said Aziza. "We only have two guns, there's three of them and I'm in front with her and don't even have my gun."

"Quit whining," said Oleg. "You got her in front of you. If they come from the front, they'll get her first, you just duck down on the ground and we'll shoot over you—oh—Viper, make sure you got it on full automatic." He looked at Aziza and laughed.

"They just ate half a six-hundred-pound forest hog," said Zora.

"They'll be slow as molasses. In any case, we'll find them before they find us. They're probably sound asleep right now."

The foliage was dense at the tree line, but there was a clear game path that cut through, like a low-ceilinged tunnel. They had to bend down to pass through, which seemed to increase Aziza's unease, but the heavy ground growth only lasted forty to fifty feet when the jungle floor opened up, and once again they were back among the giant trees where the trail switched back and forth, winding like a snake as it led them around the ever-present maze of buttress roots. The level of illumination had dropped, and the sounds of the creatures that cluttered along the river began to fade. When they did hear something now it was usually a voice arriving from out of the darkness with an eerie echo, somehow well paired with the damp coolness that permeated the air.

Much to Viper's chagrin, he and Aziza were told to switch positions. He responded to his new task by jerking back on Zora's rope. "Just a reminder—I'm in charge now."

The jungle floor was deep in leaf litter, occasional mushrooms hovered above on elongated stems, solitary fronds unfurled upward, looking like soft, almost semi-transparent hairs, vines dropped from above or grew from below, reaching upward in search of light. Man-sized palms and ferns, sparsely spaced came out of the ground and softened the pattern of mold and moss-covered roots and trunks.

"What's that?" asked Viper, after they had walked for almost an hour.

"What's what?" Zora responded with her own question.

"That noise—up above—sounds like something way up in those branches."

"Chimps," said Zora. "I think they've decided to join us."

"Same ones took Oleg's gun?"

"Could be—but there're a lot of them out here."

"Let's hold up." Viper stopped walking and looked back toward Oleg who was lagging by thirty or so feet. "I need to tell Oleg—maybe if he blasted them with the automatic, we might come up with his gun—boy, wouldn't that be sweet."

"Keep going," said Zora. "It's good to have them up there. They're like an early warning system—they're likely to see the lions way before we would. They always scream and raise hell when they see a predator. Oleg shoots at them, and they'll just take off"

"Hmm," Viper pondered on what she said. "Yeah, OK—early warning system." He shook the rope like a surrey driver signaling his horses to move on. "Keep going."

Zora led, and Viper followed, nervously, his face white with concern. Constantly on guard, his head shifted from side to side in anticipation, and each time he looked one way, the light stroke of some long leaf or vine would brush against him from the opposing side and he would quickly flinch, brushing it away with one hand, then again with the other. Each time he raised his left hand, Zora could feel the pull on her neck. She could tell exactly where he was and how far behind her he trailed.

"Hold up," he said after several more minutes. "I don't see the others." He stopped and looked back for Oleg and Aziza. "Oleg," he called out as they rounded an eight-foot high root obstruction. "Can you stay a little closer? Remember I don't have a gun."

"Of course you've got a gun—use your Glock if you need a gun and stop worrying. I had to pee. Keep going—Aziza will take over after our next water break."

"At least tell me when you stop."

"We will."

Viper shook Zora's rope again and nodded to her. She turned and resumed walking.

Zora walked slightly stooped over, looking at the ground and constantly scanning ahead and to their sides. Small lizards darted off from time to time and an unseen bird took flight, startling Viper, who stopped again, causing yet another choking jolt to Zora's neck.

"Just a bird," she said to him as she reached up to pull on the neck binding with her two hands, trying to relieve the discomfort.

"Huh? Keep going, cunt."

She continued on with her slow pace, stepping ahead, looking, listening.

They began to pass between the high ridges of two opposing buttress roots, each one going in the opposite direction from the other, one side getting higher as the other got lower. Small saplings and vines interspersed along the route, formed a natural obstacle course and forced them to step from side to side on a zigzagging route. Zora ducked down low as she passed under a spider web. Viper, seeing her movement, followed suit when he got to the web. Oleg and Aziza did not see it and suddenly Zora could hear Oleg swearing as he ran directly into it. She smiled and glanced back over her shoulder to see Viper also looking back.

Once again Oleg and Aziza had fallen behind. Viper didn't seem to have noticed, but Zora did, and she kept moving. Suddenly something caught her eye; something deeply buried in a mound of dead leaves. She knew what it was, and her mind and body responded instantly. She stepped wide to the left, away from the mound and turned abruptly back toward Viper who was now quite close behind her. As Viper realized that she had unexpectedly turned, his immediate reaction was to pull back hard on her rope, but because of her close proximity there was no tension in the rope, and the movement threw him off balance. In an attempt to keep from falling, he stepped far back with one foot, partially regained his equilibrium then immediately lunged forward at Zora. Anticipating his move, Zora stopped abruptly, rotated toward Viper, and, as he came toward her, stepped out of his way and stuck her opposing leg out and between his feet. At the same time, she grasped the rope in her left hand and placed her right hand on the back of his shoulder. With the rope, she pulled him in the direction he had begun to fall, and, placing her hand on his back, she pushed.

"Fuck!" said Viper as he spun out of control and onto the ground. He reached both arms out to break his fall but landed hard, on his forearms, facing downward. As he lifted his head, the expression of unexpected surprise shifted instantly to rage; his hands were open, fingers spread in a clawing posture—and then he froze. Viper froze,

331

for here, as he lay where he had fallen—or where Zora had skillfully guided him in his fall, Seryoga Ivanov found himself looking directly into the eyes of a Gaboon viper.

The Gaboon viper is generally considered to be a placid snake and not particularly aggressive with the rare reports of humans being bitten, often the result of someone unexpectedly stepping on one. In this instance, Seryoga Ivanov had not stepped on the Gaboon viper, but his right forearm had slammed down on the serpent's tale and was pinning it hard to the ground as the two of them—human and serpent—locked eyes for the split millisecond that passed before the viper struck.

The Gaboon viper's venom is not nearly as toxic as some of the world's other venomous species. In fact, it does not even rate in the top ten. It does hold several other records, however. It is the heaviest of the vipers, weighing as much as twenty pounds with an empty stomach and, in spite of its massive size; it has the fastest strike of any poisonous snake. It also has the longest fangs, with reports of some measuring even longer than two inches. And its venom, although not the most potent, is delivered in the largest quantities of any species of poisonous snake on earth.

This was Viper's deepest and worst nightmare finally coming to fruition. Viper was dead, and he knew it, and within that brief second it took for the snake's strike to arrive, time, as measured in human terms, screeched to a halt while each cell in Viper's brain lit up and vomited out every memory, every longing, and every fear that had been sealed away and accumulated throughout his life. Viper was physically frozen, an inanimate block, and as the snake's wide-open mouth and dripping fangs approached in ultra-slow motion, he could hear the scream of every victim that he had ever brutalized or murdered. Each face came back to life and passed across the movie screen in his brain, from the old man who had guided them to the Amur tiger to the business rivals who had disappeared at his hands, and all the girls—the young virgins he had violated from the hordes that were being shipped to brothels throughout the world, the girls

332

who thought they were being sent to some better life—they flowed past him in a long waving file that vanished into the horizon like a long Chinese kite. The void in his heart of one who had never known love or been loved loomed in a formless black cloud while walls of squirming worms imploded inward, blotting out all else, smothering him in a foulness, unbearable and vile.

The Gaboon viper was large. It was almost six feet from head to tail with a girth of fifteen inches and a head, six inches across. Its fangs were just shy of three inches in length, and when they made contact, each one landed in perfect alignment with Viper's eyes, piercing the corneal membranes and penetrating on into his brain. Again, a unique quality of the Gaboon viper—when biting its prey, where all other snakes bite and release immediately, this species holds on and patiently pumps its full prodigious content of venom into its hapless victim. For Viper, slightly over nine milliliters of the toxin was injected in three pulses, equally spaced over five seconds—thirty-three times the amount needed to kill a human being. The last conscious sensation that Viper experienced as his life was snuffed away, was that of absolute and intense pain.

Zora quickly pulled the loose end of rope out from under him and stepped back as the serpent's wide-open mouth covered Viper's face and remained latched on. She watched as his body stiffened and began to quiver. Her eyes searched down the trail to where the sounds of Oleg's voice nervously expounded obscenities as he picked and pulled the clinging silky threads of spider's web away from his face and upper body then glanced back at Viper. Out of the corner of her eye she could see the others approaching. The snake had finally released its hold and was gliding away, through the leaf pile and into the entanglement beyond. She quickly stooped and retrieved her own knife that Viper had been carrying. The other two getting close, she didn't have time to cut her bindings so she concealed it in one of the ammo pouches she had been carrying, then rolled Viper's writhing body over and called out to the others, "Snake! Viper's been bit!"

Oleg and Aziza dashed forward as they saw their companion

on the ground and when they arrived, standing over him, they both stepped back in horror. Aziza dropped her gun and screamed, "No! No!" She covered her face with both hands and wailed uncontrollably.

"Where's the snake?" Oleg yelled, looking around on the ground.

"It slid off over there," said Zora, pointing far to the left of where the snake had actually gone.

Oleg lifted his AK47 and wildly emptied the magazine, spraying the ground and then arcing upward, bullets tearing through clumps of vines, slapping tree trunks and buttresses, splintered wood flying. When the gun was empty he stooped down but quickly recoiled in disgust as the stench of urine and defecation emanated from the rapidly swelling corpse.

Blistering was appearing in a sunburst pattern from the two dark voids that once were Viper's eyes. A gray, bloated tongue bulged from his gaping mouth and everything gradually became covered in the blood that issued forth from his empty eye sockets like thin red lava flows. His entire body twitched violently as if an electrical shock had been sent through it. It twitched again and then a third time, and finally lay still.

Aziza collapsed onto the ground, crying like a hysterical child, her hands holding her head, fingers digging into her scalp as she rolled onto her side and into a fetal position, rocking back and forth. In the canopy branches above, the chimpanzees had joined her screaming.

Oleg and Zora stood, speechless, their eyes glued to Viper's body as if under a hypnotic spell. Finally Oleg turned to Zora and asked, "What kind of snake was it?"

"Viper," she answered.

54 – THE RETURN OF NGIOME

"Drink," said Oleg as he held the water bottle in front of Aziza. "Come on, take a drink. Try and relax. We're going to sit here for a few minutes. You're OK—we're OK. He's gone now, and we're all in shock. We knew it would happen someday—just weren't ready for it." He wiped the sweat from his brow and sighed, "Not like that."

Aziza took the bottle. Her hands were shaking wildly, and she could hardly hold on to it. Water spilled down her chin as she drank. She put it down and, looking at Oleg, said, "We can't just leave him back there. Not in this place."

"What do you want to do with him, Aziza? We can't dig a grave. There're no rocks—you can't pile rocks over him. All we can do is leave him where he is."

"He'll be eaten by those disgusting vultures. The worms—fucking worms and bugs." She bowed her head and started moaning again.

Oleg stroked the back of her head, massaged her neck and shoulders for a minute then sat down, facing her. He looked toward Zora who was loosely lashed to a small tree trunk. He stared at her for a minute. "The snake bit him in his head. How the hell did that happen?"

"He tripped—probably a root. I just heard him yell out, then he fell—pulled me with him. When I turned around he was lying on the ground and the snake was biting him. It was a big snake, really big. I stayed back as far as I could, which was not easy. I was still tied to him."

"You're telling me you walked right by the snake and never saw it, but it was big? How's that?"

"Gaboon vipers—they look just like the leaves they hide in. You simply can't see them sometimes."

They sat in silence for a while then Oleg asked, "How far do you think we are from the lions?"

"I can't tell for certain, but I would guess the lions came down this path just a few hours ago. Oh—and there's only two sets of tracks now. One of them wandered off to the south." She pointed to the right with her bound hands. "Toward the river—the small river we followed yesterday from where we left Carver," she looked at Aziza and continued, "unburied and exposed—just waiting for the worms and bugs."

Aziza slowly lifted her head and stared at Zora. The two locked eyes and continued to stare at each other while Oleg watched, his right forefinger nervously moving back and forth along the stock of his gun. Finally Aziza broke the silence. "You led him into that snake, you fucking bitch. I know you did," then she stood up and shouted, "You fucking led him into that snake—tell me! Tell me, you fuck, you!"

She took a step toward Zora, but Oleg jumped up and intercepted her. "Calm down—she didn't do that." He grasped her arms. "Aziza, you're upset—you need to calm down. We can't stay here much longer, so sit back down—sit down until you get your head cleared. We need to keep moving."

"Yeah, OK—OK." She began to step away, then turned suddenly, both hands out and holding her Glock, pointing it at Zora. "I know you did it you bitch—I'm gonna blow your fucking head off!"

"Aziza! No!" yelled Oleg. "Listen to me—we can't afford to kill her. We need her—we need her to find the lion, and then we need her to take us out of here—Aziza!" he screamed, and as he screamed, another scream echoed back from above. The chimpanzees were still with them.

Aziza looked up, then turned and pointed the pistol at Oleg. "Don't get in my way, Oleg. We don't need her. Can't you see what she's doing? She's gonna kill us both if we let her keep going." She moved her arms back and forth pointing the gun toward Zora, then

336

to Oleg, then back to Zora. "Oleg, you know how to find your way through the woods as good as anyone—we don't need her—she's a fucking liability."

"No, you're wrong. This is not like the woods you and I know—look at all the people who've died around us here. We need her, Aziza."

As the two of them traded words, the chimpanzees turned up their volume, but no one noticed—at least Aziza and Oleg didn't.

"She's blinded you with her fucking pussy, Oleg. I'm telling you, she's just waiting." The pistol was pointed back at Zora now and Aziza slowly started toward her. "Open your mouth cunt, I'm going to put this thing in your mouth, like a steel cock, and you're going to tell me what really happened or I'm gonna blast the back of your head off."

Aziza stopped, still glaring at Zora, then abruptly pounced toward her and screamed, "You're dead, bitch!" But, as she raised the pistol again, something flashed through the air and glanced off her arm, knocking the Glock from her hand as it fired, missing Zora by several feet. "What the fuck?" she yelled. She took a step back and there, embedded in a tree was Ngiome's spear. She stared at it as she rubbed her forearm, then looked into the direction from which it had come, jumped back and shrieked, "Viper!" She staggered backwards several feet, then wiped her arm across her face. No more than fifteen feet away, towering above them on the ridge of an eight-foot high buttress root was Ngiome. His face and body were entirely coated with a chalky white paint in a pattern that resembled a shattered eggshell. His eyes were fixed on Aziza and Aziza's were on him. For a split second she had thought he was Viper—the chaotic patterns on his face made him look like a negative of Viper—white on black as opposed to Viper's black on white tattoos.

She stared in disbelief, still clutching the arm that had been grazed by the spear. Then she scrambled to her pistol, fumbled with it, and, grasping it in both hands, turned. She pointed, and frantically fired off several rounds, but Ngiome was no longer there. He had dropped off the back of his perch and was gone.

"It's him!" screamed Aziza at the top of her lungs. She threw her pistol to the ground, grabbed her AK-47, and darted off after Ngiome, screaming, "The fucking pygmy! He's mine—his fucking head is mine!"

"Run!" Zora screamed in his language, "Run, Ngiome—she's coming!"

"Shit," said Oleg. He bolted after Aziza, shouting at her, "Aziza— come back—you'll never catch him like that!"

The instant Oleg started after Aziza, Zora reached into her ammo pouch and pulled out the knife. She quickly picked it up and in one swipe, cut the ropes that bound her feet, then stood up and ran her hand bindings across the edge of Ngiome's spear. She was free.

In the same instant, as Oleg was about to disappear beyond the high buttress, he stopped and looked back at her. "No!" he screamed frantically, as their eyes met. "Zora, no—I won't shoot—stay!" He stood motionless with his mouth open, and as he slowly raised his AK47, Zora, with Ngiome's spear in one hand and her knife in the other, vaulted the root wall and was gone. Oleg fired off one shot in frustration as he changed directions and took off after her.

Zora flew through the jungle like a dart. She ran up one long-reaching root, leaped, grabbed a vine, swung to another, ran down onto the ground, vaulted over a fallen tree, and continued, full speed, following the screams and gunshots of Aziza who was now on a parallel course, not far off. She altered her course and began to slow her pace, wanting to converge with Aziza and catch her from behind. Further back, she heard Oleg's clumsy footsteps, the clinking and banging of his water bottle and the cartridges that hung from his belt. He was moving on a skewed pattern that was taking him in the wrong direction.

The pursuit quickly took them toward the river. Zora could smell it; could feel its coolness as she began to close on Aziza. The AK-47 had stopped firing, and Aziza was no longer screaming but Zora could hear the pounding of her footsteps and her missteps as she slipped and tripped her way after Ngiome. Then she heard the sound of Aziza's gun hitting the ground, followed by her agitated voice as it erupted into a fusillade of self-deprecating obscenities.

Aziza was unable to run along the root structures or fallen trees. The constant detours she was forced to take left her completely lost and confused, but she continued to rush blindly ahead, looking back and forth. Finally she began to slow down. Out of breath and breathing hard she yelled out, "Where are you, you little fuck? Come out, come out so Ziza can see you." Then she stopped, blinked and with a sinister smile cracking its way across her face, she raised the AK-47. "There you are, you little…" And there he stood, no more than twenty yards, straight in front of her. He seemed to have just jumped out from behind a tree. He looked straight at her as she raised the gun, but the bullets just sprayed out harmlessly and once again, he was gone. Re-energized, she bolted after him, more determined than ever.

Like a ghost, Ngiome sprinted ahead each time he heard the sound of her gun. He sniffed the air and could smell water—the river was close. He looked back and realized he was losing her again, so he waited. He listened and realized she was wandering off course. In a move to cut her off, he changed directions, and then, a minute later, he saw her. He quietly skirted around to get in front, hopped up onto a large fallen branch and revealed himself once again, then simply dropped back off as she raised her weapon. He continued to draw her on, and within minutes he was at the river's edge, close to where the fallen tree lay across like a bridge. The mad she-*bilo* was close behind.

He made a dash for the tree, jumped up, and was half way across when he heard Aziza come tumbling out of the thicket. He stopped, watched her, and waited. She looked upstream first, then down, and just as her eye caught his movement, he dove into the vegetation beyond. Again, she wildly fired off another volley.

She swore, then ran toward the tree, attempting to fire into the foliage where he had just disappeared, but her gun was empty. As she ran, she ejected the empty clip, reached into her belt pouch and reloaded. She had to transfer the gun to her shoulder, carrying it by the strap, in order to use both hands to climb onto the fallen tree. Once up, she started firing into the foliage, running full speed across the natural bridge. She was half way across when her foot slipped on the damp moss that coated the tree trunk and she went down, face first. Dazed from the impact, she slid helplessly off and into the river.

Her arms flailed about spastically as she desperately tried to regain equilibrium. She sputtered water and screamed as she bobbed up and down, her head disappearing under the surface then reappearing. Her feet finally discovered the bottom and she stood up; the water came up to just below her armpits. "Fuck, fuck, fuck!" she screamed as her fists pounded the water. She looked back and forth, "My gun—where's my fucking gun?"

With all her frantic screaming, her state of disorientation, her maddening frustration, she never heard the crocodiles.

The crocodiles spent most of the day quietly reposing in lairs, hidden within the deep banks of the river, accessed only from below the water's surface. It was late afternoon now, however; dusk was setting in, and it was time to eat. They had just begun to leave their mud dens and were quietly gathered in the deep shade just below the fallen tree where they would normally wait for their evening meal to appear. At times it came in the form of a fish or the bloated body of some creature that had perished upstream and was only passing through with the river's current, but on occasion some small or mid-sized mammal would come down to drink or even attempt to swim to the opposite bank. Although these were of the smaller crocodilian species known as dwarf crocodiles and not normally considered dangerous to humans, this group was hungry, and Aziza had managed to land right in their midst.

Zora had just arrived at the river and was looking across as Ngiome reappeared. Neither of them said a thing; they just looked at each other, visually confirming that each was safe, and then they watched. Aziza was pulled under for a few seconds, but then came bobbing back up, her eyes as big as chicken's eggs, bulging out and staring at Zora as if in wonder. The water thrashed wildly as over a dozen crocodiles grabbed and pulled. Aziza's eyes remained fixed on Zora as her body was simultaneously pulled in different directions. Within minutes she was ripped to shreds, only her head still floating like a buoy; and then a long, razor-edged mouth opened and clamped shut with a loud crunching noise, and Aziza Meyer, one-time Polish orphan turned adopted Jewish-American princess, and, finally, international diamond tsar and hunter of men, ceased to exist.

55 – ALONE IN THE DARK

Oleg was seated on the ground, his back settled into the curvature of a large tree where a pair of towering root walls splayed out across the moss-covered forest floor. The night was black as India ink, and a damp chill had settled in. Oleg's legs were bent, with his knees drawn in close and his feet planted firmly on the ground, a tension running from his feet up and through his legs as though he were trying to slowly push himself further into the tree. He held his Kalashnikov with both hands, the stock pressing into his armpit. It was set on full automatic, the safety was off and his right hand gripped the stock while his forefinger, straight out, just barely touched the trigger. His eyes were dilated, they flicked back and forth, and he was shivering. The sound of his teeth chattering blended in with the nighttime sounds of beetles, crickets, and frogs.

Oleg had to urinate, but he didn't dare to move. One second of distraction could be fatal, so he held it in until his bladder was ready to burst. At some point he realized that he couldn't hold it any longer. He took a long deep breath, strained his eyes to see if anything was moving, then, maintaining his ready-firing position with his right hand, he slowly released his left from the AK, slid it down to his fly, opened it, fought with his underwear as he tried to find the opening in the pocket, and finally pulled his penis out and relieved himself on the ground. His urine gushed out and saturated the moss he was sitting on. It dripped all over his hand as he fought once again to replace his penis, then, unable to complete the procedure with his left hand, he left his fly open and went back to his former position with both hands on the gun. Noting the scent of urine on his hand, he nervously wiped it across the moss.

The night continued to tick by and Oleg began to tire. He started nodding off, then snapped his head up, shook it, took a deep breath, and whispered to himself, "Stay awake—must stay awake." He widened his eyes, stretched the lids up and down, and rolled his eyes from side to side. The darkness was ubiquitous. He had assumed that he would experience some level of acclimatization and eventually shapes and objects would appear; he needed something to focus on—to help keep himself awake, but all he could see was the occasional flicker of some fluorescent insect, a moth, a small speck moving along just above the ground. There were sounds, so he concentrated on them; the wings of a bat perhaps, but for the most part it was the sound of mosquitoes that dominated this night. He had left his Deet behind and didn't dare swat them, so he allowed them to land and bite and suck his blood. At one point he wanted to cry. It was torture—slow, persistent, nightmarish torture. One landed on his eyelid, and when it drilled its proboscis into his skin, he twitched in agony, slapped himself with his urine-scented hand and let out a whining gasp.

A distant scream snapped him back as he started to drift. Some carnivore had just dispatched its prey. *What was that?* he asked himself in silence. He stretched his eyes again. He could feel his entire face swelling from the mosquito bites, and he released the gun again to wipe his eyes and to touch the surface of his puffed flesh. He could feel the stretching tension of his skin as it bloated out and away from his eyes. *Never assume anything,* he thought to himself. *Never assume that you're coming back. There are certain minimum supplies and equipment you must always take with you. All we took was water and ammo. No fucking food, no mosquito net. At least I have my compass and the map. Fuck the lion—fuck the lion—if I make it through this night I'm going straight back to the camp, get what I need and get the hell out of here. I can find my way—get to the top of the ridge and out of this fucking sunken nightmare. I'll be able to use the radio then— and the GPS.*

343

He carefully scanned the blackness again, and then slowly rotated the gun so that he could see his watch. "Fuck!" he said out loud. "Only eleven. I'm fucking dying here. I've got to stay awake—got to."

Fifteen minutes later Oleg was sound asleep. He could hear himself snoring, but he was so exhausted he couldn't force himself to wake up. He had become semi-aware of the snoring and within his dream he was telling himself that he shouldn't be asleep. Over and over he kept repeating to himself, *Oleg, you need to wake up. You're dreaming, but you need to wake up.* He became agitated, and his snores went into an irregular pattern and got louder, and then he suddenly couldn't breathe. He gasped out for air and was jolted into consciousness as a pain ripped through his hands. He felt something pushing into him. His eyes opened and the shivering chill of panic tore through his chest. He tried pointing his gun into the darkness and pulled the trigger only to discover that the gun was no longer there.

"You smell like piss, Oleg." It was Zora's voice. She was standing directly above him, and she was holding his gun.

"Zora, is that you?"

"Of course it's me." She stepped away from him, knelt and began to strip the AK-47. "Why don't you get up and move somewhere else? You're sitting in your own piss, you know. That can't be very comfortable. If I recall correctly, you and your two goons left me tied out in my own urine not too long ago—so, I speak from experience."

Oleg put his hands on the ground to push himself up, but pulled them back quickly as he felt the damp urine-drenched moss. He reached up and applying pressure outward and against the wall of the tree root, lifted himself off the ground. "Where did you go?" he asked.

"After Aziza. Had to make sure she wouldn't harm Ngiome—not that he wasn't able to take care of himself."

"Where is she—Aziza?"

"She's gone."

"What do you mean, gone?"

"I mean gone. She no longer exists—at least not as you knew her. She had a little accident—fell into the river. It was full of crocodiles,

Oleg—not a pretty sight. I'm glad for your sake that you didn't have to see it."

"Crocodiles?"

"Yes, crocodiles—a lot of them, and they ate her. Like I said, she doesn't exist anymore." Zora had completely disassembled Oleg's gun and started throwing the pieces, one at a time off into different directions.

"What are you doing? I can't see you—it's so God-damned dark."

"Getting rid of your Kalashnikov. You won't be needing it anymore."

"What do you mean getting rid of it? Are you crazy?"

"It's like I said when we started this trip, Oleg. These weapons are completely unnecessary out here—just extra weight. Think about it, Oleg. How many of us were there when we started? You three, Denis, his men, Carver, Ngiome, me—did I forget any one? That makes eleven. Between them they had a Swiss army semi-automatic, seven AK-47s, three handguns—Glocks, weren't they? And then, your Browning. And, as if that weren't enough, we stumbled on Hoyt's camp and picked up all the hardware they'd left scattered around. My God, Oleg—there was enough of an arsenal to have held off a small army. All those guns and all that ammo—and what good did it do any of you? Just think of all the food you could have carried instead of those guns and ammo. And, Oleg—tell me—who's still alive, huh? You, Ngiome, and me, that's who. Ngiome only needed his short spear and a machete, and I've managed to get by with just my knife—which Viper stole from me, but which I have now recovered."

Zora tossed the last piece of Oleg's Kalashnikov off, and they could hear the impact of metal hitting wood. Without a sound she moved up next to him and quickly removed the pistol and knife that he carried on the back of his belt.

"What the hell are doing?"

"You don't need those either." She stepped back and then she said something to Ngiome, which Oleg couldn't understand.

"Where's the pygmy?"

345

"Standing right next to me—you blind?"

"No, it's dark—I can't see."

"Too dark for you? Take this." Zora grasped one of Oleg's hands and placed the end of a rope between his fingers. "That's been my rope for the past several days, Oleg. Now I'm going to let you use it. Hold on tight. You're coming with us."

56 – THE YELLOW BRICK ROAD

"What?" stammered Oleg as he awoke, groggy and disoriented. He moaned, rolled over into a sitting position and realized he was still gripping the end of the rope. He dropped it and flexed his fingers, shaking out the numbness. It was light now, and he could see; he appeared to be alone. But he'd heard something—something had wakened him. He looked back and forth, then reached around and felt the empty holster on his belt. "Shit," he said to himself. He bowed his head briefly then sat up straight, sniffing the air.

"Lose something?" It was Zora's voice.

"What was that? I heard something."

"You mean Ngiome? He was singing."

"Where were you?"

"Making breakfast. Smell the smoke?"

"Yeah, smells good—that's mushrooms?"

"Ngiome caught a fish—you hungry?"

"Thirsty. My water's gone."

"Here," she handed him her water bottle. "Take all you want. When you're finished you can go over there—" she pointed—" and relieve yourself. Then just follow the smell of the smoke, and you'll find us—you might want to hurry up though. It's not a big fish."

Five minutes later, Oleg sat facing Zora and Ngiome across a small fire. They had given him a piece of fish on a large leaf. It was full of bones. He was forced to eat slowly and when the fish was gone he took a stick full of mushrooms, roots, and something else. He stared at it then asked, "What are these—more mushrooms?"

Zora said something to Ngiome and they both laughed, then she said to Oleg, "Go ahead. They won't kill you."

He bit into one, chewed slowly at first, then swallowed, took another, and worked his way down the skewer. Zora and Ngiome watched as he finished, then took another.

"Those were grubs," said Zora.

He looked at her then wiped his mouth with his forearm, sat back, and let out a small belch. He realized they had been observing him; he shifted nervously and, looking at Zora, blurted out, "OK—I guess you have the upper hand now."

She attempted to translate to Ngiome but did not respond to Oleg. "So what's your plan?"

"My plan? I never wanted to be here in the first place. I should be in Alaska right now. I came here because I was paid a lot of money to safely guide Carver and find Hoyt. I found Hoyt, but I guess I failed as far as Carver goes. What's your plan, Oleg?"

"My plan, I guess is shot. I came here to hunt a melanistic lion— but now I have no way of shooting it, even if I did find it." He looked at Ngiome breifly then went on, "Chimpanzees didn't take my gun—it was him, wasn't it?"

"That's very possible, why don't you ask him?"

He glanced at Zora, then back at Ngiome. "Right—I don't need to ask him."

"And I got rid of your Kalashnikov and your pistol and your knife. I would have left you the knife, but you seemed a bit unstable. I was concerned you might hurt yourself."

"Zora, I can accept the fact that I'm not going to get the lion—at least not this trip. I am a realist, though. I need to get back to the base camp. If you and the pygmy can get me back there, I can reward you. I will pay you ten times what Carver's company offered you."

Zora laughed. "I have no interest in your money, Oleg. You people—you think of nothing but money. Everything's money— money, money, money. I realize that outside of this forest—back in your world and the world that I've been living in, money is God. It's all an illusion though. Humanity has evolved technologically to where it can potentially have or do anything. But what have they done? They've turned our world into a box lined with mirrors. No matter where they look, all they see is themselves. Our existence in this universe is but a tiny speck in time and, within our own timeframe, the frenzied state of greed and self-importance that we have evolved into is but a speck on that speck, and yet we think we see everything when we in fact, we see nothing—just our own insignificant image. And those who have the most, seem to see the least. When are you ever going to wake up and realize how pathetic you are?"

"What do you want, Zora—revenge? I didn't want Viper to hurt you, I did everything I could to make sure—"

"What I want has nothing to do with revenge, Oleg. If I wanted to kill you I would have put you out of your misery when we found you sleeping against that tree last night. Let me try to explain it to you, Oleg. There are three reasons I'm still here."

"Three?"

"Yes—starting with your agreement with Ngiome?"

Oleg looked at Ngiome, then back at Zora. "Yes, and I fully intend to make good on that agreement."

"You and I both know that you have never intended to make good on your agreement. You realize," she pointed at Ngiome, "to him, a person's word is sacrosanct when he makes a promise to another person. The kind of deception that is par for the course with someone like you is nonexistent in his world. He cannot comprehend that you would promise something with no intention of ever keeping that promise." She looked sternly into his eyes and continued. "Oleg, you kidnapped his entire extended family, then you promised him that you would bring them back if he would guide you to the *zabolo-yindo*."

"Not how it went down at all—the idea that we kidnapped anyone is ludicrous. Those people were overjoyed that we offered to take them to Ouésso. They'll find jobs there, live easier lives—for God's sake— he offered to help us find the lion out of appreciation!"

"Don't make me throw up, Oleg. I know exactly what happened.

Viper basically murdered his cousin in cold blood—right in front of his entire family—a horrific intimidation to get them to board the helicopter. Those poor people had never been exposed to the kind of savagery that you dwell on in your daily life. Do you realize that no one in that tribe had ever seen one human being kill another? You totally destroyed an innocence that is almost nonexistent in the world today. They were like children, and you and those two diseased monsters you brought with you destroyed their world!"

Zora stood up, stepped over the fire and looking down on Oleg, said, "My first reason for being here is to make sure that you make good on your agreement with Ngiome. You told him that you would return his people if he helped you find the black devil. I'm going to make sure that you find your black lion. Upon full satisfaction of Ngiome's part of the agreement, you will tell me where his people are and what we need to do to get them back."

"You're going to find the black lion for me? Shit! You took my gun! What the hell do you expect me to do without my gun—and what if it attacks us? Huh? They killed everyone in the other expedition!"

"Oleg, you only told Ngiome that he had to help you find the lion, not kill it. We intend to take you to the lion."

"What good is it to me to find it if I can't kill it? You're a fucking nutcase."

"That brings me to my second reason for being here. We're about to find an animal that, as far as the rest of the world knows, does not exist. It is highly possible that we're about to discover a totally unknown species, or subspecies—something that is absolutely unique in nature," she bent down, her face no more than six inches from his. "And you want to kill it?" She laughed. "If this creature really is a black lion, there's no way in hell that I'm going to allow you to kill it!" She stepped back from him, avoiding the fire that had almost burned out. "If you want to kill it, you're going to have to try throwing rocks at it."

"What the hell are we going to do if the lion comes after us?" he yelled at her. "It will come after us if we stay here. You haven't answered that question. Without weapons, what are we going to do?"

"I don't know about you, Oleg, but Ngiome and I? We'll climb a tree—and fast."

"Climb a tree?"

"Of course. Look Oleg." Zora pointed upward. "You see the chimpanzees up there?"

He looked up. "What the fuck are you talking about?"

"The chimps—how do you think they survive? Half the group stays up in the tree and keeps a lookout for danger while the other half forages around on the ground. They're up there right now. If they start raising hell, we climb up there with them."

"How the hell am I supposed to climb up there?"

"That will be your problem. We'll just scramble up a vine. You can do the same—or you can stay on the ground and throw rocks." She looked at him and smiled. "In any case, if the lion comes to us, it will have just made our job easier—Ngiome will have taken you to the *zabolo-yindo,* and his part of the agreement will have been fulfilled. He seems to think that the lair is close—so," she looked him in the eyes, intensely and speaking in a low tone, said, "We're going to go find it, Oleg. Are you ready?"

"Listen—tell him I consider his side of the deal as delivered. He's taken me to the black lion, and now we need to return. As soon as we get up to where my SAT phone will work, I'll call for the copter. I'll tell them to bring his people back. We need to leave this place—do you understand me, Zora?"

She looked at him then exchanged words again with Ngiome.

"What did he say?"

"He said he's willing to take you back, but only if I agree to it."

Oleg smiled nervously, "Good—we need to stop by our old campsite next to the big tree. We stashed the satellite radio there."

"Oleg—he said only if I agree to it."

"Z-Zora, we–we need to g-get out of here." Oleg had begun to stutter; his lower lip quivered, and one eyelid began to twitch. "Zora—he said it was OK—he said—"

"It's not OK, Oleg." She said, her eyes drilling into him. "My third reason for remaining here is the forest, Oleg. Your initial interest in coming here might have been to poach some new subspecies of lion, but as I've managed to eavesdrop on the many discussions you and your two dead associates had—it seemed apparent to me that you had every intention of obtaining an illegal deal with whoever you have on your payroll back in Brazzaville. A deal that would give you the right to basically raze this forest—cut all the wood so that every wannabe successful creep can have exotic paneling in his yacht—kill all the wildlife so some Chinese lecher can waive off impotency with powdered bones—to lay waste to the land, suck it dry, and leave it barren. All of that just because you think that everything in this world has been put here for you. You had no intention of letting Carver get out of here alive—not after you saw what this was."

"Zora—listen—why do you think Carver came here? He was here for the same reason. Don't you think his company has their own people of influence they pay off? I guarantee you that he or at least Hoyt—when they saw what this place was—didn't come here without bringing a box full of unmarked cash. The peons that run this place— ha! They all have their own little villas in France, Switzerland— everything here is for sale—everything! It all comes down to who gets it first. In ten years, this whole country will be one big empty swamp." Oleg stood and began to stumble erratically toward Zora, his arms reached out, his eyes wide, and a leering smile of madness split across the bottom of his face.

Zora put her hand up and touched Oleg's chest. "Control yourself, Oleg. I know why Carver came here. I also know that when he saw what this place really was—its unfathomable beauty—its uniqueness—he knew he would have to alter his mission. At the end, he had determined not to let this place fall victim to your world, Oleg."

"Carver was a pawn, Zora. He was totally conditioned by the system. He said what you wanted to hear. As soon as he got back he would have been sticking an envelope with twenty, or maybe fifty million cash into the clammy hands of one of the ministers— maybe even the president."

352

"Well, Carver's dead now, isn't he? So it's a moot point. Viper cut his rope—he murdered Carver, like he murdered Ngiome's nephew and God knows how many other innocent people before that." She looked at Oleg, an expression of distaste on her face, and she stepped back, motioning with her arms as if to usher him away. "Viper pulled the trigger, and he cut the rope, but it was just a mechanical action wasn't it, Oleg? It was you who really killed them. You're the mother monster."

Ngiome recognized his name in the conversation, and he took a step closer to Oleg, gripping his spear in both hands and pointed it toward him.

Oleg looked at Ngiome, then back to Zora. "Zora—you can have this fucking jungle—you understand me? You can have it. I'll take care of the pay-off myself—and I'll tell them they'll have to do whatever you want. You'll be in charge—you can call the shots, alright? Just get us out of here."

Zora looked at Ngiome, and they exchanged words as Ngiome pointed his spear past Oleg.

"What'd he say?"

"He said it's time to go—that's the way. This is their trail we've been sitting on, you know—eating our breakfast."

Ngiome walked to what appeared to be an opening in a dense growth of cascading ferns. He pointed to the ground with his spear and spoke to Zora.

"He said they come this way often—maybe every day. He said they drag big kill here—come and look." Ngiome motioned with his spear, pointed, spoke again, and Zora went on with her translation. "Black hair of a giant forest hog. They dragged it from the river last night before we got here. The lair is obviously close."

Zora smiled at Oleg, "This is the path we want."

"The path we want?"

"Yes, Oleg—you don't recognize it? The yellow brick road—same one you've been following all your life."

57 – OLEG

"Don't worry, Oleg. They're still with us," Zora said when she noticed him glancing up into the trees.

"I don't see them," he said, looking up—then tripping.

She caught him as he stumbled into her then pointed up into the trees. "Look, follow where I'm pointing. You see that slow movement in the branches? Follow the movement along the branch until you get to a dark form—it almost floats, going from one branch to another. They move faster up there than we do down here. They move for a minute then stop. Sometimes they stop because they found something to eat, but I think they also stop to wait for us. What you care about though is that they haven't started screaming bloody hell."

"Why would they be following us?"

"Carver and I had a friendly encounter with them—we exchanged gifts, you might say. I was afraid that Denis had ruined it all when he shot one, but now I feel pretty certain they at least didn't blame us. It might also be because of Ngiome. When he sings to the forest early in the morning or at night, they sometimes gather to listen—at times they'll answer him."

Oleg wiped the sweat out of his eyes and tried to find the chimpanzees again. "I don't know. I can't see anything—just shadows in the leaves."

"Don't worry about it. Ngiome and I see them. It's the sound that's important anyway. Of course, they're not always totally dependable—I mean, you know—every now and then a chimp gets eaten too."

"What do you mean?"

"Well, they're all the way up there. They have great eyes, but who says there isn't some predator that's been patiently waiting half the day, hidden away—not visible from above. And then one of them wanders down to check something out on the ground."

She motioned with her head to Ngiome to continue on, put her hand on Oleg's arm and tried to pull him along. He wouldn't move.

"Come on, Oleg. You need to keep moving."

"No—we're going the wrong way. You're taking us in the wrong direction. This path is coming from the river and we're going away from the river. I want to go the other way."

"Oleg, at least one of the cats has been stalking us for days now. If you go back that way, you're just going to run into him."

"Don't try to scare me—I'm going back." He backed away from her.

"You're losing it, Oleg. You should see yourself—the big-shot millionaire. Oh! Excuse me—I meant billionaire. You're scared. You're all alone, none of your goons around to help hold you up, your money's no good here and, of course, no gun—ha!" she laughed. "Oleg without his gun is like Oleg without his penis. Go ahead then, go back the other way. In three minutes you'll be running back to us whimpering like baby." She turned her back on him and started after Ngiome.

Oleg stood alone in the middle of the path and stared after her. The sweat ran off his forehead and into his eyes, where it stung. He blinked and wiped his face with his arm, which was already slippery with sweat. He grabbed the short sleeve of his shirt with one hand and lifted the other into the air so that he could reach his eye with the shirt and wipe, but everything was soaked. He became frustrated and began to shake; his jaw twisted, his eyes narrowed, and he screamed. "I should have let Viper slit your throat—you hear me?"

Zora and Ngiome had both disappeared. He looked at the empty trail ahead, then turned and looked the other way. He took a step, squinted, straining his eyes, trying to see into the menacing voids that lined the trail. He wiped his eyes again, and spoke in a quiet tone, almost crying, "Fuck—fuck!" He reached to the empty holster on his back; it was still empty. He stooped forward slightly and beat his two hands against his sides and repeated, "Fuck," then he turned and started after Zora and Ngiome, lumbering in a slow, uncertain jog. He hadn't gone more than a dozen strides when he tripped over himself and sprawled to the ground. He went down face-first, his cheekbone cracking hard against a root. Grunting and moaning to himself, he scrambled to his feet and continued up the path.

"I'm going to kill you!" he screamed as Zora came into view. He ran at her, now completely hysterical, his arms reaching out, screaming, "If I'm going to die here, I'm going to kill you first."

He lunged at her. She stooped over slightly and placed her shoulder into his midsection as he made contact, then lifted up, allowing his momentum to carry him, and flipped him onto his back. He landed hard but quickly recovered and came back up. He took a swing at her, missed, and lost his balance once again. Turning wildly, he flailed out again. This time she blocked his arm and pummeled him under the chin with an open palm, sending him once again onto his back. This time he remained still—unconscious, blood forming between his lips.

Zora rolled him over and poured water onto his face. He didn't respond so she stepped back, looking at Ngiome and said, "I think he's not very happy. Let's allow him a short nap. Maybe he'll calm down."

"Are all white *bilo* mad like this?" asked Ngiome.

"Not all, but many."

"Ngiome likes how Zora knocked the big white *bilo* to the ground—like a leopard that takes a much bigger buffalo. Zora is like a cat."

Zora returned his smile as she poured more water in Oleg's face. He sputtered and coughed lightly as his eyes fluttered open, and he looked up at Zora. His face was colorless and he was clearly dazed, but the hysteria had subsided.

"Give me your hand, Oleg."

He held out his hand and she pulled. He was much heavier than Zora and his efforts to assist were minimal. She braced her feet and grunted as she pulled. Ngiome quickly joined in, taking one of his arms and pulled until finally, Oleg was upright. He made a couple of short staggering steps, reached out and put one hand on Zora's shoulder to steady himself.

"What happened?" he asked.

"You had a little breakdown, Oleg. Here, take a drink—wash your mouth out, I don't know if you bit yourself or what, but you're bleeding from the mouth."

Oleg took a swig of water, swished it around in his mouth, spit it out, then spit again as something solid projected out and onto the ground.

Zora bent down and picked it up, holding it for Oleg to see. "One of your teeth—that was a bad fall you took. Here—you can put it under your pillow tonight."

He waved her hand away, reached up to his mouth and began exploring the new gap that now separated his front teeth. He fidgeted with his fingers then held up another tooth.

"Two teeth!" exclaimed Zora. "And it's the two front ones—you're going to need a little dental work, Oleg." She laughed and Ngiome joined her. "You look like a cartoon of yourself—very nice!"

"You hit me?" he looked at her, "You knocked my teeth out—my fucking teeth!" There was a slight whistling sound as he talked now.

"You're lucky I didn't castrate you."

He stood, speechless, still weaving back and forth. He breathed in deeply and looked at the tooth in his hand, then threw it away and took another swig of water. His hand shook as he pulled the bottle back from his mouth. He attempted to hand it to Zora but dropped it. As she picked it up he ran both hands up his forehead, back through his hair, and then to the sides of his head where he pressed them into his temples. "Ahh," he groaned. "My head—my fucking head."

"Think you can walk, Oleg?" Zora asked.

"No—need to sit a minute." He grabbed a vine and carefully let himself down onto the ground again, leaned back against a tree and allowed his head to flop back with a painful thump.

Zora and Ngiome spoke for a minute, then Ngiome continued alone up the trail while she sat opposite Oleg.

"Where's he going?"

"Scouting ahead while you recover. Drink some water—you didn't spill it all. Might help your headache."

He drained his bottle, let out a little burp, then started to put the bottle back into the loop on his belt, couldn't seem to get it, got frustrated, and dropped it on the ground. He sat looking at the bottle, then turned his gaze to Zora and began to speak.

"Zora, you have to listen to me. I know when I talk about money you reject my words outright. You don't want to hear about it so you don't really listen, but you're letting your emotions—your ideals— cloud your thoughts. I'm worth billions, Zora—billions."

She just looked at him and said nothing.

"Over half my wealth is hidden—impossible to trace. I keep it invisible—stashed in secret places."

"Do you get something out of listening to yourself talk, Oleg?"

"No—I'm not saying this to hear myself. I'm telling you this because I am willing to offer you half of everything. Zora, I know I forced myself on you but—you have to admit—you were starting to like it. I know you were."

"Oleg, your perception of reality is so far off. My God—you're pathetic. Let me untangle your twisted mind and set something straight—when you raped me, I coped by taking myself away—far away. Oleg, I was not even there with you. Yesterday morning at the river—when I knew it was inevitable—I simply closed my eyes and my mind took me someplace else. While you were violating me, like a primitive beast, I was with someone else."

"Someone else? That cowboy botanist back there—that loser who's rotting on the ground back at that tree?"

"No, not him—although he would have sufficed. No, I was with someone who was a real man. Someone who loved me and whom I loved—and always will. You could never understand that though, could you? Love is beyond your level of comprehension."

"You can try to convince yourself that it didn't happen, but it did. You were getting pleasure out of it, I could tell—and if things had gone my way, I was not going to hurt you. My intention has always been to take you back with me—it still is. The threat to get you hooked on heroin—I was just trying to scare you." He paused, looked down at the ground, then back at her. "You can still go back with me, you know. I'll make you a goddess. God, you could be the richest, most beautiful, exotic woman on the planet. Us together—Caesar and Cleopatra!"

"Oleg, please. You know, one reason some people are so obsessed with getting rich and then even richer, once they've become rich, is because they're never satisfied. They spend their entire lives looking in the wrong place—and that's you. You understand that, don't you? No—that was stupid of me to have asked. Of course you couldn't possibly comprehend something like that." She stared at him as he blinked several times as though he were short-circuiting.

"Oleg, you explained to me—more than once—how you perceive yourself as the center of the universe. Whatever preceded your arrival into the world is not something you perceive as real, and the same goes for whatever will come after you. Reality to you is nothing but you and you alone. The reality though, Oleg, is that you're so fucking afraid of what life is all about that you've invented your own insane scenario—where you are God and everyone else is here to serve you—everyone and everything—this jungle, the air, the dirt you're sitting on. Now, you sit here, the terrified child in the wilderness that you actually are. Frightened because you're beginning to see the light at the end of your deranged tunnel, and that light is a big black formless face with huge white fangs and it's waiting for you." Zora leaned toward Oleg and lowered her voice, like an adult whispering a secret to a child. "And Oleg, it's really close now—so close you can smell it. We both smell it. Just sniff the air, Oleg—we're almost there."

Oleg suddenly flung himself across the space between them. Zora shifted back, and he landed on his chest, his arms reached out, groping, his head twisted up, mouth half-open, and he stared up at her. She took one of his hands and bent his fingers back causing him to wince. She stood and stepped over him, taking his hand and arm with her, forcing him to roll over then she dropped his hand and stepped back. As she looked at him again, she noticed that Ngiome was back, quietly watching. She nodded to him then looked down at Oleg.

"Oleg, your entire life—everything you've taught yourself to believe—all your possessions, your money, the women you've either raped or bought—it's all one big wasteland. You never even knew your own mother—and she never knew you. As I understand it, your father had you removed from her at the birthing bed. You never tasted her milk. Oleg, you never knew the most basic, the most important thing that all humans must know in order to at least have a chance to lead a fulfilling life—love. You never knew the love that binds a mother to a child from the moment life out of the womb begins. The real tragedy is that a mother's love, as well as her joys and fears—the energy of those emotions—they say that they're all transferred automatically from mother to child while the child is still in the womb. To come out of that womb and have it all just vanish and not be there—the warmth and joy of that love—not having ever known that love might be the worst horror any creature can be subjected to." She paused, took a long breath, then continued, "And that was how you came into this world—into the arms of some steel-faced robot of a father—some power-mongering automaton. And your mother, knowing that she would never be able to keep you as her child, she knew she was just being used and would never be allowed to know you. She must have just bathed her little fetus in angst—emptiness—and it's all still there. I can see it now, eating away at your soul. You're not afraid of the black lion, Oleg—you're afraid of finally seeing the pitiful vacuity of your own life—and knowing that it's too late to do anything about it. No wonder you're starting to lose it." She stood up, stretched her arms, took a long breath, and shook her head. "I don't know why I'm not feeling sorry for you, now that I think of it. Perhaps—just perhaps—the little bit of empathy I do have is what kept me from slitting your throat when we found you last night. That and a promise I made to myself a while ago."

Zora stood up and held her hand out to him. "Come on, Oleg. Ngiome's waiting. You should be nicely rested now. We're getting close."

58 – THE FIELD OF BONES

"Oleg, if you're really concerned about your safety, maybe you should stop your incessant blabbing."

Oleg's rambling had not ceased since their last stop, and it appeared that the more he chattered, the more incoherent he became. For the most part, he muttered under his breath, but on occasion his voice would rise up, usually with a question. "Did you know that Forbes listed 1,826 billionaires in the world last year?" he asked. "Only 88 were Russian and the richest has a net worth of only16 billion. They have me listed with less than half that. If they only knew—I would be up there—and I'm still young. You know how old I am, Zora?"

"Shut up, Oleg, I need to be able to hear."

"Chimps—I don't hear the chimpanzees."

"They stopped, Oleg. They're no longer with us."

"Well, if they come back—tell them I need my gun."

Ngiome had slowed his pace and was looking up into the trees. As Zora caught up to him he looked at her, then motioned upward with his eyes. The landscape was changing. The lower levels of the canopy were much higher than they had been since their departure from the big tree. Now the large trees seemed to be getting larger again. They were further apart and there was a sense that the understory had begun to inflate outward into a vast cavernous vault, much like the initial impression that had struck them when they first arrived in the sunken forest.

"Why are we stopping?" asked Oleg.

"We're not," answered Zora. She looked at Ngiome and, with a subtle nod, motioned to keep going.

Within minutes, the surface growth that lined their path began to thin. Enormous trees paralleled the trail, creating the impression they were entering a heroic entryway or corridor. It was open across its sixty- to seventy-foot width and continued ahead for almost a hundred yards before it curved into a bend. Although the open corridor and their direction of travel were straight, the trail itself continued to switch back and forth as the obstacle course of crisscrossing roots had now been joined by a myriad of ponds of standing water.

Random vines dropped down from above like spiraling strands of green silk and Ngiome pointed at them and said, "If the black devil comes, we climb these." He looked at Oleg and shook his head.

"I don't think he can climb anything the way he is now," said Zora.

Oleg didn't seem to notice the exchange. His eyes were glazed over, his face withdrawn into blankness.

A deathly silence hung over this strange forest passageway. The chirping and squawking that normally hovered above remained discernable, but only barely.

"Something smells," said Zora, as they neared the bend. "Sulfur." She and Ngiome looked at each other, sniffing the air. They slowed their pace, then the quiet was broken by a deep grating cluck followed by the sound of movement—a sifting of something large through pieces of broken pottery or shells.

"Vulture," said Ngiome.

She nodded in agreement, and they proceeded, now with increased care. They rounded the bend in the trail that was defined by one of the many large trees and peered ahead to what appeared to be the source of the clucking. A misty cloud floated in the air, further obscuring their view. The clucking sounded again. Ngiome held his finger to his lips, pointed ahead and lifted his hand indicating the others hold their positions while he proceeded.

As he slipped into the cloud, Zora tightened her grip on Oleg and urged him to remain quiet, but he pulled away, gagged, then blurted out, "Stinks! That sulfur shit again."

"Quiet!" snapped Zora. "There's some kind of geothermal source up ahead."

Oleg brushed past Zora and staggered after Ngiome. "What's that?"

"Vultures," said Zora.

"No," said Oleg, "That—what's all that?" He waved his hand across the misty space that spread out before them.

"The lion's den," answered Zora. "And its set right in the middle of some kind of hot sulfur spring."

As they attempted to adjust their eyes, a black object could be seen moving on top of what resembled a pile of broken pottery shards, sticks and rocks. An ugly gray head popped up—a vulture—with something dangling from its beak. The mound was almost Oleg's height, and the pieces of randomly shaped objects were scattered throughout the open area. Just beyond the vulture, two more mounds could be seen and between them, a massive tree set behind a screen of smaller, tightly spaced trees.

Zora stepped cautiously toward the first mound, Ngiome followed, and then Oleg. She stopped and picked up the first fragment she came to, turned and held it up for Ngiome. "Bones," she said. As they got closer, the vulture let out another of his greedy clucks, flipped the object it had been holding off to one side, took a couple of hops back, and then spread its wings, which in the erie mist looked like the cloak of a vampire. It rose slowly up through the drifting clouds, flapped down hard as it lifted off the mound, flapped again, and began to glide up in a slow spiraling climb.

Ngiome circled to the side of the mound where the vulture had tossed whatever large morsel it had found. He bent over, pointed the end of his spear to the ground next to it and tapped it over toward Zora. "*Bilo*," he said.

"What's that?" asked Oleg as she stooped to examine it.

"Lower portion of a human head—mostly jaw. Hmm—little bit of flesh clinging to it—probably what the vulture was interested in. Most interesting though—the fact that it's not totally picked clean and dried out suggests it's not that old." She picked it up. "Could be

Nabu!" She dropped it and continued inspecting the debris, rolling pieces aside with her foot, then looked up and focused on the other two mounds. "This must have been their lair for years. These mounds are nothing but bone fragments—most are from animals. Looks like the hogs have been their most common prey." She climbed onto the second pile. "Here—this must have been from an elephant—wow, and it wasn't an infant either." She leaped back to the ground and bent over again. "Another human. Might even be one of Hoyt's expedition members—or Hoyt himself." She returned to Oleg who hadn't moved from where she'd left him. "My guess is that whatever they don't finish off immediately, they carry back here—probably started when the mother or father would bring food back for their cubs. Ever seen anything like this, Oleg?"

Oleg was staring at the tree. "The pygmy," he mumbled.

"Ngiome? What about him?"

"Inside the tree."

"Ah, yes—I see him. That's not the kind of tree you're used to Oleg. It's some form of strangler fig—or more likely, several stranglers. In fact, it's quite amazing. The host tree is long gone, and the strangler has expanded up and outward. It looks like a massive web of entwined tentacles—not an uncommon phenomenon in rainforests, but I've never seen one quite like this. Come, let's look.

The central root mass of the strangler stretched out for at least forty feet across at its base and the winding pieces that formed its walls ranged up to three feet in diameter with hundreds of newer vines or roots, some as small as delicate strands of thread or string, clinging to the larger vines and working their way up, continuing the parasitic process. The additional trunks that formed an outer set of concentric circles appeared to be separate trees, each with its own collection of roots and vines, but all were part of the original. The mass of roots and trunks became denser the further into the center they grew.

Oleg watched as Zora slid sideways between two of the outer ring's trunks and carefully picked her way in. She could see Ngiome, who must have been close to the center and just below the original host tree shaft, as a column of light fluttered across his face. "This is where the *bisi ndima* have a big advantage over someone like me," she said to him. "You can squeeze through the tightest openings."

"Ngiome looks to see if the black devils come here."

"And do they?"

"Only cubs—we can come here if we need to be safe."

"Any snakes?"

"Just bats—many bats. Smell is very strong."

Zora maneuvered her way in until she found herself alongside Ngiome. The opening at ground level where they stood was the size of a small room and as she looked straight up, the top of the shaft was so far away that it appeared to be no larger than a coin. "Wow ... it does smell like bat guano. Feels like it too." She looked down at her calloused, but nimble bare feet, which had sunk into at least an inch of black gooey substance. She looked up again and now knowing that bats occupied the space, realized that the walls of the central shaft above were covered with them.

"Hey!" It was Oleg shouting.

"What do we do with the white *bilo* now?" asked Ngiome.

"Not sure. I ask myself what he would do if we were to trade places. In any case, we need to decide soon. We cannot stay here long. The black devils can come any time."

As they both started working their way back out of the maze, Zora debated in her head, the various options and problems imposed on them by Oleg. *If we get him out of here alive, he will never be held responsible for what he has done—people with his kind of money can commit murder in broad daylight, and they always seem to get away with it. If we get him back alive, he will not only get away with murder—he will obtain the timbering rights to this place. He'll come back and end up shooting the animals, and Ngiome will never see his people again. I can't kill him though. Can we just abandon him? If we do, he'll be dead in a day.*

Oleg had attempted to follow the other two into the strangler but never got very far. By the time Zora and Ngiome had exited the maze, he was standing, stoop shouldered and shaking out his arms and hands like competitive swimmers sometimes do. "Need to sit down for a minute," he mumbled, and then awkwardly stumbled his way to the smaller of the bone mounds where he plopped himself down. Zora followed him.

"Zora!" Ngiome called out in a loud whispering tone. "Look!" He was pointing up the trail, from where they had come.

Zora looked and immediately her heart began to pound. She put her hand on Oleg's head and said, quietly, "Oleg, turn around—slowly."

59 – THE LION'S DEN

"What?" asked Oleg, his head snapping up.

"Your black lion, Oleg." Zora spoke quietly, looking at him, and then motioning beyond with her eyes. "It's here—but I'm afraid you're going to be disappointed."

Oleg bolted to his feet. "Where?" he asked. He was still disoriented and had difficulty focusing. He blinked and looked back and forth, until finally his eyes came to rest on what at first read as a dark smudge. It was black. Blacker than any of the shadows or shaded areas that gave depth to the forest that engulfed them. It was black like an empty, formless void that might appear through a tear in a picture. Two almond-shaped golden orbs appeared floating within the darkness. They disappeared then reappeared.

"Ngiome was right from the beginning," said Zora, still maintaining a hushed level in her voice. "It's a leopard—a black leopard. Your black lion is a five-hundred-pound black panther—Panthera Pardus—a leopard." She placed her hand on his shoulder and smiled. "Imagine that," she continued. "A leopard—as big as any lion that ever roamed the Serengeti. It could be the most lethal land predator on the planet—the king of kings! And Oleg—you don't have your gun, do you?"

The cat's posture was relaxed as it observed them—it could just as easily have been watching three birds foraging along the forest floor. It looked at them and the humans looked back. A slow rippling, like a wave, softly flowed across the creature's back, starting at the back of its head and ending at the base of its tail. The end of the tail twitched.

367

The cat sniffed the air and calmly blinked again.

"It's not poised to attack. Do not panic, Oleg. If you panic, it will come, and it will come fast—do you understand?"

He didn't answer. Zora looked at him. His complexion was that of a cadaver: his lower lip trembled, and a strand of drool appeared and slid down his chin. His breathing was irregular. She kept her eyes on the leopard and speaking just above a whisper, said to Ngiome, "If he attacks, jump back into the tree." Then, speaking in Russian, repeated herself for Oleg's benefit.

"Get my gun," Oleg suddenly blurted out. "Get it now!" he snapped as he looked at Zora. "My gun, you dumb bitch—get my gun!"

Ngiome and Zora both started to back step, slowly inching their way into the strangler. The leopard's tail twitched again, and then it stretched its head forward, its ears flattened out along its head, and it went into a low crouch and began to creep forward.

"Oleg, he's going to attack, keep quiet and back up—you have to get into the fig tree. Do you hear me?"

Oleg ignored her and, as if in defiance, began to jump up and down, screaming like a child throwing a tantrum. "For God's fucking sake, where's my gun?" He bent over, picked up a bone, and threw it randomly into the ground. He slipped, fell to his knees, and jumped up with another bone, now screaming incoherently. He turned and violently threw the bone toward Zora and Ngiome, both of whom were now within the outer perimeter of the strangler. The bone flew past them and bounced harmlessly off one of the smaller trunks. He turned back toward the leopard, and scrambled erratically to the top of the mound.

Within seconds the leopard had covered half the distance to Oleg, but stopped. It lifted its head high, raised its ears, and began sniffing the air. It went back to a more erect and relaxed stance again, and then started to move laterally at a slow pace, maintaining a constant distance from the humans. It stopped, and from out of nowhere a second leopard appeared. With uncanny stealth, the creatures moved as dark shadows with the ability to blend into their surroundings, disappearing, and then reappearing from out of nowhere. The second cat was about the same size as the first, and the two stood no more than ten yards apart now.

"Oleg!" Zora now shouted. "Get back here—they can't get you in here. Oleg—listen to me!"

Oleg, now on top of the mound, turned, and looking toward Zora, laughed. He couldn't see her at first; she was too deep into the strangler. His eyes darted nervously back and forth, searching into the obscurity of the maze. His face, already drained of all color, became ever paler, and then his eyes found her. He bent down, picked up another bone, and threw it at her, screaming, "You did this—bitch!" Then, he fell to his hands and knees and broke into a stuttering tirade of sobbing interspersed with ear-piercing screams.

"Oleg, stop screaming and get over here. You'll have a chance if you get over here. Come on!"

Slowly, Oleg raised his head. His tantrum slowed to a quiet whimpering, and then he began to crawl down from the mound. When he reached the bottom, he pushed himself up off his hands into a hunched-over standing posture and, one foot at a time, began to stagger toward the maze of the strangler fig.

"Hurry, Oleg!" yelled Zora. She was joined by Ngiome, but Oleg couldn't understand him—whatever he said was heard as gibberish, and Oleg's confusion only worsened. He stumbled, seemed to lose his direction and began to meander aimlessly.

Somehow Oleg managed to arrive at one of the strangler's outlying trunks. He grabbed it with both hands, braced himself, then searched into the darkness, trying to find Zora's face again, but seeing only the darkness, he let out another cry of exasperation and lunged toward the next trunk, grabbing this one as he had the first. "Zora!" he cried out.

"Look out!" he heard her scream. He turned and found himself staring directly into the gaping mouth of one of the leopards, just as it lunged toward him and roared. The boom of the roar was so loud that Oleg's eardrums burst, and the putrid stench of the beast's partially digested morning meal engulfed. Oleg's heart stopped, and he stood frozen, unable to move. Drool and mucous began to run down his face; he sank to his knees and collapsed onto his face.

The cat sniffed his still body. It nudged him slightly with its nose, then grabbed his right shoulder in its mouth, dragged him several feet, then dropped him. The second cat joined the first, sniffed at Oleg's head, then worked its way down one side of his body, sniffing and nudging. The first cat made a light groaning sound, then bent its head and pushed against Oleg's rib cage, partially rolling him over. Both cats stood side by side now. One licked the face of the other, then retreated several steps and lay down on the ground while the other climbed to the top of the mound of bones where it lay down.

"White *bilo* is still breathing," said Ngiome.

"Yes. The black leopard frightened him. I fear his heart might have stopped."

"The black leopard frightens me too."

They both began to retreat further into the sanctuary of the strangler's core. Ngiome placed a hand on Zora's arm and looking up to her said, "Zora, while the leopards watch the white *bilo*—you and I must climb through the tree and go out the other side. We must go quietly. We must go to the river before darkness comes."

Zora hesitated, looked at him then, looking back toward Oleg and the two leopards, said, "Wait, Ngiome—the white *bilo* is still moving."

He had raised his head and was looking toward them, but didn't seem to see them. His half-closed eyes looked like empty slits. "Look at the white *bilo*'s hair," said Ngiome. Oleg's hair had begun to turn white and as he rolled his head away from them, they could see where blood was running from one of his ears.

Zora realized he couldn't see them so she moved back to the perimeter, stuck her head out through an opening and called, gently, "Oleg—Oleg—look over here—we're here." She stuck an arm out and waved it back and forth. The leopards looked at her but showed no signs of concern or interest.

Oleg seemed to see her and raised his head a little higher. "Zora," he gasped. He raised himself and pulled his elbows up, resting on them, then, very slowly, began to crawl toward her. His shirt was torn where the leopard had taken hold of him, and there were small splatters of blood, but nothing looked broken. "Zora," he groaned again. He kept crawling and had gone almost half the distance to the edge of the strangler grove, when he stopped and craning his neck to his right, let out a short cry. "Ahhh—no—please!" he pleaded.

Zora and Ngiome followed his gaze and there, standing right alongside one of the outer trunks of the fig grove, was a third cat. Ngiome gasped as Zora exclaimed, "My God—it's even bigger—it's the mother!" *Six-hundred pounds*, she thought to herself. *If that's the mother, imagine the father!"*

Like the two younger cats, the female appeared relaxed. Her ears stood upright, she sniffed the air and her tail undulated in a soft rolling motion. She took a few steps toward Oleg, stopped and looked directly at Zora, then took another step toward Oleg and lay down on the ground, her head about eight feet from Oleg and her side pressed up against the outer wall of the strangler.

Oleg looked up again at Zora. The rapidity of his breathing increased while short groaning sounds began to emanate from his throat as if he were trying to push words out. Then he let out a cry—a pathetic cry of loss—and dropped his head, face first into the ground and his body shuddered as he began to silently sob.

The mother cat rolled its head back and with her eyes closed began to rub her cheek against one of the root offshoots. Her eyes opened halfway, and as she gazed lazily toward Zora and Ngiome, she began to emit a deep soothing sound that resembled that of a large muffled motor—she was sighing. It was almost a purring sound.

Zora and Ngiome both returned the cat's stare, then Zora called out once again, "Oleg." He didn't respond. "Look at me." He stopped shaking as she repeated, "Look at me, Oleg. Lift your head up and look at me."

His head rose up slightly, dirt now stuck to the wetness of his face. "Zora."

"Oleg—the cat's lying down—keep crawling—you only need to

371

go a few more feet. Just go slowly and when you get close, we'll pull you in. Now come."

He rolled his head and looked at the big cat. His face gave the impression of being sucked inward like a prune and he quivered as if he were about to start crying again, then he turned his gaze back to Zora and Ngiome. "I can't."

"Yes, you can. Listen to me. That cat is either going to kill you or she's not. You've lived your life taking chances. This is a fifty-fifty chance. If you don't even try, your odds are zero. Now come—crawl."

Oleg shuddered one more time, took a deep breath, and very slowly began to stretch his arm forward. He bent his leg and pulled his knee up, and as he moved his opposing arm and leg, his body slowly inched across the ground and he was eight inches closer. He peered carefully over his shoulder at the cat, and repeated the process. Inch by inch, Oleg crawled, gradualy closing the distance to the tree trunks. As he approached, Zora stooped low to the ground and positioned herself so that she could reach out and grab him. Finally, Oleg was within reach. She extended her arm out to him and their hands clasped. She pulled, slowly at first, getting him just a little closer so that she could grab with both hands and as her second hand came out, the female leapt and in a single bound—a fraction of a second—it pounced across Oleg's back, straddling him with all four paws and snarled at Zora, whose hands slipped away from Oleg, causing her to fall back.

"Shit!" she swore in frustration. She watched as the cat backed up, took one of Oleg's feet in her mouth, and in one sharp movement, jerked his body backward—just enough to keep him out of Zora's reach—and Oleg's ankle snapped with a stomach-wrenching crack.

He screamed, sat up straight, and grabbed for his foot, but fell onto his back, thrashing and crying, "Ah—ah—oh God! God—God—God," he cried over and over. He finally flopped his arms out on the ground toward Ngiome and Zora then folded them over his head as he settled into a rhythm of sobbing and choking. He went on for several minutes while Zora and Ngiome watched in hopeless silence.

"We cannot help him," Ngiome said. "He made his own life, and now this is how it is to end. We must go."

"Zora." It was Oleg's desperate voice again. Zora looked out through the opening again, and Oleg's ashen face now looked back at her.

"I'm fucked," he said, and then his mouth bent into a sickly grin. "Zora—my child—my son—I know—need to see Martel." His face dropped onto the ground. He coughed, then lifted it again and continued, "Tell Martel—business for him—the child—you— you take the rest—cash—gold—the villa." He paused, gasped for air, wheezing. He choked, spit on the ground then looked up again. "The vault—Raskolnikov—spelled backwards, then 1866—bypass reader—just use code—no one knows. Not even Martel."

"Oleg, I'm staying here. I don't know why—you don't deserve it, and you know you don't deserve anything. But I'm going to stay here. We won't let you die alone. You came into this world alone, but we won't let you die that way."

He pushed, his hands on the ground, straightened his arms, and with his back arched, lifted his head up. His mouth was open, gaping at her like a foul hole and he blurted out, "You have my child! My heir! You have no choice—I order you! He will be a god—I am—I—I," his ranting became louder and louder and finally, the leopard rose up, let out a short growl, leapt up beside him and with one paw, slapped him across the back of his head, embedding his face deep into the ground.

Now the two younger cats were standing again and lingered along each side of Oleg and their mother. The mother cat's tale twitched, and Zora detected a subtle glance as it made eye contact with one of its offspring. An instant later it grabbed Oleg by the shoulder with its mouth and in one quick flick of its head, sent him flying through the air, screaming, his body crashing into the mound of bones. The seated cat quickly jumped sideways, its rear end up high and its front down low, like a kitten preparing to play with a ball of string, and it pounced, landing next to Oleg. Again, with its head low and its tail end up, it made a short jump and swatted Oleg's lower torso, sending

373

him spinning away from the mound. The cat quickly followed his prey and repeated the action. Oleg screamed madly.

Zora watched in horror, and then, as Oleg rolled to a stop, his head flopped over. She could see his face and their eyes made contact. "My gun," he yelled out hoarsely. "Get my gun." The second of the young cats then cut off her view as it charged and pounced. She could see its head go down. It shook quickly from side to side as the sickening sound of crushing bones mixed with the cat's mischievous growling could be detected through the hysterical screaming of Olegushka Levkov.

"We go now!" said Ngiome, his urgent voice breaking as he regarded Zora, his eyes wide with fear.

60 – INTO THE DARKNESS OF ERROR

It was raining again, and the night brought an added chill that ripped through the two humans' souls. Ngiome and Zora had made it out of the leopards' den, but the night had plunged down upon them too swiftly, and they knew they didn't have time to get to the river. They found a suitable tree, climbed it and quickly fabricated a shelter, much like they had done that night after Denis had killed the young chimpanzee, and the chimpanzees had killed Denis. They hadn't eaten anything since early that morning. They were hungry—they were cold—they were desperate—but they were alive. The two sat huddled together in the dark, listening to the rain, feeling the slow dripping wetness that filtered through the hastily fabricated roof.

"Leopards climb trees," Ngiome said, finally breaking the silence.

"I know, but the rain might wash our scent away—just in case they come. They might not come."

They remained quiet for a while, and then Zora broke the silence again. "I ask myself, Ngiome—why? Why didn't they come for us before this? They knew we were here. At least one of them has been stalking us for days. They attacked Carver's friends as soon as they found them—but not us. I ask myself why."

"The *bisi ndima* eat the meat of many animals," said Ngiome. "We hunt *mboloko*—sometimes the big ones with horns that spiral up like vines, but mostly we hunt the little ones—for their numbers are great. We eat fish, sometimes civet cat, pangolin, and sometimes the red river hogs—one time, many years ago, we caught a forest elephant. It took many suns for our family to finish the meat of the elephant. When it was finished, we had almost forgotten how to hunt, and then we had great difficulty finding meat, so we ate nothing but roots and mushrooms for many days. That is why we do not hunt the elephant. The *bisi ndima* hunt only when we need food, and we only hunt what we can eat. That is why we eat the smaller animals, for they are many, and they come to us when it is time to hunt. We never hunt the chimpanzee or the big ones—the gorilla. They are cousins. Some say that we all the same family one time, but the family got too big and become three small families. The leopard hunt the same animals that the *bisi ndima* hunt, only he prefers the river hog and the giant black hog while we prefer the smaller antelope. We do not hunt the leopard, and the leopard does not hunt the *bisi ndima.*

"We are careful when we see a leopard. When Ngiome was young, a leopard killed his uncle. They say the leopard had two cubs and did not hear him come, and he did not see or hear the leopard. The leopard killed him, but it did not eat him. They say it caught a small river hog later the same day and that was what it dined on with its cubs. *Zabolo-yindo*—the big black leopards—they did not try to kill us because we are *bisi ndima.*"

"Then why do you think they killed all of the people in the group that Carver's friend came here with? And also, the soldier who came here with us?"

"They were *bilo.* White *bilo*—black *bilo.* Not *bisi ndima.* Bisi ndima* are of the forest, *bilo* are not, and when bilo come into the forest, they kill—not to eat, just to kill. *Bilo* are destructors of the forest—they are a sickness. The *zabolo-yindo* kill *bilo* to protect the forest. *Zabolo-yindo* are not like other leopards that live and hunt in the forest like *bisi ndima.* What Zora calls the *sunken forest* is sacred. It is the first forest. The *zabolo-yindo* protect the forest like they protect their cubs."

"Ngiome—the night after I came down from the big tree—after Carver was killed, the white *bilo*—the ones who called themselves Oleg, Viper, and Aziza—they hurt Zora. They bound me with *bilo* vines and left me under the rain and when I was there, one of the *zabolo-yindo* came to me. It touched me with its nose and licked me with its tongue, and I could not move, but it did not hurt me. Why did it not hurt Zora?"

Ngiome laughed. "Because you are not *bilo*, Zora—you are *bisi ndima*."

Zora looked at Ngiome. She smiled, reached her arm around him and hugged him. "I am *bisi ndima*. Thank you, Ngiome."

Ngiome nodded, then looked out into the night as thunder rumbled somewhere in the distance. He sighed and so did she, and then they listened as the rain began to pick up again. It fell hard for a while, then slowed again to a steady drizzle.

As exhausted as she was, Zora was unable to fall asleep. She sat, her back against the trunk of the tree and her knees pulled up close to her chest. Ngiome had fallen asleep, and his head lay cradled by Zora's arm. Her hand held his upper arm, and every few minutes she tightened her grip on him as if to assure herself that he was still there. As the rain slowed, she tried to focus on the sound of the water as it dripped with a steady rhythm onto their makeshift roof. It had a soothing effect and soon she was able to clear her mind, and sleep entered. Her head settled down onto Ngiome and the muscles throughout her body finally relaxed into a peaceful smoothness; each cell began to release the maddening tension, like air slowly leaking out of a balloon, and for the first time in days Zora began to sleep—in peace.

She was in a deep sleep when she heard a voice. Her eyes snapped open, and Ngiome was sitting up straight next to her, his eyes wide, and he repeated, "What was that?"

"What?" she answered. "Did you hear something?"

"Listen." He looked at her and they both sat in silence, listening.

At first, she only heard the slow dripping. The rain had completely stopped, but the canopy continued to shed water as it dripped downward from leaf to leaf to leaf. "There!" he said, as a far-off cry broke through the night. It could have been an owl or night bird of some kind, but it wasn't. It was more of a mammal sound. They both listened. It came in random spurts at first, but then moved into an elongated, drawn out wailing cry. Finally, as the night air shifted directions, the sound came to them with renewed clarity.

Zora felt her heart stop, and then she felt it pound. It pounded hard, and then harder—like a crashing hammer forcing its way through her chest. She gasped for air as her throat became blocked—blocked with fear—with the sudden recognition of the horror that would not leave her alone. It was Oleg.

Like a mourner at a Greek funeral, Oleg's pain-ridden voice droned out in a long crying wail. It drifted through the forest like a lingering fog as it transported the pain of his empty soul, winding and rubbing against everything in its way.

Zora looked to the ground below, and in the fog that hovered there she could feel the melancholic disease—that essence of Oleg Levkov, the monster, as it searched in a final belch from within his black soul, and his final horror, his fear that he knew not for what he searched. For hours, his long and soulless cry lingered, and when it finally stopped a profound peacefulness fell across the forest. That vile malignancy that Oleg Levkov had so diligently spread throughout his life to everyone and everything he touched had finally been drawn down into the sulfur-spewing cracks that opened across the bone field where his empty corpse now lay. Down into the confusions of Erebus, through the circles of suffering and to the eternal emptiness—the darkness of error that eagerly awaited him below. And a peaceful silence followed.

"He's gone," said Zora as she looked at Ngiome.

61 – THE TROPHY

In the few hours that remained before the onset of dawn, Zora and Ngiome were, at last able to fall into a restful sleep. Zora was awakened only by the pressure from a full bladder that needed attending to, and by then the morning was half gone. The two descended from the tree with caution, looking, listening, smelling; all their senses open wide in anticipation for what dangers might lurk below. Although famished, they set aside their need for nourishment and headed directly for the river where they found themselves upstream from where they had witnessed Aziza's fatal encounter with the crocodiles. The river was narrower here, and they were able to wade across without incident.

Within another hour they were back at the big tree where they found what the scavengers had left of Carver's body. Zora attempted to build a pyre to burn what was left, a final attempt at some kind of funeral; some way to acknowledge his life, but the rain had returned, dampening her efforts. She thought of attempting a stone sepulcher, but there were no stones to be found. Finally she placed his remains into the deep junction where two large roots sprouted from the base of the trunk. There she covered him in an interlacing construction of damp broken boughs—a tomb that would rot, but never burn. "Most of him has already returned to the earth through the stomachs of scavengers," she said to Ngiome. "The rest will go more slowly, one day perhaps to feed the beginning of a new tree."

As Zora stood and stared down into his final place of rest, her mind drifted back to those final moments. His words, as he lay broken across the branches, his head in her arms; those final words returned, and she paused. Quickly, she dropped back down between the roots, disassembled the wooden sepulcher and began to pick through his bones and tattered clothing. She found his belt and a zippered pouch, set them aside, then carefully rebuilt the chamber and pulled herself back up to sit on one of the wide root ridges. She opened the pouch and found his passport along with several other papers. Next she examined the belt and found that it did have a small zippered security pocket on its inner lining. She opened it and found a key, which she recognized as the one he had used to access the metal box back in Brazzaville. She looked at the key for a minute, thinking to herself, then dropped it into the pouch, zipped it shut and slid it onto her own belt. She then looked at Ngiome and said, "Carver was a *bilo* but he was a good *bilo* and he loved the forest—he would be happy if you were to take his belt and his knife."

In the hope that she might retrieve the satellite radio, Zora returned up the big tree. The second climb was much more difficult than it had been the first time. The days since her ascent with Carver had drained her. Not only, was she much weaker physically, but her spirit had suffered. Now she carried a weight that strained both her heart and her mind, and the climb progressed more like that of a sloth than the monkey she had been when she danced her way up the first time. She passed through the dense canopy with its myriad of twisting branches and continued on, finally arriving at the *ramure*. She found Carver's backpack and the tote bag that she was supposed to have sent down to him. They had both been ripped apart and the contents were strewn about.

"Little bastards!" she said as she dashed to the backpack first. She looked inside then threw it down. "Damn!" she exclaimed. She looked around frantically. Although some of the bags' contents were scattered about, many were simply gone. Finally she saw what she had been hoping to find; a reflection of light, indicating something metallic and partially concealed behind the ferns in the smaller niche. It was the satellite radio. She dashed over to it, and her heart sank. It had been smashed apart; the battery and antennae were missing and what was left had been thrown against the tree trunk.

Zora slowly gathered up what she could find and put it all into a pile. She sat down, looked through the mess and found his measuring devices, his compass, a pair of binoculars, and several notebooks. She quickly skimmed through some of the notebooks then stopped, took a deep breath and looking around, bit her lip as tears began to run down her cheeks. She sniffled, wiped her arm across her face, and said to herself, "This was our little garden of Eden." She stood up, ripped Carver's notes into pieces and grabbing hold of a thick vine, pulled down to test it, grabbed a second vine as security, stepped off the edge of her perch and returned to Ngiome below.

Although they moved quickly, they took the time to forage for food and gradually replenished themselves. By nightfall they had reached the waterfall at the base of the slope and Ngiome washed off the last of his face and body paint. They detected no signs that the big cats had attempted to pursue them, but they took no chances and once again, climbed up into a tree where they made preparations for the night. It did not rain that night, and the soothing sound of the waterfall eased them both into a deep and peaceful slumber.

◆　◆

As soon as it was light enough to see, Zora and Ngiome were down on the ground and began their ascent up the switch-backing trail that led to the rim. Where two weeks earlier it had taken the entire party of thirteen several hours to descend from rim to base, Zora and Ngiome were able to make the return climb in just over an hour. As they neared the rim, it ran as a dark wall, backlit by an intense sprinkling of light from the sun which had just begun to break through the canopy above. They stopped for an instant to gaze, each smiling with a sense of joy.

They covered the remaining distance in minutes, and as they stepped into the brilliant light, Ngiome turned to Zora grinning, his lips spread taught, revealing his white teeth. Then his smile faded as his eyes shifted to something behind her. Following his gaze, she turned and noticed a dark form to one side of the trail; a termite nest perched on top of a small tree stump. It looked like the form of a man with a large head standing silently at the edge of the rim. A shiver ran down her spine. "Just a termite nest she said." But she knew what Ngiome was thinking—Oleg. For a brief second, they both saw him standing there. She placed her hand on his arm. "It's time to go home," she said. He nodded, lifted his spear onto his shoulder, and the two started down the path that led back to the *bai*.

And far behind, deep within that place where Ngiome said that man had been forbidden to go, a large feline, black like ink, lay peacefully at the base of a mound of shattered bones. With slow, smooth strokes it licked its paws and groaning with satisfaction, glanced up to where at the pinnacle, there sat perched, the rotting head of the former billionaire and hunter of exotic trophies, Olegushka Levkov.

62 – ADIEU

A pervasive calm had settled across the rain forest as Ngiome and Zora retraced their steps. Where once again they waded across the great swamp, the water had settled, reaching only to Ngiome's chest, and when they arrived on the far side, the bees that had stung one hapless soldier to death, now circled harmlessly about as the two travelers sated themselves on honey.

Each morning Ngiome sang to the forest, and each evening Zora sang to him in Spanish, the songs her mother and grandparents had once sung to her. When Ngiome noticed spots of red on Zora's leg he smiled and said to her, "You are like bees that give honey—you start new cycle. The forest is happy today."

They stopped at Ngiome's vacant hunting camp and looked for signs that someone might have been there, but found none. Ngiome retrieved his *molimo*, which had been concealed in a tree hollow then they went on to the *bai*. As they entered the open glade they could hear the sound of breaking limbs as elephants browsed along the far side of the river. They searched for signs of the former camp, but the only evidence that it had ever been there was a lone pyramid of muddied wood protruding out of the ground—the corner of an ammunition crate that had become submerged when the last flood inundated the open glade and washed everything away that was not firmly secured by a system of roots.

It had been a while since the last helicopter had landed; probably a final effort to find evidence of what might have happened. Whether it had been Oleg's people or Carver's, it was no longer possible to discern. The ruts it left when landing were almost gone, silt from another cycle of floods had washed the ground clean, and the grass had come back thick and strong. The *bai* hummed with the sounds of birds, frogs, and crickets.

They crossed the open area to the fallen tree where the two of them had sat when they had first met. Here they sat again and watched the cornucopia of life that flowed in and out of the forest and across the open glade.

A large male mandrill foraging for fallen fruit on the ground along the far bank exchanged glances with them, his face a splendid arrangement of outrageous colors framed within an orange-fringed, olive green mane. A dragonfly hovered in front of Zora, inspected her with its multi-faceted eyes, then jumped to Ngiome to examine him as well before zipping off.

Finally Ngiome turned to Zora and asked, "Will your people come back for you?"

"They might come back again—they might not. They were here while we were in the forest where one must not go, but now I think they believe that we have all perished—like the *bilo* who went before us."

"Then you stay here. If you go, you must go without the big bird that brought you."

"I would like to stay with you, but I must go."

"Will you go to your own village—see your family?"

"I would like to go to my own village, but not now. I want to find your people and bring them back and I also have other work I must do."

"They said they were taking my people to a big village, far beyond any villages we know. Do you know how to find this big village?"

"Yes, I think I know where they took your people. It will take me a long time to get there, but I will find them and I will bring them back."

"When do you go?"

"I should go today. Perhaps you can come with me."

"No, Ngiome will stay. Ngiome cannot leave the forest. None of my people remain here now—only me, Ngiome—but I am part of the forest. I have the forest, and the forest has me. It is important that Ngiome stay."

Zora stood up on the log, stretched, arching her spine and head back, then twisted her torso from side to side. "I am not happy leaving you here alone, Ngiome, but I must go. Will you take me to the path which goes to the *bilo* village?"

"It is here." He smiled and rolled his arm out toward the river. The river is the path to the village. We ride on logs that the bilo use for travel on the river."

"Ah," exclaimed Zora. "A log. Do the *bilo* have a name for this log?"

"Pirogue. They cut the log in half, then cut out middle where we sit or stand inside." Ngiome stood up and dropped down to the ground. "Come, I will show you."

Zora followed and as the two of them started across the *bai*, Ngiome continued, "It takes three days to go to the *bilo* village, and the *bilo* tell us another village lies five days beyond. None of my people have ever been to the other village. I do not know what lies beyond, but I know the big village where they took my people must be many days beyond the second village. They have told us that where river becomes wider, there are more and more *bilo* villages."

When they arrived at the bend where the river flowed out of the *bai* they continued onto a narrow game trail that paralleled the river. Eventually they came to a promontory of rock where a small cove lay concealed beyond. Ngiome parted the thick foliage that lined the inlet and stepped into the dark shade beyond, continued for several strides, then stopped. A long pirogue lay hidden beneath the overhanging fronds of a small palm. It was secured to an arm-sized sapling by a piece of vine-rope. "My people take game to the village, and the *bilo* give us metal, cloth—sometimes knife or machete. One day, the village elder gave us two pirogues. He said we could carry fresh meat to them quicker. When the men who guided the white *bilo* to the forbidden forest were banished, they took one pirogue and went to the *bilo* village. Now, Zora can take the second pirogue. It will take you to the big village where the *bilo* took my people, then it will take you to the village of your own people." He paused, looking at her, and added, "And maybe you will find the rest of Ngiome's family, and send them back."

"That is what I intend to do, Ngiome. But we must see if this pirogue still floats." She wanted to ask him again to go with her, but she knew he would refuse. Ngiome would never leave his forest. The forest was just as important to him as his family, perhaps even more important. His family might have been taken from him, but the forest was still there, and he was not part of the world of villages and towns that lay out there somewhere, down the river, he was part of the forest. She had learned to understand this relationship; she accepted it wholly and she admired it.

Together they dragged the pirogue to the edge of the water and pushed it in. While Zora held the end of the vine-rope to maintain it, Ngiome took what had once been Carver's knife and hacked down a long sapling, trimmed it, then sharpened one end. He handed it to Zora and said, "Use this to push the pirogue downriver. I sharpened this end so you can spear fish when hunger comes." They stood looking at each other; they each smiled, reached their hands out and held each other's arms, and then she bent down and their foreheads touched, and pressed firmly together.

"I will find your people, Ngiome—and I will bring them back to you. That is my promise to you."

"Follow the flow of the river," he said. "In three days, when you smell smoke, you will be at the *bilo* village. You will find some of Ngiome's people—those who were banished. They will feed you and give you shelter. When you go on to the next village Ngiome does not know what you will find. Our people only know the second village from *bilo* stories."

"Why don't you come—just to the village?" she asked. "You can return with those who were once banished. You can bring them back to the forest."

"No, Ngiome must remain. You should tell my people when you see them, Ngiome asks for them to return. If Ngiome were to go and not come back, the forest would no longer exist—the *bisi ndima* would no longer exist, and the world would die."

Zora stepped into the pirogue, then turned and placed her hand on Ngiome's shoulder, bent toward him, and they touched foreheads again. She pushed the pirogue out into the water with her pole and began to propel herself away from the bank. She picked up speed as she caught the river's current, and, with each push on the pole, she looked back to see her friend, who had begun to walk along the bank, looking out toward her. Finally as she neared a bend in the river she turned once more for a final glimpse and as he disappeared, she saw him lifting his *molimo*.

Zora could no longer see Ngiome. The wall of mighty trees and tangling vines had finally obscured him from her view but he had begun to sing through the *molimo*. He sang as he had on that wet morning long ago, when she first heard him. He sang his song to the forest; he sang his song to his friend, the *bisi ndima* who had come into his world in a strange flying pirogue. He sang to the only human being, along with himself, to have ever entered and returned from the forbidden sunken forest. Now she was leaving, and he did not know if she would ever return, but like him, she was *of the forest,* and so he sang his song to her as he, Ngiome, perhaps the last of his people to live completely free as one with his ever-threatened world, bid adieu to Zora de Rycken.

EPILOGUE

The rainy season had finally come to an end, yet the current of the river remained strong as it carried the long, slim wooden pirogue and its lone passenger swiftly along the watery highway that wound endlessly back and forth through the forest. A cool breeze drifted up the open corridor of the river and lifted her hair, which had begun to grow long, like a headdress of soft black feathers. She stood tall in the back of the vessel, and, with a slow consistent motion poled herself along, gracefully rounding each bend, picking up momentum as she curved into the turns, then propelling herself forward and down to the next bend. She had thought carefully about the trip that lay before her and knew that until she came to a large village that was serviced by power boats or had a satellite radio, she would be spending a long time in her pirogue—it could be weeks, a month; even more—she had no idea.

Coasting smoothly along the water's surface in the pirogue was to her, soothing and meditative. Zora loved being in the jungle. It was, in fact, preferable to be returning this way than to be suddenly catapulted back into the realm of 'civilized man' via the convenience of a six-hour helicopter ride.

Pushing herself into a long straight run, she would close her eyes, lift her head slightly and absorb the scents and sounds that filled the air. Everywhere she looked she saw life—some she had become familiar with in recent weeks, but often it was new. In each hour that passed she discovered wonders she never knew existed. As she rounded another bend, she looked up into the branches overhead and a small creature with large round eyes looked down at her—a *potto*, in some places known as a bush baby. Minutes later, a golden cat stopped to watch her pass; she recognized its skin from the old cap that Ngiome always wore.

With plenty of time to think and a lot to think about, so she thought about the past several weeks—the pain, the love, the despair. In a month, she had experienced more than most would know in a lifetime. She had seen what no human being had ever seen. She thought about the sunken forest with its enormous trees, the animals and birds that had never known human beings, and had no fear. And her mind kept going back to the black leopards. Mutations of some kind or perhaps holdovers from a past era, they had managed to remain hidden away in their remote forest, tucked into one of the last unexplored and inaccessible regions in the world. Or were they something else? Something she dared not to even suggest to herself. She thought about what Ngiome had said—the black leopards were the guardians.

Ngiome had never been outside of his forest. His forest was his universe. He was a part of it, an integral part and, as he had said, if it were to be destroyed, he would disappear. He and his kind were looked down upon by those who inhabited the outside world—the others—the *bilo*. They were considered primitive, savage, laughable, living in the forest like wild animals. Yet they dwelled in an existence that was devoid of fear, hunger, jealousy, hatred, murder, ownership, consumption—destruction.

Olegushka Levkov on the other hand was highly educated, cultured, a billionaire—what everyone envied, what so many strived to emulate, but he was the personification of everything humanity claimed to abhor. Yet, it was Oleg's road that the flowing tide of humanity chose to follow—a road that was clearly headed to a world devoid of trees, where the fauna would become reduced to a few rodent species, insects diminished to heat-resistant scorpions, dung beetles, and cockroaches living off the rotting ruins of a human civilization that had lost its connectivity to the very earth that had birthed it and nurtured it for millions of years. Ngiome and Olegushka Levkov were the absolute antitheses of one another, and, if asked which life they would prefer, most humans would select Oleg's.

Darkness began to set in. She poled the pirogue to a low-hanging branch where she secured it with the rope that had remained tied to its bow. It took no more than a few seconds for her to spear a fish, which she quickly scaled, cleaned, and filleted. Smiling, she took her first bite and thought to herself, *Sashimi!* When she was finished she lay down in the hollow of the pirogue and looked up. The current had pulled the small craft away from the branch that held it in place and she was able to see the sky above. It was clear and full of stars. The wind picked up; a shooting star zipped across the sky; an owl hooted deep in the forest, something splashed in the water near the far bank. *I will find his people, and I will get them back to him*, she thought to herself, *and then I have a lot of work ahead of me—a lot of work.*

And as Zora deRycken closed her eyes, three hundred miles to her north, where she, Carver, Luke, and Prince had flown out of the town of Ouésso, where they had crossed the vast open wasteland that spread out beyond the river, an endless horde of human destroyers continued to chew their way through the forest like oversized army ants, cutting, killing, devouring everything in their path as they moved ever closer to the Sunken Forest.

AUTHOR'S NOTES

Several people I have talked to when discussing *The Sunken Forest*, have told me they find the term *pygmy*, pejorative, or politically incorrect. The fact is, unless the specific ethnicity is known, there is no single term to replace it, and most members of the scientific community use the term pygmy. Major ethnic pygmy groups today include the Baka and the Aka, both on the western side of the Congo Basin, and the Twa and Efe (Mbuti), on the eastern side. A smaller group, the Bakola, live along the border between Congo and Gabon, south of the Baka and Aka populations. There is a rather large unpopulated and undeveloped region that lies between the Baka, Aka, and Bakola groups in the Republic of the Congo. It is there that I have set my story and in doing so, have invented the name, **BaKaya**, for Ngiome's isolated family group.

Throughout the novel I have used non-English words in some of the dialogs in order to achieve a particular effect. In each case, the meaning should be obvious. Most of the non-English words used by Ngiome and his people, are Lingala, the language of the Bantu people. *Nyanna* (animal), is a Lingala word. I have also used a few words from both the Baka and Mbuti ethnic groups, in spite of the fact that these two groups are separated by almost five hundred miles. *Bisi ndima* (forest people), *bisi mboka* (*bisi ndima* who have left the forest, live with the Bantus, and no longer know the forest), and *bilo* (Bantus and others who are not from the forest), are from the Baka. The word, *molimo*, the forest flute used by Ngiome was taken from Colin Turnbull's book, *The Forest People*. It is a *Mbuti* word and would not likely be found by tribes living on the opposite side of the Congo basin, although *jengi* (spirit of the forest) does occur in many of the different languages. Ngiome's name is my own construction, based on the French name, Guillaume (William in English). The spelling is based on how I might imagine a pygmy pronouncing the French name.

Ngiome's group is fictitious, as is the Sunken Forest, and I have taken some artistic freedom in creating them, however, I have also made great efforts to present characters and locations that do reflect the real world. My descriptions of the forest are based on my own experience in the rainforests of West Africa, India, Hawaii, Mexico, Guatemala, and Costa Rica. One might say that the *Sunken Forest* could easily be an ancient, primary rain forest, but on steroids.

Other than the liberties I have taken with vocabulary and musical instruments, the pygmies, as I have presented them, are based on people and a culture that do exist. The number of pygmies who continue to live as true hunter-gatherers has diminished dramatically in recent years. These unique people may not survive in this state much longer, and the recent history of the pygmy culture's decline is a true tragedy of our times. They have been subject to slavery, murder, cannibalism, and every type of abuse possible. With such a bleak future, it is my hope that by bringing these wonderful people to the attention of a wide audience through popular fiction, my book might aid in awakening public awareness, not just in their plight but, in what the rest of us might learn from them.

If you ask a Pygmy why his people have no chiefs, no lawgivers, no councils, or no leaders, he will answer with misleading simplicity, "Because we are the people of the forest." The forest, the great provider, is the one standard by which all deeds and thoughts are judged; it is the chief, the lawgiver, the leader, and the final arbitrator.

The Forest People, by Colin M. Turnbull

ACKNOWLEDGMENTS

The seed that germinated and ultimately grew into *The Sunken Forest*, began when I first read anthropologist, Colin M. Turnbull's book, *The Forest People* (1961; Simon & Schuster). The book describes in detail, a three-year period in the late 1950s that Turnbull spent with a community of Mbuti hunter-gatherers in the Ituri Forest. By the time I finished the book, I felt that one day I should write a piece of fiction that would focus on, or at least include, the pygmy people. It took a long time to finally do it, but now that I have, my first offer of gratitude goes to the memory of Colin Macmillan Turnbull.

I am enormously indebted to my daughter, Adriana Anderson Boudoiron, who invited me to join her in a novel writing class at the University of Virginia, where I wrote the first four chapters of the book. And, I thank Meredith Coles who taught the class and provided the encouragement to continue on. Further encouragement came from my beta readers, Gordon Matthew, Paul Gold, Vic Caruso, Dr. Melvin N. Wilson, and Mary Sproles Martin. Mary also did the final edit and proof. Others who played critical roles include my editor (both structural and technical), Erica Orloff, and my graphic designer, Jen Fleisher. Joseph Armand Anderson, my oldest son and veteran mountain guide, provided technical information and editing for the Denali chapter. Those friends and family who have taken me deep into the rainforest and allowed me to see, hear, smell, and love it at its deepest level include Adrian Forsythe, Manuel Sanchez Mendoza, Max Villalobos, Manuel Ramirez Umana, and my youngest son, Frederic Anderson. To each of these individuals, I offer my deepest gratitude.

In addition to Colin Turnbull's book, I give credit, as well as praise to photographer, Michael (Nick) Nichols, who, from 1999 through 2002, documented Mike Fay's 2,000 mile Megatransect expedition from the north central Congo Basin to the Atlantic Ocean.

Nick was kind enough to have invited me to some of his earliest video and photographic presentations of that most extraordinary expedition. The expedition itself has been a direct influence on the setting I chose for my book. National Geographic's publication, *The Last Place on Earth*, a collection of Nichol's photography and Fay's journals served as a resource throughout the novel's development. I also want to thank Nathan Williams, former team member with Nick Nichols, for sharing some of his recent video work from the rainforests of Gabon.

Current information on pygmies and their living conditions has been made available to me through *Survival*, a non-profit dedicated to the protection of tribal peoples throughout the world. And, the book, *Hunters-gatherers of the Congo Basin: cultures, histories and biology of African Pygmies* (2014, Barry S. Hewlett, editor), has proven to be an outstanding source of detailed information.

Finally, I must thank my wife, Dominique Astruc Anderson, who, in addition to putting up with my countless episodes of late-night writing, proofread, advised, and provided a final, most crucial edit for *The Sunken Forest*.

THE AUTHOR

    R. Barber Anderson is an architect, artist, and writer. His early formative years were spent in Hawaii where he developed a life-long interest in rain forests. He has lived, worked, and travelled through rain forests in West Africa, India, Mexico, Central America, and for the last seven years has been a planning consultant with a conservation organization on the Osa Peninsula in Costa Rica. Today he resides in Virginia next to the Blue Ridge Mountains where he draws, paints, writes, and sometimes wanders off to lose himself in nature. The Sunken Forest is his first novel.